Bonds of Attachment

Also by Emyr Humphreys

NOVELS
The Little Kingdom
The Voice of a Stranger
A Change of Heart
Hear and Forgive
A Man's Estate
The Italian Wife
A Toy Epic
The Gift
Outside the House of Baal
Natives
National Winner
Flesh and Blood
The Best of Friends
The Anchor Tree
Jones
Salt of the Earth
An Absolute Hero
Open Secrets

NON-FICTION
The Taliesin Tradition
Miscellany Two
The Triple Net

POETRY
Ancestor worship
Landscapes
The Kingdom of Brân
Pwyll a Riannon
Penguin Modern Poets 27 (with John Ormond and John Tripp)

IN WELSH
Y Tri Llais (*novel*)
Dinas (with W.S. Jones (*play*)
Cymod Cardarn (*play*)
Theatr Saunders Lewis (*essays*)

Bonds of Attachment

EMYR HUMPHREYS

MACDONALD

F HUMPHRIES

A *Macdonald* Book

First published in Great Britain in 1991 by
Macdonald & Co (Publishers) Ltd,
London & Sydney

Printed and bound in Great Britain by
BPCC Hazell Books
Aylesbury, Bucks, England
Member of BPCC Ltd.

0020287
British Library Cataloguing in Publication Data

Humphreys, Emyr *1919-*
I. Bonds of attachment.
823.914 [F]

ISBN 0–356–19134–6

Macdonald & Co (Publishers) Ltd
Orbit House
1 New Fetter Lane
London EC4A 1AR

A member of Maxwell Macmillan Pergamon Publishing Corporation

I
ELINOR
ETO

'O voi, che siete due dentro ad un foco . . .'*

Inferno XXVI

* 'O you, who are both bound together in one fire . . .'

One

i

I listened to their voices and to my heart beating.

'The carving-knife. The one with the white handle. Remember it?'

We three remembered it. I saw it suspended in the air before me now, like Macbeth's dagger. My two brothers smiled as they remembered. I trembled inwardly.

'I hid it,' Bedwyr said. His smile was preparatory to an amusing revelation. Reminiscence deserves a smile. 'I hid it in my tool-box. In the garden shed that smelt of creosote. Remember it?'

I could see the padlock on his tool-box. Carefully oiled. How old would he have been? I saw a twelve-year-old still in short trousers. White knees and a scab drying after a recent fall off his bicycle. My eldest brother Bedwyr, for whom I had a rooted admiration. Now he was a successful architect and paterfamilias, serious and responsible, and nothing he had ever done allowed my restless and suspicious mind to doubt his integrity.

'I just thought he was going to kill her,' Bedwyr said. 'I was scared stiff.'

'He' was my father. 'Her' my mother. Why are they so detached, my two brothers? They stretch back in their hotel chairs like two men of the world. Any moment Gwydion will glance at his empty glass and make a gesture and ask us both whether we would have the same again. The notion that my father had hated my mother so much that he might have wanted to kill her was no more disturbing to him than the dregs at the bottom of a glass. A fine fellow, my brother

1

Gwydion, selling himself and his gift-wrapped television package deals with a cool confidence I could only envy. One man of the world smiles at the other. What is it they have in common: medieval names; harmonies of inherited gesture; remembered tribulations; the complacency that comes with limited success each in his chosen field? I am caught in the cross-fire of their indulgent smiles as they both study simultaneously their youngest and smallest and ugliest brother. A restless and ill-adjusted creature. A potential but unpredictable family pet, amusing to watch indoors, but to be kept on a tight lead outdoors. Capable of causing a wide range of embarrassment. Bedwyr has noticed how intently I am listening to his words. He at least is uneasy about me and my intentions. He lowers his voice to a level of ironic detachment.

'Mind you, it was as blunt as the nose on my face.'

I suppose that was soothing enough. I felt more for my brother than for my parents. A boy in the tool-shed nursing his nightmare fears. Until Gwydion supplied his gloss. His voice pricked my skin.

'More likely she would have killed him,' he said. 'Old Amy was a damned sight fitter. And more aggressive.'

He speaks with authority. A tough negotiator to whom frankness comes more swiftly to hand than a handkerchief.

'Old Cilydd wouldn't hurt a fly. Except with his tongue, of course. That was sharp enough.'

Words push the years back. He calls his father 'Old Cilydd'! Dead seventeen years. That much out of reach. But was he his father? A playground remark is spat in my face and almost as hastily shut out of my consciousness. 'He's not your brother . . .' We were a family like a fortress in hostile territory. I adored my brothers. Belief in them was the bedrock of my existence. Was it a girl or a boy that screamed in my face like a Red Indian hurling a cinematic tomahawk? We were a family. I could never bear to hear ill spoken of either of them. How do I measure now what they think of me? Do they share any of my devotion to that familial ideal? True they have allowed a modified memorial to our father's memory. A slate block, executed under Bedwyr's tasteful architectural direction. A discreet plaque. And for this

2

limited gain, in return I have exercised restraint concerning our mother. Affairs of kith and kin. This is an interim conference. Negotiations are still in progress. No treaty has been signed.

'Sharp! Forensic!'

Bedwyr raised an index finger to signal a joke was being offered. It was a fact that my father used to cross-examine us. Them certainly. And even me, child as I was. He longed for conversation, but all he could achieve were sequences of awkward questions that seemed designed to test the veracity of whatever replies we contrived to make. Was there always more to hide than to reveal? I could see now the haunted expression on his pale face: the mute longing for an affection that would always be withheld.

'Up to a point,' Gwydion said. 'But when it came to the push, he wouldn't discuss anything, would he? Not "discuss".'

Their recollections carried more authority because they went that much further back. Their money-boxes were always bigger than mine and I'm sure I never resented it. They were senior. I was very junior. That was the natural order. And now their hands rose and fell in barely perceptible counterpoint as they drew out the old threads of their conclusions about my father's character arrived at all those years ago.

'She would,' Gwydion said. 'Up to a point anyway. But he wouldn't ever. As if his lips were sealed with cement.'

Pleasant reminiscences. They shared just that much more of the past with each other than with me. They were my seniors after all. But I could still hear my father's fist battering the locked bedroom door. I could still see my mother thrust her head under the pillow and see her whole body shake. Was it with sobbing or with rage? I was in her bed. Seven years old, was I, or eight? Somewhere the exact age was recorded. But lured there on what pretext? She was never that fond of me, was she? I was the unwanted child that put paid to her parliamentary ambitions. I was the heaviest link in the chains around her feet . . . Children are such helpless pawns in adult warfare. What had she done? Where had she been? Should I interrupt my brothers'

3

pleasant discourse to ask them. On such and such a day or night, what had she done and where had she been? They would know enough to rekindle a fire that, even at seventeen years' distance, had power to scorch and etch red patches on my skin. I was there and I heard it and I felt it. The hatred that kills. I should not allow personal discomfort, boils, blisters, redness, itching or eczema to impede an analysis or investigation . . . But now there were decisions to be made about the future that had more pressing claims on my attention. Today the struggle.

'Family life stinks,' Gwydion said.

Their discursive recollections had brought him to this abrupt conclusion. Cheerfully he swept up our glasses and prepared to journey to the bar. He seemed slow to appreciate that Bedwyr found his blithe generalization unacceptable. Bedwyr was, after all, a happily married man with an adoring wife and three adoring children. Even I was aware that his hearth and home glowed with refulgent happiness and contentment. Gwydion was professionally insensitive and self-centred. His programmes and deals about programmes shrank people in order to tread on them and their most intimate relationships, like cullers clubbing seal cubs on the ice: bloodstains and cheerful shouts blossoming in the cold air, and all in the sacred name of entertainment. He was sitting down again, intent on repairing the damage.

'I'm being objective,' he said. 'Nothing personal, my old chaps. Did a programme with this police johnny. My private police informer. Chief Inspector Williams. Nice chap. A bit garrulous after the third pint. Nothing like inside information in my business. Seventy-five per cent of homicides occur in the bosom of the family.' Bedwyr was still reluctant to smile. Gwydion turned to me. Not that I was a softer target, but teasing me might bring back a smile to Bedwyr's face. 'Seventy five per cent, P.C.M.!' he said. 'Did you know that? How's that for a piece of social analysis?' My unpublished thesis. Always good for a laugh. 'It's a cesspool,' he said. 'Have you ever seen the Black Museum at Scotland Yard?'

How travelled and knowledgeable he was. A life

4

measured out in programmes, not coffee spoons. Anodyne footage, inane commentary, reducing the mystery of existence to the vagaries of a white ball booted or potted around a four-sided screen. The window of a coffin.

'Look,' he continued. 'If we have to be blunt about it and come to some conclusion, I would say he killed himself instead of killing her. That's a theory as good as any other.'

He gathered up the glasses again and made for the bar. Bedwyr and I sat in silence. Did he, too, find Gwydion's detachment deeply distasteful?

ii

I woke up and saw the single yellow light reflected in the dressing-table mirror. It was in the form of a brown candle and the light was solidified into a flame bending before a breeze. Except there was no breeze. It was warm in the hotel bedroom. Outside it was raining. I could hear the tyres of cars sizzling on the wet streets as they passed through the centre of the city. The hotel and all its rooms and corridors were a dark citadel and I was secreted inside it and my nostrils were twitching nervously. My breath rustled in the dry mucus. The room was too warm. How could I sleep? I raised myself on my elbows and saw that the double bed in which my mother should have been sleeping was empty. What could I do? She had deserted me. A tide of panic rose in my breast like an asthma attack. I lay back to think.

I had never set out so exultantly on a journey. I was her chosen companion and she filled our compartment in the railway carriage with an elation as sweet as the discreet perfume she was wearing. She seemed to love me with a wholeheartedness I had never experienced before. My head lay in her lap while her fingers played with the curls of my hair and her voice flowed over me in warm confidences I barely understood. I was her boy, her youngest son, her very own, and there was a unique bond between us, a trust that nothing could break because we understood each other so perfectly. I could tell her everything and she could do the same for me so that when I grew up I would qualify to be

5

closer to her than any other living being – even Bedwyr who was so gentle and perfect, even Gwydion, so naughty and loveable, and of course it went without saying, even closer than my father who was morose and fault finding, absorbed in his poetry and in his work, both of which he put invariably before his wife and family. He was a father and a husband who rarely understood us, not because he couldn't, but because he didn't choose to.

The train was carrying us to a treasure house of marvels, a prodigious city through which she would lead me by the hand. We would visit the halls of her former happiness and more than that: by that magic that is the exclusive prerogative of mother love, with my hand in hers, we would come across those portions of time and space where, in the future which recaptures the past, there would spring up crystal castles in which we would wander together, free spirits bound only by silk threads of mutual devotion. This hotel seemed such a place when we first took possession of the numbered bedroom. I heard her murmur 'how nice' under her breath as the porter in uniform opened the shutters and the November sunshine flooded in. She used the words 'free' and 'independent' as she addressed me and examined her face in the dressing-table mirror. Her eyes followed her own lips moving. Which preoccupied her more: what she was saying or how she looked? The question pressed in on me as I lay in the cot-bed which I thought had been put in the room so that she could be near me. She had let go my hand far too soon. The bed was empty. My mother had gone.

There was that man we met for tea. Mr Everett. He seemed lost in admiration for my mother. His hair was not entirely attached to his head and he kept dabbing his lips with his serviette as though he were drying sentences with blotting paper as they came out. My mother had told me he was a brilliant man, but that my father disliked him for some unaccountable reason and so this tea was another feature of our excursion it would be better not to mention when we got home. That seemed reasonable enough. When he withdrew himself from adoring my mother and took notice of me he transfixed me with a penetrating smile and promised to take me around the House of Commons the next time I was brought to London. My mother urged me to smile and be exceedingly grateful. I did my best to do as I was told. She leaned towards Mr Everett and I saw him shiver as he surreptitiously covered her hand with his. Her voice was low but I knew she was complaining about my father.

'He allies himself with people so petty and provincial. He goes to the local eisteddfodau now, which he never used to do . . . The things he used to say about them. He'll stand at the back and listen to the same piece being recited or sung over and over again. As if he were listening to Gielgud or Gigli.'

Mr Everett's eyes disappeared behind his spectacles and unaccustomed mirth possessed him like a private earthquake. I glanced about the restaurant and was relieved to see that no one noticed his indecorous behaviour. He became serious and intense again. He had plans for my mother's benefit. She sat up and listened. His homage made her happy. He was determined, he said, to advance her cause and extend the sphere of her influence because he knew better than anyone else how much she had to contribute. I heard the word 'contribute' and wondered if this process involved money. Money was one of the more sensitive of many sensitive subjects in our house. My mother took the view that we had plenty of it if only my father could be prevailed upon to unlock the cash-box and distribute it. Her philosophy favoured applying money like manure to support the growth of superior projects. My father used obscure legal phrases and made tying-up gestures with his fingers that underlined his intention of providing for the education and future security of his children. There was a great wall between my parents: an ice barrier. Transparent but impassable. And no one could have been more aware than I of the daily effort they both made to keep it in refrigeration.

'It's a trap,' my mother said.

She was referring to our tall terrace house in Pendraw, not to those metal objects Robert Thomas the molecatcher secreted in soft hedgerows. She sighed as she said it and I saw Mr Everett's meagre chest expand with heroic

7

determination to rescue this fair lady in distress. Marine Terrace in Pendraw had become a moated grange. His fingers clutched and crumbled his serviette lying on the table.

'I don't know what I can do about it . . .' my mother said.

Mr Everett's forehead set in permanent waves under his loose hair as his brain revved with an attempt to slam in the clutch on a scheme that would carry her away to unfettered freedom.

'The boys . . .'

She muttered the phrase and it was heavy with meaning. I understood that she sacrificed herself for our sakes and even as I bit into another buttered teacake my shoulders sagged, weighed down with gratitude. She would never desert us so long as we continued to be grateful. Was that why she was not asleep across the room in that double bed? Had I somehow been guilty of a temporary relapse and forgotten to be grateful?

'Mam . . . Mam! . . .'

I felt the pile of the carpet under my feet. This hotel was a palace, but a palace could be a prison for a solitary boy. I pressed the sheet of her open bed with the palm of my hand. It was smooth and uncreased with a cold and seamless perfection. She walked the corridors with total confidence, but I knew the whole place couldn't be hers, even if it was all laid out for her convenience. She had pointed out a card mounted on an easel in the reception office that read 'We aim to please', and murmured a remark about American influence which I knew from the tone of her voice was intended as a humorous comment.

The clock at the end of the corridor had illuminated rectangles of equal size instead of figures. It suggested the paradox of two in the morning and the depth of night. What could I do except stand there in the open doorway of Room 222? The number was engraved on my mind. The world was two of everything except one of me. To move left or move right would be equal mistakes: paths that were long passages to deeper confusion. My forlorn hope was to remain rooted to the spot without moving a muscle under the number on the door.

8

She emerged from a room further down our corridor. She wore her blue silk dressing-gown that rippled as she moved. And a man appeared to take her hand and kiss it. He wore a red dressing-gown that reached down to his naked ankles. A man I had never seen before. Strange and unfamiliar in a way that frightened me. Was my mother frightened too? She seemed to snatch her hand away and long to leave him even before she saw me. How tall was he? A giant? Did he have a beard?

She swept me up and closed the door behind us. She was frightened. She was shivering. She clutched me to her and her voice choked in her throat.

'Peredur. Darling. You are a lump of ice.'

She took me into her bed. I could hear her heart thumping. She looked down at me imploringly as if she were at my mercy. She was still staring at my face when she switched off the light. On the dressing-table the imitation candle burned in its own yellow haze. Our heads were on the same pillow as she whispered to me.

'He's a famous painter from France. He is painting my portrait, you see. But it's a great secret. When you grow up, perhaps I'll give it to you. It's a work of art. A great work of art. And artists are unusual people, Peredur. Different from the rest of us. He has this strange idea that I'm very beautiful. I don't believe him, of course. I inspire him, he says. I don't know about that. He stayed with us once, you know. When you were a baby. But you wouldn't remember that. No reason why you should. But you shouldn't mention it to anybody. About our being here. This is a terribly expensive hotel. And he's paying for it. Paying back old hospitality, he calls it. When he was a penniless refugee. But he's rich now and he's famous and he wants to pay us back so I suppose we should let him, shouldn't we?'

Her voice murmured on. It was delightful to lie beside her. In some strange way I had never experienced before, she was in my power. I could reach out my hand and touch her, stroke her even, and she didn't seem to mind. This amazed me. The satin of her nightdress shifted against her skin until she suddenly became aware of my hand and pushed it roughly away.

9

'You're warm enough now,' she said. 'Get back into your own bed. Quickly. And go to sleep. It's very late. You should never have woken up in the first place. That was naughty. You are a bad boy.'

I lay awake staring at the yellow candle on the dressing-table, more confused and afraid than ever. There were secrets pressed down tightly inside me, one on top of the other, that nothing on earth would ever persuade me to release.

iii

In the Land Rover Gwydion had hired we sat, the three of us, contemplating the grey pile of Brangor Hall across the breadth of the park and wondering, each in his own way, what could be done about it. It would be a strange inheritance. Whether we liked it or not, our mother was Amy, Lady Brangor and this was her Brangor Hall. Perhaps, if we stared at the place long enough, three reluctant heirs apparent would metamorphose into three hereditary priests equipped to return to some imagined orient laden with revelation? We had only to wait in silence for the rays of the setting sun to gild those trees and lawns and lakes and baronial turrets with significance. Autumn here was beautiful enough to give any world a new meaning.

That excited me. The whole landscape was trembling with the brief translucent beauty of a falling leaf. Whatever was beautiful could be inherited. This way aesthetics could contribute to universal propositions. The notion was ripe for development until my hesitant process of reasoning was broken up by Bedwyr muttering his professional disapproval of moss and dampness. He had noted several trees in the western avenue that needed drastic surgery. At this distance he could still point them out. His gesture invoked the wearisome intricacies of estate management. My predisposition towards philosophical detachment should not delete awareness that there was always something to be done: without constant attention and repair every environment would revert to a brambled forest. We should never forget

10

that there was always something that needed to be done. The concern on his face activated the feelings of admiration and respect for my eldest brother that were rooted in my breast. He had shaved his beard and the lineament of the thoughtful boy illuminated his familiar features. How many times in my childhood had he come to my rescue?

'Look at it!' Gwydion said. 'Do you know what I'm thinking?'

My other brother's mouth was already twitching with amusement. How early in his existence had he been licensed to indulge an inclination towards misrule? Was it my mother who first issued the permit? Besotted by his black curls and rosebud mouth, a cherub on a sepia postcard: so loveable and cuddly in a silver frame. I was here between them. Not the counterfeit presentment of two brothers so much as the poles of my childhood existence. The responsible and the irresponsible, the calm builder of Meccano towers who somehow managed to contain his temper when the twinkle-eyed destroyer pushed it over and told him to build something different. The marvel was how far the bonds of tolerant affection could stretch. Bedwyr was smiling now his patient, indulgent smile as he waited for Gwydion to tease out the colourful distractions of his mischievous mind.

'You have to laugh,' Gwydion said. 'I mean it's no joke being an ageing beauty. But you have to admit old Amy has done pretty well for herself. What a history, eh? From rags to riches. It's quite a story.'

A small boy rasping his stick on iron railings and grinning at the sound he creates. Gwydion usually disturbs me more than he diverts. I respect his enterprise and daring, but could he possibly be contemplating making one of his ridiculous television programmes about our mother? I could not put it past him. Or her, when I come to think of it. She is indulgent and foolish enough to allow it. They come of the same mould. But then, so do I. I would never allow it. He would encapsulate history in a thirty-minute strait-jacket of visual clichés in order to extricate himself from any responsibility for it. And free himself for what purpose? To get on with his next daisy-chain of profitable floss and flotsam. He and his medium had the miraculous power of transforming fact into

11

palpable untruth. Like 'rags to riches'. It was untrue. Not rags at all. No more than frugal, honest poverty of a kind not so far remote from the world's last hope of salvation.

I visited the ruin of that crippled quarryman's small-holding where Amy was brought up. Poor soil perhaps, but enough for independent subsistence. I felt infinitely tender towards the place. It had charm and variety and dignity and its own spectacular view. If I ever succeeded in establishing a meaningful and rational dialogue with my mother, I intended to question her about it. No doubt she would make some reference to the romantic urges in an academic never obliged to bend an aching back over ditch or furrow. But my memory stored evidence from her own lips which I would like to re-examine with her. Had I not heard her swear that her Aunt Esther, the sainted aunt who brought her up, whose goodness was also unparalleled in her experience, made the best butter she had ever tasted or hoped to taste? I would like to establish again how many times that smallholding had featured in a range of anecdotes related to exemplify spontaneous joy of living. So how dare Gwydion equate that upland *tyddyn* with rags – or for that matter this grey pile across the park with 'riches'? I needed a sharp remark that would shatter the misconception here and now and perhaps put a spoke in the wheel of a dubious enterprise. It had to be quick and sharp and final – and not one of those stammered preludes to an interminable debate incapable of conclusion. Before I could formulate effective words, Bedwyr had spoken.

'If you ask me . . .' He was prepared to think aloud and it was our business to listen attentively. '. . . she should get rid of it.'

Gwydion's reaction was immediate. 'Oh, she'd never do that,' he said.

'I don't see why not,' Bedwyr said. 'If it's put to her properly. She's a sensible woman. Not beyond rational processes.'

I would have liked to point out that my mother's capacity for rational processes was at all times directed by her will; she was always a woman who directed her intellect and her energies into getting whatever it was at a given moment she imagined she wanted. Fortunately I realized there was no way I could express this thought without sounding hostile and spiteful and even venomous, so I had the sense to remain silent. I knew they both suspected me of an irrational hatred of my mother. I knew there had been grounds for such suspicion. But now I was a man in better command of himself with a more clearly defined purpose. I had abandoned exile, but silence and cunning were still at my disposal.

I sit back and listen to the plain pragmatic speaking that passes between two men of the world. My brothers belong to the executive species: each in his degree controls enterprises. They are familiar with all the testing intricacies of banking, buying and selling. They deal with trade unions and board meetings. They understood planning and the slitheringly devious practices of local politicians. They had no need to take into account the nervous speculations of an academic. At different moments in my career each in his own way had urged me to pump my small energies into published theory; and each had made reference, more or less snide, to the untried teaching the untrained. I would not resent this or hold it against them – only use it as a spur. The day was fast approaching when I would astonish and surprise them, invading fields they had assumed were far outside my reach.

'In a place like this,' Bedwyr was saying, with accompanying gestures that drew my attention to his hands and their comforting resemblance to my own, 'the rate of deterioration is alarming. There's no other word for it. Moisture seeps into everything. As old Connie used to say, it really does need twenty-five indoor servants and a fire in every room. Or the modern mechanised equivalent that would cost a fortune to install. That antiquated central heating system eats more coal than an ocean liner. And since Barr died there's nobody left that really understands it. She really has no choice. She has to get rid of it.'

It distressed him even to think of depriving my mother of something she might be attached to. The house was turning black against the golden sky. The light was spectacular. From the trees on the knoll on the south side of the park the

13

single tower of the ruined medieval keep seemed to stretch up in an attempt to survey its territory with a petrified intensity that transferred itself to me. There was everything here that I sought: the fallen cromlech, the traces of an iron-age fort, the mound that had been an abbey, stripped by the rapacious ancestors of Lord Brangor in order to widen the base of the family fortune. It was all here like original sin.

'Rid of it,' Gwydion said. 'How can you get rid of it with those Huskie females holed up in the garden cottage? They don't pay a penny's rent but they're sitting tenants. If they were sitting ducks you could shoot them. Who would want to take on a pair of gabble-gobble spinsters and a mongoloid idiot like Milly? It's not easy, is it?'

'I didn't think it was easy,' Bedwyr said. 'But I can tell you this. It won't get any easier. The sooner the problem is tackled, the better. We've just got to tackle her about it. That's all there is to it.'

Confronted with a problem so intractable Gwydion had to be flippant. 'She could always marry again,' he said. 'She married into it, so she could marry out of it. After all, she's only had three husbands.'

He was pulling that fleeting mask-of-comedy face I used to glimpse in the sideboard mirror at meal times. Always it made me giggle and earned me a rebuke from my father. The pall of silence between our parents never seemed to worry Gwydion. I wanted to ask him about that at this moment. Instead I identified the ruined tower in the trees with my father. He was the only husband that really mattered. It was with him that she created me. If this estate was hers, I myself was obliged to be part of the inheritance. The fact that I once hated it so much reinforced the new affection I had begun to feel for it.

How could it have meant so little and now mean so much? The proposition was simple: if love can turn to hate so can hate convert to love. The road to Damascus carries two-way traffic. Avoid such windy generalizations and be specific! To distance my tender self from her and from the confused torment of prolonged adolescence I submerged myself in academic work. It was as simple as that. And on such a precarious base I had constructed a superstructure of absurdly complex and unmeaningful relationships. All those I had blown away like the cypsela of a dandelion clock. By a triumphant act of will I had reasserted my autonomy; that restored to my own keeping the control of my own destiny.

I wanted to laugh at my two accomplished brothers, sitting in the Land Rover like a pair of estate agents brooding over an unsaleable property. If they only knew it, I was there to relieve them of a needless anxiety. I know how comic they would both find me as the improbable heir to the last Lord Brangor. I could see the funny side of the succession myself. His inheritance stretched from the dissolution of Brangor Abbey by his Tudor ancestors to the sipping of pink gins in the Atlantico Hotel in Cascais. My mother wintered in Estoril and carried snapshots of her three sons in her purse. Snipped with her nail-scissors to make them fit. Mine was the smallest and, I imagine, the least displayed. The last Lord Brangor was lost in admiration for a handsome woman on the right side of the menopause. And by such transient affections are the main avenues of history restored. That tower in the trees was built to protect an earlier inheritance and repel barbarian invaders. That was the original Brangor purpose and I have been called by the invisible magic of history to restore it. The secret of the centuries has to be available to the individual with the vision to perceive it. How many days would it take me to make manifest to my brothers a process of reasoning that was so lucid and obvious to me? We sat like a tribunal in session in Gwydion's hired Land Rover, but so far my opinion had not been sought. What could I do except bide my time and take habitual refuge in silence.

Bedwyr was paying me attention. His voice sounded reproachful, so I was instantly on my guard.

'She's worried about you, you know,' he said.

'Why about me?' I was even more puzzled when the expression on his face implied I knew full well. I did not. Unless she had taken to worrying about finding me generally antipathetic, which was unlikely.

'Not much sense in it, is there?' Bedwyr said. So he was worried about it too, whatever it was.

'Sense in what?'

15

'Resigning one job before being appointed to another,' Bedwyr said. He seemed to resent stating the obvious.

I had to display unqualified confidence. 'You may as well say I'm on a shortlist of one,' I said. 'They're bound to appoint me.'

Gwydion slapped me with unnecessary force on the back. Bedwyr remained ominously silent.

iv

On the artificial lake I saw what I took to be a family of ducks floating on liquid twilight. Their motion disturbed gold clouds so that the sky rippled. Their home was an islet containing bushes like a bunch of evergreens in a shallow brown dish. The swing on which I sat squeaked as I moved and I found the noise repeatedly pleasant. My father was a silent black feature watching me. I gripped the cold chains of the swing with fingers protected by woollen gloves. I could assume that my movements were sufficient to maintain me as the centre of his attention. The whole experience was strange but not unpleasant. The swing was a pendulum that created its own hiatus inside which I could enjoy the illusion that time was under my control.

I could not tell whether his patience had given out or whether he had determined on a course of action. His hand was as cold as the chain of the swing as he dragged me along, then bundled me into the back of his car with more force than was necessary. I would never have stayed alone in the park. Night was falling and this was a strange town. There was hardly any speech between us but I was bound more closely to him than I had ever been before or ever would be again. Knowledge and foreknowledge assembled in the back of the car with stifling power. My best plan was to move as little as possible, to transform the totality of my being into dependent obedience.

I stared at my father's head and shoulders. They were like a mountain range that marked the horizon of my existence. His hands were on the steering wheel. He drove the car with monotonous persistence around the artificial lake. I recognized the railings and the boat house and the row of four weeping willows each time as we passed them, but since it had not occurred to me to keep count when our journey started I had no real notion as to how many times we had circumnavigated the lake before darkness fell and he was obliged to switch on his headlights. It was in the glare of those headlights that I saw a man with a beatific smile raise his hand like a celestial policeman. He was bareheaded and bald but a fringe of red hair hovered above his ears like a halo. The bonnet of my father's car came to a halt within an inch of his chest. I could see the same red hair grew out of his ears. He never ceased to smile. I thought his face, even in the white light, was like an advertisment for goodness. He seemed extremely fond of my father.

'Dear Cilydd,' he said. 'Old friend. Won't you come in so that we can have a quiet word together?'

My father's response was silence. This was nothing new and did not surprise me. It was the custom in our terrace house when the doorbell rang that we got there before he did so that the harmless caller should be spared his silent, suspicious stare.

'You know I have a great concern for you both . . .'

I saw his large hand hover above my father's shoulder. I wondered whether or not it would land. It trembled like a naked bird uncertain of its physical capacity to execute a hazardous manoeuvre. The voice, a bell-like tenor with an exhortatory note, could have belonged to someone else.

'Concern . . . What am I talking about? I mean "love". Real love. That's the word. I love you both. I married you, didn't I? I baptized that boy on the back seat. We have shared so much of life's adventure together. Cilydd, my dear. Do I have to tell you?'

His hand had finally landed on the black hillside and it had not been shrugged off. My father was listening. So was I. Suspended as I had been in the swing, the motion of the pendulum remained a pleasant sensation. My tongue hung out. The man's words reached me across a vast distance, in the sense that the prevailing wind buffets everybody and does no real hurt.

'It's not practical, is it, dear fellow, even on the lowest

17

level. Where would you go? And who would look after him? The little one, bless him. If you went to England and you managed it somehow, just think of how much he would lose. How much you would both lose if it came to that. You a rooted man if ever I knew one, with a great cultural responsibility. Oh dear, I'm so distressed, dear friend, I'm not doing my job properly. My job, if that's what I should call it, is reconciliation. A wonderful word that. At the core, at the very heart of the Christian faith. God was in Christ, reconciling the world unto himself . . . and hath committed unto us the word of reconciliation. The word is the work! Oh dear, listen to me. I'm preaching and that's not what I meant to do at all. Cilydd, John Cilydd. I come to beg and implore you. In the name of the love I bear you. All my own personal love which as I confess before God is more for you, my dear man, than for her . . . but above all for the sake of that child in the back seat and for the sake of his future . . .'

The hand on the shoulder was more insistent now than the voice. And my father was responding to it. I could just hear the words as he muttered them at the bottom of his throat.

'She's not fit . . .' he was saying. 'She's not fit to have charge of a child. She's a . . .' Whatever the word was he did not utter it. 'She's not fit . . . not fit . . .'

He was repeating himself as if he were caught in a fever. Or had he been drinking? I had not been close enough to him to smell his breath. Drinking made him incoherent. Not that I listened when he battered his fist on the locked bedroom door. If my mother put her head under the pillow, that was the best thing to do. When he found sufficient words he seemed to be blaming himself.

'I packed her bags,' my father said. 'The bags with labels on them she was so fond of using. Cannes . . . Nice . . . Rome . . . I packed them and carried them down. I told her to go. Go and never come back. Go where ever it was she wanted to go. Join whoever it was she wanted to join. She wouldn't. I wanted to take hold of her and throw her out. I didn't.'

'Of course you didn't,' the man said. 'Of course you didn't.' My father's fists were clenched. Was he going to hit the man who was smiling at him. It would not have been a nice thing to do. 'Why not?'

Was my father choking? Was he swaying or was he trembling? 'She's broken me, Tasker. That's why . . . Broken me . . .'

The man was comforting my father. His arm was around his shoulder. He drew him closer. My father was shaking and sobbing. This was something I had never seen before. Sobbing and crying in another man's arms. This was Tasker Thomas whom I had heard my mother and my father refer to as a near saint and as one point at least upon which they were both agreed. This was the good Tasker Thomas stroking my father's hair as if he were a little boy. This was what 'suffer little children to come unto me' really meant.

'It's because you are so sensitive,' Tasker was saying. 'That's why you are a poet, John Cilydd. Your whole nature is exposed and raw. I understand. I understand. The harshness of this old world is too much for you sometimes. But there are comforts, you know. There is consolation. Our disappointments and our sadness and our fears can be transformed . . .'

My father was stiffening. Tasker was talking too much. I could have told him that. My father was liable to get irritated and angry when talk flowed too freely. He had shaken off the man's embrace and was gripping the steering wheel. He would make a pronouncement to dam the flood of speech.

'I should have killed her,' he said. 'That's what I should have done. At least that's clean. Part of an honourable pagan code. I don't want all that mealy-mouthed rubbish about forgiveness. I want retribution. I should have killed her.'

It was the word 'kill' that upset me. By myself in the back seat I was howling. At last both men had noticed me. They could see I was in the grip of a sudden panic and they were both quite unable to understand the phenomenon or to calm me. I could see my father forcing my mother's head over the end of the kitchen table and plunging a knife with a white handle into her neck and I could see her blood pouring down into a bucket encrusted with dried blood like the one Hughes the butcher used in his slaughtering shed when he was killing sheep. That was what killing meant and that was what I could not bear to happen.

19

'You must take him home.' The man called Tasker had come into the back of the car to sit by me. I wouldn't let him touch me. 'The poor little chap is upset,' he said. 'I'll come with you. You'll need a mediator. I'll mediate between you.'

My father had become a dark mass of indecision. He was ready to accept help now, from any quarter.

v

My mother was having her hair done. She was enjoying the experience. The contraption had been set up behind her chair so that she could gaze through the wall of glass and see herself as monarch of all she surveyed. The view was extensive, as far as the mountains of Eryri, so that this royal metaphor could not possibly be the truth. Yet the framing was her property and the hairdryer was a crown poised over her head. There were jewelled rings on her fine fingers. A nylon robe had been draped over her shoulders and tied with a pink bow under her chin. The afternoon light poured on her face through the plate glass to show both the enticing softness of her skin and the ageing process working on it. Her eyes at this moment were rounded and youthful and as coy as a rococo cupid's. Those grey irises were flecked with glittering blue. I was on my guard. What was she up to?

Miss Maude Hopkin was in charge of the coiffure coronation. Her large feet shifted about in court shoes and her beaky nose could have belonged to an ecclesiastic of indeterminate sex. We three sons sat around the drawing-room like chamberlains or officers of state being granted informal audience. She was up to something. Offering Miss Maude a brief share in the spectacular view framed by the wall of a window designed by her architect son fresh from a student visit to Scandinavia would not be sufficient to account for so much suppressed ebullience. She had received a greater stimulus than the envy-tinged admiration of a hairdresser and amateur soprano.

Miss Maude was one of my mother's failures that she had somehow contrived to transform into a satisfaction that was a more than adequate substitute for success. I had stood on

20

the Jacobean staircase in Brangor and heard that powerful soprano reverberate in the empty chapel. It had seemed a marvel, then, that so timid and nervous a woman could be capable of such resounding arpeggios. But she never had the will or resilience to launch out on the operatic career my mother had mapped out for her. As a Centre for the Advancement of Creative Women, or whatever it was my mother liked to call it, Brangor had not been a success. And I knew perfectly well why. It had not been properly rooted in the community. Would-be-creative females descended on the place from four points of the compass and had a whale of a time, one assumes, for a weekend or a week, or even for much more extensive periods. But in the end they went and the place therof knew them no more. There were those two Maggies from California. The entire stable area was transformed into a silk-screening workshop just for their benefit. They came and went at great expense and the place thereof knew them no more. The doctor from East Berlin and her Bulgarian lover engaged on a feminist saga that was to reach five volumes. During their six months' fellowship at Brangor they fell out and nearly set the whole place on fire. The Arts Council could not stomach my mother's autocratic methods. The County Council caught whiffs of imagined scandal and withdrew their meagre support. My mother's purse and patience wore thin. Connie Clayton, her faithful housekeeper, fell ill and my mother, with what seemed to me uncharacteristic selflessness, devoted herself to nursing the old woman. Without her concentrated care and attention the Centre for Creative Women unravelled like neglected knitting.

The hairdresser was the very proof of the validity of my critique. I went so far as to point out to my mother that authentic living culture was not cherries and icing on bread and butter pudding. I put the question to her quite forcefully. 'What is your aim?' I asked. 'To bring art with a capital "A" like missionary skirts to the naked fuzzy-wuzzies? Or is it to nurture the local product, to cultivate our own corner of the garden so that a multitude of new blossoms bloom?' Her immediate reaction was to tell me not to mix my metaphors – but I think she took my point. Or at least as much of it as she could bear to assimilate. Miss Maude Hopkin's singing and the women's *Côr Cerdd Dant* remained among the few abiding legacies of the Brangor experiment. This would be the first point I needed to drive home when I took the initial steps of introducing my mother and my brothers to the schemes I myself had in mind as soon as I took up my new appointment.

'You haven't met Maude's brother have you? Mr Gareth Hopkin.' My mother was looking through the window. I was slow to realize she was addressing me. 'He is an extremely intelligent man,' my mother said.

Such praise generated a blush in the hairdresser's cheeks. Myself, I was on my guard. Why should my mother announce her discovery of Gareth Hopkin's intelligence as though it were a treasure he had hitherto kept hidden? She had known him long enough. I seemed to recollect her expressing disapproval of the man's selfishness. Had he not stood in the way of his sister's progress by insisting she kept house for him when his wife died? Whatever he had done I was certain it had found a place in her private black museum of male chauvinism. So how had he so suddenly been transformed into a specimen of shining intelligence? My mother had shifted her head to look at me. My suspicions made me unable to return her stare.

'He had such a trying time at the Secondary Modern, didn't he, Maude? He had enemies on the staff. And the Head wasn't nice at all. Gave him horrible, unruly classes to deal with. Didn't he, Maude?'

The hairdresser spoke in a nervous whisper, concentrating on my mother's hair. Had she not been inhibited by our presence she would by now have been engaged in softly singing its praises: a Te Deum for elderly tresses, a carol for her ageing curls. As it was she was stricken dumb by Gwydion's bold and penetrating stare.

'In the Teachers' Training College at least the poor man has time to breathe,' my mother said. 'Although I myself would have described him as a pure academic. Research is what he's really good at. Isn't that so, Maude?'

The hairdresser nodded, too nervous to venture audible agreement.

22

'He's writing a book about Wales and the Spanish Civil War,' my mother continued. 'Did you know that, Peredur?'

'No, I didn't,' I said.

How on earth could I have known? I spoke as politely as I could. This was no juncture in my scheme of things in which to alienate my mother. My giant step, my leap in the dark – according to both my brothers – had already been taken. I had resigned one secure tenure of university teaching before being appointed to another. Now caution had to be my watchword. Especially with my mother. At the right moment I had to remind her of an offer she had once made of turning Brangor Hall into a research centre for my benefit. Somehow the essence of that offer had to be extracted from the emotional upheaval of the occasion when it had been made as some kind of peace offering and when I had angrily rejected it. Timing was everything. I had to wait with iron patience until the right moment presented itself.

'He's very interested in the man I should have married instead of your father,' my mother said. 'Now what do you think of that?'

Her outburst of light-hearted laughter at her own daring made me want to flee from the room and all it represented. I gripped the arms of my chair to make sure I didn't move. Gwydion was laughing too and Bedwyr was smiling obligingly. Some hidden source of pleasure was responsible for this outburst of frankness. With my mother it was always the undertow that I had to watch out for.

'Pen Lewis,' my mother said. She uttered the name with unnecessary clarity. She was listening to a distant clarion call. She smiled wistfully at the view through the window as if it were all being illuminated and given a special significance by a fond memory from her past. 'Mr Hopkin has seen his picture hanging in the Miners' Institute at Cwmdu. A faded photograph in a heavy frame. And an inscription about the supreme sacrifice. Killed on the Jarama. A head-on clash between the Moors and the International Brigade.' She sighed. ' "You are History, you are Legend". Words are not much good, are they? And yet what else have we got?'

She did not seem to find the silence that followed

23

uncomfortable. The hairdresser trod softly on the thick carpet in her court shoes.

'Your old boyfriend,' Gwydion said. 'Well I never.' As usual he was resolved to be cheerful come what may.

'He should have been your father,' my mother said. 'If he hadn't been killed. You know, sometimes I think how on earth did we come to be what we are? It's a very great mystery, isn't it, Maude?'

The hairdresser was compelled to agree with her. Lady Brangor sat in her chair in complete charge of the order of events. She could display so much confidence about her own past because any official history would need her approval. Would her hairdresser's brother be called upon to write it? Was that what she was up to? And when my turn came to put in my request, would I have to supplicate on my knees?

' "Why don't you write your memoirs, Lady Brangor?" he said to me the other day, didn't he, Maude? And do you know what I said to him? "Dear Mr Hopkin, I have far more to conceal than to reveal." ' Her laughter was restrained and almost musical. She was so much in control of herself and her circumstance. ' "Reserve all news", eh Gwydion?'

Now he was laughing too. It was a phrase they both regularly used in their letters when he was away at school. The bitterness of that enforced exile seemed to have completely vanished. All that remained was the grace note of a pleasing reminiscence.

'It's always been my view,' my mother said, 'that words are no substitute for deeds. That was the common Welsh weakness your poor father suffered from. A few lines of *cynghanedd*, a couple of verses, the equivalent labour of rebuilding one of the walls of the temple. My inclination was always for action. And it still is, my boys. It still is. Let others record my doings if they must – but my duty as long as I have breath left in me is to get things done!'

The hairdressing was complete. Reverently Miss Maude undid the pink bow under my mother's chin and removed the nylon cape. She stepped back and clasped her hands together high on her bosom to survey her handiwork. Now that my mother was standing and had become the undisputed cynosure, Miss Maude could relax, and even derive some

24

pleasure in being on the fringe of a family conversation piece. My mother's head of hair was a fair example of her work. It crowned whatever was left of her good looks. She straightened her back in a conscious effort to keep any incipient dowager's hump at bay. She looked as wholesome as an idealized line-drawing of a wife and husband picking up the first instalment of a well-earned pension – except there was no husband. She had buried three on her journey to this one-storey modern dwelling and the twin set and pearls.

'Now for my bit of news,' she said. She smiled at each of us in turn as though she were examining her refurbished appearance in a triple mirror. 'I've been appointed to a quango. By two secretaries of state. You can't get to be more important than that, can you?'

Here was the true source of her elation. All her life she had longed for political power and importance in one shape or another. Being pregnant with me and the responsibility of bringing up three boys had put paid to her early parliamentary chances. She had been forced to forego a safe seat and in one way or another I had never been allowed to forget it. Even during her second and third marriages the announcement of the promotion of a political contemporary would send her into a silent sulk that could last a minimum of forty-eight hours. When both the men she had defeated for the Labour nomination in North Maelor entered the Cabinet, she disappeared for the best part of a week. I remembered these things better than my brothers. I was still within the orbit of whatever it was she designated 'home'. She was pointing at each one of us in turn.

'I know you are worrying about me. And the burden of Brangor and so on. I want you to stop it. It's very, very sweet of you and I appreciate it more than I can say . . .'

'A quango for what?' Gwydion said.

My mother forgave the interruption. She could see her son was overcome with curiosity. With a coquettish gesture she tapped the side of her nose.

'All in good time,' she said. 'But I can see a future for Brangor. And I can see promising developments that can do nothing but benefit the both of you. Let us leave it at that for the time being. Now let us take tea. Earl Grey for Gwydion, Assam for Bedwyr. And Peredur can please himself. It's so nice to have you here, all three. It really is.'

I was in our back garden with Harry Duff. We were waiting for tea. My mother had made a special effort and a card-table covered with a white cloth was already planted on the narrow lawn. Harry Duff was my mother's best friend's favourite nephew. 'Best' and 'favourite' were necessary adjectives. We were penfriends under a long-standing arrangement arrived at by my mother and his aunt Margot. Somehow our primitive attempts at communication would help to shore up what was left of an ancient and fading friendship between Amy More and Margot Grosmont. Dear Harry and dear Peredur would make up for the absence of dearest Amy and dearest Margot. But face to face the penfriends had little to say to each other. That did not prevent me from prowling about him with an inextinguishable pride at such a precious acquisition.

For the few days he was staying with us he was the prisoner of our hospitality and his own politeness. His greatest shortcoming was that he found every single place-name around us impossible to pronounce. My mother told me to overlook this and pointed out the perfection of his table manners. He was varnished in Englishness. Glazed all over in confidence. Blissfully exempt from and immune to superfluous emotions. As cool as his blond curls. As composed as his underwear with his name-tapes on them. These qualities my mother admired and I did too. His mere presence imposed a truce in our troubled household. My father and my mother were polite to each other and it seemed as if a new age could dawn.

Talking to Harry should have been an exhilarating experience. My mind worked overtime trying to assemble the necesssary words that could introduce a range of topics I would like to consult Harry about. My mother was convinced that talking English to Harry would widen my horizon and I was sure she was right. So why should it be so difficult? I could start off with a single question. My mother had said at suppertime the day Harry arrived that there was so much more to laugh at once you acquired a complete command of English. I could not make out whether she had said it merely to annoy my father or whether she was making an authentic revelation of the true nature of the human condition. Do all the best jokes have to be in English? There are match-boxes and Christmas crackers to prove it. So there wasn't much point in cross-examining Harry about that.

There wasn't much point in cross-examining Harry about anything. He sat as motionless as a judge on our blistered green garden bench. He looked solemn and suspicious. All I could do was watch the toes of his shoes rise and fall with the impartial detachment of the scales of justice and wait for him to speak.

'Cricket,' Harry said.

'Yes.'

I leaned forward too quickly. I was eager to sit at the feet of this visiting Gamaliel. He looked at me with the grave caution of an explorer moving through hostile territory. It was probably my father who had put him unnecessarily on his guard. He had tried too hard to demonstrate he could be jovial. He had told a silly joke about an old parson in Wiltshire who had a notice on the back door: 'Beware of Jews, gypsies and Welshmen'. He had shaken up and down with soundless laughter because neither Harry nor I could see the point of his joke. I think it would be fair to blame my parents for our inability to communicate. So much of what they said put up barriers instead of pulling them down.

'Cricket,' Harry said.

I nodded encouragingly. We were on the brink of a breakthrough: a revelation even. There wasn't enough room in our narrow back garden to play without breaking windows. That is probably what he was going to say. I had a bat of sorts inherited from my brother Gwydion, but there were only old tennis balls to hit and they might be beneath Harry's contempt. At some point I had to make clear to Harry that we lived in this grim terrace simply to satisfy some inexplicable whim of my father's that had something to do with walking to the office and the post-war shortage of petrol. He was not to think that we lacked the means to possess a better property where cricket could be practised on a lawn like a calm illustration to an English schoolboy story.

'You need plenty of sun,' Harry said. 'Too much wind around here.'

This thought had never occurred to me before. It was like fresh light on the nature of the universe. I knew Harry had been preoccupied with the prospects of the English Test Team on their next visit to Australia, but his remark implied that the Southern Cross had been fixed in the sky in order to guide chosen cricketers like the magi to a continent where an inexhaustible supply of pitches of regulation size would be available with sufficient sunshine and regulated wind. I also perceived that the fortunes of the English team were exceptionally close to his heart and I wanted to ask whether he expected me to support Australia or find a place for his team in my own heart. But voices rising in the house distracted me. My heart and my mind were flooded with foreboding. A row had broken out. Not an argument or a fleeting point of friction: a full-scale row. And Harry was here to register the shame and horror of it. So far he had heard nothing. I had to get him away.

'Let's go to the dunes,' I said. 'We could go looking for golf balls.'

He stared at my inane grin with manifest suspicion. 'It's teatime,' Harry said. 'Time for tea.'

I groaned inwardly. This was another law of the universe. What could I do to subvert it? On an impulse I tried a cartwheel and then standing on my head. They were feeble attempts but I grinned and capered about like a clown who seeks to disparage his own expertise. The level of sound in the house was rising. Harry had heard it. My mother was screaming with rage. He had turned his head to listen. I could not even attract – let alone hold – his attention. He witnessed the carving-knife with a white handle burst through the window like a cricket ball and land on the worn grass not far from his feet. My mind was numb as Harry stared at the knife. I wanted to tell him not to touch it. I

28

wanted to explain everything but my mind was throbbing with suns and galaxies instead of words. When the glass broke everything was nothing. I looked up in search of any available succour or comfort. I saw my father's face as pale as a ghost beyond the jagged edges of the shattered glass before he disappeared from my sight for ever.

Two

The walls of the Reading Room were lined with leather-bound books that were not often opened. The windows offered views of the sea and the mountains and below us the slate roofs of the old town. The sea was one blue, the sky another and the hill beyond the town covered with bright bracken in the sunlight. I was in the mood to be magnanimous. It wasn't a shortlist of one, of course. There were two others in the room. A dark handsome South Walian called Adams and, to my surprise, no less a person than Wesley Dilkes. A distinguished figure in our field but also noted for his uncertain temper. It seemed odd to me that he should be trying for this job. He knew nothing at all about Wales and at the moment I guessed Adams was biding his time to make just such a point.

The sunlight in the room seemed to be there to reassure me that magnanimity would be the key to revelation. Without wishing to separate myself from the others I was impelled to move closer to the window. Under the blue water of the bay one of the sunken cities of our folk imagination lay hidden. By the timeless harbour a penniless prince came fishing and caught a talking infant with shining brow. There was room on the horizon for a fleet of ships conjured out of seaweed and it was all part of a plan to force a malevolent mother to provide her son with an official name, with the armament of a decent occupation, and with an impeccable wife. I was a place before I became a person. Everything I looked at was part of an inheritance. Even the air I breathed was refurbished with myth and magic. My only problem was to contain my excitement and continue to allow the light to shine in my head. The trick was to stand as calm as a scholarly statue in the vaulted Reading Room and pay the others the grave and benevolent attention due to colleagues teasing out a problem with the combined force of three minds trained and tempered with rationality.

'It's disgusting,' Dilkes said. 'There's no other word for it.'

Adams offered him a piece of four-sided buttered toast with the cautious respect of a lion-tamer feeding a new addition to his troupe. Abruptly Dilkes declined it. Adams smiled politely as he folded his hands and tilted his head to one side with a readiness to listen. Dilkes noted his attitude and he became more guarded. He tapped his briefcase with the toecap of his black boot.

'I've brought some proofs along,' he said. 'Just in case something like this would happen.'

'A new book?' Adams displayed a genuine interest.

'My Dusseldorf study,' Dilkes replied.

Adam's inquiry allowed him to relax a little. His plump fingers deserted his beard and went to play up and down the inside of his vivid blue braces before settling on the mound of his extended waistband. He was renowned for his punishing work schedule. His wife left his meals for him on a tray outside his study door. Large meals that he wolfed down with one hand as he went on writing with the other. There was some celebrated remark he had made to a post-graduate student about keeping his fat arse fixed to his study chair. I could see the drift of the message without remembering the exact text.

'It's on the workshop floor it all happens,' Dilkes said. 'And in the minds and motivations of the operators. Therein lies the secret.'

Adams showed too much eagerness to know more. Dilkes's cheek bulged as he removed fragments of college toast from his upper dentures.

'I can tell you this much,' Dilkes said. 'If we don't buck our ideas up, British manufacturing industry will be dead in ten years.'

I had to rein in an urge to ask Dilkes why on earth he was

putting in for this job. It was a chair he should be looking for – perhaps in Ibadan or Abu Dhabi. In this United Kingdom his reputation had gone before him. Every department in the British Isles knew by now how difficult he was to live with. Perhaps he had his eye on a cheap property in the outback, where he could labour at his books and his wife could cook him enormous meals with fresh eggs and he could pop in here twice a week to deliver disquieting lectures and Common Room tirades to subsidize his arcadian existence.

'I'd say we were in here for good.' Dilkes had settled on a jovial approach. 'They'll open this place up a hundred years from now and find three skeletons covered in tattered academic cobwebs.'

His stomach shook with approval of the humour he invited us to share. Over the carved oak fireplace there was a large oil painting of a former principal at ease in his library, smoking a pipe. Dilkes pointed at it.

'The old boy was trying to look like Thomas Hardy,' he said. 'Assuming he knew who Thomas Hardy was.'

Adams had raised his hand a few inches away from his mouth. 'The unions,' Adams said. 'In Dusseldorf and so on. They're Americanized, aren't they? They don't have any power.'

Dilkes gave a deep sigh. 'You a Marxist?' he asked.

Adams sat back. His physical stance was defiant, but his speech was more cautious. 'Yes,' he said. 'In a manner of speaking. You could say that I was. As a tool of analysis and diagnosis, I would say Marxism is indispensable. Unsurpassed.'

Dilkes was already shaking his head. 'Socialism, my friend, is a busted flush,' he said. 'A twentieth-century myth already exploded. It will take time to work itself out, of course. Through the various bodies politick. But for scholars and scientists it's in the morgue waiting for the post-mortem.'

'Oh now . . . steady on . . .' Adams's dark, handsome features had begun to flush.

'I expect you're emotionally involved,' Dilkes said. 'A miner's son from the valleys and all that sort of thing. Fair

32

enough. But we can't let things like that stand in the way of scientific objectivity, can we? That way chaos lies. Intellectual chaos, that is, and economic stagnation. Two things that often go together. But there we are. I'm not here to deliver a lecture, am I? Where the hell are these people?'

There was an ornate clock-face set in the oak pediment above the heavy door of the Reading Room. Dilkes pulled out his watch from his trouser pocket by its silver chain and caught it expertly in the same hand.

'That clock is slow,' he said. 'Like everything else in this place. Either of you fellows been to the States? You'll never get far in this business you know, without going there first.'

The knock on the door was playful and by the expression on his face when he poked his head in, Simons, the assistant registrar, could have been engaged in some childhood game, like hide-and-seek.

'Bad news I'm afraid,' he said. 'I hope you won't shoot the messenger.'

The three of us looked alert. Dilkes's mouth hung open as if to facilitate the emergence of indignant comment. Someone at some stage in his development must have told Simons that he had a puckish smile, and the information had pleased him so much he was determined to display it on every possible occasion. He seemed equally proud of his red hair which was set in tight waves close to his head in a style favoured by pre-war film stars.

'Show's postponed,' he said. 'Until two-thirty this afternoon.' He stood in the room smiling and rubbing his hands together.

'Good God,' Dilkes said. 'That's unheard of. I never heard of such a thing. What kind of a place is this?'

The assistant registrar placed a hand over his heart and shook his head in deep apology. I felt curiously detached, as if the whole affair had very little to do with me. Without drawing attention to myself, I shifted back close to the window in the hope of renewing the state of mind I had enjoyed when I last looked out at the harbour and the bay and the headland.

'You will be guests of the college,' Simons said. 'For lunch or dinner or any additional expenses. Meanwhile the

Principal suggests that you might like to look around the establishment. I am here to offer my services for a conducted tour. At your service, gentlemen.'

Adams tried to catch my eye. I could see what he was thinking: let us demonstrate a united front and walk out on the bastards. That was all right for him – he had a position to go back to. I had burned my boats. I could not indulge in any fine gestures. Besides, the professor had virtually assured me on the telephone that the job was mine. The situation was delicate: putting my magnanimity to the test and driving a pleasing sequence of mythological inspirations clean out of my head.

'Mr Dilkes,' Simons said. 'Are you coming?' He was looking forward to giving us a guided tour. It was an escape from the boredom of routine administration in his office and clearly one of his hobbies was taking light-hearted roles in amateur dramatics.

'You've seen one, you've seen them all,' Dilkes said. 'I'll just clear that table and get on with correcting my proofs.'

ii

Simons was inviting Adams and myself to admire the sequence of refurbished coats of arms embossed on the ceiling of the Old Library. I understood it was the workmanship that pleased him and that he found the Victorian medievalism endearingly absurd. Adams was more interested in the undergraduates working away at the long oak tables positioned between the shelves. It flashed through my mind that if the undergraduate vote had any part in deciding who got the job, Adams would win hands down. I could see young women's heads moving in incipient admiration whichever way he moved. Nevertheless the place was congenial. My eye was taken with a discreet display of eighteenth-century Welsh manuscripts in an alcove illuminated by stained-glass windows. My interest seemed to intrigue Simons.

'Not your field, is it?' he said.

I refrained from acid comment about specialization and

34

academic strait-jackets. There was no point in alienating persons I might need to collaborate with if this place was ever to be transformed into an authentic Welsh university college. I had begun to assume that Simons paid closer attention to me than to Adams because he was already certain that I would be appointed. We were on a staircase on our way down to inspect the library stacks that had only recently been installed, when I grasped the true reason for his interest in me. He brought it up quite abruptly, as if his curiosity could be contained no longer.

'You're Gwydion More's brother, aren't you?'

I had to admit it.

'He's got a way with him, hasn't he?' Simons said. 'I'm a bit of a fan of his, to tell you the truth. I thought that *Behind Closed Doors* series of his was terrific. It's not as easy as it looks, is it? To poke and probe and get away with it. My wife says it's his cheeky charm. We never miss his programmes.'

There was an echo on the stone staircase that enlarged the hollowness in the fellow's words. I racked my brains for the appropriate quotation from Morgan Llwyd, but it didn't come until the occasion to use it had passed: 'The mouth of a man who talks too much offers the devil an unbridled mount.' A college with a vow of silence wouldn't be such a bad idea. Did this mean that television was, after all, the work of the devil? The tumbling torrent of words bursting out at the turn of a switch to flood minds like Mr and Mrs Simons and turn them into regurgitating sewers. The one word I murmured was 'Superficial.'

Adams heard it. He nodded enthusiastically. 'I was about to say the same myself,' he said. 'But since he's your brother I didn't want to sound offensive. Mind you, I would admit he's very good at his job.'

For some reason Simons was blushing like a man caught out in a weakness it would have been wiser to conceal. 'I suppose we all watch too much telly, don't we?' he said. 'A weakness of the age. What I was going to ask you was this – not that I have any right to ask. But since we're on the subject . . . Why doesn't your brother ever do anything in Welsh?'

Was it my turn to blush? In view of the nature of my

mission it was embarrassing. But the question had to be faced. Adams, too, was poised with one foot on the stair, the other in the air, waiting for an answer. There was nothing for it but to blurt out the nearest approximation to the truth.

'Money,' I said. 'There's no money in it.'

Laughter from two mouths mingled in the stairwell. Whatever their separate sources of amusement, for me it was a form of relief and I was able to smile.

Simons grappled with the mechanism of the moveable stacks and made confident remarks about technology and storing information. After the exchange on the stairs he behaved more familiarly with us both. I imagined our tour would end with an invitation to join him in a drink at the Senior Common Room bar. I was considering the wisdom of accepting such an invitation before being elected when I noticed that a man beyond the stacks was winking at me. He was half concealed by a row of shelves and his antics were comic as well as disturbing. He contrived always to wink when the other two were looking in some other direction. I was forced to perceive how urgently he was intent on communicating with me. He was grey-haired, bespectacled and solemn-looking: a member of staff, some kind of librarian, and not a deranged undergraduate. I could either ignore him or respond at once to his signalling.

When I was within earshot he whispered urgently, 'I've got something to show you.' He winked, nodded and beckoned until I joined him in his hide behind the bookshelves. He had a worktable of his own and box-files heaped on either side. One shoulder was higher than the other, his skin had a laminated pallor and he was given to friendly, conspiratorial sniggers.

'The bowels of the ship,' he said. 'The least distinguished section of the college library, but in my view the most important.' He offered me his hand and withdrew it quickly as soon as I had taken it. He swayed back and forth on the balls of his feet like a bird summoning up the courage to engage in a courtship dance. 'Hefin Mather.' He pressed his fingertips against his chest to indicate he was naming himself. 'Come back when you've got rid of them. I've come across some of your father's papers. They could be important. Not a word to anyone. Especially that one.'

Simons and Adams had caught up with me. Hefin Mather turned to the files and papers on his table with a great display of industry. He barely acknowledged a serene greeting from the assistant registrar.

The conducted tour petered out when Adams expressed a disinclination to visit the extended gymnasium. Simons rubbed his hands together and suggested it was not too early to present ourselves at the Senior Common Room bar. It wasn't easy to escape from his clutches but eventually I found my way across the quadrangle to the main entrance of the library and down the two flights of stairs to the dim underworld of the stacks.

Hefin Mather was nibbling systematically around the sides of his sandwich. A plastic box containing his lunch and a large thermos flask occupied the only uncovered corner of his worktable.

'So you found your way,' he said.

I was not put off by his confident smirk. He had more to give than receive. It was interesting to distinguish his mode of utterance from the way Simons and Adams used their Welsh. It was nothing to do with dialect or accent or class. The other two used their mother tongue as a social lubricant: a useful adjunct, for example, to social-climbing career-making or private jokes. Their mental processes remained rigidly Anglo-British. The bounded systems of their minds were concurrent with the even edges of the columns of any middle-class London newspaper. They were trained like performing seals to exchange English received opinion in Welsh. This library troglodyte was different. The underground cunning of an authentic cultural survivor gave his simplest statement a subversive edge. It seemed so inevitable that I should have so immediately sought him out.

'I wouldn't trust Oliver Simons too much if I were you.' He was articulating an unease I had already felt. We were natural collaborators. 'It's none of my business, of course, but you may as well know he is very much the Registrar's errand boy. And the Registrar runs this place. And in spite of the fuss he makes about rugby, that man is basically anti-Welsh.'

37

I was being inducted into an ancient fellowship that was at the core of a miraculous resistance to dominant power structures and cultural imperialism. The sensation stimulated me so much I began to shiver. You could say that the imagination of the defeated, Celts, or whatever they were, was still at work, ready for renaissance and revolution, the great undertaking of reshaping the world. I sat watching Hefin Mather finish his lunch with the patience of a disciple still outside the mouth of the cave. He wiped his mouth and screwed on the cap of his thermos with deliberation.

'I'll be taking another cup,' he said, 'in the middle of the afternoon.'

He exercised the quiet confidence of a man who appointed his own rhythm of time and season. His imagination would not be restricted by the soulless schedules of a college calendar. He was essentially a shape-shifter: a Gwion Bach on the long flight to illumination and rebirth.

'You know that your father was a national poet of real importance?'

It was the question I had been waiting a lifetime to hear. My father had not been a cranky poetaster, a mere eisteddfod winner who had failed to go from his bit of a prize to a proper life's work. The oracle could only issue from the lips of a total stranger. I followed Mather to what had been a large coal-cellar next to the boiler-room. In the artificial light I saw great heaps of magazines, documents and books covered with dust. Mather sneezed and rubbed the end of his nose with the back of his hand.

'I sometimes think most things of value are underground,' he said. 'King Arthur's cave or a coal mine.' As he giggled I understood how much he was enjoying the occasion. He dragged a rusty tin trunk along the uneven floor. 'Look,' he said. 'Poetic justice.'

Painted in white capitals on the lid of the trunk were the words MUNIMENTS AND TITLE DEEDS. He unlocked the small padlock with one of the keys on his ring. He opened the lid slowly as if he were about to show me a heap of precious jewels.

'It's a mess,' he said. 'You have to realize that. Some of the loose papers are badly damaged. Goodness knows where

38

they've been. Some damp outhouse, I shouldn't wonder. But the notebooks are not too bad . . . We have to be grateful . . .'

I kneeled down to look at pages covered with my father's small, secretive handwriting. I was overwhelmed with emotion, like a man on the verge of the discovery of a lifetime. It looked like rubbish. It could have been rubbish if my mother's attitude were to be credited. But this man attached great value to the hoard. All so remote – and yet nothing more than fifty years old, mostly far more recent. What divides ancient from modern? Deteriorating paper . . . I could have been gazing at the glittering contents of a newly opened Egyptian or Etruscan tomb.

iii

My problem was to contain my excitement. The interview had become a remote occasion, a distraction. I was alone in the Reading Room with Dilkes. He had put away his precious proofs and wanted to talk to pass the time. Adams was being interviewed.

'I thought the sherry was pretty disgusting,' Dilkes said. 'South African, I shouldn't wonder. Wouldn't put it past them in a place like this.'

I clung to the window. I didn't want to listen. My heart beat faster as I wondered what revelations awaited me in that muniment trunk. Alongside it in the cellar was an untidy heap of sets of *The Illustrated London News* from 1915 to 1945. Mather told me how he had saved them from the incinerator. Part of his concern for them had arisen from the fact that they had come from the same house in Pendraw. During all my investigations into my father's elusive history this stuff had been lying in the defunct outside lavatory of an obscure terrace house in Eifion Street. It all meant something. What was missing was the peace and quiet for uninterrupted concentrated study. The secret lay as much in the angle and intensity of analysis as in the raw material, so that by some alchemy that had little to do with logic, the curriculum of my present life had to acquire a sufficient cutting edge to make effective cross-sections of my father's petrified thought in order to penetrate the riddle of his past. I wished Dilkes wasn't there. His nervous shuffle and nailbiting intruded on trains of thought that were themselves as elusive and changeable as the shifting cloud formations in the sky I was staring at. Dilkes was talking to me.

'I said they call this "The Land of Song", don't they? Don't you hear anything I say?' He was expecting me to apologize. He had no idea how rudely he was interrupting my effort to concentrate on my own thinking. 'I suppose you're wondering why I'm putting in for a job in a place like this?' Nothing on earth was further from my mind. Dilkes wanted to unburden himself and since there was no one else around I had to suffer the process. 'I'll tell you this much,' he said with an air of confidentiality. 'The age of university expansion is over. Now the time to get out is before the ship starts to sink.' He grinned and stirred in his chair like a spoon in a cup of tea. 'It's not quite this place or Saskatoon,' he said. 'It's not that bad. But a sociologist who can't read the signs of the times is about as much use as a paper paddle.'

I couldn't wait to go through my father's papers. There were diaries there and illicit notebooks written in pencil when he had been under-age in the trenches. Nothing I had discovered before was comparable to this. I wanted Wesley Dilkes to oblige me by shutting up. I wanted this whole interviewing process to accelerate and get itself finished and done with so that I could get back to Hefin Mather and his treasure trove. The contents of that trunk were in some sense the title deeds of my very existence. My father's secrets were the secret of my universe.

'Why should you want to be moving in any case, More?' Dilkes was saying. 'I should have thought Redbatch Abbey was a very go-ahead sort of place. Just the place for a thrusting young academic.'

He was drivelling on to gain my attention. Perhaps I should feed him a pack of lies and watch the expression on his face as he gobbled them up. But I had far more important things to engage my mind. At the moment he was sprawling in the oak bardic chair like a thwarted monarch biting a corner of his beard. It was only by a great effort of will that I was able to concede to myself that he had as much right to apply for this post as he had to exist, and that he had as much right to exist as I had. In the ceiling of the Reading Room I could hear the Fates spinning. It was my being that was suspended like a spider's thread. It was Dilkes's breath that was blowing on it disturbing the still air.

'I can't see how they'd dare, mind you. I can't see how they ever would.' Dilkes was getting agitated. The Welsh language was worrying him. 'How could it ever be a requirement in our field, for Christ's sake? It would be an intolerable encroachment on academic freedom. I'd have the whole lot of them up before the UGC before you could say Aberjabber. Not to mention the Race Relations Board. Wire-pulling bloody lot, they are. All this fuss about Welsh. It's a patois that should have died out years ago. Sentimental lot. They'd never dare, would they?'

He would be gone tomorrow at the latest. And the place therof would know him no more. Yet another one. So why bother to attack him? *'Dr Dilkes, you don't perhaps realize it, but that is a tidal wave of detergent waste flowing out of your flaccid mouth . . . a torrent of linguistic pollution . . . a mid-atlantic admass oil slick . . .'* Why bother. Why bother?

The Adams who returned from the Council Chamber looked uncomfortable and crestfallen. It was not like this that he had gone forth with Arthurian confidence to pick up his just reward at the academic Round Table. He had taken with him the ring of worthiness that belongs by right to the working-class lad who had climbed the educational ladder by dint of his own unaided effort. I glimpsed the shadow that travelled over Dilkes's face when Adams let us know with unforced pride that his father was a railway porter at Pontypool Road. He slouched back into the Reading Room, his cheeks red with white patches and his lips swollen with protest. Dilkes seemed pleased to note that the candidate's worldview had changed so much.

'My political allegiance was none of their business,' Adams said. 'I told them straight out.'

'Good for you,' Dilkes said.

41

Adams sat down by the oak table. He was deflated, as if some inner structure of his anatomy had been weakened. He looked in immediate need of comfort, a mother perhaps or a wife, that reservoir of domestic comfort reserved for just such an occasion as this. He muttered in spite of himself.

'I cooked my goose,' he said. 'You can be sure of that. You want to watch out for Mared. He's an absolute bastard. A man can smile and smile and still be a villain.'

Adams's fist was tight on the table. I recognized symptoms of self-loathing. They would account for the depth of his dejection. Against his own principles he had crept and he had crawled just to get a measly job that he now suspected the college president, Lord Mared, would withhold from him out of sheer malice. His image of himself as an outspoken champion of fearless working-class virtues was damaged. His face was flushed and he was sweating with embarrassment and humiliation.

'You want to watch out for him. Gaitskell sacked him from the Shadow Cabinet and he's been taking it out on the rest of the world ever since. The man was never a socialist. Just taking a ride on the party bandwagon in the hope of easy advancement. You mark my words, he'll turn his coat at the first convenient opportunity. My God. I'll expose the bastard if it's the last thing I ever do.'

He was talking to himself. It was the only comfort available in the Reading Room. Dilkes was preparing for his ordeal by surreptitious deep-breathing exercises, and I myself was still thinking about my father and barely in touch with my immediate surroundings.

iv

The Council Chamber had been designed to invoke a distinguished past which could hardly ever have existed in reality. Above the table at which I sat keeping my critical wits about me hung three elaborate brass candelabra suspended from a ceiling of vaulted stone. The reproduction William and Mary chairs surrounded the length of the table like silent witnesses who found council meetings of the past

42

of greater interest than the present proceedings. The carved cresting rails of the back uprights were like fixed frowns on loan from the former presidents, vice-chancellors and principals whose images hung on the walls behind them. The half-dozen members of the selection board were lost among so many imposing appointments – except for Lord Mared, who sat like an actor in a spotlight at the head of the table. Behind him, Simons the assistant registrar was tucked in at his own little table, keeping the minutes and cradling a silver propelling pen in both hands. I had to avoid his puckish smile. In the canopied fireplace behind him a single bar electric fire glowed as a forlorn substitute for the log fire of the designer's imagination.

'Well, now then, Mr More . . .'

Lord Mared's manner was crisp and military. It gave the interview something of the atmosphere of a court martial, to which I did not object. Straight questions validated straight answers. I was prepared to speak out as far as the nature of the occasion allowed.

'Professor Morris Pritchard has assured us that all three of you are equally brilliant in your field and we are quite happy to take his word for it.'

Professor Pritchard leaned forward and it seemed as if a chair-back had become temporarily animated. He exposed his teeth in my direction before sinking back into obscurity. The members of the board were hidden among the chairs. I could see the fingers of an old man drumming the table-top and the head of an old woman made its presence visible by an involuntary oscillation on a short neck embellished with a string of pearls. Professors sat back, council members sat forward. I counted six present, including Lord Mared. The Principal was said to be attending a conference in Vienna. Simons I did not count.

'You are the youngest candidate, Mr More, and I am sure that is to your credit. Now would you like to tell the board in as few words as possible why we should choose you?'

I was overwhelmed by unforeseen panic. This was not the kind of question I anticipated. I had no idea what to say. I could see all the faces turned towards me, waiting for me to speak. There was Morris Pritchard's, like a boiled pudding going cold. Why hadn't he prepared me for this? Simon's puckish smile was alight with *Schadenfreude*.

'Come along, Mr More. The rules of the market-place operate in the most unexpected places these days. No one is privileged any more. Sell yourself.'

A spurt of anger blurred my vision. My persona was disintegrating and in the process an unnaturally vivid awareness of my immediate surroundings was taking over. There were reflections and highlights everywhere as if the room had been invaded by luminous hobgoblins. I could see the old woman's face reflected in a polished candelabra; the shaking of her head threatened the stability of the Council Chamber like the first tremor of an earthquake.

'No,' I said. It was some relief to speak. The long room was assuming its normal dimensions. 'I filled an application,' I said. 'You have all the papers in front of you. I am what I am. It's not my business to sell myself. I wouldn't know how to do it.'

I had cooled down. It was a satisfactory response and I was prepared to stand by it. I was no longer tempted to push back my chair and storm out of the room. Lord Mared was smiling at me as if I were a convenient mirror in which he could contemplate his own reflection. He lifted his chin and adjusted his hard collar with an index finger.

'So why do you think you are here?' Lord Mared asked.

For that I had an immediate answer. He smiled as though he approved at least of its promptness.

'To discuss what contribution I could make to the college,' I said. 'In the light of possibilities and principles.'

'Good,' Mared said. 'Good. What principles. Let's begin there, shall we?'

I wanted to be lucid and I wanted to grip the attention of the lay members of the committee. A display of intellectual pyrotechnics was called for if Adams and Dilkes were all that good. I had to impress on their collective consciousness the unique nature of what it was I had to contribute. Nothing else could account for my embarking on a dissertation concerning the sociology of the early Celts. I was swept forward on a wave of uncharacteristic eloquence.

'. . . Thus in total contrast to the power structures of the

44

Roman imperial power, the early Celts relied on language, religion, custom and practice, art forms and mythology to provide the necessary minimum of social cohesion. I think I would be prepared to argue that this Celtic substrata remains a fundamental element in the more liberal aspects of European sociology.' When I paused for breath I thought I saw oscillations of the old woman's head adopting a more negative emphasis. To stop that shaking, or at least to reduce it to its normal level, I had to gain sympathetic interest. 'Take the role of women,' I continued, 'in what one may call the archetypal Celtic social pattern. Both in myth and in reality. Let us compare Rhiannon in the Mabinogi and the remarkable tomb of the Princess of Vix. They controlled their own destinies in so far as they owned their own property. In this respect their status was equal with that of men . . .' I went on as though I were incapable of controlling the afflatus that had taken possession of my speech. It wouldn't stop until someone interrupted the flow. 'This great common store of myth ensured that each generation in its turn retained its awareness of the genius of place. They knew they shared the occupation of the land with gods and spirits and that these supernatural forces used natural phenomena like mounds and hills and rivers and mists and phases of the moon to come closer to humankind and give it a deeper understanding of the nature and purpose of its existence . . .'

I looked at Lord Mared with gratitude when at last he cut across me.

'This is all very interesting, Mr More,' he said. 'But this isn't exactly your field, is it?' He shuffled the papers in front of him and made a show of examining his cyclostyled copy of my curriculum vitae. 'Your thesis was to do with pay differentials and family stability among skilled and unskilled labour in post-war car manufacture in the English Midlands. Are we to understand that you are making a radical change of direction in your research work?'

Professor Pritchard had leaned forward again. His eyebrows were raised. There was also an expression of vague reproach on his flabby face. How much had I told him and how much had I withheld? Boldness was the only policy left to me.

'Cultural ecology,' I said.

There was an extent to which I was obliged – no, compelled – to take this lot into my complete confidence. This was the turning point. The tide in the affairs of Peredur More that had to be taken in the flood. They had to understand that this was no ordinary job. A visionary touch would not go amiss. This was a mission. At the same time I would be pragmatic, placing each foot in correct order on firm ground. There were things to be said about the topography of forests as a social force and the pride of lineage that bound the whole of a given society together on the grounds that they were all, male and female, rich and poor alike, of gentle birth. But these would have to wait along with my ideas about a common aesthetic and the function of art in securing freedom and unity in the social pattern.

'Let me put it this way,' I said. 'It seems to me that this college is ideally situated to initiate a new and exciting synthesis of sociology, economics, political philosophy and what is becoming known as environmental studies. We have a mission. Let me give a concrete example. I envisage a designated area where cultural conservation and growth will be given a first priority. This is of the first importance not only to the British Isles but to Europe as a whole. The pluralistic basis of European civilization, it seems to me, has an unmistakeable Celtic undertone. This is the place to explore that concept. By doing that we might well bring a fresh impetus to the economy of this corner of Wales and maybe set a creative example that could be followed elsewhere.'

The old woman wanted to speak. I hoped she might want to ask an intelligent question. Her head as it trembled was turning towards Lord Mared. Her voice rumbled with surprising depth.

'Mr Chairman. I do hope we are not going to have too much of this Welsh business disrupting the life of the college. I would just make that point.'

When her head turned towards me again it seemed to me that her powdered features were filled with undisguised loathing. It was a relief to hear Lord Mared laugh. I took it he was politely overlooking an old woman with a familiar bee at work decorating her tattered bonnet. Members of the panel were glancing at their wrist-watches. But Mared was the man. Not one of them would dare attempt to expedite the proceedings without his signalled consent.

'Mr More,' Lord Mared said. 'There is one question I would like to put to you. You don't have to answer it, unless you want to. I'm sure the board would not hold it against you. Why exactly did you leave Redbatch? Was there something wrong with the place?'

I spotted the hidden implication in the question. What he really meant was, was there something wrong with me. Adams was right. He was a dangerous, smiling bastard. He was drawing the attention of the entire panel to the fact that I had resigned from one lectureship without a guaranteed prospect of a fresh appointment. I was over-prepared to answer this one. I was a bachelor. My needs were few. I travelled light. I had a small savings account. Ideas were more significant than security. I wanted to live nearer to my widowed mother? (That seemed to have the more general appeal even if it were less than the whole truth.) There was a post-graduate student stealing my ideas with the tacit approval of the Head of Department who was in league with the post-graduate's rich father . . . That would have been entirely true, but not helpful at this juncture. I did not wish to appear a malcontent. An honest simplicity would be my best remedy.

'I wanted to come back to Wales,' I said.

Lord Mared smiled broadly as though he entirely approved of such sentiments. There were no further questions.

v

Adams had a migraine. He lay on a sofa against the inside wall of the Reading Room with his eyes closed. A casualty in a comfortable dressing station. I wanted to get at my father's notebooks. Even at a glance sentences had taken root in my mind. *The cattle wagon stinks because we stink . . . the straw*

47

under our feet is as filthy as the language in our mouths. A seventeen-year-old on his way to the Front, carrying his chapel upbringing with him like the down on his cheeks. It seems amazing to me . . . *The dead can't do anything to you. I crawl among bodies buried three years ago exhumed by the shelling. Spades would not have dug so deep.* This was my father. This was how his reticence was shaped. These were experiences that never left him all his life and it was out of them that I came. His task, then, was to search out living wounded like a young sniffer dog among the skulls of an earlier Golgotha. This was what haunted him: this, too, was part of my inheritance. Unbearable suffering on a barbed-wire cross.

There was no binding obligation for me to linger in the silent Reading Room while Dr Dilkes was being interviewed. I had to make contact with Hefin Mather. I saw him now like a new Merlin in his underground lair devising a looking-glass through which I would see my father and my progenitors come to life again. That same glass should also give me prismatic glimpses of my own future. Nothing could be more urgent.

He was not at his table. I scurried about the library looking for him. He was the man who had my future under lock and key. It was vital I came to an understanding with him as quickly as possible. Were those discarded papers to be regarded as part of my father's residuary estate? In which case did they belong to my mother, even though she would prefer that they did not exist? Or did they belong now to the college library as they lay in the anonymity of the institution's lowest circle. The darkness in which they hid was neutral and so was the range of colour in the seed of an uncatalogued flower.

I found him in a research-room in the turret, his nose in a box of books. They were from the library which a deceased Congregational minister had left in his will to his old college. Behind the lens of his spectacles Mather's eyes looked large with a guilty surprise that verged on alarm. Did I really look like an avenger with snakes standing up in my hair? It was necessary for me to calm down. Too much excitement would activate the rashes on my skin.

48

'Could we come to an arrangement?' Breathlessness did not inspire confidence. Was my instinct about the urgency of the affair so infallible? If the papers had lain in mouldering obscurity for so many years, what was my tearing hurry? 'About the papers,' I said. 'Perhaps we could edit them together? And, in the meantime, keep them secret.'

Did he see what I meant? They were too important for my mother, or even my brothers, to be allowed to tamper with them. I was the only member of the family who could bring to the uncovenanted hoard the degree of sympathetic attention and scholarly care that they required.

'They are important, aren't they?' I said. 'You said so yourself.'

'I think so,' Mather said. 'But what I think doesn't really count for all that much. Here or anywhere else.'

I wanted certainties not equivocations. 'You said he was a poet of national importance. Isn't it true?' I wanted to drag him out of his defensive earthworks. He was getting to look more like a mole the longer I looked at him. I hadn't noticed before that he rolled his 'r's'. It could develop into an irritation unworthy of any merlinesque role.

'It's relative, isn't it?' he said. 'Like everything else. I mean there are some very worthwhile books in this box. But if this were the British Museum they'd be more excited if it were filled with Winston Churchill's old bedsocks.'

He giggled merrily at his own joke and rubbed one ankle against the other. This, too, was something I would have to put up with. The more intimate we became the greater the number of extempore quips and jests I would have to put up with.

'You've had a look?' I said.

'Oh, there's some excellent stuff in there,' Mather said. 'No doubt about that. But a great deal of repetition. A lot of fragments.'

Fragments of what? And why repetitions? I held back from asking. What I yearned for was immediate and untrammelled access to all the material. Every scrap. To get that I needed Mather's collaboration and goodwill. Would I get it?

'Do you agree, Mr Mather?'

I tried to sound cool and rational. He showed willing and yet he seemed preoccupied with a different issue.

'Have you heard?' he said.

'Heard what?' I must have sounded obtuse.

'Have they made the appointment?'

It was impossible trying to be in two places at once. I sped down the spiral stone staircase and along a sequence of echoing corridors and up yet another staircase to the isolated Reading Room. Its position was ideal for academic incarcerations. Dilkes was back. Adams was sitting up, frowning and smiling at the same time because Dilkes in a heightened emotional state was recalling an incident in his protracted interview in minute detail. The old boy I recalled drumming his thick fingers on the table had dozed off and farted in his sleep. His intense coughing fit came too late to disguise the embarrassing sound. Dilkes himself was a changed man. Like a student after a gruelling examination he was light-headed with relief. He was dancing around the carpet as he embellished his anecdote. My return was an unseemly interruption. I should have been present to appreciate the nuances of his narrative. A shaft of sunlight caught drops of spittle in his beard.

'Where the hell have you been?' he asked.

I had no intention of telling him. 'Just looking around,' I replied.

'I don't know whether it's wise or not to take it,' Dilkes said. 'It's a bit out in the sticks, to say the least. Who wants to be a big fish in a small pond? But that is not entirely the point, is it?' He looked at Adams and myself like the man-in-charge who invites comment from his subordinates out of sheer politeness. He stalked to the window. 'The scenery's very agreeable,' he said. 'Especially if you like climbing or messing about in boats. I don't happen to go in for either. And after all we're here to work, aren't we? Not just to mess about like repatriated colonials in semi-retirement. I've got a magnum opus to finish. And this may be the very place to do it. Away from the rat race. Peace and quiet and creative fulfilment.' He lifted a plump hand in a gesture of episcopal benediction. He was a senior figure speaking for all in the courts of academic enlightenment.

'What magnum opus?' Adams asked. He passed a hand wearily over his forehead. He had the shape of a rugby forward and the face of a nervous child. I could see how much he would appeal to women.

'*Purpose and Power: Sociological Theory from Machiavelli to Marx*. In four volumes.' Dilkes smiled at each of us in turn as he unveiled his glittering project. 'Quite a catchy title: *Purpose and Power*. Will it be a bestseller? Give old Bertie Russell a run for his money. Put our discipline bang in the centre of the academic map, which is where it belongs.'

He was expecting us to be grateful. I could see that. All his Herculean labours were being taken, in some mysterious way, on our behalf. He really was a pompous idiot. Yet his self-assurance made me uneasy. There was a tap on the door and Simons popped his head in. He went through his routine of behaving like a puckish Mr Punch. Then he paused until he had gained the undivided attention of each candidate in the Reading Room. This was the climax of his performance. He spoke at last.

'Dr Dilkes,' he said. 'The committee would like a brief word.' Simons's grin had momentarily vanished. Somehow he contrived to turn the corners of his mouth down.

'What's the trouble?' Dilkes said.

Simons was teasing him. He smiled. 'The job,' he said. 'They want to make you an offer. It's yours if you want it.' Simons winked and lowered his voice. 'My God they were impressed with the scope of that book of yours. *Purpose and Power*. Just the thing to put this old place on the map. Congratulations.' He held the door open with mock obsequiousness. As Dilkes marched out he bestowed a parting grin on Adams and myself. 'And our commiserations to the gallant losers,' he said.

He closed the door. I looked down and the ground seemed to open under my feet.

Three

There was sympathy in Hefin Mather's soft and self-effacing voice, but underneath I thought I could detect a profound curiosity.

'What will you do now?' he said.

It was not merely the question of a sensitive fellow who suffered with those whom he saw suffer, or felt his own fate tremble in the weather-front that settled the destiny of another representative of his species. I guessed him to be the cherished offspring of working-class parents with a pious regard for the power of education. Sacrifices had been made to enable the young Hefin to get first one foot and then the other on the steep educational ladder. He had struggled with one exam after the other to reach his present haven in the basement of the college library. He was the properly qualified assistant librarian with special responsibility for modern Welsh manuscript material and he had letters to prove it and a table and a filing system and a temporary muniment room next to the boiler. In me he was confronted with an academic who had no responsibility for anything except his own failure: a man who had gambled with his own career and lost; a subject of reproof as well as commiseration. As we talked in subdued tones between the stacks and the open shelves he cradled one hand in the other as though there had been a death in the family.

'Nothing ever really changes,' he said.

I was disturbed by the depth of his pessimism. He observed the world from between the bookshelves in the library basement. It was as good a vantage point as any to judge the times and the seasons. He could arrive at his own shrewd and scholarly verdict in the fullness of his own quiet time. If he had concluded that nothing changed then there was little point in any effort to improve matters. How could I accept that? My resignation from Redbatch was in itself an act of defiance against the conspiracy theory of history. That kind of fatalism was suitable for serfs under the hatches whose lives depended on the whims and machinations of their masters strutting about on deck posturing as captains of their souls and architects of empire; or for the hangers-on of an academic system created to service the superstructure of capitalist industrial technology. But not for me. The more evidence he accumulated the more fiercely I needed to argue, at least inside myself, to combat it.

'These people choose one another,' Mather said. 'That's how the system perpetuates itself.'

I had spent hours trudging on the foreshore trying to walk off the shock and disappointment and humiliation of my rejection. My self-confidence had been even more absurd and ephemeral than the fleet of ships conjured out of seaweed that I had seen darkening the horizon from the high window of the college Reading Room, that cold retreat for quiet and meditation and unsuccessful candidacies. I could hear the echo of my mother's laughter at the spectacle of yet another contretemps in the comical career of her accident-prone youngest son. This would be what she wanted. Being appointed here, I would have encroached too closely on her sphere of influence. What had seemed a destiny and a high adventure, an exercise in enterprise and daring, had ended up all loss and no profit. There was no myth or magic in the evening air. Only a cold wind that chopped up the sea and made my nose drip and my eyes water. My feet sank in the pebbles and loose sand of the foreshore until my heels were as sore as those of the bankrupt prince in the story.

'What will you do now?' Hefin Mather had said.

I saw again those high-backed chairs ranged around the table in the Council Chamber. They moulded the people who sat in them like an Act of Uniformity. Should I seek an appointment with Professor Morris Pritchard in order to protest at the outcome, to reproach him for having misled me, to demand an explanation, to fill the air of his room in college with the steam of indignation? To what end? As Mather said: these people choose each other. You only had to look at them.

I still had no idea what I was going to do, except gain access to my father's papers before any other member of my family took wind of their existence. And for that I depended wholly on the goodwill of this man in front of me. From now on I could only be here on sufferance. I was not a member of the staff. I did not even possess a reader's ticket. I could be shooed away by any cleaner or part-time porter unless Hefin Mather protected me and accounted for my presence. This man was the living link with all I had to salvage from my misadventure. It was his wink and beckoning finger that allowed me to stumble across the jewel in the dark.

An apparent accident could be more fruitful than the ponderous planning of my intellect. There would be light in the darkness the moment I came to appreciate how far my father's suffering outweighed my disappointment. Understanding his past would give me the mastery over my own future that this defeat had taken from me.

'Have you thought of extra-mural work?' Mather asked.

In fact, I hadn't. This man was unremittingly helpful. I should sink to my knees to ask forgiveness for all the unworthy thoughts I had entertained about him.

'There's the WEA, of course,' Mather said. 'But the Extra-Mural Department pays better. I know that from my own experience. I have a class in "The Poets of the Princes" in Uwch Digell. An out-of-the-way place. They pay for a taxi to get me there. I don't drive myself.'

I had to put aside all reservations. This was a man after my own heart. He had bad breath and his jacket was impregnated with the smell of stale sweat, but these were trivial blemishes that accentuated rather than diminished his worth. Besides I was no oil painting myself. What mattered and what bound us ever closely together was the purity of our intentions.

'Look,' I said. 'I can't tell you how grateful I am to you for all your help. It's been worthwhile coming here, just in order to meet you. What I wanted to ask . . . since they are still uncatalogued and so on . . . could you let me borrow just one or two of my father's notebooks? Just for the time being. I know how much work there is to be done and so on. I sincerely hope we can collaborate. But if this could be a secret between us . . . It's what I need at the moment more than anything. I don't know quite how to put it. Make contact with his spirit, I suppose . . .'

In spite of my revulsion at so much emotional exposure, I was prepared to go even further to get my hands on those notebooks. If I attacked this timid and defenceless creature it would still be impossible for me to drag out the contents of the trunk and escape from this place without being stopped.

'It's very difficult for me to express in so many words,' I continued, 'how much these papers mean to me. Especially now. Especially at this juncture . . . How can I put it?'

His beady eyes seemed to be scrutinizing my motives like a bank manager calculating the credit worthiness of a new customer. From a shelf concealed by his desk he produced an account book with a pencil attached to the spine by a piece of string.

'Whatever you take,' he said, 'you can sign for it here. An informal arrangement. For my benefit more than anything else. The stuff hasn't gone into the system. But all the more reason for keeping a check on what goes in and out, so to speak. I hope you don't mind? But my mind would be easier then, you see.'

Of course I didn't mind. I was so pleased and relieved I could have embraced him.

ii

Those trenches. Those trenches. I saw them opening across the green fields outside the window as I deciphered and copied out my father's minute writing on the stained pages of his buttoned notebook. I also envisaged, in confused abstracted forms, parasols, silk hats, starched shirt fronts, long skirts and heavy underwear blasted to all points of a square bourgeois compass, and as the smooth skin of

55

existence cracks, colour drains from the picture and the brushes choke with earth. Mud and blood belong to each other. What a trite conclusion. How comfortable it is to be an academic. Even a failed one. With all the time in the world, it seems, to digest other men's experience. But this is not just another man. This is my father whose seed, at one time or another before they were estranged and grew to hate each other, entered my mother's womb like a loving signal and initiated my existence. There was an Eden before the Fall; and before Eden there was this journey through Hell. In my father's record even the rubrics of the bourgeois life-cycle materialize in the wrong order.

'. . . The dead can't do anything to you. I crawled among bodies buried three years ago exhumed by the shelling. Spades could not have dug so deep . . . I have heard voices inside me I never heard before. Officers commissioned or non-commissioned are accredited agents of Providence and it is only unquestioning obedience that keeps the sky from falling in. I can hear the voice of Alice Breeze's father echoing from the pitch-pine pulpit: "As Abraham of old was ready to sacrifice his son Isaac, so let us in our day of anguish, of travail, and of trial, learn to give up even those things we love and cherish most . . ." I can see Alice's hat beyond the music stand of the organ which is centrally placed in our chapel under the pulpit and the deacon's pew and exactly halfway between the two aisles. Our pew is a cross-bench so I can study these things as the minister's voice reverberates like distant gunfire over my head . . . I crawl as close as I can to the earth. Above the labyrinthine trenches the sun has come out to intensify the smell. Soon the flies would be out. I was more afraid of them than the corpses. I had to turn back, to get up and run, but the weight of the war held me down. I saw a khaki-wrapped body stretched out on the sap-head like a corpse sunbathing, which was ridiculous. I recognized the face even with the eyes closed. I knew him. Over-age, they said. And I was under-age. They warned me not to talk to him. A dirty old bugger looking for bum boys, Frankie said. You want to keep well clear of him. He was still enough to be dead until he opened one eye and winked at me. As I came close enough to examine him, he opened both eyes and said "Kiss me, Hardy", in English. The grin grew slowly on his face, turning his cheeks into a pair of bloodshot apples. His breath stank of rum. He had no need of my first aid. He was alive and well and drunk. His mittened fingers fumbled among the folds of his khaki clothing. Under his tunic he had a money-belt and from it dangled at least half a dozen small flasks. "Nothing you can do for this lot, comrade," he said. "What would you like to drink?" He saw me shake my head. "Chapel lad. That's what I was. Chatham Road. Doesn't mean much here though, does it? Didn't mean much there either, come to think of it. You know what I call this?" He displayed his belt again. "The eternal arm," he said. "Would you like me to get you one?" I was shocked by his blasphemy; but he wanted me to laugh. "Where's your mate, then? Frankie, do they call him? Nice lad. Very nice-looking. And so are you. How old are you then? Would you like to tell me that?" His false teeth were loose in his mouth and saliva spilled over his lips. He was old. He could have been as much as fifty. As old as my Uncle Gwilym in his office on the slate quay with the war map all over the partition wall. "Sweet seventeen." He had to say that in English. The silence in the trench was as unnerving as the smell. I could hear nothing. No cries for stretchers. The war had moved away. Just above the drunken soldier's head a weasel poked its head over the parapet, less nervous than I was. "I'm Arty," the soldier said. " 'B' Company, if you want to know." The hessian on his steel helmet was like Mrs Roberts, Belan View's Sunday hat. His pockets were bulging. More bottles or was it rob-all-my-comrades? "Come and lie by me, boy, and open your coat. Feel the sun on you while you still can. We'll have a little drink. One sip. Two sips. And a little snooze in the sun." Someone was shouting. It must have been for me. And the gunfire in the distance. "I'm going," I said. "I've got to go." Arty wouldn't move. "I'm too drunk to move. That's the truth of it. I'm better off dead to the world. I can hear the hymns." He began to sing in a quavering tenor. *"Cofia'n gwlad Benllywydd tirion /Dy gyfiawnder fyddo'i grym . . ."* (Remember our land, merciful Lord and Master /Let your righteousness be her strength) . . . and wave his hand around as if he were conducting a choir. It was disgusting. A sacrilege. And yet it made me feel an unexpected twinge of longing for the home I had run away from. "*Cofia amdana'i fachgen annwyl.* (Remember me, dear boy.) Kiss me, Hardy." He was revolting. He would have been better dead.'

What I felt was deeper than twinges of scholarly excitement. There were other accounts in larger, neater exercise books. Attempts to make sense of his experience and reduce inchoate perception into formal permanence. He would try out a piece in strict metres, then prose, then an experimental narrative poem that was clearly an extended fragment of autobiography. I had to establish to my own satisfaction the reasons for his failure. He had the talent. But the society in which he spent his life was insufficiently supportive. There was nothing there to give him the help he needed.

As a child I watched that thin figure stalking across the cob in the rain on his way home from the office. I saw how blue his hand was as he held on to his sober solicitor's hat. Even then I was sorry for his solitude. I had no idea of the memories that would not leave him. I only saw the absent, haunted look on his face. There were certain times he could never bear to hear about. And there were public occasions he would lock himself in his study to avoid. These papers only gave me partial access to his secrets. How often and when in the lengths of unspecified time after the event did he make these several attempts to fashion votive objects out of his traumas? He tried so hard. Sisyphus himself could not have tried harder or received less thanks.

'I sat next to Frankie on the tailpiece of a transport next to the horse ambulances. The captain said he bore a charmed life so that was something to which I could well shift closer. Frankie knew so much more about everything than I did. He was as solid as those stout legs of his in their puttees. I could see them run their crooked race through the bullets and the five-point-nines. He was as solid as all life itself; more solid than shattered trees and ruined houses. Whenever I could I laid my hand on his arm. He squinted up at our aeroplanes buzzing overhead like wasps trying to singe their wings in the midday sun. He used the Woodbine in his hand to count them. Sixteen, he said, and he knew why they were there. That was what was so comforting about Frankie. He always knew.

' "No shelling around here today," he said. It was such a relief when he said it. My lungs expanded at the prospect of sustained release. We could smoke together longer than a lifetime. The smoke had time to explore the depth of our lungs.

' "The King is in St Omer," Frankie said.

'With leisurely kindness he told me how he knew. I basked in his insights.

' "Willie Williams, you know, that Willie that waits in the Officer's Mess, proper creeping Jesus, he had twenty-four hours and he saw the old bugger having his picture taken driving a railway engine. Playing bloody trains behind the Front. And that sod General Plumer was with him, monocle stuck in his eye. So there you are, my little More and More, dog doesn't eat dog."

'He could see I didn't quite follow and this made him grin as he blew cigarette smoke through his nose.

' "Boche knows everything, don't he? So Kaiser Bill knows his cousin George is popping down to visit the Front. So Kaiser Bill tells the big guns to lay off and no shelling behind the hill. And those aeroplanes are arsing about up there to make sure the old bastard keeps his word."

'Was that really why the shelling had stopped? Certainly everything seemed strangely different. I could listen in peace to Frankie, and the second phase of his lucid argument became as unshakeable as the ground under the transport we were sitting on. I had faith in Frankie.

' "Who makes the rules and decides on the uniforms? The King's this and the King's that? It's a bloody game, you see. That's all it is. Who says you're a Taff and yonder's Froggie or Fritz or what have you? It's just that the bloody game's gone wrong, you see, and we're paying the price in corpses instead of pawns and checkers. That's all it is."

'Everything Frankie said was as solid and right and resilient as his body. I couldn't understand it but so long as I kept close it gave me comfort. He had subtle theories about shadowy figures who were making fortunes out of all that

59

was going on and about the intimate link between blood and shit and money. He would draw on his cigarette until it was lower than his fingertips and find new discernments with which to astonish me.

' "Who says it's got to keep on going, More and More? Somebody lending money to both sides, mate, and the longer it goes on the More-more the interest goes up. Get it? You should, boy. Got any more fags?"

'Some were killed and some carried on. That was obvious enough. If the King came this far he would see the camp was neat and in good order. The Army looked after us: fed, clothed, equipped, sheltered, nourished, organized all of us. In the canteen fags would be waiting for us as white as flowers of forgiveness smelling of asphodel.

'At the gate we saw a soldier tied with his back to a gun-carriage. His arms and legs were lashed tight to the wheel in the cruciform of Field Punishment Number One. I had seen it before. In the rest area outside Lillers. I was watching a crowd outside an estaminet in the middle of a village. Frankie said my mouth was open. They were setting up a game of housey-housey and I couldn't decide whether or not to join in. Alice Breeze's father and my grandmother pronounced gambling a cardinal sin as bad as drunkenness. I hadn't been drunk then. I had bits of Arras Chamber of Commerce tokens in my pocket. They didn't seem like real money. If I used those it would be like playing poker with dead matches. In the middle of it all, two Red Caps marched a prisoner in handcuffs. They tied him to the wheel of a limber in the village square. I could see the poor chap's head hanging limp as a dead pheasant's. Something about him gained everyone's sympathy. It was like a miracle. Even as I watched, two Tommies started a fight and the housey-housey game started like a noisy riot. The Red Caps rushed over to separate the fighters and I saw a soldier giving the prisoner on the wheel a swig of wine. It was like a station of the cross. They were even able to loosen and ease the prisoner's bonds before the Red Caps could notice. But it wasn't the same here. The man on the wheel was Arty. And I shared his guilt. I had been tempted to drink from one of his illegal flasks. Like the notebooks at the bottom of my

60

kit-bag, it was an offence in itself. They had caught him. I was still at large. But only just. Frankie was pulling at my arm. There was no sympathy at all from those who passed by Arty. "Come on," Frankie said. "Never mind that dirty bugger. We need some fags."

'Arty had seen me. He had spotted me. His voice quavered out the same hymn he had sung lying on the saphead. It was for my benefit and no one else's. I had to make some sign. "*Cofia amdana'i . . .*" He was saying it again. Should I raise my hand? He was not supposed to speak. A burly Red Cap struck him across the mouth. His false teeth flew out and landed in two separate pieces on the ground. Were they still grinning on his behalf? I couldn't take my eyes off them although they were the last things on earth I wanted to see. I should pick them up, wash them, and put them back in his mouth. Or keep them for him. His mouth was slack and bleeding. Frankie dragged me away. "Come on," he said. "There's no knowing what that slippery bugger has been up to." '

iii

I did not have absolute confidence in my second-hand Triumph Herald but it was all I could afford and it was as indispensable to my new way of life as Hefin Mather, who sat alongside me, well wrapped up and determined to enjoy the outing. He looked like a delicate child being taken out for the first time after an old-fashioned illness. He was inclined to make a cult of being old-fashioned. I overheard him being asked by an inquisitive local journalist his views on Sunday closing. He said that most things that had happened in Wales since the Great War were changes for the worse and the best thing that could happen would be for the petrol to turn into water so that he could live to welcome back the pony and trap. As far as I could see, the petrol in my tank did nothing to impair the undiluted pleasure our excursion gave him.

He had a trick of raising his right hand encased in its woolly glove to hint that we were about to commit an act of unconscious vandalism by passing some site or other of incalculable historical importance. Over-anxious to avoid such tasteless solipsism, I would jam my foot on the brake and furnish him with the question that would allow him to indulge in an impromptu but not inelegant lecture once he had recovered from lurching forward in his seat. The Welsh world around us was his aesthetic stamping ground. If he had had his way we would have stopped at every churchyard and he would have threaded his way through the tombstones with the combined confidence of an art expert and criminal investigator to point at an inscription as though once again he had uncovered a pearl of great price and was delighted to share its beauty and significance with a fellow traveller on that stern highroad of historical research that had no real ending.

'We are all born somewhere and we all die somewhere.' He had his own way of throwing out sage pronouncements and then sniggering happily as though he had made a joke. 'Does it mean anything? It's like the existence of God. You can believe or not believe. I prefer to believe.'

By the grave of Silas Fardd, a poet cleric of the last century, he was moved to recite the sonorous verses from the Welsh translation of the Book of Job about man that is born of a woman being of few days and full of trouble. 'He cometh forth like a flower and is cut down: he fleeth also as a shadow and continueth not.' That was certainly true of my father. His papers were all that were left of him. He walked the earth for more than half a century. His existence had been as substantial and solid as my own; as Mather and I stood by Silas Fardd's elaborate slate gravestone and the wet seeped from the grass into my shoes, I was filled with that elusive longing the living have to communicate with the dead. Without such conversation we shrink into febrile by-products of the machine age: creatures to be standard-ized into convenient units of consumption. Discuss. Would I ever set an examination paper again?

In another graveyard, following Mather on his route to his prey, it was a shock to realize that here in this very place, with her white sports car parked on the uncut grass, I came with Maxine Hacket on my first attempts to find my father's grave. She took it all so lightly, eating grass seeds and spitting them out. A small, slim figure like an advertisement for scented soap, half hidden in the green haze of long grass. The same place at a different season. Not so long ago but nevertheless another existence less real than my father's spidery writing. It was an experience I had to suffer but it was safe to say now that I had survived it. What did I ever see in that loathsome damsel who drove me to the brink of desperation? Her frankness – was she so like a red red rose? – her untamed youthfulness, her uninhibited sense of humour, even her voice with its odd Birmingham accent that foraged among English words like a hen's beak rummaging among old corn for fresher content. To be honest, none of these. The binding excitement was her interest in me: that so attractive a girl should have made the first approaches in my direction and found me worth her notice. The illusion I cherished, until she tired of my self-absorbed melancholy, was that she loved me for myself alone; and for that benediction, gratitude could know no bounds. Now I chose to regard that experience as a purgatorial fire through which I had to pass in order to reach my present status: a man armed with a purpose, with spirit and intellect tempered to a cutting edge.

'Look at those kids,' Hefin Mather said. 'Just look at them.'

Were they six- or seven-year-olds? Three girls and two boys in caps and scarves and overcoats sent out to play on a fine November morning engaged in an odd ritual of their own making. They were dancing around a slate sarcophagus and throwing on it withered flowers they had snitched from ornamental pots on recently tended graves. The ringleader was a girl. It was obvious that the game they were playing was of her invention and that she herself still wavered between frolic and sober ceremony.

'That's how witches are born,' Mather said. 'I think she's trying to frighten herself.'

He was prepared to elaborate but I did not encourage him. From him I wanted hard fact. I was myself only too capable of providing fantasy. There was much ground to cover.

Within twenty minutes my Triumph Herald was parked on the deserted promenade at Pendraw. We had to draw up a more meticulous plan of campaign. We found a café open on the corner of the promenade. We sat at a table in the window extension and enjoyed an illusion of summer warmth. Mather had removed his scarf and was soon beaming over his coffee. He had an Ordnance Survey map at his elbow and a notebook with a list of references and addresses we needed to visit in the course of our researches. For him it was a magical mystery tour.

'Nice little place,' Mather said. 'Always nice to find a nice little place.'

Certainly nice to escape from his den down in the stacks. Through the side window there was a vision of the harbour and the water of the ebb-tide, as smooth as a pale mirror. It reflected the railway yard and some of the houses on the hill behind the town. Birds skimming over the faint images looked like missiles, black and three-dimensional. From the clear horizon of the bay the sun sent a sparkling triangle of light over the waves to point straight at us. Mather murmured an eisteddfodic incantation about facing the sun and the eye of light. He was very ready to wax lyrical.

'Nice little place, Pendraw,' he said. 'We used to come here on our Sunday School trips. Not every year. But I always voted for it.'

As far as I was concerned, the place filled me with misgiving. Only in a superficial, cosmetic way had it changed since I was a child. The woodwork of the terrace house where we lived was painted in garish yellow, but the grey stonework was impregnated with old sadness and I could see the ghost of my father crossing the embankment holding on to his hat against the same old stiff breeze from the sea. He had practised here as a solicitor and as a champion of lost causes for almost a quarter of a century; a substantial slice of historical time about which Mr Hefin Mather knew a great deal more than I did. I had to fill all the gaps in my knowledge in order to exorcize the phantasmagoric dance of anxieties and fears. Why should I dread meeting people I might know in the narrow streets? We moved away when I was twelve. It was true that my mother had dealt parsimoniously with the Town Council when they asked for her support in putting up a memorial to my father. Was I obliged to bear the burden of her guilt, to behave like a man revisiting a place where his name is tainted with a disrepute which verges on scandal?

'Now then,' Mather said, opening his Ordnance Survey map with relish. 'The best way to get there . . . There's no question about it. John Cilydd More was born at Glanrafon Stores. And here it is on the map. Marked. Glanrafon.'

Mather tapped the tiny symbol where it was situated at the junction of two minor roads. I stared at the pale contour marks, the green patches, the dots for rights of way and open pits and bracken, as if I were learning to read music.

'It's not every day I have the privilege of leading a young man to his father's birthplace,' Mather said.

He was generous with his time and attentions. I should never show resentment that he knew more about the life and times of my father than I did. The difficulty was to appraise the degree of gratitude I needed to display. It was a subtle business. The strand of Welsh peasant nonconformity from which he sprang I knew to be excessively polite. At one remove my mother and father had emerged from the same social strata. Lady Brangor had been born poor little Amy Price adopted by her aunt and uncle, Esther and Lucas Parry, whose surname she took. They had been poor enough. And my mother always said her aunt was excessively polite and kind. The vestiges of ancient gentility ingrained in the vernacular which this class used, when mixed with the self-effacing humility fostered by their chosen brand of evangelical religion, could produce manners that bordered on the servile. That was a superficial pseudo-academic sociological assessment and nothing to do with my present mission.

Deep in the cultural tradition to which this man Mather clings as to a life-raft on an ocean of mid-atlantic indifference, there are deposits and rare elements that defined my father's entire existence. Whether Mather understood it or not, to rescue my father's work from oblivion also involved demonstrating that these hidden virtues had a universal validity. Therefore I needed to smile at him and nod at regular intervals. His pencil hovered over his notebook, prescribing tight circles of businesslike enthusiasm.

'We need to construct an exact genealogy,' he said. 'I quite enjoy drawing up family trees. Ancient Celtic habit, I suppose. It's a popular hobby still in these parts, like fishing. I'm told the Americans are taking it up in a big way. A different motivation, one assumes. Filling up empty spaces. And, of course, if you became unexpectedly rich and powerful you get to face an overwhelming need for illustrious ancestors. With us it's different, isn't it? A question of keeping the title deeds up to date. Dusting them down and giving them an airing.'

I had to admit there was more to Mather than met the eye. Secure in his dug-out he had a sophisticated assemblage of intellectual periscopes through which he could study a dangerous terrain without having to venture too often across it. Hence his relish of our present excursion.

'It's a most interesting family,' Mather said. He spoke with such speed and in such a low tone I had to lean forward to catch what he was saying. His excitement made him conspiratorial as if any information he parted with was liable to be picked up by some concealed listening device. 'Your grandfather Robert Samuel More was lost at sea under mysterious circumstances, it seems. His first command. Off the coast of Newfoundland. No survivors.'

This was something I had known and forgotten. Now, coming from Mather's researches, it assumed a new importance in the scheme of things. This was why my father had a love-hate relationship with the sea. One of the few tales he used to tell us was about a pink sailing boat owned by young friends of his. How he went out with them one day against his grandmother's strict prohibition and how they were nearly drowned. One of those rare glimpses of a world he seemed to prefer to keep hidden from us, or not to revisit.

'His father, your great-grandfather, who added the Stores to Glanrafon Farm, was the author of *A History of Calvinistic Methodism in Rhosyr and Dinodig*. Did you ever read it? A very useful work. A rare book, of course, now.

66

We have a copy in the stacks. You must let me show it to you. The style is a bit convoluted, of course, as it tended to be in those days. He was a man of his time. As we all are, come to that.'

Had I ever seen it? I must have. One of the never-read behind the glass doors of the bookcase in the drawing-room of our terrace house. Imposing bindings, uncut pages. Part of the furnishings of a room which I never liked sitting in. A room for drawn blinds and uncomfortable family occasions. I associated it with my mother's worse moods. I could see her knuckles white now as her fingers worked over her forehead and into her hair.

'William Lloyd died in early middle age. There is a pencilled note in an unknown hand on the flyleaf of our copy in the stacks that says the author's hair turned white with the labour of composing this book far into the night. They were an industrious generation. No doubt about that. What happened, as far as I can gather, was that your father's grandmother, your great-grandmother, took command of the Farm and the Stores and ran it all like a great merchant ship, with a very tight hold on the tiller and the till, shall we say?'

Mather was amusing himself even more than me.

'Now she had two daughters and three sons. That's all on record. The widow of the sea captain, your father's mother Elizabeth Rosina More (née Lloyd), died of grief, we can assume. So your father and his sister were brought up by Mrs Lloyd, their grandmother, the energetic and no doubt puritanical widow of the aforesaid prematurely white-haired William Lloyd. Now what I can't help asking myself is this. Was that why John Cilydd More, your father, ran away to the war? Joined up under-age? We have to face the question. Right at the onset. Don't you agree?'

It was easy enough for him. Objective. Dispassionate. He was not obliged to dig and probe painfully into his own past. In the mythology that was left to me from childhood, the place called Glanrafon was like a dark ruin in the country where the worst of our family secrets were buried. My mother would never go near the place. It was there my father's sister had set herself on fire and for that reason

67

alone the place could only be spoken of in whispers. Bedwyr and Gwydion had played there as children but I had only glimpsed it from a distance: a house under a curse with the windows of the shop front blinded by boards. There was an ancient aunt who survived in the Cottage Hospital that used to be the Workhouse. My father took me to see her and she put a hand on my head. Even now I could feel the dead weight of it. He stopped going to see her when she could no longer recognize him.

There were poems he had written which were rooted in the place. The house he was born in. 'The ladder between heaven and earth' and 'the voice and shape of the folk who gave me birth . . .'

'What we need is an accurate chronology of the main events in your father's life,' Mather said. 'And then all the material would fall neatly into place. I'm sure of it. Should I have another cup of coffee, I wonder?'

Of course, that meant that he wanted one. I ordered it.

iv

'A cuckoo sang in the distant wood,' my father wrote, 'but it brought me no comfort. I have mastered the strict metres but I shall never sing the praises of manual labour. A poet is not an earthworm. My knees are sore. My back is aching. My Uncle Simon's backside is several feet ahead like an elephant pretending to be a snail, between the rows of swede plants and rampant weeds that stretch ahead interminably as if to prove the curve of the earth's surface. My fingers thrust like tender fork tines through the gritty soil to snatch at weeds and unwanted plants and tear them out at rapid intervals. My knees are meant to be protected, but the sacking has a way of working loose and impeding my progress. I'll never catch up with my uncle and when he gets to the headland he will look back and grin at me and prepare one of his nasal sarcasms as I crawl towards him. This is worse than war. Nothing gives my uncle more pleasure than the spectacle of my servitude. All those idiotic conventions about arcadia and the pastoral. I could blast the lot. Which is

68

what I will do. The subject in itself is a cliché-ridden anomaly. 'The Garden of Eden'. Where does the Eisteddfod Committee think it is living? What a subject to set in the middle of a great war. I covet the three guineas. How can I win it and say the truth? Impossible. I shall send in two hundred and twenty lines of received opinion mellifluously expressed in skilful variations on the twenty-four measures of Dafydd ap Edmund. To hell with the lot of them. I bide my time.

' "Do you know something, John Cilydd?" He puts his words together as if he is lifting up a load of hay on the end of a pitchfork. "Farming and competing in eisteddfodau don't mix," he said.

'I stared at his hands. They were so broad and earth-encrusted. His whole body was carapaced with unremitting physical labour. He was my uncle and it was assumed I would be his heir. But he was the last man on earth I wanted to be like. He makes me hold the rear legs of bull calves as he shows off his expertise in castration. My grandmother sends me here to be the butt of her eldest son's stunted wit. When he had something on his mind except work he would masticate it like a cow chewing the cud.

'When we sat in the shade of the hedge to eat the tough beef sandwiches his wife had made us and swill the strong tea in the tin can, he went on about "competing". He saw it as an hereditary family flaw. I tried to compose lines in my head instead of listening to him. It was easier to do this eating than when crawling between the rows intent on mindless labour.

' "Your Uncle Gwilym has it badly," Uncle Simon said. "It's a taint all right. Like original sin. That's why he sticks a fancy name on himself. Gwilym Glaslyn. Bardic. Very bardic. For a penny-a-liner with a weekly column in the *Glaslyn Herald*."

'My Uncle Simon was eaten up with envy. It was a fact of his life like the weathering on his skin. There was a feminine pink around his ears and along the top half of his forehead shaded by his cap and in the depth of the creases around his weasel eyes. I could shape him nicely into the pleated mould of the *cynghanedd*. At least his brother Gwilym had that skill and had passed it on to me while I was still a child. At least my Uncle Gwilym had the rudiments of culture and had ventured into the bigger world. I knew about his erratic career because it was a favoured topic with Simon. There were few things he enjoyed more than recalling one or other of his brother's misadventures. Gwilym Glaslyn had been a candidate for the ministry until he had been discovered reeling drunk under the Menai Bridge on the night of the October Fair. He had been an elementary school teacher until a group of mothers found the strength to denounce his weakness for beating little boys with a birch. My grandmother had despatched him to work with Simon when they were both still bachelors but this had been the most disastrous course of all according to Simon. And from my own experience I could well believe it. Then there was a brief sojourn in the office of a cotton importer in Liverpool. It was, according to Simon, sheer desperation and exasperation that drove my grandmother to get him his place as a clerk in the Slate Office on the quay at Glaslyn. Now the slate quarries were closed for the duration he was allowed to use the office for part-time work for the Council. And it was there he composed his weekly column and entertained his literary friends, as my Uncle Simon sarcastically liked to call them. It was there he championed causes like teetotalism and the war effort; and Uncle Simon gave me to understand that was something to be profoundly grateful for, if only for the honour of the family name.

' "Competing and farming don't mix." He had a way of repeating these worn phrases as if they had just occurred to him. "So why do you do it, John Cilydd? Tell me that." For a moment he appeared to be genuinely curious about me.

' "I don't like competing," I said.

'He couldn't believe this. "Then why do you do it? You've been at it since you were twelve."

'Anyone would have thought it was a form of self-abuse.

' "Practice," I said.

' "Practice? For what?"

' "To become a proper poet," I said. "What else?"

'His lips opened and shut. I was pleased he could not find a comment. If I could sharpen my wits on his leathery skin, that would make my servitude easier to bear.

70

'All I want to be is a poet,' he wrote. 'Instead I am measuring out my life in root crop rows. The same field. Another row. I am marooned in a monstrous green sea of servitude. I miss the focal point of my uncle's broad backside and the stretched patch on his corduroy. Without him to hate I am an earthworm with a nose so close to the soil I can smell it. This is all my grandmother's doing. She has a tyrannical obsession with the worthiness of hard labour. She knows I have a prosodic gift superior to Uncle Gwilym and whatever he puts in his weekly causerie, but she is bent on teaching me that sweat is the sweeter virtue. She knows exactly what she's doing. "Get your nose close to the soil, John Cilydd," she says. "That will bring you inspiration." Then invariably she will quote some hymn or other from her own private treasury, such as "In Eden let us ne'er forget /We lost blessings more than drops of dew in number." Sailing that close to the rocks of blasphemy merely to mock my true vocation. Even as she busies herself with her myriad Glanrafon concerns, I hear a hen's cackle escape from the corner of her mouth.

'Let me rebel. Crawl back to the headland and the hedge where I hid my stolen packet of Woodbines in a heap of stones. I say stolen, but I consider I am entitled to take them from the Stores since neither my grandmother nor my uncle pay me for my labour. I smoke, therefore I think; I think, therefore compose. The Muse will permit me to see Alice Breeze, the minister's youngest daughter, sitting demure and beautiful in their family pew which is providentially opposite ours. The scar trace on her swan-like neck is the discreet signature of an artist pleased with the golden-haired, peach-skinned excellence of his creation. I could work on that. Not so keen on her father. Moves about as smoothly as an advertisement for clerical clothes of the best cut. There is so much suspicion in his eyes that I can never hold his glance.

'O what a sweet gesture of defiance to inhale cheap

tobacco smoke, stretch my legs, unstiffen my knees and dig my heels in the soft earth where a real mole has been burrowing. In my jacket I secrete a grubby notebook and a stump of pencil. Anything to write with. The humble tools of my trade. Let the Muse haunt my green prison. The world exists only to be translated in my words. Out of my trance I hear my name called. The thin column of tobacco smoke has betrayed my presence. There are two voices calling my name. My sister Nanw, more excited than usual. And, with her, Alice Breeze. My heart misses a beat when I recognize her silvery laugh. I had to hide. Why had my sister brought her to witness my humiliation: the earthworm in his shabby working clothes, the convict in his chains? Through the hedge I could see them down the lane, both leaning on their bicycles. There were folds of yellow tulle wrapped around the crown of Alice's straw hat like an embrace. The tilt of her nose as she looked up and, I hope, saw only the hedge, made my heart race. Nanw said Alice had a question to put to me. Did she imagine herself some appointed love-messenger between the poet and his mistress with one foot on her pedal?

' "John Cilydd!"

'Alice's voice was uttering my name and bestowing upon it a new resonance it would never lose. It attached itself to my skin, a farm labourer hiding behind a hedge like Adam in the original garden aware of his nakedness.

' "I was asking your sister Nanw, John Cilydd, if you don't want to be a minister what is it you want to be?"

'How could I stand up straight and utter the magic word "a Poet" in all its unqualified radiance without being laughed at by both of them. I could hear Nanw, I if had not already heard her, respond with a "but what will you live on?" How could my sister be so insensitive as to bring the minister's daughter here to ask such a question. Had Alice interpreted my negative approach to the conspiracy between my grandmother and the minister as some slur or reflection on that man's pulpit perfection, his clear-cut and clean-shaven rectitude as elegant and columnal as a new pencil. The elements of a poem centred on the delicious scar on Alice's neck were already blown away like the seeds of a

72

dandelion clock. I had to say something. Try and be self-possessed and even lofty.

' "I'm thinking of going in for the Law," I said.

'And there could only have been one good reason why I said it. The chap I admired most was already articled with Pritchard, Jones and Caddle, Solicitors and Commissioners for Oaths, in Glaslyn High Street. Owen Guest wore a stiff collar, a watch-chain, shoes not boots, and his red-gold curls were pomaded on working days and reduced to ordered waves that anyone could envy. I was lost with admiration for his lordly manner and I longed to have him as my best friend. If the Law had room for him, it might have room for me too. It was an honourable estate and an imposing arm of the structure of imperial might we were all called upon to defend.

' "Did you say the Law?"

'I could see Alice's eyes looking up, filled with the light of curiosity that could also be interpreted as elation. I had said the right thing.

' "Like Owen Guest, you mean?" Alice said.

'Now they were both laughing. If you could call it laughter. An interweaving of giggle and cackle and only a trace of the silver note in Alice's voice. They were shifting about their bicycles, disturbed by an excitement I could not explain. It could only have to do with some joint esteem and regard they shared for Owen Guest rather than for me. Nanw was quick to sober up.

' "Well," she said. "I wonder what Nain will have to say about that."

'It was my future, not my grandmother's, we were supposed to be discussing. I mumbled words to that effect, but they barely heard me. Alice had declared she had to go. I straightened up to peer over the hedge and watch them ride away.'

vi

It wasn't a place I could recognize at all. Mather sat in the Triumph Herald staring at the apparition as if it were a spaceship set down in an otherwise familiar landscape. No

73

boarded shop windows. No haybarn with a map of rust the shape of Africa on its corrugated iron roof. No ivy-covered outbuildings. No midden and no hens strutting about in the mud. There was a sign painted in tasteful gothic letters calling the place 'The Glanrafon Arms'. It offered bar food and holiday flatlets and in the field behind the house there were caravans drawn up on concrete bases.

'Behold thy gods, O Walia,' Mather said.

It was a theoretical response. Standard from his point of view. It was my roots that were obliterated, not his. Such an odd figure of speech representing human beings as plants. But at this moment I felt the metaphor like a physical reality. Such roots as I had were lying about on the face of this landscape for any passer-by to tread on or any vehicle to ride over. And yet this was absurd. A form of inane passivity to which I should not surrender. My mission was to recreate, refurbish, renew; not lie back in a foam bath of nostalgic inertia.

'Now we've come,' Mather said, 'we may as well go inside for a bit. We may as well look around.'

I was stirred by unexpected twinges of affection as I looked at him. It was time I called him Hefin. True, he was probably ten years my senior and his lifestyle was more cribbed and subterranean than I would ever choose, but he was loyal to the things that mattered. If any of my schemes of rehabilitation were to reach fruition, Hefin Mather and his descendants would be my chosen legatees. It occurred to me suddenly that I did not know whether or not the chap was married or where exactly he lived. Our point of contact, and our only real bond, was the trunks of books and papers lying next to the boiler-room under the college library. His impulses were more generous and altruistic than mine. It was time I showed him more respect and found out more about him – especially what he had written and what he hoped to write out of the depth of his scholarship. He did not spend his life lurking between the stacks and among all those old papers without the hope of producing something one day that would at least stir the academic pond, if not astonish the Welsh bourgeoisie.

There were no other customers. It was out of season and

the choice of bar food was limited. The stone walls were exposed and pointed. A log fire smouldered in an open grate. The place was meant to be cosy. I wondered how it all corresponded to the lost interior of Glanrafon Stores. Mather and I drank lager and ordered ham sandwiches. The woman who served us wore a thick woolly jumper and skirt over her thin form and large spectacles that tended to slip down her nose. She was eager to be friendly and treat us as her personal guests. She had a raw Scottish voice and in no time she had told us she came from Dumfries. Mather blossomed under the warmth of her attention, unbuttoned his overcoat and stretched out his legs in front of the log fire as she stirred it into flame. Could he possibly turn out to be a ladies' man? He twiddled his thumbs and looked up at her with a beatific smile I hadn't seen before.

'Very nice,' he said. 'Very nice place you've got here. Shall I tell you something that might surprise you?' He looked ready for an extended chortle and she looked very willing to be surprised. 'This young gentleman here,' Mather said in his deliberate, rather bookish English. 'This gentleman's father was born in this house. *Poeta nascitur non fit.*'

The woman was astonished and I was embarrassed.

'And what is more,' Mather said. 'He was a famous poet. John Cilydd More. Have you ever heard of him?'

'Oh dear, no,' the woman said. 'I'm afraid I haven't. Am I dreadfully ignorant?'

'It's not your fault,' Mather said gallantly.

He was smiling at me as if he thought he had just done me a favour. Perhaps he noticed how self-conscious I had become and he was trying to put me at ease. Whatever affection I felt for him vanished, supplanted by a turmoil of emotion I found unpleasant and difficult to control. Unintentionally, I hoped, Mather had pushed me into the very pool of introspection I was struggling hard to escape from. I had been on the verge of confiding in him and now his absurd effusion was widening the gap between us.

'I'll call Idris,' the woman said. 'Do you mind if I call Idris? He's a proper Welshman. He would have to know about it. He really would.'

75

I assumed this was her husband. Mather was reluctant to let her go. He launched himself on a brief etymological excursion among the place-names around Dumfries. They were Brythonic, he told her, and cognate with the place-names among which she was now living.

'Is that so?' she said. 'I never knew that.' She was shifting back to detach herself from the threat of Mather's pedagogic embrace. 'I must get on with your sandwiches, mustn't I?' she said. 'A round of tongue and a round of ham. And Idris will be along. I know he'll be thrilled to bits to learn a famous poet was born here.'

I should reproach Mather for that epithet. What concept was he trying to convey by using such an inflated word? 'Rare' would have been more accurate. One of those wildflowers of delicate hue only to be found on inaccessible ledges between the mosses and ferns that still flourish over two thousand feet up the mountain side. He was moidering happily on about Dumbarton meaning 'the Fort of the British' and the Bannock from Bannockburn being the Welsh 'Bannog'. How the centuries roll away if you spend your working life down in the stacks and feed on a philological diet as rare as the milk of asphodel.

Idris bustled towards us with evident enthusiasm. He did not feel the cold like his wife. He was in his shirtsleeves and he wore a sleeveless pullover and a claret-coloured bow-tie. His hair was cut *en brosse* in a vaguely French style and he carried an old box-file under his arm. He spoke rapid Cardiganshire Welsh and displayed a thrusting determination to be agreeable.

'I love this old place,' he said. 'Strange, isn't it, how it gets you? We've only been here eighteen months and it would break my heart to have to leave it. Not that we make a fortune. We break even. Let's put it like that. I was a civil servant you know. In London. That's where I met Moira. We decided to pool our resources and get out while the going was good. Sold up in Clapham and came here. The country life for us. Mind you, five acres and a cow aren't practical nowadays. So this is the next best thing. I was so interested to hear your father was born here. Is that right?'

'Yes,' I said. They both looked at me expectantly. What

else could I say? Please respect my reticence? 'And, of course, he was a poet.'

Idris gave a knowing smile and tapped his box-file.

'I think I have some of his work in here,' he said. 'Very interesting. To tell you the truth I've been wondering for some time now how I could best get it reproduced and hung up here somewhere. For people to know, you know. That sort of thing. I've got pictures too.'

He opened his file and handed us a meagre collection of four old postcards. They were all views of Glanrafon General Stores from different angles. In one, a woman in a black bonnet and widow's weeds sat in a governess cart on the cobbled forecourt in front of the shop. Could it have been my father's grandmother? The formidable widow of the author of *A History of Calvinistic Methodism in Rhosyr and Dinodig*?

'You see that tin-plate advert for Colman's Mustard?' Idris said. 'On the side door. There. You can just make it out. I came across that in the woodshed. A bit rusty. But I'm going to clean it up and put it on the wall. Frame it, maybe. Haven't decided yet. Now here's a poem.'

He took out a printed broadsheet that had a line-drawing of Glanrafon on the top and the words William Lloyd, General Dealer, Glanrafon Stores and Post Office. He held it up and began to recite some verses.

' "The shop at Glanrafon, a notable haven / Is more than a warehouse, we hope you'll agree? / The prices are low but the quality fancy / Nothing is missing and the welcome is free." Good, isn't it? Straightforward, simple stuff. The work of a country poet, of course. But just the stuff to adorn these walls, as I see it.'

'That wasn't my father,' I said curtly. 'He never wrote stuff like that.'

'William Lloyd.' Idris pointed at the name printed at the bottom of the sheet. 'Ah.'

Mather's bony index finger shot up to show that he knew the answer to the riddle.

'That would be this gentleman's great-grandfather,' he said. 'And at a guess I would say they were verses written as a form of advertisement when he first opened his shop. We

77

have quite a collection of that sort of rhyming from Mid-Victorian times onwards. Judging from the general appearance of your broadsheet, I would put that down to the mid 1880s.'

Moira appeared with a tray of sandwiches elegantly garnished with slices of tomato and onion.

'He's thrilled to bits to find somebody connected with this old place. Aren't you, Idris? Did you tell them about the ghost?'

She was still smiling to show that we could safely assume the story would amuse us. I was inhibited by my inability to devise a form of words that would convey to these people the information that my father wrote illustrious verses with imagination and vision, not antiquarian doggerel. How could I expect them to take my word for it? And even if they had the sensibility to appreciate the nature of his artistry, which I was inclined to doubt, on what authority did I make such a pronouncement? What doctoral chair was reserved for the justification of fragments? I would have to tell them that he had in mind the celebration of one particular landscape throughout the aeon of its being and the mystical relationship nurtured in time between the genius of the place and the genius of the people? A huge ambition encompassed in a modesty of means because it would have been a continuation and extension of a poetic tradition which had itself been sustained for centuries by talents as skilled and anonymous as the medieval cathedral builders. My lips were sealed with a ham sandwich.

'You never know whether ghosts are good for business or not,' Idris said. He sounded shrewder in English. 'You can have clients with a nervous disposition,' he said. 'In the Annexe, for example. They wouldn't sleep a wink all night.'

'It's the way you put it, isn't it?' his wife said. She seemed to have more confidence in her own ability to handle people, and so was better suited to the hotel and catering business. 'It's the same with food, isn't it?' she said. 'Presentation. The eye has its own appetite. Isn't there a French proverb that says that?'

Idris was scrabbling among the contents of his box-file. He had more letterheads and postcards. There were pictures of the old smithy which was now a whitewashed private house with black cart-wheels on the wall; of a halt on a railway line which no longer existed; of old-fashioned buses; coal-wagons; boys carrying water from a well with a bare bicycle wheel to balance the buckets; cows being milked by women in long dresses; and preaching meetings in the open air.

'Now, Idris,' his wife said fondly. 'You must let these gentlemen finish their meal in peace. And you promised you'd finish the shelf today.'

She was in charge. I could see that. But he was her willing vassal and no doubt within the context they had devised for themselves that was how it should be. It would be time enough for me to extol my father's merits when they themselves were moved to seek them out. There are forms of heritage that only become available when we become aware of a need to inherit. My business was to equip myself with the capacity to praise my father as a famous man and give thanks that he begat me. That could well involve remembering my grandfather who was drowned at sea and my great-grandmother who bullied on land and governed this place with an iron hand. There is also my mother's side, which I seem to prefer not to think about even when munching a sandwich. Her mother who died, if I remember rightly, when she was two. Her father who ran away to sing with the Carl Rosa before being killed serving with the Canadian Forces at Pilckem Ridge. The facts of history are bric-a-brac on a tidal wave. That is reason enough for the urge to be anchored in one landscape.

Mather and I strolled around the place when we had finished eating. Behind the breeze-brick toilets that had been put up for the caravan holiday-makers there was an oak tree that could not have changed much since my great-grandmother's day. Had Mather not been with me observing my reactions with his customary cautious curiosity, I would have stretched out my arms to embrace the trunk of that tree. No wonder oak trees were once the objects of worship and veneration. Without continuity the individual human being withers quickly like a leaf with a loose base in the branch, born and dead in the same year. The fields around the house were all for grazing. Little sign of the intense cultivation my father's youthful effusions complained about. There were store bullocks out showing glaucous inquisitiveness about our movements. Mather had a particular sympathy for them.

'I always think,' he said, 'those eyes were made for a depth of feeling. They seem tragic somehow, set in those pendulous dumb heads.'

Before we reached the car I was accosted and taken aside by Idris. He had a coat on and it had been obviously his intention to waylay me before I left. Mather walked on to the car.

'If I could have a brief word,' Idris said. 'I hope you won't mind my asking. But it is an opportunity I can't let slip, as they say. This nonsense about a ghost is neither here nor there. Of course I know that. But what I wanted to ask was – and after all who else can I ask, what else should I do but come to the eye of the stream and the source of wisdom? There is a story that a woman burnt herself to death in that part of the house where we have the bar now. Would you know anything about that?'

I established an expression of judicious inquiry on my face. Idris was waiting too anxiously for my verdict. Why should I tell what little I knew? It could only do harm. It could have happened. It could have been an accident. My mother was inclined to cloak facts in secrecy for her own purposes. Now I would do the same. Until I had examined the facts and circumstances for myself, why should I help the outside world to believe that both my father and his sister had committed suicide? That wasn't at all the kind of inheritance I was looking for. At last I shook my head.

'Sorry,' I said. 'I'm afraid I can't help you there.'

When I stepped into the car Mather was curious to know what the proprietor of The Glanrafon Arms wanted. I didn't tell him.

Four

'I was on my way to meet Owen,' my father wrote. 'I leapt out of the compartment all arms and legs, to collide with Hugget Hughes the station master, holding his flag. He bared his canine teeth and looked like a bull-mastiff in a green uniform with silver buttons. He knew my grandmother. The whole world knows my grandmother. He said that if I broke my stupid legs as I was bound to do one day he would have the doleful duty of going to Glanrafon to tell her about it. He said I looked like a giraffe escaping from a circus. I don't know how it is, but every Tom, Dick and Harry seems moved to try and say something clever whenever they see me, or maybe anyone of our family. Is it because my Uncle Gwilym has a weekly column in the local paper? Or because I won a local eisteddfod chair at the age of fourteen? In any case I arrive panting outside the offices of Pritchard, Jones and Caddle, Solicitors and Commissioners for Oaths, concerned with not being late and with the cut of my waistcoat and the bulbous toecaps of my boots. I would like to wear Owen's shoes as well as tread in his footsteps. But my grandmother insists on boots and her youngest son, my Uncle Tryfan, whom Owen considers verging on the simple-minded, makes them in his workshop in the outbuildings of Glanrafon – yet another member of my family engaged in fashioning fetters for my winged feet. They have no conception of the depth of my desire to be like Owen. It drives me on like the steam in an engine.

'Out of the office comes Owen, dressed, it seems to me, like a prince. How much in this world we need heroes. I admit he is mine. Even as I walk at his side I fall in behind him. We march towards the harbour. The sun is still shining in the late afternoon but Owen is frowning.

' "This place is finished."

'I feel a thrill as if I were being given a glimpse of the meaning of history, even though I know Owen is in a bad mood.

' "You'd think at a time of emergency even an old fool like Caddle would get his priorities right. 'Shooting practice, sir,' I said. 'In the old quarry.' You'd think the old fool would recognize an essential part of a cadet officer's training. 'After hours, Mr Guest. That will be all.' And that was all he could find to say. And there he sits behind his glass door. Like an old wax fruit."

'Owen winks and we both laugh in an explosive outburst of unstinting appreciation. Owen is a wit from a wider world. I am allowed to sip at his fountain and I am awed at the privilege.

' "Old Creak, I call him. His boots squeak as if he hadn't paid for them. And the influence he has in this place. You wouldn't believe it. The epitome of hypocrisy. The incarnation of narrowness. The quintessence of complacency. Get your pen out, Killy-Willy. I give you leave to record for posterity the impromptu coruscations of my caustic wit."

'I was nodding eagerly to show him that I would do it. It would be a pleasure and a mark of my devotion.

' "We have to face up to it, don't we?" Owen said. "Just look around you. *Circumpsice*, Killy. *Circumspice!*"

'We were outside the boarded windows of the Mutual Ship Insurance Society. The massive portico, built as a symbol of mercantile power and reliability, served now merely to highlight the decaying state of dry-docks where ships were no longer built and the still water of the old harbour was covered with scum like a duck pond. There had been a *Guest Line* owned by Owen's family. In its day it had been successful. But Owen's father quarrelled with his grandfather and fled to the United States. I record this as something we have in common: both brought up by ageing tyrants. At the appropriate time I shall draw Owen's

82

attention to this significant fact. But not when he is in the middle of impassioned utterance.

' "What is this war all about, my friend? In one word. Just one word." He pokes a finger in my ribs and I delight in our familiarity. "Expansion. Expansion, Killy."

'I would prefer him to call me "John" or "John Cilydd", but it is a small price to pay for being close to him.

' "It's so obvious. But do you know what I've noticed? People never see the obvious until you shove their noses right under it."

'The voice of a true leader. I was privileged to hear it. It furnished me with an energy and a confidence that would elevate me out of the cart ruts and earth rows, so that I could look down on Glanrafon and my family and my three uncles and rejoice that I would not become like them, as empty as an old jacket on a hedge.

' "If you don't expand, you contract," Owen said. "It's a basic law of nature."

'Now that he mentioned it, of course it was.

' "There had to be a blood-letting. The whole damn place was so run-down and scruffy. Not just here, Killy. The whole country. The heart of the empire threatened with lassitude, lack of oxygen, fatty degeneration. Do you follow? Do you see what I mean?"

'I tried to. It was like climbing a cliff to reach the vertiginous height of his viewpoint. It didn't entirely coincide with the doctrine of my other candidate for hero-worship, the distant and illustrious O.M. Edwards, who wrote in his red magazine "The strength of the Empire rests on the affection and understanding the member nations feel for each other." That was nice. But it had the drawback of being an article of faith espoused and cherished by all my uncles. My Owen had the advantage of combining iconoclastic irony with the thrill of a clarion call to arms. As I walked through the dusty avenues between the stacks of dressed slate that made no contribution whatsoever to the war effort, I was fortunate to be the recipient of Owen Guest's confidences.

' "I never tire of reading about Napoleon," he said. His voice was as calm as the subtle light that softened the rugged landscape and smoothed the waters of the bay. "I imagine the handicaps he had to overcome. Five foot two. I mean, Ajaccio was hardly bigger than this place. And the people were just as narrow and mean and petty-minded."

'There was a gaslight already burning in the clerk's office of the Glaslyn Slate and Allied Trades Company. That was where my Uncle Gwilym pushed his pen, on that second floor. He was a man who kept constant vigil. I had to say that for him and I hoped Owen would spare him from his deluge of disapproval. He had a great map on the partition wall with flags stuck in it that kept him in touch with the progress of the war as he wrote his weekly column for the *Glaslyn Herald*, clerked for the company and the fringes of local government, and composed somewhat platitudinous verses, I have to confess, in the strict metres with which he was perhaps over-familiar.

' "Modern Knowledge and British Grit will win this war," Owen said. "Do you follow me? That is the secret. This war allows us to harness the natural impulse to Expansion and Progress to a nobler vision of Empire. Do you see what I mean?"

'I saw proper nouns with capital letters moving through the dusk in pillars of fire. If there were questions, this was not the time to ask them.

' "When we've won, John Cilydd . . ." I melt with gratitude to hear him use my real name. ". . . Modern Knowledge . . ." I see English encyclopedias rise in cloud-topped towers. ". . . Modern Knowledge will make our British Empire the greatest empire the world has ever seen. What a choice: living to see it, or dying to bring it about. One way or the other, the road to glory."

'In ghostly fashion the pink boat was sailing into harbour. The brothers Harri and Sam had seen us. They were both waving. They were inviting Owen and I aboard. My Uncle Gwilym had only to raise his head to peer through the grimy window and take note of my exposed position. If I boarded the boat it was still light enough for him to recognize me. If I went on board in my second-best suit he would report the misdemeanour to my grandmother. How could any man flourish under such a regime, let alone a promising poet?

These were my friends. Harri, Sam and, above all, Owen, and it was in their company that my gift would grow to adult height and my Muse blossom like the rose.'

ii

'This is where the world falls best into place. A sailing boat drifts gently on the tide. Freshly painted, pink and white. New now and for evermore. We are out in the bay, well beyond the white line of the bar. The breeze lifts the red-gold curls around Owen's head, transforming them into a sun king's aureole. He is singing. His voice reaches me like Ariel's music and I lie under its spell. Harri and Sam move about noiselessly in rope-soled shoes, captains of their craft attaining their perfection of good order. I strained to make out the words of Owen's song. Something about people never believing him when he told them how beautiful the girl he was serenading was. A haunting, plangent tune to such hackneyed words. Alice Breeze was beautiful. I could give him more meaningful lyrics for his song. He was teasing Harri now.

' "Where are the quicksands, Harri Bont? And the mighty rollers. Let's have the sea gushing over the gunwhale. At the very least."

'It was all in fun, of course, but it made me uneasy. Harri wasn't smiling. That could be because he had had all his teeth taken out. We met him on the station the day before his second medical. There were bloodstains on his scarf. Inside that boyish, sunburnt face his gums were a raw portent of old age. His youth had vanished with his smile; sacrificed on the altar of his determination to join the Royal Navy. Nelson was his hero. He also had a good word to say for Black Barti the Welsh pirate and Prince Madoc whom he swore had crossed the self-same bar we had crossed, on his voyage to discover the Americas.

'For me it had been no fun crossing the bar. Harri had snatched the tiller from Owen just in time. I would never

85

have dared to do that. I rolled at the bottom of the boat expecting to be swept overboard in a sludge of sand and salt water, to go to the bottom as a boy well warned by his grandmother and weak, wailing mother to keep well away from the Bont boys Harri and Sam, and never forget that his father had been swallowed up by the sea. An aspect of the sea's nature that I particularly suspected was its sameness, whether it washed the shores of Newfoundland, Hong Kong Island, the Red Sea or Glaslyn Bay. At any moment as the boat capsized I could have joined my father in the same green fathoms. It was thanks to Harri's skill and the instinctive seamanship that passed between the two brothers that we emerged from the maelstrom where I had been stricken with too much fear and guilt even to think of being sick, to drift with god-like calm on this timeless ocean where no disaster could strike.

'We were floating on a sea of myth and even then I knew it. The question that arose was, could submarines, especially German submarines, see cities under the sea? Owen said in any case they did not exist. I was moved to speak. For once I knew more about a subject than he did. He had never heard of Tir-fa-tonn or Caer Is or Lyonesse; and to him Cantre'r Gwaelod was a fictional feature of a Standard-Four children's poem.

' "There is History," I said. "There is Legend. And there is Myth."

'I stretched out my arm, excited by the sudden acquisition of an inner power that seemed to be related to divination. But the others weren't listening. Owen and Harri were engaged in childish argument about how to make the boat sail faster. Sam followed Harri's instructions, not Owen's. The boat rolled as he tacked and I began to feel ill. The sheets tugged and the leech quivered and more seagulls appeared above the mast like volunteers flocking to the colours. Harri was sailing straight towards the dangerous causeway as if to prove to Owen once and for all that the city under the sea existed. An untidy bank of stones and boulders created its own scar of turbulence in the waters of the bay. It must have been against such rocks that my father's ship went down. As we sailed closer I saw rows of sea birds perched like mourners waiting for a funeral procession. There were others nudging each other off slimy pinnacles like parasites on the back of a monster indifferent to an angry sea churning away at its adamantine scales. If I had to die I would go with a poem on my lips. Harri gave an almighty yell and snatched command of the tiller, shoving Owen to one side. He knew of the gap in the causeway and he was making straight for it. Should I trust in Owen's heaven-sent gift to command, or Harri's seamanship? Either way it didn't matter. All I could do was close my eyes and pray. I saw my grandmother's grim visage in our family pew as they held a memorial service for me in our chapel. Alice wasn't at the organ; she was too overwhelmed with grief to play. Instead there was a mysterious female with her face hidden in a black veil. One of the Fates? When I opened my eyes I saw shags and puffins to the leeward looking benevolent and friendly and I heard Sam and Harri and Owen cheering and slapping each other on the back. They were so emboldened by success they determined to go through it all again. Once again it seemed as if the world would disappear in a cauldron of boiling water. Harri was so confident of what he was doing he was jabbering excitedly. He pointed at what he called slabs of fallen masonry covered with seaweed and barnacles, and visible slabs of worked stone, and the traces of mortared walls that once held the sluice gates of the sunken city. There was a point to be made about the mythic significance of the legendary figure of Seithenyn, but I was too weak to make it. The function of the watchman was to look out for the signs and the seasons. It was no use Owen lecturing poor Harri about geology and glacial deposits. Harri hadn't had the education. The landscape that really mattered was the landscape of our lives. I would write a poem about it. As we reached calmer waters, I vomited over the side and the other three cheered.'

iii

'My excitement was so intense I could barely master it, contain myself and continue to sit and scribble at my grandfather's roll-top desk in the side parlour. The door had been removed and when I leaned forward I could see Alice Breeze had called in the shop to gossip and whisper with my sister Nanw over the drapery counter. I longed for a cigarette but my grandmother was also in the store attending to customers and she would detect the smell of the weed and put an end to my inspiration. I was being visited by the Muse. There was no question about it. Words ran ahead of my pen and poured over the edge of my notebook in their own invisible ink. All to do with the application of myth to history and tracing the reverse process. It was an idea raging in the red turmoil of my heart. There was one of Arthur's knights whose spear could draw blood from the wind. Would it be Bedwyr? In any case I had a royal choice of names: Cai, Culwch, Peredur, Pwyll, Pryderi, and this band of heroes would set out for France to shave the Giant of Potsdam's beard with the shears and comb secreted between the ears of the Teutonic High Command ravishing the fair fields of Picardy. And could I include Mabon as a symbol of mankind, languishing in the dungeons of dark servitude and yearning to be set free? Nanw could see me. She raised a hand to gain my attention. Alice was looking at me. Did they realize they were watching a poet in the fury of composition?

' "John Cilydd," Nanw said. "Nain wants you."

'That was it. Down to earth with a thud. Errands. Beck and call. I suppose I had to be thankful I wasn't out in the fields with Uncle Simon. It would have been unwise to tell my grandmother that I was engaged in one of the higher activities known to man. My Uncle Gwilym and his weekly column had muddied that pool for ever. If only the scriptures had taken the trouble to record that there could be other honourable methods of earning one's bread apart from the sweat of one's brow. Nothing seemed to amuse my grandmother more than the recollection of my falling off a cart-horse's back or being buried under sacks of Indian corn or falling over in the pigsties – especially if she had been present to snigger at my expense.

'She was at the grocery counter filling up a basket. Behind her the door with the word "Dispensary" etched into the glass panel was open. Inside was the holy of holiest where she mixed her witches' potions and her remedies for wild warts.

' "Since you have nothing much to do, John Cilydd, and you have your bike, you will take this basket down to Foryd Isa. That poor woman's legs can hardly bear the weight of her any more."

' "That poor woman" was called Mrs Klugman. Harri Bont said he thought she might be a German spy. Sam agreed with him. Foryd Isa was a solitary smallholding overlooking the estuary and within winking distance of the open sea. "Signals," Harri said. "From a bedroom window. Enemy subs. Easy." Owen wasn't so sure. He said Harri had subs on the brain. Mrs Klugman was a German Jewess, according to Alice. She had lived in London and was an authority on accents in the English language. Mrs Klugman's hair was dyed black. Unless it was her wig. Her head wobbled on her shoulders. Her eyes were as big and as mournful as a bullock's and Alice said her ankles were thicker even than her accent.

'It always amazed me who and what my grandmother chose to be sorry for. Mrs Klugman was an old grievance in everyone else's view. She had come from nowhere for no apparent reason. It seems she had owned a shop in one of the South Wales mining valleys. Perhaps that was what she and my mother had in common? No, it was more than that. The shop windows had been smashed in a riot. No. More than that. She had a son in the army. Her only son. Mrs Klugman said her only son was missing, but so far she had received no message from the spirit world. That would be gipsy talk of which my grandmother in normal times would have disapproved. Also, she bought cigarettes and my grandmother strongly disapproved of women smoking. The last time I saw Mrs Klugman in the shop my grandmother had called on me to act as interpreter. She couldn't recall the English for "sympathy".

'As I fixed Mrs Klugman's basket on the carrier of my bike, Alice emerged from the shop. She bade me farewell in my grandmother's hearing. Once we were out of sight of Glanrafon she said that if I liked she would accompany me, just for the ride, on such a fine day. I trembled and had momentary difficulty in controlling a bicycle with a full basket and a satchel on the cross-bar stuffed with the magazines and old newspapers my grandmother provided Mrs Klugman with.

' "Did you notice something?" Alice asked.

'As if I had not noticed her eyes were violet and her lips as sweet as honeysuckle. We were faced with a hill. She dismounted and decided to take off her hat. I watched her draw out the hat-pin. The operation was so delicate. Her arms rose with perfect symmetry and the bright metal of the pin was like the evening star that kept the firmament in place. She tied the hat to the lamp-bracket of her bicycle with a piece of ribbon and I wanted to write a poem about it.

' "Did you notice," Alice said, "she buys cigarettes and there are no nicotine stains on her fingers." She wanted me to appreciate how observant she was. "I think we ought to keep an eye on her, don't you?"

'Was that an excuse for her to accompany me to Foryd Isa or was it the other way round? It was easier to compose an epic poem than fathom Alice Breeze's mind. The bicycle was an encumberance. How could I get close enough to touch her, petite and perfect as she was, replete with uncelebrated merits? Inside her clothes, her body was a dazzling mystery.

' "And Nanw says she buys cough mixture," Alice said. "But she's never heard her coughing."

'Should I confide in her that I was composing an epic poem? I long to do so. She was so absorbed in the mystery of Mrs Klugman.

' "Robert Thomas the molecatcher says he's heard her talking," Alice said. "You know he creeps around the place setting his traps."

'Robert Thomas wore moleskin leggings and chewed tobacco. His cottage stood on a mount so close to an inlet that when the high tide was in he could spit into the waves.

' "And do you know what her excuse was?"

'Fleetingly I wished Alice would talk less. If I told her that I loved her and asked her to love me, would she ignore my request?

' "She said she was a medium talking to the spirits. And when he said 'What spirits?' she said the spirits of the soldiers killed in France. On both sides. Well, we'll see about that."

'From the top of the hill we surveyed an exposed landscape. The narrow road wound down past Foryd Isa and petered out in a belt of gorse bushes that hid the foreshore. Alice examined the contents of Mrs Klugman's basket. It was more than I had thought of doing. Mouse-trap cheese, margarine, biscuits, baking flour, a large tin of Colman's mustard, a bottle of linctus and a lump of beef dripping wrapped in greaseproof paper. Alice looked like a dove peering into a rubbish dump.

' "I'll go down first," she said. "I'll hide my bike in the gorse bushes and have a look around while you talk to the old woman. Then you come to meet me in the bushes." She burst out laughing. I must have looked puzzled. "Meet me in the bushes," she said. "Sounds naughty, doesn't it?"

'I watched her speed down the slope with the panels of her linen jacket flying out and the hat bouncing on the handlebars. She could have been a goddess enjoying her human disguise and it would have been poetically appropriate to love her. The green cords threaded through the holes along the rear mudguard of her Sunbeam could be compared to the strings of a harp. Sunbeam! What a fitting vehicle for the apotheosis of Alice Breeze.

'Foryd Isa was in a morose state of dilapidation. The faded blinds were drawn on all the windows. There was no answer when I knocked. Mrs Klugman was either asleep or dead. It looked like one of those houses where the front door was never used except to carry out a coffin. I couldn't go around the back if Alice was snooping about. I knocked again. The slate slabs under my feet were loose and there was barely room for the basket and my feet. I heard Mrs Klugman grunt and groan as she stretched and bent to unbolt her front door at the top and the bottom. When she hung out her large head I tried not to stare at the blackness of the rings under her eyes. She caught up her dewlapped throat in a greasy shawl.

' "Good Mrs Lloyd's grandson," she said. "You walked in

my dream. Did you know that? And here you are." Her eyes lowered to settle hungrily on the basket. "Ah, she's good and she's kind and you'll never meet her equal let alone her better as you walk through the wilderness of this world. Remember I told you that. If you forget everything else, laddie, remember that."

'My balance on the slate slab was precarious. I could not turn away to avoid her smouldering stare.

' "You walked in my dream," she said. "I told you that. And I saw the golden calf dance out of the fire. And a little black pig ran after it. What do you suppose that means?" She pushed her jaw towards me, challenging me to answer. "Everything in my dreams means something, laddie. And I'll tell you something else." She wanted me to move close enough to hear her whisper. "There's more diseases to come from all those dead bodies. Don't you go near them trenches. Lift it for me, there's a good laddie. I'm a poor one for bending."

'The corner of her mouth disappeared into her puffy cheeks and the door was shut smartly in my face. She had snatched her prize and vanished, leaving me disturbed with fear and revulsion that could easily have turned to hatred. What on earth did my "nain" see in such a woman? Was there a secret commerce between witches? The confidence that came from composition and the exercise of prosodic skill was gone; there were so many things about which I knew nothing. I rode down to the gorse bushes to wait for Alice. She came breathless with excitement.

' "There's a man in there,' she said. "I was right. A deserter."

' "I didn't see anyone," I said.

' "I saw him. Crossing the yard on all fours. Like a dog. And I can tell you something else. He was wearing khaki trousers."

' "I thought he was missing," I said.

' "He's not missing," Alice said. "He's in there. Hiding. Now you are going to be a man of the law, aren't you? You should report it."

' "To whom?"

'I know I sounded disturbed and almost frightened. She

smiled and took pity on me.

' "Owen Guest," she said. "He knows everything, doesn't he? Your sister Nanw says you follow him about like Bo-Peep's pet lamb."

'We were close together in the bushes. She put her hand on my cheek.

' "You are a nice boy," she said. "And you're a poet. Are you going to write anything about me?"

'I nodded eagerly.

' "You can kiss me if you like."

'I trembled with excitement at such unexpected good fortune.

' "Since we're here," Alice said, "we may as well have a cuddle. So long as you are a good boy and do exactly as I tell you."

'She took my hand and for the first time I felt the softness of her breasts.'

iv

'The chapel was full. This was a meeting to pray for the fallen heroes of our district and the demarcation lines and petty enmities between denominations had melted away. The old Baptist pastor stood in Mr Breeze's Calvinistic Methodist pulpit droning on about the consolation of the Gospel in the face of loss and tragedy. He was sincere enough, but I could tell Owen didn't think he was up to the job. In the gallery Owen sat next to me in his cadet officer's uniform, his arms folded across his chest, his face as impassive as a memorial carved in marble. I knew what he was thinking. This was remarkable. In the intense atmosphere of the packed chapel his thoughts transferred themselves to me. The old man in the pulpit was inadequate. What he had to say was written down but he could not read his own writing. He had a voluminous white handkerchief in front of his mouth in case his loose teeth dropped out. He stumbled and fumbled over his words as an embodiment of the bewildered lack of comprehension of the older generation. He had no idea what the new world was all

93

about. All he knew and felt was the grief of family after family pressing in on him. I realized that they were all families he knew and cared for from all the chapels in the district and I realized that history was cruel. Owen was as inexorable as a graven image. The old man's head shook and his hands trembled as he shuffled through his notes. He had lost his place. A crisis was approaching. He would collapse in the pulpit and have to be carried down like some stricken captain from the bridge of his ship.

'Mr Breeze was equal to the occasion. As the old man in the pulpit flopped back on to the bench behind him, he rose to his feet and took control of the proceedings. His delivery was as polished as pitch-pine. I looked at Alice in the second row of the gallery opposite, next to my sister Nanw. This was a brave occasion and her father was in command, a prince among his people. She herself was a pearl in her setting. Her curls were only half hidden by a velvet cap of military cut. How could my words ever encompass the roundness of her breasts. It was disconcerting to feel my verse skill was muffled and inadequate. If she smiled in this direction it would be dangerous. I gave her father my undivided attention. He was about to take over the task of reading the Roll Call of Honour. He asked the congregation to stand as a mark of respect.

'Mr Breeze was an artist at work. His voice with its distinctive nasal intonation brushed over the surface of throbbing silence. I dared not glance at Alice. If our eyes met I would blush and Owen might disapprove. Mr Breeze was a paragon.

' "He fell on the field of blood leading his boys to victory . . . His pure spirit gave its last sigh before it fled upwards from this world of pain and sorrow to the safe bosom of the Lord our God . . . He has joined in the wedding feast of the Lamb of God in the world beyond where the merciful hand wipes away every tear, where . . ."

'From somewhere under the gallery where Owen and I were sitting came a howl of grief that brought an expression of cold disgust to Owen's face. Some weak woman had gone out of control. The iron law of discipline had been broken. The security of the rampart threatened. Our defence work momentarily breached. He wanted her cleared out with the minimum of fuss. Some of the ministers and deacons in the big pew were twisting their necks with unseemly curiosity. I saw Alice was upset. She had shrunk against my sister Nanw as though under physical threat. But her father stood erect, and motionless behind the communion table, in control of himself and the occasion. The howl subsided into sobs as they led the woman out.

'When the service was over the people filed out in an atmosphere of impressive silence. When we were a sufficient distance from the chapel gates I suggested to Owen that the Reverend Breeze had handled a difficult situation well and I was pleased when Owen expressed complete agreement. His uniform was conspicuous in the twilight and when he took me by the arm and led me down the road so that we could speak more freely, I hoped as many people outside the chapel as possible had noticed this.

' "It's all fixed," he said.

'I was slow to react. He slapped me on the back.

' "Your old Uncle Ezra has stumped up," he said. "Eighty pounds to cover the stamp duty. Your grandmother will pay the hundred and thirty pounds premium. Which is as it should be. And I can tell you more, old boy. In strictest confidence."

'The news was good, of course; the warmth and increased friendliness in Owen's manner was even better. He had his arm on my shoulder. Owen and I were friends and colleagues: all for one and one for all.

' "You are the heir to the old boy's estate," Owen said. "Your great-uncle Ezra and Alfred Caddle the ancient creak are old comrades on the temperance campaign trail. I just caught a glimpse of the will on Caddle's desk. The house Cae Golau, the substantial outbuildings, the orchard, the walled garden and sixteen acres of tolerable grazing land. So there you are, Killy boy. You're a man of property and a man of law. But mum's the word, of course. Let nature take its course."

'There would be no need to look up another sophisticated phrase from Calvin's Institutes the next time my great-uncle Ezra asked me if I had heard the Call. Every week I visited

95

Cae Golau, loaded with delicacies and groceries prepared by my grandmother for her reverend brother-in-law for whom she cherished the most profound respect. And this was my reward. And my friend and brother-in-arms to be was the messenger appointed to invest me with the good news.

' "And what are you two up to?"

'My sister Nanw and Alice Breeze had caught up with us. They gathered about me with the warmth of congratulation and inside knowledge. They all seemed to know more than I did. They had pieced together their separate segments of information to produce a credible diagram of my immediate future and I could only quietly rejoice that the day of my release from the servitude of the soil was at hand. I would be allowed to do what I wanted to do, in spite of all my grandmother's reservations and misgivings.

' "John Cilydd," Nanw said. "We were thinking, Alice and I. The annual outing of the Glaslyn Antiquarian Club. Aren't they going to Llys y Foel this year?"

'Nanw and I were close enough for me to know that she was up to something. In the confined and tightly ordered world my sister and I inhabited, the exercise of a certain deviousness was often called for to achieve the simplest ends.

' "Uncle Gwilym is giving the address this year," Nanw continued. "We were thinking could you ask him if we could come. The four of us. If it's an edifying outing, I'm sure Nain wouldn't object. And your papa wouldn't either, would he Alice?"

' "What a jolly good idea," Owen said.

'It dawned on me that he knew about the plan already. A bilious light flashed in front of my eyes in the twilight as I took in for the first time my sister's interest in Owen. I wasn't the only creature under Glanrafon roof capable of falling in love. A kaleidoscope of instances and occasions in chapel, in the shop, on the street, and in the local train trundled through my mind. Why was I always the last person to find out anything? This was the price of hiding my head in a cloud of verse. Owen slapped me cordially on the back and I was reminded that, as things were, he was the one I was supposed to please.'

'I never saw my sister Nanw look happier. Both she and Alice wore white linen suits and straw hats. They posed together for a picture of girlish innocence. Owen and I sat opposite them in the second wagonette. There was a spectacular view of the estuary beyond the tops of the pine trees as the horses toiled up the track towards Llys y Foel. Alice was talking to me about London and Owen was listening. Nanw could barely take her eyes off Owen. Something my grandmother had said about our mother surfaced in my mind. "That poor child was born with one layer of skin less than anyone else." I knew how like our mother Nanw was. So sensitive mere words could set her skin on fire. It seemed dangerous on a day like this for her to look so happy.

'Alice was inclined to repeat herself. She had told me before that an elder in the Reverend Breeze's London church had tried to entice her father onto the Board of a firm manufacturing indoor sanitation. There he would earn, for far less stress and strain, three thousand pounds a year instead of two hundred. It was a growth industry and there were other directorships he would have been offered. But such was her father's devotion to the church and the Connexion and by extension, to little Wales, that he gave up such worldly temptations in order to dedicate his business flair towards the smooth and efficient direction of our denomination's affairs. It was clear that if I loved Alice I would have to love her father as well.

'She called me her "funny boy" and "next-best-friend" and said, "I know I can always rely on you, John Cilydd". In return I had to respect her confidences about difficult deacons and certain jealous colleagues of her father's. It was not until we sat all four in the wagonette that I began to suspect that she frequently addressed me in order that Owen could overhear what she was saying – gently tapping the post so that the partition could hear. It was, of course, a beautiful day and a happy occasion, but I began to wish that Nanw

97

and Owen were not there.

'Owen was a resplendent physical presence in his uniform; not that he needed that additional source of admiration and respect. He was handsome and there was no reason he should not know it if everyone else did. He was giving my sister Nanw casual instruction in the art of handling men. Handling women was too easy for him to constitute any sort of a problem. The way her eyes glistened as she listened made me realize just how easily Owen handled me.

'He was helpful. I couldn't deny that. Being with him was a joyful experience. He showed me the ropes in the office. The scent of his hair cream or the fern soap he used gave me pleasure. He made me over-eager to pass on secrets, it occurred to me as I watched my sister glow under his spell. I should never have revealed to him the reason why my Uncle Gwilym wore high, stiff collars. It was a dark family secret I was not supposed to know myself. Uncle Simon had passed it on to me with quiet satisfaction one afternoon when we were sheltering under the hedge from a shower of rain. During his brief career as a council school teacher, Gwilym had lost his temper with a stupid boy whom he took to be insolent, and nearly beat him to death. That night in a fit of remorse or under the influence of the demon drink he tried to cut his own throat. That was the story. Certainly he always wore high collars and he had a nasty temper. But I shouldn't have seeped the story so willingly into Owen's ear.

'Uncle Gwilym was riding in the front wagonette, flanked by two of his cronies, a poet and a singer. Owen found this amusing. My uncle had a sheaf of notes in his overcoat pocket and he kept tugging them out and pushing them back. Owen found that funny too. Gwilym Glaslyn was a local bard and penny-a-liner, not a scholar, and he had no gift whatsoever for public speaking. An incorrigible mumbler. Owen said he looked like a man on his way to his execution. He whispered in my ear, "Do you think he's brought those two along to stop him cutting his own throat?" I pretended I hadn't heard. I blushed and sweated until the seat of my trousers stuck to the bench. "Vicious lot, really, aren't they?" Owen whispered. He was talking about my Uncle Gwilym, who had been kind enough to guide me

98

through the intricacies of *cynghanedd*, and his cronies, who foregathered in his dingy office on the slate quay to discuss poetry and politics. "These would-be poets," Owen said, "tear each other's efforts to bits or soft-soap each other to the skies. That's why they suck up to him. Waiting to see their names appear in his weekly column. It's the same everywhere, I suppose, but here it seems worse. You need to learn the rudiments of psychology, Killy."

'Indeed I did. It was all very well being in weekday digs in Glaslyn where I could smoke to my heart's content. I seemed to spend a lot of time there waiting for Owen. Letters arrived there for him, addressed to me. Sometimes he dropped in to collect them. But much more often I dropped them in the drawer in his desk in the office he jokingly refered to as his P.O. Box. If only he dropped in as often to my gaslit digs of an evening so that we could chat about things that mattered. I could have told him in detail about my Uncle Simon's rage when he learnt that his mother, my grandmother, had shelled out the equivalent of two years' rent of his farm in order to deprive him of his nephew's unpaid labour and of enjoying the exercise of petty power over a putative heir. I knew that what tipped the balance with my grandmother was great Uncle Ezra's approval of old Mr Caddle and that the unseen hand of Owen Guest had some part in that. There was also the fact that I wore spectacles. She reckoned that would keep me out of the army when the call-up came. Owen and I knew differently. When he called, I would follow; that was understood. But I wished he would call in my digs a little more often. There was much I longed to discuss with him. His manner was always so frank and open. He would never withhold any information, once I had the chance to put the question.

'Was I to understand that women in general were to be classified with wild duck and pheasant and collected for stuffing by qualified huntsmen only? And why should writing about love be so infinitely inferior to making it? Was a poet only as functional as a decoy duck? Why should Mrs Katie Caddle, the wife of our junior partner, Captain Caddle, stationed on Canvey Island as part of Coastal Defence, send letters addressed to me at my weekday digs, intended for Owen Guest? I had to ask. Comradeship was all very well, but I also had a duty to Nanw. As an authentic officer and gentleman, he would understand my obligation to defend my sister's interests.

'The three wagonettes carried the Glaslyn Antiquarian Society and its guests above the tree-line of maritime pines towards the medieval stone-roofed Chapel of Ease alongside the ruined stronghold of Llys-y-Foel. There were hurried confabulations concerning whether to hold the meeting outdoors or in. Uncle Gwilym drifted about, uncertain whether he should control his hair or check his sheaf of notes with his busy hands. Owen managed to waylay him to say there was nothing that gave young persons greater pleasure than to listen to an acknowledged authority discoursing freely on his chosen subject. Uncle Gwilym kept his hair out of his eyes with a handful of notes and squinted suspiciously at the young man in uniform standing respectfully to attention. Owen winked at me when my uncle wasn't looking.

'I had to be taken up with my concern for my uncle. If he made a fool of himself through lack of support I would have to share the responsibility. His lecture, like his notes, was all over the place. He began outside, standing on a rock. It was too windy. He moved and the company shifted and we stood like a patient flock looking up at Gwilym Glaslyn standing on an old mounting stone in the shelter of the gable end of the farmhouse. His voice went up and down as he told the antiquarians the things they knew already: Llys-y-Foel was the stronghold of a warrior aristocrat of impeccable lineage who followed the Black Prince, campaigning in France. He mumbled several times from fifteenth-century *Cywyddau* and then got carried away by an impromptu eulogy of Lloyd George. He treated his audience to a garbled version of his vision of his hero prancing through Westminster on his white charger like a second Arthur. His thoughts and his words were scattered by the teasing wind and he decided to move us all indoors. He led the way, waving his notes, into the medieval Chapel of Ease which now served as a haybarn in one half and a winter shelter for store cattle in the other.

100

'I held on to Nanw and told her we could not possibly leave. He was our uncle and it was our duty to give him our support, and to be seen to be giving it, in his hour of need. Uncle Gwilym had taken it into his head to point out members of his unsettled audience who were related either to the warrior of Llys-y-Foel or to the Prime Minister of England and supreme bailiff of the British Empire, within the prescribed limit of the ninth degree. It was a ragged attempt at oratorical audience flattery and it didn't really work. I realized Owen and Alice had not followed us into the chapel. They should be listening. Much of what my uncle had to say was relevant. In his own untidy way he was doing his best to celebrate the genius of the place. They were not to be seen.

'Alice had made use of me. And so had Owen. The two people in whom I had invested my deepest affections, in whom I trusted. The pain twisting in my chest was so great I almost cried out. At this moment, while my uncle rambled on, she would be telling Owen what he should do to her as she told me. Would there be "that's enough" and "so far and no further" and "if you can't be good be careful" and all the tawdry phrases with which she tarnished the image I cherished? And my sister Nanw, too, had been manipulated. The whole notion of joining this outing was to allow Alice to get her hands on Owen Guest. Her sainted father would never have allowed her to join the expedition except in Nanw Glanrafon's sober company. Had there been collusion between two or three? I glanced at my sister. She was listening to the lecturer with dutiful attentiveness, her head tilted to one side. Her vulnerability was unbearable. I needed to slap her across the face to awaken her from her dream. Could she see nothing? How her precious Alice had made use of her!

'The lecture had turned into a slow torment. My uncle had abandoned long quotations from an ode to read extracts from seventeenth-century documents he had copied with misplaced zeal in Mr ap-something-or-other's muniment room. He got lost. The audience was restive. Gwilym Glaslyn's musical crony saw his chance. With finger and thumb he extracted a tuning fork from his waistcoat pocket and tapped it against his knee. While the company stood or sat around singing a merry part-song, I saw Owen and Alice slip in at the back of the chapel. They were shameless. Her face was all innocence and he sported the confident grin of a hunter who has made a kill.'

vi

' "Keep an eye on little Alice."

'It was not the last thing Owen said to me before the train pulled out; but it was what made the deepest impression. And the quick wink. The elected hero of my epic was on his way to war and the whole poem ground to a halt. There was too much thinking to do. And re-thinking. My imagination had been quite agile in transposing traditional motifs into modern formations. It was quite incapable of containing the torrents of experience bursting in on my consciousness and flooding it like water to the roof of the cave. Owen was off to join the regiment to which he held unswerving allegiance. Training at Grantham. He commanded me to hold sacred the things that he held sacred. And yet he chose to take lightly many of the things I held sacred.

'In the office, I took over his desk. Letters from Owen came regularly to my weekday digs. They were addressed to me and they contained a hurriedly written cover-note and a further envelope addressed for some reason to Elsie Gell, who liked to describe herself as Mrs Catherine Caddle's "personal maid". As a mark of my continuing friendship and allegiance I had to deliver these things at the tradesmen's entrance at Captain Caddle's residence, Argraig. It was not a task I relished.

'Keeping an eye on Alice was easier. Owen's behaviour had taught me not to take the girl seriously. On Saturdays I often found her at the drapery counter deep in conclave with my sister Nanw. They referred to Owen in transparent code as O.G. and there were parcels dispatched to the hero from the Post Office section in Glanrafon Stores. If my grandmother sent me on errands of mercy to my great-uncle Ezra at Cae Golau or to Mrs Klugman at Foryd Isa, Alice

102

would contrive to accompany me. We had hiding places in which she could sigh romantically and I could provide her with as much sexual comfort as she estimated it was safe to enjoy.

'It was pleasant enough in its illicit, fumbling fashion, but it did no good at all to my Muse. The capacity to compose anything more than the most mechanical and mundane technical exercises had completely deserted me. In a state of cold panic I realized this when I hurried into the County Court with a briefcase under my arm stuffed with documents old Mr Caddle had to sign. There was no need for Old Creak to be in court at all. He just couldn't resist the breach-of-promise case when he had a ringside seat and he could sit licking his walrus moustache, listening to the bulky barrister's florid performance at close quarters. Old Caddle was so amused. Not the stern temperance-tyrant of the office at all. He was like a young man at a music hall, his body and his moustache twitching with the urge to outbreaks of unfettered laughter.

'It was a ritual occasion. When the judge allowed himself to smile it was a tacit signal for laughter in court. When he frowned, all present quickly brought themselves to order. The defendant was a diminutive hill farmer with a red face who had little or no English. This in itself was a source of some amusement. The barrister made great play of picking up a letter written on grubby lined notepaper and holding it at some distance while he translated extracts in a rich baritone laced with ironic inflections.

' "I feel very anxious to get married to you. It does not matter what my mam says. I hope to live with you, my loving one. I will be down there next Wednesday without fail so that we can go to have a licence and all what is necessary . . .' Would you accept that as a reasonable translation of your Cymric prose, Mr Cadwalader Roberts?"

'I was sickened by the entire pantomime. Why should this eminent barrister, a fellow countryman of Liberal aspirations, take it upon himself to turn the essence of our national being into a source of cheap laughter? He and the judge in their absurd apparel were indulging in a Punch and Judy show at the expense of the precious medium of my

103

Muse; and the little hill farmer in the dock was a symbol of the degradation of an entire people. The defendant drew a soiled handkerchief like a harrow across his furrowed brow while the eminent barrister, with nothing better to do, seemed prepared to go on tormenting the creature indefinitely.

' "Say yes or no. Do you know the difference?"

' "No," The defendant said, and then hastily corrected himself. "I mean, yes."

'He had reached that point of hunted desperation when all he could do was plunge on and enmesh himself still further.

' "I not marry," he said, licking his dry lips. "My mother not let her in."

'The features of the judge's worn face twitched and Mr Caddle's cheeks went through identical contortions. The court relieved itself with laughter.

' "You told the plaintiff you were off to join the Army. Is that correct?"

'The defendant clutched his waistcoat with both hands and whispered "Yes".

' "But you already knew that the medical board had decided you were unfit. You already knew the military tribunal had directed you to continue to work on your family farm. Being unfit for the Army does not mean you are unfit to marry, Mr Roberts. One exemption does not automatically provide you with another now, does it?"

'The defendant gazed at the judge: if someone explained the joke to him perhaps he could smile too. Captain Caddle had sidled into the court. He bowed to the bench, sat beside his father and touched his arm in filial greeting. His black hair was plastered down close to his skull and his moustache was trimmed with a precision that went with his uniform. Canvey Island had to defend itself without him. I placed the documents on the table in front of Old Creak. He pushed them to one side anxious not to miss a word of the cross-examination.

' "It says here you have been a patient of Dr Parry-Jones for the past two years. Would you tell the court the nature of your complaint?"

'The defendant had not understood the question. With an

104

air of gracious condescension, the barrister translated it into Welsh. The farmer detected at last a sympathetic note in the diapason that flowed out of the barrister's mouth. It belonged now to the order of solemn injunction he heard from the pulpit every Sunday: stern and unbending, but pertaining to his salvation. He leaned forward, at last eager to give an answer. It was like watching a small animal tumble into a trap.

' "Heart trouble," he said.

'This time the court exploded with laughter without waiting for the judge to smile. The barrister bowed reverentially to the bench. It was at this point that I felt Captain Caddle grab my arm. He led me out of the courtroom. Intent on the case, his father did not notice. The bulky policeman raised his eyebrows as he let Captain Caddle and myself out into the corridor. The Captain greeted the policeman by name. I knew that every sensible practising solicitor cultivated good relations with members of the Force. In the draughty corridor there were minor officials and council employees trafficking bits of paper in order to provide themselves with an excuse to leave their desks and eavesdrop on a breach-of-promise case. The Captain led me away from them, as if we were a pair of lawyers deep in confidential consultation. It was raining heavily outside. Captain Caddle stared in silence through the dirty window. In spite of the smart uniform he looked worn and unwell.

' "Since when have you been acting as a bloody little postman?"

'The question came as such a shock that I broke into a sweat. I had no idea why the Captain had arrived home on leave. I had no real idea about anything. His wife dressed expensively and fancied herself as a singer. Owen said Katie Caddle deeply resented being left at home with Old Creak while her husband was popping up to London every chance he could get. She played the piano and sang songs from *Chu Chin Chow* and *Maid of the Mountains*. I didn't give a damn about Owen and Katie Caddle and now here was the irate husband clutching my arm in a neurotic vice and blaming me.

' "You don't know much, do you? A bloody day-old kitten."

'I was ready to agree with this and with anything the man chose to say. Would Owen Guest's indiscretions cost me my job and would that be poetic justice? And if I was sacked, would my grandmother get the premium back? Those one hundred and thirty pounds, my thirty pieces of silver. Whom had I betrayed? The sum was engraved on my heart. And Great-Uncle Ezra's eighty pounds worth of stamp duty lost for ever.

' "They came addressed to Elsie Fell."

'It was all I could think of in my own defence. I should have been in the dock with the little farmer. Whose side was I on?

' "You are a wet little fart," Caddle said. "That's what you are."

'How could I accept that? What little pride I had was unavoidable. He was vested with every known form of power and authority and I was stripped of my inadequate trappings of self-respect. Any form of freedom was beyond the dirty window against which I could only press my nose like a child kept in after school.

' "Tell him this," Captain Caddle said. "If he comes within a hundred yards of my house, I'll shoot him dead. You just tell him that. Have you got it? And of course the same applies to you."

'He did not release my arm. He was no bigger than I was, but he had power and authority on his side.

' "And let me give you a piece of the best advice you will ever get. If you want to succeed in our profession, if you want to become a tolerably decent solicitor and a decent citizen, don't let people make use of you. And now for Christ's sake, get out of my sight." '

vii

'I make the journey on foot from the office to my digs in Snowdon Street like a man burdened with a guilty secret. Glaslyn had lost all its charm. I smoked one cigarette after another until the dowdy room was barely visible. I seemed condemned to sit alone in front of dying fires. "The grasshopper shall be a burden, and desire shall fail . . ." My songs no longer flourish and my career as a poet is cinders and ashes. Cast-iron grates become the focus of my discontent. In my resentment I throw letters addressed to Elsie Fell on the fire, and out of my disloyalty and despair what is left of my imagination weaves arid illusions. I hide like a bird among the yellow roses that grow in profusion on either side of the portico of Caddle Castle. Inside there is a woman singing a song to her lover on the Western Front. Is she naked or liquid under her Chinese gown? "Youth is the time for loving/So poets always say/The contrary we're proving/Look at us two today . . ."

'Captain Caddle's thirty-six hours' leave came and went, but his absence brought me no relief. My best friend had tampered with the junior partner's private property, had tumbled and sweated in his bed. How could he return to a place of honour in this firm and secure my prospects of promotion? I crept around the place with an invisible bell around my neck, guilty by association and unclean. I had a duty to inform my sister Nanw of Owen's gross behaviour, but how could I bring myself to do it? It didn't matter about Alice. She was her father's responsibility. Let him look after his daughter although from my limited experience she was very capable of looking after herself. Nanw was vulnerable. She had a glass swan Owen had given her. Something he had won in a shooting gallery in a fair. I noted that she had placed it among her sentimental souvenirs and precious ornaments in a childlike way which would not become a grown woman.

'It could be that the first step back to my lost power over poetry would be to tell the truth. But how to tell it, recognize it, discover it? Travel back to the beginning and start the journey again. I cycled back the eight miles to Glanrafon Stores to take my old place at the family table. I crouched in my corner of the horsehair sofa under the aqua tint of *The Broad and Narrow Way* and studied my grandmother in her stick-back chair in a light more penetrating than the firelight flickering on her face. She was a tyrant but she nourished her own wisdom. If only I knew how to extract the guidance I needed without incurring the injunctions I resented. In any case there was nothing she could do about Nanw's infatuation except make it worse. The burdens accumulating on my back were getting too heavy to bear. Would our well-worn religious practices offer any consolation?

'A mid-week service of Intercession. How religious we get in time of trouble. Would some revelation grow out of the sunlight and the silence of the sky that pierced the tall windows of the west side of the chapel? My expectations are punctuated with solemn evocations. I am willing to believe every word he says from "O Lord God" to "Day of Wrath". He stands in the polished pitch-pine pulpit, tall, remote, lit with an other-worldly radiance, no longer Alice Breeze's father but a possible conductor of lightning. Even the small grey curls on his head look trained to convey a vital message.

' "It is to Thee we turn in the Day of Wrath. Thy strong right arm, O Lord of Hosts, alone can deliver us from the snares of the enemy. In these days of bitter darkness, the Light of Thy Countenance is the one beacon of hope . . ."

'I saw Owen again on the hillside, his arms raised and mouth open as he rushed down towards me, and for one moment as I caught him in my arms I imagined I had captured and held the essence of sunlight. He was life. He was my leader and my friend, purged of earthly weakness and reduced to his bright essence. How great our cause must be if Owen was so ready to lay down his life for it.

' "Take now Thy Son, Thine own Son Isaac, whom Thou lovest . . . and offer him there for a burnt offering upon one of the mountains . . ."

'Out of the trenches, Owen said, men went over the top singing. How hard was a hail of bullets? How many Isaacs were hit? There were women in the congregation snuffling and suppressing their sobs. Handkerchiefs were in general use. My grandmother's chin was sunk deep on her chest and I could see a pulse between her jaw and her temple.

' "Come unquenchable grace, possess our hearts and minds with the spirit of sacrifice and with the same irresistible power, break down the fierce rage of our enemy and scatter his evil intentions. Furnish our young men with courage and the purity of spirit that will drive them on and keep them through the heat of battle to the full and fervent joy of total victory."

'I missed the emotional climax. My peripheral vision had seen my grandmother's blue eyes wide open and her gnarled hands teasing a hole in the linen fabric of her small handkerchief. It was unmistakeable dissent. A form of protest I could not fathom. I saw Alice slide along the pew to reach the keyboard of the organ. She shot a red-eyed glance in my direction while her father read the first verse of a stirring hymn that was intended to reach a note of victory in the last verse. I became increasingly concerned with my grandmother's condition. She was pulling on her black gloves. Alice's fingers pressed down the keys of a tremulous opening chord. The congregation rose. I saw my Uncle Tryfan in all his simplicity filling his lungs in preparation for a hymn he so much enjoyed singing. My grandmother's gilt-edged hymn book lay unopened in her gloved hand. As soon as the singing began she stalked in her customary busy stride up the aisle. Making an unscheduled exit. I could see she was not unwell. Just leaving. What should I do? Dash after her in the hope that Alice and her father and the entire congregation would assume Mrs Lloyd Glanrafon was in fact ailing, and that her grandson, John Cilydd More, whose father, grandfather and great-grandfather had each in his time occupied a place in the deacon's pew under the pulpit, filled with concern, was intent on catching up with her.

'She was speeding down the road in the direction of home. The chapel behind me was as conspicuous as a temple, standing among the fields outside the small village, built to serve Calvinistic Methodists over a wide area. I had to run to overtake her.

' "Nain," I said. "Nain. What's the matter? Aren't you well?"

'She marched on shaking her head.

' "I don't know what words mean anymore," she said.

'That was something I could agree with. Perhaps we were both in the same condition. I had to keep up with her.

109

' "Practical Christianity," she said, "marching forward to a better world. I never took to that man. He wasn't safe on the Five Subjects."

'I tried to remember what they were. One, the nature of divine predestination that granted unconditional salvation to the elect; Two, that Christ's death was an atonement limited to the elect; Three, man's total incapacity due to his corrupt nature . . . What about Four and Five?

'My grandmother had stopped muttering to herself. She stared at the hedgerow, examining it closely as if she was looking for something she had lost. Then she turned to look at me. I was a disappointment to her. Like someone recovering from a physical attack, she breathed deeply and weighed against the hedge. It was such an unusual posture for her that my mouth hung open in surprise.

' "Was it you that went to the police to report that poor lad hiding in Foryd Isa?"

'I was the offence. I blushed to the roots of my hair.

' "The minister said I should," I said.

'Was it in fact me or was it Alice or Owen? Perhaps I was thinking of something else at the time: holding her Sunbeam while she popped into the police station. These things are very simply done. If the minister approved, why should my grandmother object? I would share the credit or blame. Surely in wartime it was a laudable act. He was a spy. That was Owen's theory and Alice's and by osmosis it became mine.

' "He was a deserter, Nain," I said. "He could have been a spy."

'Everything I said upset her. Her head was shaking from some grief beyond my comprehension.

' "That poor woman's son was little better than an idiot. But he was all she had in the world. Everything else had been taken from her. Now they'll take him back to France, tie him to a post and shoot him. And that poor woman will walk into the sea."

'She was bent on making me feel uncomfortable. She pointed back at the chapel. Her finger was trembling.

' "That place was put up by people who understood that sin is inside each one of us, John Cilydd. Sin is the enemy.

110

Not your Germans and your Kaiser. That place wasn't built to bang a drum for the King of England. You try and grasp that simple fact."

'She marched away from me. A figure of authority reducing itself to a dot in the landscape. I couldn't go back and I couldn't go after her. I had to flee to some place where they would never find me. Put on uniform – what else? – and let it become my cloak of invisibility. Once inside I would reassemble my essential self and, even more important, nourish my delicate Muse. What else could I do? I was not prepared to spend the rest of my life in this place doing daily penance for a flaw that was never my fault in the first place.'

Five

The windscreen wipers on my Triumph Herald were fighting
a losing battle against twilight and the driving rain. There
was a settlement here in the process of being washed away:
the church, the yew trees in the graveyard, the public house,
the two chapels, the council school in which I was told I was
to hold my evening class. Had the people gone, leaving a
deserted outpost in a wet Welsh wilderness? Pant Gwyn was
a place with a name on it, with its own little history and a
people I could warm to. This was a ghost village in which I
had to find my way about. Which was the turning to the
school and the schoolmaster's house? The only signs of life
were the coloured reflections of television screens where
curtains had not been drawn against the winter evening.
They proved the outpost was in touch, partaking of the
universal comforts of the global village. The messages of
cosmopolitania were being received.

The course on offer at Pant Gwyn was 'Welsh Social
Theory' in twelve weekly classes. A staff member of the
Extra-Mural Department, a perky chap with exclamatory
hair and a mischievous grin, tipped me the wink that the
illustrious Doctor Wesley Dilkes had asked if there was such
a thing. I was glad the fellow passed on the comment since it
gave me time to prepare an effective answer should Dilkes
amble in on a class out of the night on some kind of
inspection tour during the session. That sort of thing could
happen. I was new to the Extra-Mural circuit. In fact his
comment had stimulated me towards giving the course a
missionary edge. By the time the course was finished at least

the minimum enrolment would have become aware that we could be on the brink of a great turnaround in world history, could be instrumental in initiating it even. You have to start somewhere. Why not here? We would be the first people consciously to use their culture as a basis for economic development. Thus far would we be obliged to move beyond Marx and Engels if the entire planet was not to be torn apart by the knee-jerk worship of the tin god of technological progress. Historical necessity was not some elaborate spacecraft pursuing its self-existent course on automatic pilot, with individual consciousness like a piece of chewing-gum stuck on the nose-cone by some careless engineer. To extend the metaphor, I would say to my attentive class, we have an inalienable right to take control of the machine. I would even go so far as to describe moral imperatives as rocket fuel and referring in passing to my father's papers, perhaps even suggest that digging into the past was the best way to provide the aptly named fossil fuel for our journey into the future. It was a matter of conviction: a matter of transferring the same mental and physical energy that had transformed the economic structure of the planet to the rehabilitation of culture values that had been mutilated or crippled in the historical process. The basic structure in cultural ecology was a community of communities, not a conveyor belt. The seeds of regeneration lay dormant in people's minds. It was my mission to awaken them. In an extra-mural class a tutor encountered that elected handful of people who came of their volition to drink at the well. What better place to start?

The weather could do nothing to dampen my mood of warm exultation as I peered about and recognized the white gates of the schoolmaster's house. I had met the man briefly in Mather's lair under the library and had taken to him. A bearded, jovial man who shook my hand firmly and announced that he rejoiced in teaching small children. He called it working at the coal-face. Some people would call him overqualified, since he held a doctorate in philosophy, but it was his opinion that there could not be, in the context of our crisis, a more important job than giving children an unshakeable grip on their linguistic heritage. He, too, was a man with a mission.

I left my car at the roadside. I felt a twinge of anxiety as I scampered up the gravel path to the half-verandah over the front door and tried to remember the schoolmaster's name: was it Dr Howells or Dr Hughes? In any case, did he use the title? Had he not said something jolly about discarding it as an object lesson to others?

A young woman opened the door. She had a pretty, square face. It was suspended in front of me like a portrait lit from the side. I couldn't make out whether it was reproach or resentment I saw in her eyes. She was wearing black slippers trimmed with coloured beads which also caught the light. She held one hand on the door and did not invite me in.

'Dr Howells?' I spoke hopefully. 'The schoolmaster. My name is More. I think he's expecting me. He asked me to come early. Nasty night.'

I threw in the last comment for good measure. Was this the wife or the daughter? Too young to be one and too old to be the other. She seemed to know who I was but withheld any welcome.

'You've come to the wrong place,' she said. 'This is Tuesday. Your class is on Thursdays.'

This was Carreg Wen, not Pant Gwyn. I was in the wrong village. She could see I was embarrassed and had no intention of relieving my condition. The heels of her small feet and her black slippers remained close together like a ballet dancer's in attentive repose. In some way I was being scrutinized and found wanting. I heard the cheerful chime of an older woman's voice in the corridor.

'Who is it, Wenna? Someone to see me?'

This was the mother. When they were side by side in the light of the open doorway the generic resemblance was obvious. The mother shorter, but the same square head and oddly enough the same decorated black slippers. But the mother was welcoming and cheerful. She carried the extra weight of years with gaiety that was absent from the daughter. She took my mistake to be a charming mishap. She was in fact the mistress of the village school and she had been expecting me on Thursday and the arrangements for the class were well in hand. There would be the hard core of faithful class members and one or two new faces.

114

'Including Wenna, I hope. While she's home.'

The daughter made no response. Had they been quarrelling? The mother seizing the chance to make up in the presence of a third party?

'Such a night,' the mother said. 'You must come in, Mr More, and let us make you a cup of tea. "Don't ask, give", isn't it, Wenna? I'm Morfydd Ferrario, as you must have guessed. It's a funny mixture, isn't it? My husband was an Italian prisoner of war.'

The room into which I was led was decorated with a profusion of pictures, ornaments and antiques. It looked like an extension of a warm and outgoing personality. Mrs Ferrario knelt to prod energetically at the fire until it burst into flame. She twisted her head to give me a roguish smile.

'I always enjoy doing that,' she said. 'My father, you see. And my husband. Neither of them could bear the way I poked the fire, for some reason.' She stood up and gripped her hands together, corseted in self-possession. 'Both gone now,' she said. 'One to heaven, and one to Rome. Giuseppe couldn't put up with the weather. Or me, I suppose. I'm so glad you called, Mr More. There were one or two things I wanted to ask you. I'll ring Dr Hughes. He'll understand.'

She left the room with the compact grace of a woman accustomed to being observed by children and by adults. In her own small way a public figure. I could hear the same confidence in her voice as she spoke on the telephone. I was not at my ease. I felt like a patient waiting to be diagnosed. The room was no help at all. It suggested a haphazard hankering for art objects of all kinds, limited by a schoolteacher's purse. The miniatures were reproductions crudely framed. Most of the ceramics were chipped or inexpertly mended. The girl Wenna brought in the tea and biscuits on a highly polished nickel silver tray. She was beautiful but also threatening, it seemed to me. Her eyes looking upwards were as soulful as a renaissance picture of an avenging angel. She moved away and stood at an angle to me, holding on to the Welsh dresser, not inclined to speak and yet not taking her eyes off me. This was her territory and she could remain silent indefinitely if she chose to. I was the stranger within the gates on whom an eye had to be kept.

115

Her mother raised both her hands when she saw there were only two cups on the tray.

'Wenna,' she said. 'Won't you take tea with us?'

The girl shook her head and left the room closing the door behind her.

'Poor child,' the mother said. 'Just out of prison.' She poured the tea. 'She gets very irritable. Not her real self at all. She's been suspended from her college for the rest of the session. I don't know what I'll do with her. Still, I suppose that is the price we have to pay.'

Part of one of the road-sign campaigns in the south. She was one of the new generation of protesters – the generation I had come in search of. When she next appeared I would look at her with a new warmth and respect.

'It marks them, you know,' Mrs Ferrario said. 'It's a big price we have to pay. The aim is to raise the political consciousness of the people. How can you when the power of an alien state monopolizes the mass media? They feel it, you know. The young people. They feel it here.' Mrs Ferrario pressed a clenched fist against her heart.

I couldn't tell her that to me she was stating the blindingly obvious. Instead I strenuously restrained myself from being put off by her effusive manner. We were all in the struggle together. Personal sensibilities had to be subordinated to principles and purpose at all times.

'This is a time of crisis,' she said. 'As a family you could say we have been forced to face the fact on a very personal level. I'm sure you come with the best intentions, Mr More. And at any other time, under normal conditions, whatever they are, I would never presume to question you so boldy. You have taken the empty manse at Rhyd-y-Groes?'

There were more networks running underground in this corner of Wales than I knew about. I suppose my behaviour could appear eccentric to those interested enough to enquire about it. Which was all to the good. Let life be a voyage of discovery as well as a mission; it added flavour, the tang of an apple under the teeth. She wanted to know all about my empty manse. There was damp in the back bedroom and the stone slabs outside the back door were always wet. The garden was too big and overwhelmed with weeds. But in the

116

empty dining-room, my father's papers were arranged like a collection of barrister's briefs all around the walls. Mather, the great and good, Hefin Mather, was once again my benefactor.

There was a sneaky lecturer in the Economics Department that he particularly disapproved of. This character, as a sideline, crept around buying quarrymen's cottages, doing them up with local authority improvement grants and flogging them off at a handsome profit as holiday cottages. He had approached the ageing trustees of a failing chapel and made them an offer for the manse, a substantial granite house in a large garden next to the chapel. His offer was too low even for the troubled trustees. When Mather stepped in they accepted my rent with a sigh of relief and on condition I should not bother them within the twelve-month with any complaints or requests for repairs or improvements. In the boot of my Triumph Herald, Mather and I transported my father's papers from the boiler-room to their new premises and no one in the college was any the wiser. Mather kicked his heels together in that empty dining-room and giggled. He was delighted with our little conspiracy.

Mrs Ferrario was leaning towards me over her cup of tea.

'Are you one of us, Mr More?' she said.

'Indeed, I should hope so,' I said.

Her unblinking gaze was fixed on my face. In the field one had to accept such allies as one could find with gratitude and without hesitation. Mrs Ferrario's analysis was correct. If the general political conciousness of our people was that low, only a combined and concentrated effort of whatever forces were at hand could ever hope to raise it.

'You can't blame them,' she said. 'The young ones. The forces of the state are overwhelming. You feel that when you've been to prison. Every hand seems to be raised against you. In the protest at Carmarthen there were police agents urging the students on, building cases against them. And there are rumours. Always rumours. About Special Branch men and so on. Infiltrators rhymes with traitors. The secret police are among us. That sort of thing.'

She was staring at me intently as she went through this litany. I was so slow to realize that it was my credentials that

117

were being scrutinized. This accounted for the look of suspicion I detected in the girl's eyes the moment she opened the door. I began to blush. How on earth could I begin to prove to this woman that I was not an infiltrator from the Special Branch? I was a man who had suddenly appeared from nowhere, trotting around the district offering extra-mural classes in a new form of social theory. I must have appeared blatantly unauthentic. When I spoke my voice was thick as if I had suddenly acquired a head cold.

'I don't know whether you've heard of my father,' I said. 'Cilydd. The poet. He won the chair when he was twenty-three. The youngest ever National Winner, I believe. Or so Hefin Mather tells me.'

Had she any idea who Hefin Mather was? Had she ever heard of Cilydd? It seemed a vital question. An absence of communication spelt an absence of community. Should I tell her this? A community, Mrs Ferrario, is not a figment of the imagination or some fancy recipe in a politician's cookbook. I felt my arms twitching at my sides with the urge to spread out and demonstrate the width of the oak tree behind the camper's latrines at the Glanrafon Arms. A community had the continuity of the rings of centuries binding the trunk of the tree, holding the damn thing up, Mrs Ferrario. Hence our fondness for family trees. And how was Mr Ferrario getting on by himself in Rome? Sitting in a traffic jam in the Via Flaminia at this very moment, I dare say? Light was dawning on the lady's face. It originated in a schoolroom power of recall. She raised a finger so that the class should listen.

'The hawk descends / With burning eyes / And where he strikes / The singing dies.'

We both laughed as though for the first time we realized we knew each other. My father had provided me with a provisional travel document to cross the frontier.

ii

Within a couple of days I was a comfortable tenant in the sparsely furnished manse. In the morning the inquisitive shoots of an overgrown buddleia peered into the kitchen. I

118

was inclined to talk to them rather than prune them. The vegetable patch was covered with brambles. I put off any urge to take up gardening. The decaying weeds and the bleached couch grass were part of the flavour of the place, like the wallpaper indoors with stark rectangles where pictures used to hang and patches of damp with the potential of abstract paintings. A shade of pink had been favoured by the wife of an earlier incumbent. This was the colour of the shadows when I brooded on the stairs or mooched through the rooms attending the silences left behind by my predecessors. My tenancy had ceased to be an accident. The vacant manse at Rhyd-y-Groes had become part of my inheritance. Nowhere in the world could have been better suited to house my father's papers. Here litter could become literature. I had the silence and the daytime hours to deepen my acquaintance with both.

My immediate predecessor had been an untidy single man with a gift for folk-song, accompanied and unaccompanied. Sitting on the uncarpeted stairs I saw the stringless guitar and the torn raincoat he had left behind on the hallstand and I heard the faint echo of his nasal baritone from the room he had used as his study. Mrs Jarvis, whose offer to clean up the place I had not yet accepted, told me that the woman he wanted to marry refused to become a minister's wife. Mrs Jarvis had watched him allow his breakfast to go cold while he struggled to come to a decision. He had capitulated and gone off to be a radio announcer and live with his lady in a Cardiff suburb. Mrs Jarvis and I understood the symbolic deprivation each in our own way. The deserted manse was the deserted village. The same old tunes lingered on. She confessed her abiding fondness for the minister. She said it was a pity some of the deacons had disapproved of his harmless bohemian habits. They couldn't understand why the young people crowded in to listen to his songs but didn't want to hear his sermons.

Underneath the veneer of mid-twentieth-century evangelical bohemianism and the well-meaning posters of Christian Aid and Third World concerns still stuck to the walls with rusting drawing-pins, were the pillars of the old certainties that first built the house. It was possible that at some early phase of a vacillating existence that could hardly be dignified with such a word as pilgrimage, I would have found the place dark and repulsive. Now it exuded a nostalgia more potent than dampness, which disturbed and exalted me. It had become an essential ingredient of my adventure, part of the vocabulary of my quest. On the attic floor an illustrated Peter Williams Bible with broken brass clasps was open at the Book of Hosea. I knelt down to pick out the verses in the dim light. The second chapter told me to debate with my mother and denounce her; the eleventh began with an evocation that had an irresistible lilt: 'When Israel was a child, then I loved him, and called my son out of Egypt.' I had an urge to make head and tail of the book. The key to his prophecies was more than the parallel between the preacher's forgiveness of his unfaithful wife and the chosen people's whoring after false gods. The music of the whole was far more than the sum of the parts. I could hear it as I recited the verses and heard the sound reverberate in the empty house. The extent of this language was greater than the limits of this world.

The side window of my bedroom overlooked the nonconformist graveyard that surrounded the straight avenue leading to the chapel doors. The doors stood on either side of the pulpit area and above them rose a pair of narrow stained-glass windows. Higher than where the preacher's head would be, there was a round casement that allowed a shaft of light to descend from above him into the middle of his congregation. Among the ranks of tilting headstones a grave had been re-opened. I watched a bareheaded man in unexpectedly formal dress place planks around the four sides. Jumping in and out of the grave, he was covering the hole with a green tarpaulin as protection against any deterioration in the weather before the funeral. He went in feet forward and came out backwards. A tidy, athletic version of descent and resurrection. Had I been the minister I would have known who in the village had died and I would have been preparing myself to take charge of the solemn ritual. I occupied his quarters without discharging his obligations. Like everything else in my new habitat it was food for thought. What did I believe? I believed in my own

120

emptiness. The processes of history, the pressures of providence had divested me of worldly preoccupations in order to bring me to this. I had been given the time to wait. That in itself was a privilege. And I was prepared to commit myself when the call came. Meanwhile I watched the gravedigger put his jacket on and survey his handiwork with a critical eye. He lit a cigarette and stepped around the excavation. Man that is born of woman may be of few days but they should be divided between craftsmanship and meditation. That was something to believe. He was scraping the soil from his spade with a piece of slate. 'Naked came I out of my mother's womb, and naked shall I return thither.' That was a disturbing thought. The last place in the universe I would choose to return to. Was it an insult to God not to bow to the inevitable? Did it have to be her?

From the front window I saw the bonnet of a BMW cautiously nose its way into the overgrown drive of the manse. It was a cause for alarm. In the middle of the morning I had a visitor. The notes I was making for my evening class at Carreg Wen were incomplete on the desk in the study. The fire in the grate was going out. I hadn't shaven. I looked a mess. The knock on the front door reverberated through the house. There wasn't time to do anything about my appearance. What did clothes matter? I opened the door and there was my brother Gwydion in one of his leather coats grinning at me as if he were renewing acquaintance with a perennial joke.

'Smelt you out!' he said. 'Smelt you out in your lair. The great man sulking in his tent.'

Sulking. Did he think I was sulking? It only went to show how little they understood me, my family.

'You certainly have a taste for the austere,' Gwydion said. 'A monk. That's what you must have been in a previous incarnation. Living in a damp cell on bread and water.'

I could only offer him a cup of tea. I hadn't done my shopping yet. Nothing much left to eat in the house. Half a wholemeal loaf. The biscuit tin was empty except for crumbs.

'So what are we up to?' He leaned against the old-fashioned porcelain kitchen sink to drink the mug of tea

I gave him. 'You're up to something,' he said. 'No question about that. You've got more brains in that big head of yours than Bedwyr and I put together. If you've got a loaf, why not use it? That's what I say. You're not miffed because you didn't get that job at the college, are you?'

I shook my head. He was my brother I suppose. He had some right to take an interest.

'Good Lord, I should think not,' he continued. 'As I've told you on more than one occasion, it never was a job for a grown man. And I'll tell you something else, too, while I'm at it. You should do something about this unhealthy obsession you've got with your father. And trying to relate his existence with your own. Or you'll end up like a tuppenny ha'penny Hamlet with nobody to assassinate. They're all dead, boy. It's even more difficult to mount the play without the King than without the Prince. I have some idea about what's going on, you know. I'm not just a pretty face.'

He slapped his mug down on the wooden drawing-board and launched himself on an inspection of the house. I moved quietly in his wake. I would have liked to take him more into my confidence if only my intentions had taken on firmer shape. It would have been dangerous. He was too close to my mother. They were two of a kind. I had never once heard him speak warmly of the things I believed my father stood for.

'Great place!' He enjoyed the reverberation of his own voice. 'Smashing place to make a film,' he said. 'We've got to try and think of a suitable plot.' To him everything was always game. I was like a child watching from the touchline and longing to join in. 'Look at that!' He stood at the side window of my bedroom which overlooked the graveyard. The edges of the green tarpaulin over the open grave were flapping in the breeze. 'Talk about living at the dead centre . . . Great place, though. Bags of atmosphere. What do you do all day? Sit here and ask yourself what it's all about?'

To parry such a shrewd thrust I put the question to him.

'What do you think?' I said. 'What *is* it all about?'

Perhaps it was the melancholy charm of the churchyard that induced him to take my question seriously. He tapped the window-pane with his fingertips. His face was close to the glass. He was proud of his hands. His fingernails were always manicured.

'When your time comes,' he said, 'just drop into that hole. Meanwhile, see how far you can go. How far you can get.' He tapped the window-pane. 'There's just this between life and death,' he said. 'Between illusion and reality, So be creative! That's my motto. Have a good time while you're at it. And complain as little as possible.'

He grinned at me. My reaction was oversensitive.

'Do you think I complain too much?'

'I think the old man did,' Gwydion said. 'I'm not blaming him. He wasn't my real father and that was a lot to put up with.' It was strangely warming that he should be so frank with me. 'If it was old Pen,' Gwydion said. 'I assume it was. At least he had a go. He went out there and fought. He got killed, of course, but at least he didn't spend the rest of his life moaning and groaning.'

It was the first time I ever heard him acknowledge so bluntly that he knew Pen Lewis and not Cilydd More was his father.

The bare front bedroom of the manse was an appropriate place to shed polite fiction. Long years of pretence fell away from us and left us brothers more than ever. Perhaps it would be easier now for me to be infected with his gaiety?

There was more of the house to see. To please me he was taking it all seriously.

'What make was this lot?' he said. 'They did their ministers proud in those days, didn't they? At least they knew what they were doing. They knew what they were for. More than we can say, eh?'

'Annibynwyr,' I said. 'Independents. A minority around here. But they had a builder in their midst so they were bent on showing the Methodists and the Baptists that they could house their minister as palatially as the local Rector.'

'Fascinating, isn't it?' Gwydion said. 'What our forefathers could get up to. Ancient tribalism finding new outlets. What's this lot?'

My father's papers and notebooks were ranged around the floor of the empty dining-room. They were kept in place under glass paperweights and books. Was I obliged to tell him? He must already have noticed the secretive look on my face. I had begun to blush.

'Cilydd's papers,' I said. 'For the most part.'

He looked down on them with increasing curiosity.

'Where the hell did you get them from?'

I could not divulge my source. That would have been dangerous and unfair to Hefin Mather.

'They were in an outside lavatory. A terrace house in Pendraw,' I said. 'Eifion Street.'

Gwydion shook his head in exaggerated amazement.

'That's what I call research,' he said. 'Proper little scholar aren't you, P.C. More. "Research is more important / Than tinkering with verse" . . . Well I never.'

'In very poor condition, some of it,' I said. 'There's a lot of work to be done on it.'

I kept expecting to see him drop on his knees and start reading avidly. There would have been no objection to that. But all he did was put his hands behind his back, under his leather coat, and peer down like a naturalist looking for signs of the passage of some hedge mammal in a ditch.

'Do you know what I'm thinking?' he said.

There was a generous expression on his face as he gave me ample time to guess. He was prepared to share his innermost thoughts as well as his intuition with me and I should not be ungrateful.

'It's no secret,' he said. 'I've been asked to set up a film on the Eisteddfod for worldwide consumption. Why couldn't this be part of it? That's what I'm thinking.' He made a sweeping gesture to include everything on the floor. 'He was the product of eisteddfodic culture, wasn't he? Of course he was. You've got to start somewhere. With a film I mean. Big budget stuff has got to have an angle. Not one of your Aunty BBC documentary plod-plods. Think about it, brother! Think about it.' He could see my lack of enthusiasm. 'You've got to face this, you know. The kind of world we live in. Presentation is all! It's no use being a shrinking violet if you've got something to get across. It really isn't. You've got to master the media. There's nothing else for it. No other way. Don't look so bloody depressed.'

He stretched out his arms and grinned. I could see he was

so full of his own notion, he would not want to be bothered with reading the wealth of material lying around him on the floor. This was more of a relief than a disappointment.

'Oh, I know you've got to have something to say. That's why I'm here, brother,' he said. 'To take you out to lunch and make you a firm offer. Work for us as a consultant on this and allied projects and we'll pay you twice whatever that measly college of yours was offering. At least that. Car and expenses, of course. No pension, of course, but since when has a chap who gave up one job before clinching another been interested in pensions?'

This made us both laugh. It was enjoyable to be with him. It stopped me taking myself too seriously. It would have been a pleasure to work with him. He was, I suppose, unscrupulous and it was a fact that he cut corners, but he had his own engaging frankness, and he had proved he was good at his job – which was more than I had done. He poked around the place while I shaved and got ready to go out. It would be pleasant to have a decent meal. Gwydion knew about food and wine. My notes for the class tonight could wait. In any case I was taking the business of evening classes a fraction too solemnly. I needed a fresh perspective and Gwydion was just the man to provide it.

His BMW was new and powerful. He gave me a brief résumé of its virtues and advantages. It certainly allowed us to speed through the green countryside like two mythological princes on a magical progress. It was a car that would be delightful to possess. I had only to stay close to my brother and in the fullness of time I would get one. Isolation had its uses, but fulfilment required relationships. If a man could not achieve a relationship with his own brother, what chance had he in a wider context? In theory, at least, an organic community required the family as a basic unit; in which case a family needs to be free, flexible, secure and as economically independent as is compatible with the welfare of society as a whole. Social theory encapsulated for instant application, like an antibiotic. There seemed no good reason why we could not cooperate. Thinking about the possibility was a stimulation in itself. Sitting alongside him in his car, I had the sensation that he too shared this perception.

'It's all go,' he said. 'You've heard the latest about old Amy?'

We had arrived. It was too early for lunch. The hotel was a converted country house. We took a walk in the grounds. I listened carefully to what Gwydion had to say.

'She has the most amazing plans,' he said. 'Xanadu has nothing on Amy. You've got to hand it to her. If an opportunity comes along, she grabs it with both hands. And she doesn't give up. You'd think after her women's centre fiasco and losing dear old Connie Clayton she would have had enough. Not a bit of it. She wants to commission a glittering glass pyramid from Bedwyr to plonk right in front of Brangor and give the place a bit of contemporary class.'

I had to stop him.

'What is it all about?' I said. 'Where is the money coming from?'

He slapped my back to allay my anxieties.

'Money no problem,' he said. 'Government's behind her all the way. She's got the Welsh lobby of the great Labour movement eating out of her hand. Do you remember that creepy little friend of hers D.I. Everett?'

Did I remember him? I could see his hand now on the white tea-table closing over my mother's. Who eats out of whose hand?

'Weird types, aren't they? These Labourist friends of hers. Have you come across that threadbare journalist Meredith? He'll do anything she tells him. Strange generation. Furtive, conspiratorial, backstairs lot. Of course, there are limits. They can go so far and no further. Mustn't disturb the basic power structure. Not that they ever would. They bend over backwards to strengthen it. Hence this Investiture lark. Hence all the money. I'm not blind, you know. Or stupid.' He had stopped to confront me challengingly. 'All I am saying, Peredur, is this. Your best chance is to work inside the system and not go banging your head against its concrete foundations and solid walls. It's the way we've survived, man, all down the centuries. Open rebellion just gets crushed underfoot. Believe me. I know how you feel.'

My heart sank. The dream of cooperation and

collaboration was evaporating like mist on the artificial lake. I stood by a bare weeping willow and a family of ducks swam towards us expecting to be fed.

'I know its a cliché to talk about putting Wales on the map,' Gwydion said. 'But that's what it amounts to. And it's vitally important the right people, the best people, should do it. That's what I mean about Cilydd's stuff and a film about the Eisteddfod. Telling the world what it really means. Exploring the real values. What the hell is wrong with that?'

'Exploiting,' I said. It was the only word I could think of. 'Exploitation.'

'What's wrong with that, in God's name?'

He genuinely didn't know. So how could I tell him? It would take a lifetime to explain. I was hungry. I suggested we should go in and eat.

iii

Over salmon in a pastry case and a second bottle of Chablis Montmain, Gwydion said you could divide the human race into those who have a go and those who give up. He was in that flushed state when the man of action feels obliged to sum up his understanding of life in gnomic pontifications. I was his brother and he could say what he liked to me. In this condition he would have said what he liked to anyone. He took a delight in frankness, which I found engaging, like the performance of an actor with the gift of transforming an audience into a single entity under the control of his hypnotic gaze. It over-simplified everything and had little relationship to truth; but it gave an experience for which the recipient felt obliged to be grateful. It emerged from a shadowy category that lay somewhere between the titilating and the life-enhancing. He was pointing a finger at me.

'Amy had a go,' he said. 'Cilydd gave up. Therein lay the difference. The charm, you might say. The abyss. He fell in. She didn't.'

How conveniently simple. And how deceptive. He was rambling on for my benefit. Doing his best to please me like the appetizing fish on its bed of young spinach surrounded by artichokes and with a side plate of distinctive and delicious vegetables. All because he wanted something. And I knew what it was: 'this Welsh business', as that old trout with a trembling head put it in my interview. What Gwydion with all his frankness and self-awareness did not realize – I assumed that he didn't – was the true nature of the role the not so mysterious powers of the ruling technological superstructure were thrusting upon him. Not that they needed to thrust very hard when there were candidates for unholy ordination; so many mouths open to be stuffed with gold. The mission assigned to Gwydion and his kind was to contain and tame that upheaval of protest and political consciousness that had spread throughout this decade from one end of Wales to the other. The moment would come when I would point this out to him in the most brotherly way I could manage.

Beyond the salmon I could see Wenna Ferrario's face gleam like the ghostly presence of an inspector of morals and conduct. She scorned make-up and sat in the most shadowy corner of the cookery room of Carreg Wen Council School. This was where my class chose to sit, at a comfortable distance from the old-fashioned range. When the firelight flickered across it, Wenna's head had the gravity of Roman sculpture. And the impassivity. She never opened her mouth to join in our class discussion. When I spun out the guidelines it was that graven image in the firelight I was trying to appease. I had to arrive at general theoretical proportions that would embrace and thereby justify whatever impulses governed the urge of her generation to protest. They had a right to become aware of themselves and of the threat to their heritage and identity. In the cool terms of an extra-mural lecture on social theory, their revolt was part of the response of the Western world to the numbing effect of universal technological state tyranny that had taken upon itself a remote quasi-supernatural authority that could never be questioned. If there was ever a quiver of approval on that girl's face as I spoke, I never glimpsed it. That did nothing to deter me from strenuous effort to gain a sign of grace.

'And that's why he took to the bottle,' Gwydion said.

128

He grinned and raised his glass of Chablis to his lips. I didn't like the contempt implied in his disparaging attitude. Perhaps Cilydd had been a secret drinker. There was a cupboard in his study that he always kept locked. And he was in the habit of leaving the house on certain evenings after dark without any explanation. There was a back room in one of the more old-fashioned taverns in Pendraw which he frequented with his cronies. Who were his cronies? Temporary fugitives from the suffocating restrictions of smalltown nonconformity; eisteddfodic types; closet bards and furtive revellers; clubbable but classless males with nothing more comfortable or congenial to resort to. It was not so long ago, and yet it appeared to be a custom belonging to another age.

'I'll tell you one thing about father figures,' Gwydion said. 'They are bloody dangerous. I've done a bit of thinking about father figures. Figuring it out, you might say.'

I was his guest. There was an excellent table between us and I was there to listen. The waiter came and went. Gwydion handled the fellow with the polite expertise of which I was still incapable. Now he was going to clarify the past for my exclusive benefit.

'I'm not saying it's a family curse or some kind of recurring decimal in the mathematics of fate or anything particularly spooky. But just you think, my lad. What have we all got in common? You, me, and the blessed John Cilydd? And Bedwyr, too, but it doesn't seem to have rubbed off on him. I tell you, Peredur, that eldest brother of ours is too perfect by half. Now where was I. Eh? Oh yes, what have we got in common, apart from dear old Amy? I'll tell you, a space where a father should have been. Cilydd never knew his father, did he? Neither did I. And as far as I can make out the poor old bugger was little better than a substitute for any of us, legit or illegit. Not much of a husband either. Never get married, brother . . . Now this is what I'm coming to . . . this is the point I want to make . . .'

He was mildly fuddled. The alcohol that heightened his urge to honesty blunted what ability he had to anaylse. He had never submitted to any academic discipline for any worthwhile length of time. He was bright but his flashes of intuition never lasted long enough to sustain systematic thinking. The waiter responded quickly to his bidding and they shared the order for black coffee like a private joke. It would be served in a corner of the lounge that overlooked the artificial lake. Like his mother, Gwydion enjoyed making use of hotels. I could see her now crossing the carpeted floors, on Gwydion's arm, in semi-regal progress, and her youngest son like a servitor in attendance.

'This is the point . . .' Gwydion hung on to his discourse. 'The missing father figure is the origin of the cult of personality. Just as it was at the root of the *Fuhrerprinzip*. Just think of it, wars great and small wiping out fathers by the thousand. To whom do the orphaned generations turn as they grow up? For authority. For guidance. The father of his people. The leader. The icon carried aloft . . .' Gwydion raised both arms dramatically. 'There you are. I give you the notion. Free gratis and for nothing. Make a nice essay in an academic publication. A nice entry for the college gazette.'

Gwydion left university without a degree. Nothing he enjoyed more than mocking academic usages. I had to allow for that.

'I don't see what it's all got to do with me,' I said.

He snorted incredulously.

'Don't you?' he said. 'Taking an empty manse to house his papers. Thrashing around in search of a cause old Cilydd would fully approve of.'

This stung me.

'You've chosen a poor example for your theory,' I said. 'Very poor. What we have in Wales is a spontaneous outburst of protest. A generation in revolt. No sign of a leader. It's hydra-headed. Imprison here and protest springs up somewhere else. It's not even coordinated. And if you want my considered opinion, that's what's so exciting about it.'

'Exciting.' Gwydion repeated the word to discredit it. 'Teenage rebellion,' he said. 'You can't call it serious politics. In any case it won't get anywhere. The steam-roller is in motion and a protest or frogs crossing the road won't stop it. Be your age, Peredur.'

He was smiling to demonstrate he wasn't being offensive.

130

I was twenty-nine. The waiter put down the coffee on the occasional table. I considered myself emotionally stable and capable of balanced judgement. Did Gwydion have any grounds for thinking otherwise? Was this the point at which I should tell him that I declined to drown my conscience in a sea of cynicism? Somehow I had to get to grips with him over a definition of integrity. Was it a fact that he rated as a non-starter this quality I admired so much? If that were the case there was no prospect at all of any collaboration between us. Just how much had to be sacrificed in the name of ambition and success? We could do nothing unless we spoke the same language.

His coffee-cup rattled gently in his saucer as he shook with amusement at a thought that had occurred to him.

'She didn't pull any wires for you, did she?'

He was talking about our mother in order to tease me. He would have all our difficulties dissolve at a touch of laughter. Or was it to compel me to face yet another aspect of harsh reality?

'She could have done,' Gwydion said. 'If that was what she had wanted. She has quite a nice little slice of local influence when she cares to exercise it. A magistrate of course. Tell you what.' An even more amusing thought had occurred to him. 'She was scared of you appearing before the bench when she was presiding over it. After one of the protests of your children's crusade. Pity really. Classic situation. The dilemma of the Welsh bourgeoisie in microcosm. An orgy of mutual recrimination! I would have driven a long way to see it.'

I was not prepared to enjoy his joke. He put his cup down to refill it and release his hand to wag a warning finger at me.

'Politics,' Gwydion said. 'Old Amy understands about politics. You don't. It's the art of the possible. In the end you can only persuade people to do what will make them more comfortable. And who is to blame them? Our dear fellow countrymen are no exception. They exemplify it far better than your mute, long-suffering English. Take your Labourists. Your devoted Welsh Labourists. North and South. It's nearly the end of the sixties and they've suddenly tumbled to the fact that they've travelled further on the tide of post-war reform than they really wanted to go. Correction!' Gwydion's lips twitched with pleasure at the subtlety of his exposition. 'They have twigged that the Labour machine to which they owe undying allegiance has fallen in love with the status quo. Reform like revolution has fallen out of fashion – and there is nothing your Welsh party operators respond to more quickly than changes in London political fashions. Now they are free to adore the monarchy and enjoy prolonged flirtations with the City and capitalist finance. They enjoy power and they positively glow with nostalgia for all the glories of Empire. Any bit of ceremony and regal trappings going and they'll devour it like ravening wolves. They won't allow any worn-out manifesto or clap-trap about the means of production, distribution and exchange to stop them. Interesting, isn't it? Reform has reached high-water. Nothing but ebb-tide left.'

He sat back waiting for my applause. I was reminded of the spurts of youthful display with which he used to seek Bedwyr's approval during the holidays. How little the essence of our nature changes. He was the one who longed to have his head patted. No wonder he had thought so much about father figures. He had no inkling of the objective discipline that governed my approach.

'What does all that prove?' I said.

He looked at me as if I were being deliberately stupid.

'If the gravy train is coming,' he said. 'You can't stop it. It will just run over you. So you may as well hop aboard.' He tapped his chest with his open hand. 'Look who's telling you,' he said. 'A natural subversive. But if you want to subvert, you've got to do it from the inside. Jumping up and down in the ditch won't get you anywhere. If you get too much in the way they'll sweep the whole damn lot of you in prison until the celebrations are over. Your protesters. They are only kids, for God's sake.'

'They've got a scale of values,' I said.

I sounded childishly petulant myself as I said it. I thought of Wenna Ferrario's implacable stare. Did it mean I was inadequate without her? She possessed the power that went with essential integrity.

'Look.' Gwydion leaned forward and pressed his hands

132

together in a final attempt at convincing simplification. 'There is only one constant factor in politics,' he said. 'The exercise of power. It's so damned simple you don't need to read endless books to understand it. Principles don't come into it. Except as coloured counters to camouflage the real power-play.'

'So what?' I said.

It was a fatuous comment but the best I could offer in my troubled state. The elaborate arguments of social theory were drained of their relevance. I was confronted by the self-confidence of my brother and haunted by the reproachful face of the girl who had been to prison. Was it reproach I saw, or did my own sense of inadequacy paint it on her impassive features?

'You take old Amy,' Gwydion said. 'Just think of her colourful progress. Her chequered career from rags to riches. From revolution to reaction. Can you think of anything more typical? From pacifism, Welsh nationalism, communism, socialism, to what? Brangor Hall. And I'll tell you something I wouldn't put past her. If she did pull any wires, and I can't myself see her resist the pleasure, it would be for the other chap, not for you.'

The betrayal was as immediate as a blow on the chest. Mared was a Labour Lord. My mother probably knew him well since they were part of the same power network. Those bonds were closer than family ties. And they were both engaged in that exercise of quiet desperation when rulers shed the slogans that brought them into power, and seek out more enduring forms to perpetuate their hegemony. Gwydion could see the pallor on my face. He had gone further than he intended. All he had wanted was amusement at observing my usual contortions of discomfort. This was different. It was beyond a change of values on her part and perhaps on mine. He had pushed me into a deeper primeval zone of feeling. In me she saw the ghost of my father come back to haunt her. That would account for it. She had made what military strategists like to call a pre-emptive strike. It fitted. Truth was always an elegant design, as incisive as a mathematic equation.

'Don't take it seriously,' Gwydion said. 'I was only joking.'

133

Impassivity was the thing. I mustn't show him what I was feeling.

'This extra-mural thing,' Gwydion said. 'How long will you keep it up for?' He wanted me to appreciate afresh that he had my best interests at heart. 'A bit of an academic dead end, surely?' he said. 'How long does it go on for?'

I had to provide him with some kind of an answer or he would suspect me of harbouring vengeful thoughts about our mother. She was old Amy after all; not Gertrude or Clytemnestra. He was visibly relieved when he saw me smiling.

'As long as it takes,' I said.

iv

'I remember your father well.'

The dear lady was offering me a cup of tea. She was as wide as she was high and she wore a hat of old-fashioned dish design that seemed intended to proclaim that the class at Carreg Wen was also a social occasion. I struggled to remember her name. Mrs Ferrario brushed past my elbow and murmured. 'Mrs Lloyd, Tai Hirion.' She knew I was not good at remembering the names on the register. It was a revelation to me to find that the cult of welcome, the myth of Welsh hospitality, was a reality among these women. Social theory certainly needed to be expanded to include this element: a vision of outgoing feminine coherence stretching from one end of the country to the other; from Môn to Mynwy an abundance of social gifts and women's hands at work tirelessly embellishing the sweet struggle for cultural survival. These were the people that mattered most and I was right to concentrate on preparing lectures that would be intelligible to all irrespective of their formal education. The burden of a message should include the condition of those who chose to hear it. I had to learn the names on the register. It was no good regarding each class as a congealed entity of students. These were all individuals with names and histories. It was an act of will on their part to cohere in the cookery room of Carreg Wen Council School on Thursday evenings and become a society in miniature capable of radiating its own consolations and comforts.

'Thank you, Mrs Lloyd,' I said.

I thanked her for the cup of tea and for remembering my father. Old Catch-me-out, a retired electrical engineer from Manchester who had returned to his native village to find it not at all to his satisfaction, was watching me closely. He had a bee in his bonnet about Oliver Cromwell. He maintained that the man's name should have been Oliver Williams and in some way this proved the vital contribution it was Wales's duty to make to the well-being of the English state. Nothing I had to say ever seemed to please or convince him. He had a sour expression on his wrinkled face from the beginning to the end of each meeting, but he never missed a class and he contrived to monopolise the biggest chair nearest the stove on each occasion. He was just biding his time now, ready to unmask my ignorance of the writings of James Harrington with specific reference to the relationship between property and power.

'Will you come and have supper with us, Mr More?' Mrs Lloyd said. 'I would like you to meet my husband Ednyfed. He's stiff with arthritis, otherwise he'd be here.'

She was smiling up at me, the invitation hovering about her lips while she waited politely for me to accept. Hesitation with me was liable to become a habit.

'Wenna will be coming,' Mrs Lloyd said.

'Thank you Mrs Lloyd,' I said.

'Ednyfed thinks the world of Wenna,' Mrs Lloyd said. 'We haven't any children of our own.'

Mrs Lloyd offered me a homemade scone and I told her it melted in the mouth. In such an atmosphere, it seemed essential to think the world of as many things as possible. This included every star in the heavens and Wenna Ferrario who was so admired by this busy collaboration of middle-aged women. She was smiling at me across the room. There was no need for me to go on hacking through a jungle of words to reach her approval.

In the schoolyard Mrs Lloyd suggested Wenna should travel in the Triumph Herald with me. Her own car was a little Austin 35. She patted it like a dog and said it had been made to fit her. It was a starlit night. And there was starlight in Wenna's deep blue eyes. She was looking up and the moment expanded into a vision.

Everything was amusing. Mrs Lloyd's little vehicle creeping ahead of us between the high hedgerows. A hare caught in the headlights. Most of all Wenna's suspicion of me at our first meeting. We were able to talk across each other and leave sentences unfinished and the interior of my Triumph Herald was transfigured. 'Tell me . . .' I said. 'I thought . . .' she said. She had a habit of touching her lips when she laughed that bewitched me. There was so much to be said. This was the confluence of two rivers of living. The process was a beautiful turbulence. An image of her life and struggle was constructed in my consciousness with miraculous speed as we laughed at Mrs Lloyd's A35 bumping up and down over the potholes in the farm road.

Wenna sketched the shock and indignation of the two fat policemen on duty when they carried their heaps of broken road signs to dump them outside the police station at two o'clock in the morning. Their campaign was like a great awakening. The shackles of the centuries were being broken by young people. There was a part for everybody to play. This was when our hands touched for the first time. It seemed an accident. Two gestures coinciding. She almost apologized. Her fingers touched her lips and we both laughed. Yet it was a solemn moment. A seal on the world. By the time we arrived in the sloping farmyard of Tai Hirion, the headlights of the two cars shining on the whitewashed walls of the long dwelling house, I had to make a stiff effort to contain my excitement. Living was something to share.

The kitchen of Tai Hirion was suffused with a miraculous light. Mrs Lloyd favoured oil lamps and polish. Her husband Ednyfed sat in his saddle-shaped seat with his legs apart, his brown leggings and boots gleaming in the firelight. There was a childlike grin of pleasure on his glossy, clean-shaven face. He nursed a pipe in his arthritic fingers that could have been used for blowing bubbles rather than smoking. Everything in his presence was polished; the stone floor, the brasses, the oak chest, the dark table, the Welsh dresser.

Mrs Lloyd had taken off her coat and put on a pinafore while leaving her hat on. She pushed Wenna towards her husband and began ferrying food from the chilly dairy. He seemed to have known that I was coming. Mrs Lloyd laid out scones and shortbread as well as cold ham and sponge cakes. Wenna kissed Ednyfed Lloyd on the cheek and laid the palm of her hand lightly on his close-cropped grey hair. She was introducing him to me. Another facet of her life to fascinate me.

'Isn't he pretty?' she said. 'I've promised to take him to Rome to meet the Pope. A year next August!'

I was sharing in a vintage joke. Like the old calendar left on the oak beam behind him because it was a full-colour picture of a prize-winning Welsh Black bull he had an affection for. This was her second home. This childless couple had always adored her. She moved about the place in her blue and black costume with the confident elegance of a mannequin, no, better still, a quintessence of youth and beauty illuminating a venerable setting. She was sent to save this. On her fourth birthday Mrs Lloyd gave her a doll with dark blue eyes and long eyelashes like her own. At five Ednyfed Lloyd, still able to use his hands and a competent carpenter, made her a toy wheelbarrow, then a doll's house and a farmyard, and at six, or was it seven, an easel and blackboard. And all these treasures were stored now in the granary. One day she would show me. And most of the ninety-six acres were rented since arthritis took its grip on his joints.

'I remember the last time I saw him,' Mrs Lloyd said. 'Don't you, Edni?'

She had settled sideways behind a teapot almost as big as herself. She still wore her hat. Wenna and I hardly dared to look at each other across the table. All Ednyfed had to do was turn his chair to the meal. Mrs Lloyd was talking about my father. It couldn't have been more appropriate. I wanted Wenna to listen as closely as I did. Ednyfed didn't remember. He shook his head and his mouth opened in admiration of his wife's powers of recall among her manifold accomplishments. These were the most important people in the world. It was my privilege that they should have wished to include me at this table.

'The Colwyn Bay Eisteddfod, I'm sure it was. It was the last time he adjudicated anyway. I'm quite sure of that. He was a shy man. Anybody could see that by the way he stood on the platform. He looked as though he wished he were somewhere else.'

I caught Wenna's glance. She was smiling at me. As if I were a commendable continuation of the virtue Mrs Lloyd found in my father.

'It was part of the adjudication, of course, but we could see the little, fat archdruid squirming inside his regalia. I could see your father's foot trembling.' Mrs Lloyd raised her hand to signify verbatim quotation. ' "The English War Office already occupies a tenth" – a "tithe" he said – "of the land of Wales; consider their threat to occupy more! In the parish of Ysgurn alone eighty-five members of the old Baptist chapel will be turned out of their homes . . . Consider the devastation of the territory of Dewi and Brynach with all the deposits of a civilization of centuries. What land are these Armed Forces supposed to be defending?" '

'Did he say all that?' Wenna said.

The light in her eyes was like the joy of discovery. We had always been committed.

'And a lot more,' Mrs Lloyd said. 'I only wish I could remember it. And then the little fat archdruid said your father was contaminating the ceremony with political protest. You can tell me, something, Mr More. Is it true your father had a picture of Gandhi in his study?'

I couldn't remember. It was painful. Should I confess I had all his papers and knew nothing about him? Mrs Lloyd was tactful. Was there ever a breed of people so sensitive to other people's feelings? She turned to teasing Wenna.

'So you see, my little one. We did our bit of protesting too. And Mr More's father was one of the best. I can tell you that.'

When could I ask her to stop calling me Mr More and call me Peredur? She had to complete her eulogy. It was a solemn note.

'That was the last eisteddfod your father attended.'

My skin was sticky with embarrassment. What stage of despair had he reached to do away with himself? How far

138

was my mother to blame? And for how long was I condemned to hold down these secrets? The bones of my back sagged under the intolerable burden. As if to alleviate my condition Mrs Lloyd plied me with more food than I could eat and asked Wenna questions about her father. The girl was so open and charming about it. There was the comedy of her father's family in Lucca. The struggle for power in the fez factory and the quarrel between her father's two brothers-in-law. Ednyfed found the idea of making fezzes funny until his wife rebuked him for his insularity. We had to respect other people's customs, she said, if we expected them to respect ours. Ednyfed's mouth hung open with pride in the depth of his wife's wisdom.

'Poor old Giuseppe,' Wenna said. 'Poor old Giuso.'

She called her father by his Christian name. A clear mark of tolerant affection. She was the child of separated parents and yet as balanced and well-adjusted as was possible for a young woman to be. Wherein lay the secret?

'So there he is, the poor old creature, teaching Latin in a Roman suburb he dislikes intensely. Longing for Lucca, as you might say, but unable to go back because he can't bear the bickering.'

'And thinking the world of his daughter,' Mrs Lloyd said. 'I'm quite sure about that.'

It was a marvel that she existed. Therefore her mouth was a source of truth that had never been available to me before. Ednyfed had caught me gazing at her.

'Have you heard her play the organ?' he said.

I had to admit I hadn't.

'There are people who come to Libanus just to hear Wenna play,' he said. 'Especially the young lads.'

He winked at me in case I should be too remote from everyday life or too obtuse to grasp that he was joking. I was thinking about her father, south of the Alps, and Mussolini's manic neo-Roman ambitions that caused the young Giuseppe Ferrario to arrive in these green hills sixteeen centuries after Magnus Maximus stripped the place of troops for the sake of an equally insatiable desire to make himself Emperor of the same old Roman dream. And now the prisoner of war was prisoner of Latin in a suburban

Roman school he hated. Did he adore his daughter? Or was he detached like one of those stray gods in the hexameters absent-mindedly begetting gifted children out of local beauties? No doubt Morfydd Ferrario had been a local beauty in her day. What beauties weren't local? 'Honour thy father and thy mother . . .' It was a lot to ask but Wenna did it without any trouble. Her days would be long in the land which the Lord had endowed with names like title deeds: Tai Hirion, Carreg Wen, Bryn Saith Marchog, Llanbedr Goch, Erging, Llanllwyda. My father was right. Wherever they occurred, we have a right to flourish.

I had left my briefcase in the cookery room. Ednyfed laughed as though my carelessness was an act of premeditated cunning. Wenna had the key. As we left Tai Hirion in the moonlight, Mrs Lloyd smiled at us like a benediction. The whole mystery of existence deepened as we travelled back alone together. Where could I begin? At last I had found the person to whom I could tell everything. Things that I had kept hidden, knowledge suppressed over a lifetime, welled up inside me clamouring for expression. From the secret sins of my mother, the litany of my early sufferings, to the injustices my father had incurred upon my efforts to restore his reputation and my urge to return to the land of my fathers, to play a useful part in the struggle for survival to theoretical concepts concerning the expansion which was the only organic antidote to contraction . . . When the Triumph Herald drew up in the Council School yard and I switched the engine and the headlights off, I was trembling as I turned to her. My lips touched the incredible smoothness of her cheek and then the softness of her lips.

In an ecstasy of gratitude I would have given her everything I possessed. By what supernatural process had we been brought together? She could lay the tip of her finger with unerring accuracy on the hidden sources of pain and joy. The shadow of the gable end of the school fell across the moon-pallor of the asphalt playground. I reached out to caress the outline of Wenna's head as gently as I could. She submitted with beautiful patience.

'I don't understand it,' I said. 'And yet I understand everything.'

140

It was all I could think of saying. The clichés we are forced to deploy when we fall in love. 'Falling' was good. A revealing metaphor. I wanted to cling on to her to allay the vertigo. She took hold of my hands. Her fingers were surprisingly strong.

'Your mother,' she said. 'Tell me about her.'

Her voice was so soft and low it could have surfaced from my own subconscious. Her finger had touched the source of my hurt. I should be free and filled with canticles of affection instead of harbouring grievances against my mother. Love would make me free of that sickness. What did it matter if she prevented me getting the job I wanted? But for that wounding fiasco, I would never have arrived in Carreg Wen, would never have embraced Wenna.

'That's why I was so suspicious,' Wenna said. 'We knew you were Lady Brangor's son. Not the Special Branch or anything like that. It was just your mother. One of our persecutors. You may as well say that. How did she come to be like that? That's what I was wondering. I know it's common in Welsh politics. People start off full of fiery nationalist sentiments. And then the system gets hold of them. The power-structure and so on. And they have to become subservient to it to satisfy whatever personal ambitions they have. It's not exactly a new story. I just wonder how it happened to her.'

I would tell her everything. Even how my mother had killed my father or driven him to a despair that was a death in itself, a lingering death. It would all need to come out. My childhood fantasies and fears; back to the very moment of conception when the beginning of my being put such an abrupt end to my mother's parliamentary ambitions. She, too, had wanted a hand in changing the world and all she got was me. The abortion that survived. Now, touched by beauty, the beast would be transformed, however painful the process. I longed for Wenna to put her arms around my neck of her own volition. My emotions were so much exposed. This is unmanly and too much to expect. Love draws love by its own strength. We would become bound together and that would end my exile. Dissolve my solitude. But she had her confidences and concerns. Her own distress.

141

Love should listen. It was for mutual comfort.

'It's not enough to get arrested,' she said.

She was not self-absorbed like me. Her burden was the cause. I had to share it. This, too, was a foundation of love and fellowship. A proper prelude.

'That's just a game the cat likes playing with the mouse,' she said. 'You've got to wound the cat. And you've got to do it in a way that wins sympathy and support.'

I was silent with admiration for the incisiveness of her analysis. She was intelligent as well as beautiful. Here was the strength of character I needed. Would it be absurd to talk of marriage so early in our relationship?

'Have I frightened you?' Her voice was as innocent as a little girl's.

'Good heavens, no!'

What could I do but embrace her. We had to become lovers. We had to teach each other to arrive at the kind of union we both wanted. Our mouths opened. Our tongues met. Longing would no longer be enough. We had to reach into each other to discover the elixir of new life. Wenna laughed as she restrained me. It was good that she laughed.

'Not here,' she said. 'Not here, Peredur!'

I was equally enthralled by her voice and her common sense. I drove her the short distance to the schoolhouse. I was reluctant to leave and she was reluctant to dismiss me. I was encased in excitement. Night or day, the world around me was being reborn.

'We know what your mother's up to,' Wenna said. 'Or, at least, we think we know. Converting Brangor Hall into a royal home in North Wales. That's what she's up to. Within a radius of fifty miles of Caernarfon Castle. Where the Labour people plan to outdo Lloyd George in deifying the royal family. And making Wales more politically impotent than ever. We can't let it happen.'

I didn't want her to challenge me. There was no need at all to put me to the test. This one night, the first kiss, was like a marriage bond between us.

My brother Bedwyr was taking measurements. He wore a green topcoat he had bought in Austria and he scrambled about while I held on to the other end of the builder's tape. He was doing someone a favour. I recognized his generosity and good nature. It was early on a Sunday morning and the centre of the city was pleasantly deserted. Sian, his wife, was getting their children ready for chapel. Bedwyr never went. It was as if he made up for his absence with surreptitious favours and good works. This little excursion verged on an escapade. A city councillor was opposed to an office development that would encroach on the serenity of the parkland, preserved more by accident than design, in the heart of the city. Bedwyr was providing him with expert advice and ammunition. It was such a good thing to do: my heart warmed towards him. How right he was about this place. Already there were far too many buildings of all shapes and sizes stuffed into the civic centre. Compared to the green expanse of the park beyond the temporary car park, it was a concrete prison. It was true when he said in his solemn way that bad planning decisions did us all harm. His breath was visible in the frosty air. I could hear him mutter measurements in the metric system to himself.

I still hadn't told him about our father's papers. I wanted to – but the right moment hadn't occurred. It was difficult in such a busy family life to take him to one side. But this was the purpose of my visit. He had to know about it. There were letters there from his mother Enid, on whose coffin he had been baptized. They showed how committed she had been to the cause to which I was now committed; and to which he also had an obligation. They would prove, if any further proof were necessary, that the notion of choice so cherished by our generation was a snare and a disillusion. The good life was not a sequence of Sunday morning favours. In the case of the tradition with which we had been born, it was a stern commitment and there were his mother's letters to prove it.

I guess from his notes and from the way he had begun to arrange the letters that my father had intended to publish them in edited form. He should have done so. They would have inspired someone. The destiny imposed upon us by the language of our forefathers would be easier to bear with the evidence of how joyfully our immediate predecessors had picked up the burden. My suspicion was that Amy had discouraged him. The hopes and aspirations of her youth differed so much from the path she had actually taken. A matter of false choice again. As I saw it, her occupation of Brangor Hall, like her new plans for its development, turned the place into a castle of illusion.

'If I were a doctor I'd be struck off the register doing this.'

He was smiling at me from the top of a grassy mound. He could have been a magician in his long green coat. He was an architect who could command landscapes to appear and disappear. I needed his help and support. He was making gestures of approval in the direction of the park. The great trees there dwelt with venerable calm among the avenues and lawns and gardens. The greenness sprinkled with hoar frost in the morning light was such a contrast to the trapped hysterical uncertainties of the overcrowded civic centre.

'We've got to do what we can to save it,' Bedwyr said in his quiet, serious voice. 'They're not making any more of it.'

I understood how much subterfuge he and his allies had to engage in, in order to save what they could of a limited environment. I wanted to make him understand how we should make common cause. One environment should complement and enhance the other.

'I tell you,' he said. 'Bad planning decisions do us all harm. Every single one of us.'

He was solemn again and absorbed in his work as I remembered him in the shed that smelt of creosote at the bottom of our narrow garden in Pendraw: kneeling down to repair his bike or finish off a patent wooden wedge for removing muddy gumboots he was making as a present for Amy. He was more devoted to her than any of us; and she loved him for it. As she would have us understand, she had loved his mother, her best friend, who with her dying breath had transferred the irresistible baby into her care. Over the

144

years my mother had elevated dubious facts into romantic fiction. Bedwyr plunged down the mound at such a speed I had to catch him. He complained about being unfit and reaffirmed his intention of taking up early morning jogging, or at least walking across the park to his office. He turned to consider the proposed site of a new office block.

'It's quite scandalous,' he said. 'They'll call it a computer centre and hope to get away with it under a smokescreen of high technology. But we won't let them, will we?' He patted me on the shoulder as we walked back to his car. 'And what about you, old son?' he said. 'Going to dedicate yourself to a life of protest? Is that what it's going to be?'

He was smiling at me quite fondly. This could be my cue to introduce the subject of my father's papers. It was one of those fleeting seconds when a decision had to be taken if the force of gravity inherent in the course of fate was to be deflected to any appreciable extent. I didn't take it because I couldn't find the appropriate formula. Or because I was so jealous of my possession of the treasure that I was unwilling to share it with anyone except on my own inflexible terms.

'It's an imposition,' I said. 'From above. It has nothing at all to do with the welfare, the well-being of Wales. And everything to do with Labour's grip on Westminster power. We are expected to make fools of ourselves in the eyes of the world in order to reinforce a system that has already squeezed out of our people all but the minimum of self-respect.'

'You've been talking to Sian,' Bedwyr said.

'No, I haven't. Not yet anyway,' I said.

'She's full of protest these days,' Bedwyr said. 'It's a bit like an epidemic.'

'Don't you agree with us?'

'I suppose I do. In theory anyway. To tell you the truth, I have such a workload it's not often I lift my eyes off the drawing-board. Laziness of a kind. And moral cowardice, no doubt.'

I wanted to speak of obligations that we could not escape from and duties that we had inherited. It was impossible to do so without sounding insufferably priggish. He was my eldest brother and responsibility was second nature to him. He did not need to be told.

145

I listened to him singing to himself as he drove down the empty streets. The light tenor voice was the sound of the happy warrior. He loved his family and he loved his work. What more could be asked of him? He had a wife who was beautiful and capable and three delightful children. They lived together in harmony and happiness in a converted farmhouse on the outskirts of the city. It was an oasis of an acre and a half surrounded by a high wall. In my new condition of love, my admiration for my brother Bedwyr and his wife Sian was intensified to a point that burned away the last traces of envy.

It was still early. He wanted to show me the progress of a landscaping reclamation he had designed for a derelict industrial valley twelve miles north of the city. It was a pleasure to share the profound satisfaction Bedwyr found in his work. On the way he enjoyed talking about Sian.

'It was quite funny really,' he said. 'You know what she's like. Straight from the shoulder. And very protective. We've got this hippy minister Cadfan Watkins. C.W. we call him. He's a nice enough chap. He'd be even nicer if he washed a bit oftener. You'll probably meet him when we get back. Red hair and a red beard. Holes in his pullover. And a voice like a thunder-clap. It used to frighten the life out of Christina until she got used to it. Anyway, what I was going to tell you? Gobroth. You've heard me mention Principal Gobroth? Know-all Yorkshire man. Very efficient in a charmless sort of way. Fixed on to me like a limpet. Partly, I think, to pick up bits of free professional advice. Anyway we go along with it – I go along with it and Sian puts up with it – for the sake of poor old Phil Magor. Gobroth leads him a terrible dance. Dangling promotion in front of him, just out of his reach. Poor old Phil still thinks he has a bit of purchase, so long as Gobroth sees how friendly he is with chaps like me and old Joe Maxen. Sir Joe. Am I boring you?'

'Good lord, no!' I said.

Bedwyr laughed at the vehemence of my denial. He pointed at an antique shop at the end of a terrace. The windows were blocked up with grimy boards.

'Nobody collects antiques around here,' he said. 'Except

146

human ones. Anyway, Gobroth wanted to see our house. How it had been converted. So I told Phil to bring him along one Sunday morning. You know how Sian likes to give her friends tea and biscuits after chapel. She says it encourages them and keeps them faithful. I have my little joke and offer them something stronger. Maybe it was a mistake but I thought it wouldn't do Gobroth any harm to see how the natives lived and might do poor old Phil a bit of good. Anyway, they came along. Gobroth in his Sunday morning polo-neck, expecting his scotch and soda, and Sian's chapel lot in their Sunday best, sipping their cups of tea. What I wasn't to know was that C.W. was on the rampage. "May I put a professional question to you Principal? Man to man." '
Bedwyr's voice boomed as he imitated the minister. 'That's all the poor sod has got, is his voice,' Bedwyr said. 'Sian thinks he's a bit of a saint and I suppose he could be in some peculiar way, but his boom can be quite unnerving. It seems two young chums of his, Arfon and Eifion, he called them, had been sent down for locking themselves in a lecture room and staging a hunger strike and demanding an increase in subjects taught through the medium of Welsh. There it was. A confrontation on the floor of our drawing-room. Gobroth versus the natives. He didn't bat an eyelid. He was enjoying it. Poor old Phil stood behind him ready to melt into a puddle of apprehension. C.W. got more emotional the colder Gobroth looked and started booming about rights and natural justice and national dignity. "What nation?" Gobroth said. "The Welsh Nation," C.W. said. And it sounded like the hallelujah chorus. "Assuming there is such a thing," says Gobroth, "the language of the overwhelming majority is English. Would you accept that?" "Why should young men suffer in order to secure their birthright in their own land?" says Cadfan. It went from bad to worse. "Far be it from me to withold their martyrs' crowns," Gobroth said. "You are responsible for your business, whatever you get up to in your church, and I am responsible for discipline in the City University. Let's leave it at that, shall we?" And that was where Sian struck. She stood in front of C.W. and told Gobroth he was an arrogant and insensitive English Hitler. Then she gave him a nice smile and asked him would he like

147

some more to drink. It was an awkward moment. Would he walk out? Poor old Phil had already shifted to one side to facilitate the great man's exit. Gobroth had gone a paler shade of pale. Sian had her eye fixed on him, in all the beauty of frankness you could say. He was out-franked. He bowed and she took his glass from his hand. And I must say from then on she's had him eating out of her hand.'

Bedwyr laughed. I could see he was glowing with pride. It was understandable. But in my view there should have been more to the encounter.

'And is there to be more teaching through the medium of Welsh at the City University?' I said.

'It's not that simple, is it?'

Bedwyr was irritated by my question. From a high vantage point where a sharp wind blew into our faces Bedwyr enlarged on the principles of rehabilitating a living land-scape. Here forests had been cut down, iron smelted, coal mined; and now a great era of frenetic exploitation was coming to an end. A healing process had started; but it was slow and painful. It would take the intelligence and ingenuity and dedication of at least one generation to repair the damage and introduce a new economic balance. Both these processes should be complementary; but the machina-tions of politicians did little to help. As I listened I realized more clearly than ever before that my brother was a man with a mission and that doing good by stealth was basic to his method. He spoke of social disintegration that followed industrial decline and a new phase of unemployment. To stand above the valley was to be drawn into the drama. Bedwyr slapped my back.

'Why don't you come south? he said 'This is where the action is. If we don't win this one there won't be much future for any kind of Welshness.'

He turned his back to the prevailing wind and squinted up at the summit of the hills that separated the industrial valleys from their rural hinterland.

'What have you got up north?' he said. 'Except scenery. I'd sooner have the scars of industry myself, than the litter of the motorised tourist.'

He was easy and agreeable to be with. It was a pleasure to

listen to him talking about his work – even the current difficulties in the office. He had a talented junior partner called Keith who was an efficient designer and solver of technical problems, but lacking perhaps in a properly grounded aesthetic sense and a coherent social vision. He had problems, too, with his wife. She wanted children and tests had proved him sterile. Should they adopt? It all affected Keith's attitude to the work and the general atmosphere in the office. This was how brothers should talk, in confidence and with confidence. Our conversation was intimate, responsible, wide-ranging. But for my mother's shadow which fell between us it would have been easy now to bring up the matter of my father's papers. As I watched him I knew his first response would be to ask why on earth I had not told her about them. He was bound to her by an affection stronger than biological ties.

vi

I could see the young minister Bedwyr called C.W. was in no hurry to leave. The last guests had departed. Bedwyr had taken the children to play in the garden. C.W.'s eyes followed Sian with such canine devotion as she moved about the room collecting glasses, cups, saucers and plates, that I wondered whether he might be in love with her. It would have been understandable. She was beautiful and efficient. She had created an atmosphere of warmth and comfort in her converted farmhouse. The design was Bedwyr's, the simplicity, the elegance, the restraint; it was Sian who brought it all to life. The whole place was a three-dimensional expression of a successful marriage. The only way to provide growing children with a happy home. Perhaps this was what C.W. was loath to leave. He also had his eye on three small cakes left behind on a plate. Sian was about to clear them away. With a gesture so characteristic of her, she held the plate out to C.W.

'Shameful greed,' he said and shook with mirth as he gobbled them up one after the other. Sian watched him with a maternal smile on her face. She wasn't Wenna, of course.

149

Less miraculously mysterious; but she belonged to the same exalted category.

'I'm sorry I can't ask you to stay to lunch, C.W.' Sian said.

He began waving his hands to show no explanation was necessary.

'Terrible, isn't it,' he said. 'This is such a nice place to be, I can't drag myself away. I've got a sermon to finish. If you could call it a sermon. And the Goliardi want an extra rehearsal.'

His long hair and beard looked buttered down. He wore a long army greatcoat dyed black and there was a hole in his yellow pullover. He had large feet and he moved with care towards the door to avoid knocking anything over. Sian stood still to smile at him with undimmed approval until he had left. She turned to register my reaction.

'He's good,' she said. 'Clothes don't matter all that much anyway.'

She sounded capable of protecting everybody and everything. Through the window I watched Bedwyr playing with the children. He gave them concentrated attention. It was Sian I should talk to about my father's papers. In dealing with Bedwyr, she was the best approach. I followed her around the house, offering inefficient help. This amused her.

'A reformed character,' she said. 'Do you know what I think?'

On the cork floor of their fitted kitchen I was caught with a plate in each hand. With Sian in the middle of it, the clinical perfection of the place came to life. She had a daily help called Mrs Peace and she and Bedwyr made great play with the surname. This was a Sunday and Sian coped with all the activities alone.

'You look so happy,' Sian said. 'There can be only one explanation. You've met a nice girl.'

I was delighted to admit it. I wanted to shake myself like a spaniel emerging from the water.

'You must tell me all about her,' Sian said. 'What is she like?'

How could I begin to describe Wenna? Not that I hadn't tried. All the way down in my Triumph Herald I practised aloud elaborate and sophisticated delineations: *that Veronese portrait . . . that St Helena with the True Cross . . . that Raphael, you know the one I mean . . .* Burying reality under icons of dark Italian beauty just to explain away a simple surname. I also launched on a fantasy about the daughter of Morfudd, the spiritual descendant of that flesh-and-blood Morfudd who troubled Dafydd into promising a sequence of seven times twenty *cywyddau . . .* The further I travelled away from her the more my imagination obscured her image.

'She's very nice,' I said.

It wasn't much, but it drew Sian and I closer than we had ever been before. Anything urgent that needed to be said should be said to her first. Like Wenna, she had to be endowed with the piercing wisdom that often went with beauty. We went back to the window overlooking the garden. We watched Bedwyr and the children play around the climbing frame and the swing. Sian was entitled to dote on her children. But she gave me her close attention. She respected the truth and gave truth in return.

'I've never liked the way she makes use of Bedwyr,' Sian said. 'You must know that.'

I did know it. We were natural allies. Against my mother and against the system. We both had personal as well as political reasons for discouraging Bedwyr from accepting any commission to design a glass hall of mirrors or whatever it was to brighten the austere facade of Brangor Hall.

'There will be special money,' I said. 'Indirectly from the government. All part of the biggest public relations propaganda campaign since the coronation. It's exploitation at its worst. It will set us back fifty years. He shouldn't touch it.'

Sian was so quiet I began to have misgivings. She was a devoted wife who had complete faith in her husband's talent and orginality. What architect could resist a commission to create a new building that would glow and glisten in the full glare of publicity, even if the offer came from Beelzebub himself? It was unfair that we should be weighed down with more choices than other human beings simply because of our allegiance to a lost cause. Most people saw nothing wrong in

151

having the best of both worlds. Perhaps I had put my case too strongly. I watched her gnaw her lower lip as she considered the problem from angles beyond my discernment.

'Who told you all this?' she said.

'Gwydion,' I said.

It was only partly true. Wenna had filled in the picture. I myself had put two and two together. It was simpler, though, to attribute the information to Gwydion. Sian raised her head in sharp disapproval.

'Just as well to keep that one at arm's length,' she said.

'That one' could only mean there had been other occasions when Gwydion had tried to take advantage of Bedwyr. I knew there had been the matter of an unpaid debt. I had judged it better at the time to know as little as possible about it. Now was the time for Sian to know about my father's papers and, even more central to her protective concern for Bedwyr, his mother's letters. They would help, as nothing else could, to discover the best method of conducting the delicate operation of detaching Bedwyr sufficiently from my mother to allow him to exercise a more independent judgement. I saw this with such disturbing clarity that I leaned towards her, my hand outstretched ready to put pressure on her arm, while I struggled to present her with the issue in the clearest order of words.

She leaped to her feet as Bedwyr brought Nia crying into the house. The little girl's face was blotched and distorted with howling. Bedwyr was smiling but mildly embarrassed. Sian applied comfort and solace. With extraordinary speed the girl recovered. Sian coaxed David to take both his sisters upstairs and engage them in a game of tents and indoor camping until lunchtime. Bedwyr said he was ready to reward himself and his wife and his brother with a sherry for exemplary conduct. He sighed with content and sprawled on the settee, pointing his glass at Sian.

'I don't know what notions they stuff into kids' heads in that Sunday School of yours,' he said. 'Do you know what she just came out with? I never thought I'd live to hear it. "When the trumpet sounds the good children will rise from the dead. But the bad ones will burn for ever in a fire that

152

never goes out." Who the hell teaches them stuff like that?'

Sian began to laugh at his solemn indignation.

'No,' Bedwyr said. 'I'm serious. Is that C.W.? He's even more cuckoo than I thought.'

Sian was still smiling. 'It sounds like Miss Esli. She is a bit old-fashioned. But she's very good with the children. It's not easy to get people to do voluntary work in chapel these days. Sunday School and so on. Poor old C.W. He does his level best.'

Perhaps because I was present Bedwyr was keen to bring their difference into the open.

'How in God's name or in anybody's name can we hope to have a sane and rational world if nightmares like that are stuffed into kids' heads. I'm just asking.'

I did not want to be drawn into the debate. There were far more urgent issues I needed to thrash out with him. It was my intention to start back on the long journey north after lunch.

'Well, that is the whole point, isn't it,' Sian said. She spoke with the calm of a person who had long faced up to the problem and arrived at her own conclusion.

'The world isn't sane and rational,' she said. 'And never will be. Because people aren't sane and rational. That's the whole point of Christianity. They – we – can only be saved by love.'

'That's a pretty tall order,' Bedwyr said. 'I don't have any trouble loving you. But I don't think I could stretch it to include the Planning Committee, let alone the City Council.'

'That shows how lucky you are . . .'

I couldn't make out if they were arguing or teasing each other. I felt like a spectator on the touchline of a game of which I had not been informed of the rules.

'You should have been in chapel this morning. Both of you. C.W. was jolly good. Text from John. Very short. Was it "Come with me"? Anyway I can give you the headings, Unbeliever.' Sian ticked them off on her fingers. 'One. Live in the company of the Father through the Son. Two. Live in imitation of perfection. Three. Live a life of service. There you are. Couldn't be simpler.'

'Or more difficult.'

153

Bedwyr sank back into his chair. He was still appalled at the superstitions being stuffed into his children's heads. To me he was the image of the man who had everything. *Admetus, rich in cattle*. A beautiful wife, as good as she was beautiful; beautiful, healthy children; a fine house exceeding in comfort Admetus's palace; a thriving practice; a full, creative life. He had no right to be gloomy. I was here with the message that would put him to the test. It was right that I should do so.

'Bedwyr,' Sian said. 'Has your mother spoken to you about a commission to design a pavilion? At Brangor?'

He looked guilty and startled. My mother indulged herself in long conversations with her eldest boy on the telephone. She chose him, she used to say. That meant I was thrust upon her. It didn't necessarily follow that he retailed the entire substances of her confidences to his wife. It was always hard work being a source of comfort and joy to two such different personalities at one and the same time.

'Just one of her notions,' Bedwyr said. 'You've got to listen to the poor old thing. I didn't take it too seriously. In through one ear and out through the other.'

'Well I wouldn't touch it,' Sian said. 'It's part of the great Investiture circus. And you know what I think about that. What we think about it.'

'Oh dear . . .'

Bedwyr wanted to laugh, but he sighed instead. This was a moment of truth. It called for action, not words. That was the essence of the message: and Bedwyr had to be made to see it. This was yet another juncture in the long history of protest when neutrality was impossible. My brother was a good man. The conflict had already reached that pitch where goodness had to commit itself, even if it found itself lined up with all sorts of elements it would never normally approve of.

'It sounded tempting,' Bedwyr said. 'Very tempting. A very nice idea.'

I couldn't keep silent any longer.

'Listen,' I said. 'You've no idea how fast things are changing. We're on the brink of a life and death struggle.'

I could see myself through Bedwyr's eyes. His neurotic

younger brother. A failed academic who had used his sheltered and privileged upbringing to nurse and nurture unhealthy notions about his mother and his dead father. An incomplete creature who knew nothing of the real world and indulged himself in fantasies about culture crises.

'You've no idea,' I said. 'There'll be action all over the place. Not just protest. Sabotage. Direct action. Why should we imagine we will be able to gain our freedom without real sacrifice. Like Ireland. Like Israel. The time is fast approaching when we shall have to put our entire effort on a war footing.'

His patience snapped. I had watched the smile disappear from his face as I wound myself up to the pitch of intensity I imagined would penetrate his protective covering of complacency and indifference. He was on his feet and waving his fist at me. I had no recollection of ever seeing him so angry.

'What bloody nonsense,' he said. 'It could only come from somebody totally divorced from the real world. Do you want to see Wales become another Ulster? If there's one thing the whole of Europe, the whole of the world, for Christ's sake, could do without it's talk like that. "A war footing". Do you think Europe hasn't seen enough of war? I've never heard such rot. From my own brother. Come down from those bloody clouds, won't you, and see the world as it really is.'

Sian was worried about me. I myself was regretting the over-colourful language I had used to try and force him to confront a critical situation. By 'war footing' I meant nothing more than a coordination of protest. Bedwyr seemed to think I meant guerrilla warfare.

'Calm down, Bed,' Sian said. 'Calm down. You'll frighten the children.'

'I'll calm down,' he said. ' "War footing". What bloody rubbish. And I'll tell you something else. If that commission does come my way, I'll count myself bloody lucky and I'll take it.'

155

Six

'There was a band playing on the promenade and it was all very cheerful. The sun shone on instruments and uniforms. A wedge of people were attached to a Punch and Judy show in a canvas booth striped in red and white. I had to wait outside the Hotel Avalon next door to the Prince's Theatre. The hotel had been requisitioned as a soldier's convalescent home. There were lads on the balcony in their hospital blue, smoking cigarettes and watching the holiday crowds shift about waiting for them all to start dancing or at least prance about under the influence of the music. I saw Owen before he saw me. An officer. Should I salute him? It took him a little time to recognize me.

' "Good God," he said. "What are you doing with that lot?"

'RAMC. I could see he disapproved. There was a lot to explain. He wasn't a patient listener. It would be no use going on about my theory of subsisting on a minimum of feeling while one state of being gave way to another, and using knaki as a cloak of invisibility. I tried to be amusing. I told him how I had borrowed enough money from the grocery till in Glanrafon Stores to pay for my one-way ticket. I mentioned spending my first night in a shelter on the prom at Llanelw; and how cold was the dawn wind over the sea. Then how I dropped my spectacles on the floor of the Drill Hall. Somebody trod on them. And how I panicked at the prospect of being rejected. And how this chap Frankie had led me to the corner where I signed on with the RAMC as nineteen years and one month instead of seventeen years

156

one month. Which was all quite funny. In the old days Owen would have laughed. Now he didn't look amused. I wanted to tell him about Frankie, my new friend. He was small and broad and red-haired and blue-eyed and his smile was brighter than a brass band. But Owen's patience had given out.

' "Come on," he said. "We'd better find him."

'I followed him like his batman. His accoutrements gleamed as though I had polished them myself. We found Harri Bont in the corner of a balcony half hidden by a flower-box. He was in pyjamas. His head was shaven and his neck was swathed in bandages that were working loose. I could see his hand gripping and ungripping the cast-iron balcony rails. You could tell at once he was filled with grievances that troubled him more than his wounds. I was glad to stand in Owen's shadow. Owen had cakes and knitted things he had just bought to give him. I had nothing. Harri looked at us and at the gifts, trying to relate them to the misery and impropriety of his condition.

' "It was all a bloody mistake," he said. "That's what annoys me." He launched himself straight away into a litany of complaint. It came out as if he spent all his time rehearsing it. "You can't win a war with incompetence," he said. "I mean, the whole bloody Empire should be on a war footing . . . We were hanging around for days. There was nothing ready for us. Nothing. No meals. No uniform. No kit. No pay. Nothing. Is that the way to win a war? I was bloody starving half the time. They'd got it all mixed up. So they put us in groups. Those who had boots. Those who had caps. Those who had knives and forks. Can you imagine it? You never saw such a bloody mess. Then they packed one half of us off to Portsmouth Barracks. Well that's all right, I said to myself. That can't be bad. At last I'm on my way to sea. Not a bit of it! When I got there it was the Army. I tried to explain but they couldn't understand me. Took no notice. It was only what was on the paper that mattered, see, and some bloody English clerk somewhere had got it all wrong. All wrong. and there I was landed where I never wanted to be. On the wrong side of a howling sergeant. In the bloody army."

'I saw Owen turn his face away to smile. He winked at me, which was like old times. He extracted a slim cigarette case from his breastpocket, lit one and put it in Harri's mouth. It didn't shut him up but it calmed him down a little. He wanted us to understand that his predicament had a wider significance and that he wasn't going over and over the same ground just out of self-pity. It all meant something.

' "It's a hell of a business," he said.

'A rash had broken out on his pale face. It was on the inside of his forearms too. He scratched one arm and then the other and the bandages around his neck worked themselves looser.

' "You know yourself, Owen Guest, I had my teeth pulled especially to join the Royal Navy. I didn't do it for fun. That was the whole point of it.'

'He concentrated on Owen, a man in officer's uniform with a legal training. He ought to help an old friend make a cast-iron, irrefutable case and re-establish his existence on a sane and rational basis. It was the least a friend could do.

' "I pull my bloody teeth, every bloody one of them, and where do I find myself? Sitting in a bloody shell-hole begging bloody stretcher bearers who take no bloody notice to cart me away. I shouldn't have been on land, let alone in a shell-hole. It's the incompetence that gets me. Do you follow me? Incompetence. That's what's wrong, Owen Guest. You can't win a war like that."

'As Harri's voice rose I looked around and saw other inmates turn away from their visitors and nod and wink at each other. All Harri's logic had turned into a joke. I saw an ancient relative alongside a soldier in a wheelchair shuffling souvenirs through his shrivelled fingers: a German soldier's paybook with family photos and postcards stained with what I took to be blood. The old man's nose was running. His problem was how to wipe it on his sleeve without dropping the souvenirs on the floor.

' "Medicals!" Harri said. "I'll tell you without a word of a lie. In Portsmouth there was a man next in line to me. He was standing there naked and he had an operation wound on his belly ten inches long and as red as a cockerel's comb. They sent him into the Navy. They passed him A1 and he

158

couldn't walk ten yards at a time. And there was me, right next to him, with all my seafaring experience. Where's the sense of that? Where's the logic?"

'Owen had to say something. "We're short of men in the Army, Harri," he said.

'This brought Harri no comfort.

' "Sea power," he said. "You were the one who used to go on about it, Owen Guest. Damn it all, I'm a seaman. You know that better than anybody. Can't you do anything for me?"

'Owen was uncomfortable and by extension so was I.

' "You are lawyers," Harri said. "What's the Law good for if it can't put bloody blunders to rights?"

'We didn't really have an answer. Owen was making comforting noises and saying he would see what he could do and what could be done. I seemed to be realizing for the first time how many things there were about which nothing at all could be done. Outside on the Promenade I didn't know whether Owen would turn on his heel and leave me because I was only an RAMC private. As it turned out we stuck together and wandered down the High Street that was thronged with trippers and, Owen said, munition workers squandering their high wages, until we found a corner in a café stuffed with people and stinking with hot food. We clambered up a narrow staircase and a sweating waitress gave Owen instant, admiring attention. She cleared us a corner with a view through the window of the crowded High Street. The buses and the horse-drawn holiday vehicles crawled along beneath us and I felt confident enough to put a case that occurred to me. There were men with me in the Drill Hall who couldn't understand English. Owen had jokes about the same situation. A little chap from Anglesey who only knew "yes" and "no" and "buggered if I know" which he had picked up after a week being lost on the barrack square in Wrexham. Owen's story was quite funny; but like Harri Bont I had begun to feel sore. There was a principle at stake.

' "Why shouldn't they use their own language?" I said. "Why haven't we got a proper Welsh Army?"

'How often I had heard my Uncle Gwilym go on about

Lloyd George having promised to look into it. There he was riding up and down Downing Street like Arthur and Henry VII on a milk-white charger. How much longer did we have to wait? Owen was staring with contemptuous impatience at my shoulder flash. I acknowledged it didn't look very military.

' "For God's sake, Killy, just shut up. You have no idea what you're talking about."

'It was rude and hurtful. He pointed through the window and spoke of the need for shells. I had a vision of millions of them pouring out of factories on conveyor belts that crossed the Channel and left them in mountainous heaps on the fields of France. I closed my eyes. The smell of food and Owen's contempt made me feel sick. When I opened them I saw the waitress' elbow deliberately nudge Owen's resplendent shoulder. He was in a good humour again.

' "What are you after, Killy? A line of bards and preachers going over the top. All in their white robes, ready for heaven. Now come on, for God's sake. Cheer up. You can't tinker about with Progress and Historical Forces. Efficiency, my lad. That's the secret. This is my treat. So cheer up and look as if you're enjoying yourself. You look as if you're on your way to a funeral." '

ii

'I conclude that Frankie O'Brien can work miracles. I watched him launch the rumour that the Swedish Rehabilitation Centre at Huddersfield was hell on earth. He said "rehabilitation" was a funny name for slavery and that Swedes were worse than Prussians on iron discipline. I could see the rumour spread from hut to hut and across the square and through the canteen like a wind-borne pollination. And I heard the warnings that followed and the way 087135 Private O'Brien, Francis Moses, acted as secret agent of error. But how did he engineer our selection, his and mine – stick with me and you'll do all right, Taff – for the publicized horrors of intensive training at the Swedish Centre, which turned out to be temporary heaven?

160

'The mornings are devoted to the techiniques of massage for damaged limbs. There are warm baths, white tiles and an atmosphere of order and cloistered tranquility. None of the chaos and vertigo of the barracks; none of the coarse din and discomforts, the barking and baying in a code I can never quite follow. I am no longer a lost name looking for a lost number, footsore with no money and nothing to eat.

'Frankie says this place is like an advertisement for Pears Soap and that it is a pity it is naked men we had under our hands and not naked women. I try to ignore his remarks so that my sensitive nostrils can respond to the atmosphere of idealism. The Swedish specialists look like high priests and the nurses are immaculate and vestal. The patients are beautiful. Their features have been refined by pain. We learn to manipulate their damaged limbs in ways which brought them solace. I was deeply moved as I listened to the thick accent of the bald Swede speaking of "empathy" and "sympathy" and "dedication". The English language too, had its exalted usages. Concepts of healing like white colonnades sustained the Centre. The bald Swede urged us to will the wounded back to health by giving them a share of our own exuberant health like a prayer from the heart. The proof of our skill would show when we began to lose weight. This moved me more deeply than the cataracts of religious parlance I had been accustomed to hear at home. It was strange to find such a haven in the cold English North Country.

' "Better than sticking bayonets in German bellies," Frankie said.

'It was strange to hear his voice, too, in such surroundings. I was intent on capturing as many glimpses of the sublime while I could. Incautiously I mentioned this to Frankie: that the place was a visionary gleam of a higher plane of consciousness. He grinned and said, "If I were you, Taff, I wouldn't put pen to paper until I'd passed the age of thirty." I didn't find that helpful. We weren't guaranteed to survive that long; and in any case visionary gleams had to be seized whenever and wherever they condescended to occur. "Look, Taff," Frankie said. "You've got to be more artful if you want to go on living. I mean, I'll keep an eye on you, but

161

I can't watch every bloody whiz-bang that whips around the corner.'

'There were free afternoons. Frankie established a visiting relationship with the catering sister in her store. I played with pencil and paper in the nurses' common room, dreaming and writing nothing. I was given cigarettes and cups of tea, considered compositions, and considered even more becoming enamoured with one blonde nurse after another. I could have paved the corridors with slabs of blank verse and out of respect for an idealized state that could not possibly last, decided not to.

'It is a mistake to suppose that Frankie's pursuit of the art of looking after number one is an end in itself. There was a method behind that apparently random decision to take me under his wing. As he put it, "We are all born such ignorant bastards. I know that and I know more than most . . . For example, I'm not Irish. I'm a red-haired Jew. My old man changed his name for business reasons. Why should he do a thing like that? Obvious, you say. Not so bloody obvious. He was a Greek Jew who followed shipping insurance from Salamis to Birkenhead. Economics, you say? Then why should he marry the daughter of an Irish tinker? And when she died, a Liverpudlian Pentecostal. Impossible to live with. And why did he keep a room at the top of the house just to say his Hebrew prayers? I tell you this, Taff, it means everything and it means nothing."

'It is in order to enlarge the scope of this inquiry that my company is necessary. I am there to catch the sparks of insight as they emerge. I am here to argue, to contradict, to sharpen up the processes of illumination. Frankie himself has said it in not so many words. "What else can we do, Taff," he says, "as we walk through the wilderness of this war." I am his collaborator and opponent: a companion, a comrade, prepared to oppose but also to be convinced, a fellow traveller with whom he can rehearse the difficult rites and ceremonies of convincing himself.

'After our Huddersfield idyll, a battle exercise. In the gorse behind the cookhouse where Frankie has somehow arranged that we serve while the rest of the unit is attached to a rigorous assault course, Frankie stares at the clouds

162

through rings of cigarette smoke and contemplates the mysteries of female anatomy and physiology.

' "You see it's like this, Taff," he says. "Their things are inward and hidden. Our things hang out and dangle. That's obvious, but it's basic. Hence the mystery. What is hidden is a mystery. And those who possess the mystery have a vested interest in increasing it. Do you follow me, Taff?"

'What else do I ever do except follow him? Almost without reservations.

' "You've got to have order when young males and females get together," Frankie said. "I quite see that. Take the Baptists in Birkenhead. All the best-looking girls were Baptists. I established that. But they wouldn't let you mess about under their skirts. So there you are. Will the number of Baptists decline in relation to the rest of the population? It's an interesting question. But the way things are going we won't be around to find out."

'I considered telling him about Alice Breeze. She wasn't a Baptist, of course, but she was a minister's daughter and she'd given me a limited amount of guidance into pubic mysteries. Frankie was more concerned with widening our sexual experience. We could listen with interest to the indecent details of visits paid by hutmates to what they called knocking shops. Frankie was more fastidious. As usual he made his own arrangements. He had influence with a plump lance-corporal in the Duty Room who did all the Company Commander's typing. It was more than influence. The plump lance-corporal was almost afraid of Frankie. It was not for me to reason why. It was from him that Frankie secured a private address to visit and a small collection of contraceptives. A mother and daughter with a husband somewhere in France. The lance-corporal had assured him they were clean and only received the best-behaved visitors.

'I was nervous to the point of distress as I trotted after Frankie down the narrow streets in the rain. A short-cut through the back streets of dark satanic mill towns did not lead to black-eyed beauties in the groves of paradise.

' "It's just a small business for the poor bitch on the side," he said. "What you've got to consider, Taff, are the mass surges of mass male urges. Just imagine the mass erections

163

that have to be met. It's like making munitions. It's a condition of war, Jack, and a slight adjustment in the great law of supply and demand. You be careful how you put it on and you'll have bugger all to worry about."

'I was touched by his concern for me. He wasn't all that older than I was. Only nineteen and a half. His coolness and detachment made me wiser in the crooked ways of the world and, I hoped, forged a lasting bond between us. Not that I dared say this, since whatever his nationality Frankie's mode was English, and he would be repelled by emotional display. I was for ever wanting to ask him questions. Too-eager interest always put him off. I knew his father spoke five languages, but not which five. He had an uncle in New York who had built a staircase shaped like a pretzel. I knew a pretzel was something to eat, but had no idea about its shape.

'The corridor of the terraced house smelled of chips, cat litter and stale scent. The woman's white blouse was luminous in the narrow space. Her daughter lurked behind her. A note of grievance in the woman's voice reminded me of Mrs Klugman, of my grandmother, of home, and I shivered.

' "What's the matter, love?" she said. "Someone walk over your grave?"

'I was deposited in the back sitting-room with the daughter. The gas mantle hissing over her dark head had more to say than either of us. She had almond-shaped eyes. She watched every move I made without fear and without interest. There was an arrangement of cushions on the floor already for us to lie on. Whether they were clean or not there was no means of knowing. The girl smelt of soap. I decided to think of myself as some kind of artist looking for plastic values. She was pliant and unresisting. Her face was unexpressive as a death mask as I uncovered her as politely as I could. Her eyes were as watchful as a cat's. There was excitement in the smooth porcelain curve of her belly, the resolute firmness of her breasts. This was a white neutrality that took the place of innocence. I preferred her body to Alice's because it existed for its own sake and did not sigh or exude the musty odours of frustrated desire. Her interest in me was minimal. In the brief length of her life that Frankie had paid for, my hands could explore her and feel the erotic power of the female waist even as it quivers under the touch.

'We were caught. A stream of abuse and a stampede of feet up and down stairs brought us to our feet. The house had been invaded. The girl swore fluently under her breath as she struggled to get dressed. The door burst open. A burly Red Cap stood in the doorway. He jabbed a finger at the girl and then at me.

' "That girl's a minor. You're for it, mate! You're for it!"

'Frankie got punched in the mouth for warning me not to say anything. I wouldn't have spoken in any case. I didn't have the strength. My mouth hung open. This incursion of a harsher reality left me paralyzed. We were marched off. I was kicked and punched each time my feet threatened to give way under me.

'The guard room was empty so early in the evening. We were tossed inside. The sawdust stuck to our wet khaki. The floor reminded me of a pig-trough at Ponciau that hadn't been properly swilled. It was a good place to be homesick. Frankie was so infuriated he was finding it difficult to breathe.

' "The bastard. The little bastard. The bastard."

'This was the plump lance-corporal's revenge. Frankie was convinced of it. His self-confidence was shaken. The lance-corporal had passed on the time of our visit to the Red Caps and we were in for it. How did crimes like unlawful intercourse or rape of a minor figure in military law? I had all night in the sawdust on the stone floor to think about it. Four drunken soldiers were thrown into the guardroom singing and swearing. One of them sank to his knees and vomited over my boots. Now I was in the trough. I spent the night thinking of Glanrafon. I saw my Aunt Bessie's floured hands plucking pastry from her glass rolling-pin. I heard my grandmother calling as she went through her favourite early morning routine of letting out the hens and feeding the geese in the apple orchard. Even Uncle Simon squatting under a hedge and drumming his bald head with a calloused index finger. We may have slept. In the morning I was so stiff I thought my bones had turned into rods of stone inside me.

165

'In the Orderly Room, Privates O'Brien and More were sentenced to seven days' detention for disorderly conduct in illicit premises, using obscene language and resisting arrest. I was so relieved I could have cheered. Frankie knew better. And so did the Duty Room lance-corporal who was present taking shorthand notes. We'd lost our embarkation leave and he knew it. This was his revenge for whatever hold it was Frankie had had over him.

' "The bastard," Frankie said under his breath. "The little bastard." '

iii

'The cattle wagon stinks because we stink. Perhaps we are cattle. But we stink. Cattle smell. Cattle don't stink. I lie stiff against my pack. A soldier leans against the crack in the sliding door and pisses into the wind. The train groans and jerks as we crawl eastward at little more than six miles an hour. In my mind I push open the top half of the shippon door at Ponciau and hold up the storm lantern so that rows of round eyes shine like angels of innocence as the cows turn to the light. Cattle don't stink. They comfort the early hour on a winter morning with the odour of fresh dung and milk. We curse. We spit. We grouse. The straw under our feet is as filthy as the language in our mouths.

'Frankie has given up talking. He is hunting lice in his pubic hair. On the ferry boat called *The Maid of Arran* he ensconced himself and his pack in the temporary dispensary and had me jammed at his feet. It was a form of privacy. I listened to his wisdom as the ferry boat butted its way across the Channel. He was sceptical about everything. All politicians were corrupt. The British Empire was a business man's backyard posing as an imperial dream. I don't know what Owen would have had to say. In dreams I heard them arguing, although they'd never met. Style, courage, purpose, Owen said. That's what we lacked. Survival. Frankie said. You can't win if you're dead. When you run out of lads who are willing to die, you'll have a bit of peace then. "Cowardly scum," I heard Owen say in my dream. "Lower orders", "flotsam and jetsam". Frankie had visions of rows of bloody airships on fire, dropping bombs like hailstones. He had brandy in a hip-flask. I sipped a little and it stopped me being sick.

'The train grinds to a halt in some god-forsaken station. We have to bribe the sergeant to let us out. Frankie would like to kill the sergeant. A sly sod from a suburb of South London. An inveterate winker when no one else is looking who plays on our hunger pangs like a god of power. He has control of the sliding door. Frankie stares at the back of his neck as if he'd like to break it. On the platform there is nothing. Men scratch themselves as they search in vain for beer or bread or fruit or tobacco or cheap wine. The dead buildings have nothing to offer. Soured and stifled by troop trains and war transport. The rudimentary conveniences are choked with excrement, "dames" and "hommes" alike. The inhabitants of the woe-begotten town have locked themselves indoors. In the main street Frankie sniffs the air and I stand close to him. Our comrades populate the spaces between the houses as they slouch about in search of any shop or estaminet that dares to open. Football supporters, Frankie said, who've lost their team.

'The engine lets off steam. A whistle blows. Soon it would be starting and I wonder whether we should get back. Frankie draws me down a street where a long midden steams along the pavement in front of the houses. These are peasant dwellings ranged side by side. Frankie is set on exploring the backs of barns and haylofts for eggs. He has a technique of piercing a shell at each end and sucking out the contents. I am to keep watch. As I lean on a wooden fence an old woman emerges from a scullery and she looks so like my grandmother I tremble with shock. The same bristling ginger hair and the same grim resolution on a weathered face. Would she raise her broom and strike me? I was willing to submit. Perhaps because of my petrified stance the broom stayed in the air. She stared at me as though I was someone she knew. She murmured as my grandmother would have done – that blend of reproach and sympathy. She brought out half a loaf and three apples and gave them to me.

While she talked to me in words I could not understand, Frankie made his escape with a capful of eggs.'

iv

'When the noise of the guns grew louder I could see flashes through the sacking. The enemy was working himself up. Frankie could still make jokes about the guns masturbating; but I felt like a pheasant. There was no point in moving. All I could do was sink lower on my haunches. There was a contest in progress inside the ruined cottage. Mr Mackay of the YMCA was engaged in persuading us to join his Christian Soldiers Fellowship, and to attend its meetings as often as our duties permitted. I would have done this weeks ago except for Frankie. He and Mr Mackay sat on either side of a cast-iron table with a candle flickering between them, contending for my soul. Frankie was a slippery wrestler. First he declared himself to be a Jew. When Mr Mackay overcame this by affirming the essential identity of Jewish and Christian virtuous behaviour, Frankie declared himself to be a free-thinker and inclined to his own brand of humanistic socialism. Frankie had his own brand of everything. Was I leaning on a broken reed? Mr Mackay's scriptural quotations took on a fatal attraction as I translated them into William Morgan's music. "Truth shall spring out of the earth . . ." was comforting and illustrated with vivid recollection of the springtime at Glanrafon and the sunlight on the stream beyond the bottom meadow and the leaves of each tree that recognized me. "Surely his salvation is nigh them that fear him . . ." could mean that those in the grip of fear automatically screamed for rescue until William Morgan's order of service elevated the concept to the proper spiritual level. It was a fact that I had chosen to consort with a sceptic and unbeliever and a bit of a rapscallion. That had been before enemy field batteries had started to flash like whips and scorpions across the unprotected night. Fear and faith like mercy and truth walk gingerly together.
    ' "Now then, More," Mr Mackay said. "We won't beat about the bush. Once he's in the heart, he's always with you.

Do you get that? And it's your job to open your heart, so that the King of Glory can ride in. Shall we go to the meeting?"

' "Hang on a minute, Mr Mackay," Frankie said. "Take the expression 'Jack Christ'. No, I'm not being disrespectful. This crucifixion business. That's the crux of the matter, isn't it? Now if this war proves anything, which is a big 'if' I admit, doesn't it prove that every man Jack is a candidate for the cross. Of course it does. Hence the expression Jack Christ. Now does that make a little Jesus out of every little twerp in that mob out there? Well I don't think it does. So what's he up to, your old pal the Almighty?"

'I stopped shivering to take close note of Mr Mackay's response. His smile was fixed anyway. His head was rocking as regularly as a metronome. Poor sod could leave us to it. He didn't have to be here at all. What sense was there in the sacrifice he was making. He should be home and dry like Alice Breeze's papa, adorning a polished pulpit. Frankie was getting carried away with a theory that the Devil was in charge.

' "He says to old Nick, 'Right, you can have them. The little buggers have more of a taste for you than for me. You've got their pockets and ninety-nine per cent of their hearts and minds. All I've got left is the last pinch of what those miserable sods down there call Luck . . .' "

' "Laddie," Mr Mackay said. "Listen to me, laddie. It isn't some blind Providence that settles the fate of the souls of the Lord Jesus Christ's followers."

'He was concentrating on me. He knew I was the weak link. Who could resist such a guarantee, brought up as I have been on the guileless milk of His Gospel? I saw Mr Mackay's shining brow full not only of theological thoughts, but also goodness and mercy ready to follow me all the days of whatever life I had left. His invitation I had to accept. It was the least I could do for the interest the Church of Scotland and the YMCA was taking in myself. When we moved, Frankie wasn't keen on being left out. It amazed me how he could go on talking. Mr Mackay and I walked ahead of him down the moonlit street.

' "If you can still think, you're lucky," Frankie was

saying. "That's the way I look at it. I mean it's all we've got left, isn't it? I suppose you could call it our bit of luck. The only chip we've got left in a pretty lousy game."

'Mr Mackay wanted to draw my attention to the planet Jupiter that hung above us in its own light in a violet sky. The ruined landscape was in the grip of a sinister enchantment. He pointed upwards and turned to Frankie as if he wanted to offer both of us something. I must have been the first to hear the shell coming. I threw myself in the ditch before my knees melted under me. Even as his mouth opened to speak, Mr Mackay was blown up so high the moon and the star went out. Frankie was unhurt. Or I thought he was since the sound of his voice was still huddled in my ear. The ditch was my bed and my cot and I was sobbing in it. When they picked me up I couldn't stand. They found Mr Mackay fifty yards down the road. His back was broken. He was dead, they said, but still smiling.'

v

'There's no way out of this. You can only apply personal salves to the sores of fear. I need nicotine and alcohol to numb the quivering rawness of my inward parts. There is no way out.

'Every ambulance and sanitary unit had to gather round and listen to a Lieutenant-Colonel standing above us like a statue on a plinth squeezed into a uniform and exercising whisky-inspired powers of exhortation. On either side of him two basilisks in the shapes of sergeants kept an eye on the assembly. The Colonel's face was red in the setting sun. If only there were a tidal wave of whisky to wipe him and his words away.

' "Now then, men. You don't expect me to tell you everything, do you? Spell it out. But I can tell you this: there's a Big Push coming soon. A Big Push!" He thrust his fist at the unresisting air. "And when it comes, as come it bloody will, you can strip off those little crosses on your sleeves and tear off those arm-bands and pick up the nearest rifle and get yourself a nice collection of bombs. Do you hear me?"

170

'Wallis Watkins whispered urgently in my ear.

' "This is out of order," he said. "It's very worrying. He's got no right at all to do this."

'There's no way out, I would have said to Watkins if I opened my mouth. Watkins was all right up to a point. Frankie called him "your shithouse pal". It was true I'd fainted again in the Casualty Station and the captain said get that sodding semi-conscious nitwit out of here. It was not entirely the excess of blood or the disposal of amputated limbs or even the shame and disgrace. It was to do with wounds gaping and gasping like mouths, with fingers twitching and pleading and eyes, the eyes of the dying, brimming over with longing for life. So I am detailed to carry buckets of chloride of lime and stinking pans with tiresome regularity. My Muse has deserted me. Where is Owen Guest now? What do they give us to eat and drink that makes this abysmal stench? I am condemned to toil in unhallowed places. There are pits and pits.

' "Do you understand, More? This is completely irregular," Watkins said.

'Watkins was a candidate for ordination with the Welsh Wesleyans. When Watkins and I talk Welsh together it gets on Frankie's nerves. Anything he doesn't understand gets on his nerves. Where was he now? This Big Push business. What did he know about it? Why should Watkins get on his nerves? I was indebted to Watkins. He understood the strict metres and he knew I was a poet. He knew all the rules and appreciated the art. Which Frankie didn't. Our buckets banged together in the latrines and pits as Watkins demonstrated he was a scholar and had been lectured to by Sir John Morris Jones. He spoke French quite well, which was more than Frankie could manage. He took me to the blacksmith's forge at the other end of the town. We were invited into the kitchen to eat cabbage soup. The two young girls and their grandfather watched us eat. The one called Sylvie gave me a slice of bread she had baked herself. Watkins explained everything. I smelt yeast on her fingers. There was an old horse turning a churning wheel. A red cockerel crowing on the midden. The girl started to giggle and the old man shooed them back to their work.

171

' "It's against regulations. Do you understand, More?"

'Watkins was getting agitated. He had a wispy moustache and it blew out at the corners of his mouth as he whispered.

' "Bombs and rifles, boys!" The colonel was waving his fist. "You make it your business to grab 'em and use 'em. Finish them off, do you hear me? The only good German is a dead German. That's what this lovely war is all about. From now on your first priority, men, is to exterminate the Boche. And the more you kill, brethren, the quicker you'll go marching home. It's common sense."

' "It's absolutely irregular."

'Watkins pale blue eyes were swollen with outrage. I just wished Frankie was with us. He would have explained it one way or another. The Colonel had run out of words. He was glaring at us. He looked as if he wanted to shoot somebody just to set an example. Would it be Watkins? If Watkins dared to protest aloud. I could still hear him mutter.

' "If ever there was a wrong man for the job. He's got no right at all to do this. It's against all the regulations."

'I thought of regular and irregular verbs. Which was which? The Colonel was lifting an arm to point in our direction. He was about to condemn Watkins and me with him. There was no room to move and nowhere to hide. His arm dropped. He snapped out.

' "God bless you all. Dismissed."

'He swayed as the two sergeants helped him down from his pedestal. In the hubbub Watkins could raise his voice to a full indignant pitch.

' "I'm a candidate for the Christian ministry. A Christian minister should not spill blood. He should not carry offensive weapons. I volunteered on that strict under-standing . . ."

'I had things to think about. On such a fine night I had a bench behind the currant bushes in the overgrown garden of the ruined convent beyond the camp perimeter. I had been wrong about so many things. Was my life itself a mistake? I had walked into the trap of my own volition. Was there nowhere else on earth where young men could go to make their first and last mistake? I couldn't pretend I was willing to give up my life any more. I was wrong about farming.

There was a sacred vocation in Sylvie's fingers and I had tasted it. The world had a myriad variations of flowers and music and it was important to survive to see and hear them. The Great Cause was whisky on the Colonel's breath and the need for sacrifice had sailed out of reach as high as the moon in the sky.

'In the minutes I had left I could start to compose again. The music of the metres was rustling in the long grass. It was time to think of new worlds and different ways of living. What else could I do? The old world lay in ruins like the streets of Arras and Albert. The young should prepare themselves for the surprise of survival, not death.

'There was a real rustle in the grass. Watkins had found my private retreat. I heard his anxiety close to my ear. The Big Push had started. The thunder of the guns was shaking the horizon. Watkins said we would be on our way to Hell in a matter of hours and he wanted someone to pray with in his own language. He was going too far. He said things like "the wheels of the juggernaut were already slithering towards the fields of slaughter." It wasn't what I wanted to hear. He was naming men I had never met and never heard of. Ivor Low, Ted Roberts, Fred Macalpine, Fred Jones, Gibbs, Griffiths, Jukes, Kerfoot, Lewis, Ralph Holmes, Bill Pryce-Jones, Bertie Rees . . . I was slow to realize these were corpses. How often did Watkins recite their names in his prayers? "O Comrades, dead comrades . . . Surely he hath born our griefs and carried our sorrows . . . he was wounded for our transgressions, he was buried for our iniquities . . . he is brought as a lamb to the slaughter and as a sheep before his shearers is dumb as he openeth not his mouth . . ." My jaw and my brain were frozen. Watkins had been through it all before. One push after another. The dead accumulating, the living dwindling. He was gripping my arm. His face was close to mine. His eyes were white and wild in the moonlight.

' "We haven't been as close as I would have wished, More. I found that very worrying. There were barriers and I couldn't pull them down. I wanted to help you. Indeed, being the creature I am, I wanted to save you. And now I've had a vision. You must let me pour out my heart."

173

'I looked up at a wide circle around the moon. I heard my grandmother utter the old saw like an incantation about the circle being distant, rain being near. The noise of the guns in the distance grew louder. Watkins's whispering rustled like grass across my ear.

' "I am to be killed," he said. "I am prepared. I saw you walk through a cloud and I knew that meant you would come through. You'll be spared, More. So you've got to carry the message home."

'What message? This worried me as much as my fear. He was muttering about a better Wales and a better world: but what did I need to do?

' "Pray for a more holy intention, More, for the dove, for the dove of the spirit to settle on your shoulder."

'He went as quietly as he had come. I think he was disappointed with my lack of reponse. I was cold and confused. What dove? What holy intention? The wind was rising. There was no comfort left in the overgrown garden.'

vi

'A mine goes up. The earth shakes. I tremble. Captain Herbert touches my arm.

' "Where *does* all this rain come from More? Any idea?"

'The strength of his character wraps itself like armour around my chest. Captain Herbert is a pattern of military perfection with a trimmed moustache and, under his clinical manner, an unhardened heart. Watkins and I follow as closely as we can in his unwavering footsteps. Watkins told me the Captain was a former gymnast champion. I know he exudes his own strength, physical and moral. A man to follow. Bombs are being passed up the line in buckets. Murder everywhere. An officer leans against the trench wall as grey as though he were already turning into mud. A bullet has passed across his back just missing his spine. He says he can manage to get to the field dressing station without help. I am glad. I don't want to be parted from the Captain.

'On the muddy trench board a young soldier lies like a sleeping child. He could be dying from loss of blood.

174

Captain Herbert talks quietly to me as he attends to the pale, sacrificial figure. Watkins is bandaging another bleeding head. He is more efficient than I. I should be doing something more useful than kneeling close to Captain Herbert. He calls himself battle-hardened. He and Watkins use names I have heard old soldiers use like tokens of romance – Loos, Givenchy, Festubert – those incantations. The Captain distances himself from human suffering by reducing the most appalling circumstances to some acceptable imitation of clinical conditions. The more I cling to my admiration for the man the better my chances of preserving some semblance of stability. No one, not Watkins certainly, not the Captain, must know of the bubbling weakness inside me. Without the pressure of this reinforced thumb of necessity it would all spurt out like a severed artery. O my Captain, he has staunched the flow of the boy's blood. Stretcher-bearers will carry the stricken youth to the rear. He will probably die on the way. Watkins and I go forward with the Captain.

'I have no idea what this fighting is about. Who gains and who loses. Watkins mutters constantly about it all being very worrying. He may as well. As long as it doesn't get on the Captain's nerves, it won't get on mine. My Captain is mine and I am his. Perhaps he doesn't have any nerves. They were exercised out of him as he trained to become a champion gymnast. He was born, bred and built to sustain the semblance of order even in the foulest chaos. He has a Military Cross because of bravery on a bridge. With a piece of shrapnel in his leg he dragged two men into safety before the whole structure collapsed into the railway cutting, collapsed with a roar that is the echo of what surrounds us now. And he will do it again and again. I am here to store up every fragment of his bravery and I shall build it into a poem like an image in a classical mosaic. The torment of Captain Herbert. The ordeals of, the hells, the horrors, the barbarous times of, and words have become as inadequate as spit.

' "Just pop down that one, More, will you?" he said. "While I attend to this chap. Estimate the dimensions. Usual drill. Look sharp. There's a good lad."

'He speaks without looking at me, but I feel like a dog whose head has been patted by his master. I bear in mind all he has taught me: how many steps down, ease of access and exit, decent overhead protection, available furnishings, state of floor and so forth. There was a light burning on a trestle table. The place looked promising until I saw the signals officer. There was a small switchboard in front of him. I didn't see his face at first because it was hidden in his hands. When I saw it, it was white and wild with anguish. It frightened me.

' "Yes," he said. "What do you want?"

'I explained that Captain Herbert had sent me down to find a space for a temporary dressing station. I was with Captain Herbert, I said. He didn't seem to hear me.

' "I haven't lost my bloody nerve," he said. "If that's what you think. We stuck it out. Do you get that? All bloody day and all bloody night and the water creeping up to our knees. Do you get that?"

'I wasn't even certain he could see me. He was conversing with some ghostly tribunal. I wanted to turn and run. I heard Captain Herbert's voice behind me. It was steadying. It was comforting.

' "What's the trouble?"

'The signals officer seized on the word. "Trouble. The bloody Colonel's the trouble. 'Get that wire out'. That's all he could say. The other end of the bloody blower. All he could think about. 'Get that wire out.' We'd been in the bloody hole two days and two nights already. There was no point in it. 'I can't send men out in that,' I said. 'It's a bloody seething boiling cauldron.' 'That's an order,' he said. 'That's an order.' So I sent them out, one after the other, like lambs to the slaughter. They never made it. And in the end it didn't bloody matter."

'He began to cry. I couldn't bear the sight of those tears. Captain Herbert pushed me up the steps. I could have been looking at myself. Should I cry? I felt the Captain's fist thump me on the back. Watkins was hard at it, patching up a sergeant with a head wound and a broken arm. The Captain asks him if he can manage the distance back to the dressing station. The sergeant goes off with his head to one side as if he were leaving a football field. We move on. At a junction of trenches I meet Frankie. He is running as usual. He stops to call out my name. He carries a map satchel. I'm curious about him. I want to ask the Captain's permission to light a fag. Frankie bends down to his running posture, off to battalion headquarters with urgent messages. He just has time to tell me he's applied for a transfer to the RFC and that if he gets it he'll make for the States the day the war is over. He was lit up with the notion. And then he was gone.

'A soldier drags himself down the trench with one leg trailing. He looks up at Captain Herbert like a helpless child. The bullet entered above the knee and tore out through the calf. I press my thumb on the femoral artery. Watkins applies a tourniquet and a temporary splint. The boy sobs with pain. Through the din I heard the Captain's quiet voice commending our work and soothing the lad's fears. We move on again in the Captain's wake. Watkins keeps on telling me that the Captain is the model of a true Welsh gentleman, as if I didn't know already. All the same I wish he didn't persist in walking towards the trench mortars falling ahead of us. Should I count the mortars or count his virtues. I had to count something: strength, discipline, firmness, fearlessness, concern, gentleness, respect, and then begin again, begin again.

' "More. Pop down that one will you?"

'He was still looking for a dug-out dressing station. If I popped down would I ever pop up again?

' "Quick sharp. And report back."

'Could I go down and stay down? I remembered a deserted communication trench that ran through a field of scarlet poppies. Frankie and I hid there for a quiet smoke. One fine day, Frankie said the war was over. The poppies reached out from either side to build a bridal arch over our heads. The sunlight filtered through the petals to create a luminous pool of colour in which we bathed like truant schoolboys smoking Woodbines out of bounds and totally content. Frankie said it felt beautiful. Just the two of us. That was the most emotional remark I ever heard him make. Only as we crept out did a stray colonel exercising his horse catch us. His leggings flashed like armour in the sun. He

177

pointed his crop at us and sent us packing. "Get back to your unit, you miserable apes."

'I loiter in the dug-out, stretch my arms out in slow motion, measuring. The next time I saw Owen Guest I would tell him to his face there was no point in this war. None whatsoever. All those regimental battle honours meant nothing to me any more. Malplaquet, Albuhera, Inkerman, Waterloo, Gehenna. My imperial epic would not be forthcoming. All I wanted was to get back whole to my green valley, my Glanrafon, even my grandmother. As for the King Emperor and worldwide dominion . . . For my impious thoughts the wrath of the gods descended. The blast hurled me against the dug-out wall. I lay with a mouthful of earth desperately winded, until an hysterical fear of being buried alive drove me to fight the earth and debris like a beast at bay. Outside I knew it as I struggled up out of the hole: my Captain and Wallis Watkins had been killed instantly. The Captain was blown to bits. I conceived it my duty to find his head. It had to be the most precious part of him. Men retreating from encircling gas shells dragged me back. I smelt the stuff. I saw my own heels ploughing the mud on the duckboards before I lost consciousness.'

vii

'Between the lock gates and the ruin they put me down and leave me choking. The bloody guns never stop. Death is the enemy. He had a thousand hands to thrash the stricken land. Why don't they move me? Poison gas. It's better that they shouldn't. All the walking wounded killed on their joyous way out of the war zone. I can't move. I can't see. There is blood going cold on my neck. How could I live in a dark world? Was it a swan on the canal? Impervious to it all? I shake like the grass until I lose consciousness again.

'It comes and goes. This grass is under cover. The bottle-green gloom of a tent that smells of chloroform and antiseptics. The guns are distant thunder. The wounded are in transit. The intolerable sufferings of others assail my ears: chokings, groans, sobs, sighs, screams. An underworld of pain and desolation. My body contributes to the clamour, not my true self who has gone absent without leave.

'In the train, in the ship, I gain shallow forms of medicated sleep. Away from the incessant thunder. Away from it. Between the harbour and the open sea I am taken with a fit of vomiting. This could be death. I cannot read the brass letters on the soldier's shoulder-straps as he holds me in his grip. Nothing matters any more. I am unconscious for such a length of time that I could wake up in another century an old man of eighteen.

'I have changed colour. I am convinced of it. The hospital blue has tinted my skin and I shall wear something of that hue in my face and hands for ever. If I ever see them again. At the foot of my bed men and women stand like trees in a mist. A stiff staff-officer in all his polished glory holds a letter in his hand and regards what is left of me with obvious disfavour. What is he saying?

' "Go no more a-roving, Moore? No. One 'o'. You're not one of those Irish traitors are you, More? An unspeakable Sinn Feiner?" He was showing off in front of a nurse I couldn't see. "A letter from the War House," he said. "Aren't you the important fellow. Sure your father doesn't know Lloyd George? Just as well he doesn't know your mother, from all I hear. I beg your pardon, Nurse. Strike that remark from the record." He was momentarily overcome with the impact of his scintillating wit. He had to clear his throat. I couldn't make out his face. "The contents of this letter. If you don't know about it already . . . Can you hear me?" He raised his voice. I didn't want to listen to it. "From the Colonel in Charge of Records, Hounslow, to a certain Reverend Goronwy F. Breeze, MA, The Manse, Glasfryn, Glaslyn, Caernarvonshire, North Wales, dated 12th December 1917. Dear sir, I am in receipt of your letter dated the first inst, with reference to No. 87144 Private J.C. More, Royal Army Medical Corps, being granted his discharge and beg to state that this man's age on attestation was nineteen years, one month, and that therefore is his official age. It is regretted that your request for his discharge cannot be acceded to. Yours faithfully, J.H. Waltham, Major for Colonel in Charge of Records, Hounslow in the County of Middlesex."

179

'My grandmother's concern for me had grown to such a size that she had swallowed her pride and gone to the Manse to beg the minister to write. I could see her hustle about the premises she loved, the stores, the farm, every nook and cranny of her domain, carrying this leaden concern in her heart. I was heavy with guilt. Innocence was useless. I thought of old Frankie and all his complex theory of Luck. Was he lucky? Was he still alive? That did it. The hot tears coursed down my cheeks and threatened my eyes again with blindness. I wanted the bandages put back.

' "Pull yourself together, man!"

'Did the fool think I was crying with disappointment? I had nothing against the Major for Colonel in Charge of Records, or Hounslow in the County of Middlesex. They preserved the names of the fallen like Wallis Watkins's prayers.

' "We're all in it together. Remember that. And victory is around the corner. Stop blubbing, man, for heaven's sake. Carry on, Nurse." '

viii

'I lie on my iron cot in the furthest corner of the Nissen hut with my face turned to the wall. Am I a malingerer? "Not much wrong with him," one doctor says. The other does not agree. "Nervous collapse," I heard, and it was on that phrase my mind fastened. "Offered home leave," that second doctor said. "Refused it." He was pleased. It clinched his diagnosis. O Francis Moses O'Brien, how you paid for your strong legs. The attack was faltering. The line of forward communication cut in several places by heavy shelling. Carefully considered plans collapsing in the usual welter of mud and blood. He had his transfer and his leave ticket in his pocket when the Colonel stopped him. "Isn't this the great runner?" It was imperative and of the utmost consequence to get this written signal to the captain of 'D' Company. Frankie's death was written up. Down for a medal. In the dressing station – the final scene, lovingly recounted (and did I believe it?) – he pulls the blood-soaked message from his pocket and insists it be delivered. He dies like one of Owen Guest's heroes, and I am a living coward left alive to malinger and ponder the mystery. The war has killed off Frankie. What else have I got to lean on?

'This wet winter. Men I recognize but don't know, cluster about the comforting heat of the stove in the centre of the hut. They were in a minor mutiny in a Blackpool convalescent camp. It was water-logged, they said. A protest against the flooded conditions brought the men surging towards the gates in a flood of their own. They shove the guard and a couple of officers into the mud. They've all heard it before but it comes out like plainsong in between talks of fronts and theatres of war and football matches. They commandeered trams and drove themselves into town. That was a great ride, they agree. They were met by the Chief Constable – " 't'were like Robin Hood an't merry men" – that was the voice that always got its applause – and laughed in his face. He parleyed with them – "Now then, lads" – and in collaboration with the Mayor provided them with shelter from the rainy blast and a hot meal in the Temperance Hall not far from the police station. Their reward for this insurrection was their rapid transfer to these Nissen huts in the grounds of a country house on the shores of Lough Neagh; which they said weren't half bad, all things considered. I marvel at them. Whatever their wounds, their minds are not like mine, suppurating with resentment. They grumble and rumble all day about the weather, the war, the world, but they have been issued with rations of contentment they can draw on like tobacco. Their bovine serenity cramps my thinking. What can I do except turn my face to the wall?

'I lie in the closest I can manage to a trance of rigidity because the eyes in which I once registered the fact of my existence are dead and buried. My image cannot be reflected in empty sockets. There is probably an order somewhere that states my place is with the remains of Frankie O'Brien, Captain Herbert, Wallis Watkins and all the men he prayed for, in soil ready to be exhumed by shells of another attack. Let it be enforced. It would be easier than facing a disjointed and hostile world alone. I had not finished my course with Frankie. The lessons are all unlearned. I never embraced him or even thanked him for the strength he gave me. His absence lies beside me on this corner cot. He will never appear, not even as a painting on the iron wall of this tomb. There is no music from a dead musician.

'The door of the hut flew open. Without turning around the men clustered around the stove yelled at the newcomer to shut that fucking door. A voice rang out in Welsh.

' "Any Welsh boys in here?"

'I was so surprised I almost responded to the summons. I saw a burly padre with his greatcoat open and the peak of his cap tilted back further than any regulation would allow.

' "It's too hot in here, you men. You need a breath of fresh air."

'His uniform and cloth protected him. These men resented any intrusion into their lair. The padre's smile was relentlessly amiable. His face was tanned and round as a sun. It was part of his mission in life to cheer men up. A fellow rubbed his nose with a bandaged hand before pointing in my direction.

' "There's a Taff over there," he said.

'They had a game of brag in progress and they wanted to get on with it. Before the padre's attention was fixed on me, I turned to face the wall. I heard his heavy tread approach on the cement floor. He looked down at me with quizzical compassion.

' "Dost thou know what day it is, brother?"

'His Welsh and his use of the second person singular were close to pulpit exhortation. One of the few conclusions I had arrived at was that the age of exhortation had come to an end; colonels on plinths or preachers in pulpits. This was a day like any other, wet and joyless on the chill fringe of a khaki world.

' "Dydd Gwyl Dewi Sant! St David's Day, brother. 'Wear a leek in your cap and a leek in your heart' . . . I've arranged a little celebration."

'At the last church parade I attended with Frankie, the chaplain yelled his head off about Jehovah in his rage vowing armies to destruction, delivering them to the slaughter and so forth. "He's a fiery little bugger, isn't he?" Frankie had said in a stage whisper and started a tittering. Half the time

182

they were never around to give a chap a decent burial.

' "Tell me. How do you come to be here?"'

'The padre was sitting on the end of my cot. Invading my privacy. He wasn't put off by my silence. Under his breath almost, he began reciting. It was a familiar hackneyed *englyn* – 'the exile' – from the last century; old-fashioned and sentimental, but it touched me.

' "*Wylaf a'm dwylo ar led*/I weep with my arms outstretched/ For the warm hearth of the place where I was born."'

'He had the sense to make it sound as if he were speaking for himself. And somehow the lilt relaxed me. But I did not speak.

' "We'll give old St David a rest this time, shall we? I'll be back for a little chat tomorrow. Tasker Thomas is the name. I have a feeling we can help each other." '

ix

'I suppose there was a law of gravity inherent in our common language that drew him towards me. He would hardly have been my choice of companion in the ordinary course of events. But what events are ordinary the moment you begin to examine them? He had rank and he could impose himself on me whenever he felt like it. In any case, taking a walk in the private grounds with the chaplain was to be preferred to watching convalescents spitting into the stove and playing interminable brag.

'There were small cyclamen nestling in the moss under the tall beeches. Constellations of snowdrops were still visible spread over cloudy banks of green leaves. Padre Thomas inhaled with such vigour that I was obliged to notice he was breathing in the beauty of the world. The daffodils were ready to open along the margin of the lake. Gardeners reinforced with soldiers fit for light duty kept the network of paths open through the woods and the evergreen shrubs so that the ladies from the castle could take afternoon strolls down to the lake. Padre Thomas knew all about the castle. He had an appetite for aristocratic genealogies and he

183

could spot Welsh connections at a distance. Even as he went on about it I could hear Frankie's voice shouting, "If there's a revolution around, Taff, I'll be joining it." If he could see me now in solemn conclave with the Reverend Tasker Thomas. All forms of rank and hierarchy he had taught me to suspect; so why should I hold my breath at the revelation that the second earl took to wife an heiress from Pembrokeshire in the next parish where Tasker had his first ministry?

'He was so eager for me to understand everything. Always specific, dotting 'i's and crossing 't's.

' "I'll never forget that morning, John Cilydd," he said.

'He breathed even more deeply. He knew I wrote poetry. Was he listening to me or was I listening to him? It was an effort.

' "A purple sunrise, I remember, and a tank stuck in a trench like a dead monster in a trap, and smoke drifting through stumps of trees. All around me desolation and in my heart a kind of joy I thought I'd lost for ever. My faith had come back!"

'It must have been very nice for him. I nodded as politely as I could. What I wanted to ask him was would one more turn of duty back there transform my paralyzing fear into some form of courage?

' "Oh, we all have a purpose in life," he said. "I'm deeply certain of that. We all have our calling."

'I heard the whistle in my great-uncle Ezra's throat when he asked me yet again whether I'd heard "the Call". What happens if you want to be a poet? At some point I would ask Tasker that too. When it was safe to ask him. It was one of the few things left I urgently wanted to know.

'He looked around him and lowered his voice so that even the birds would not overhear him. He was going to tell me something I had to keep to myself.

' "There's talk in the mess of sending the battalion down to Dublin. They are going to fill the city with troops when Sinn Fein commemorates the Easter Rising. For me this is a crisis of conscience. If that order comes I shall refuse to go."

'I saw the man in a new light. He stood on a mound near the water's edge. He and his uniform never looked as if they

184

had been made for each other. Even now his greatcoat looked as if dogs had been lying on it. Here and now, however, in an Irish landscape, he was Bendigeidfran bent on Reconciliation with a capital 'R' that lay on its face like a bridge across the water so that little men could scamper across into safety. Perhaps he was a big man. Momentarily I felt my Muse stir inside me. Had I stumbled across a new hero?

'I was under orders to take exercise every day. Padre Thomas gave me a pass which allowed me to walk where I liked inside the park. The doctor said I was like a tuberculosis patient and gentle exercise was as good for damaged minds as damaged lungs. It was good to walk on my own. The doctor seemed to think I needed to develop a more independent persona; I was inclined to attach myself too closely to stronger personalities. I could see the truth in that. On the other hand it would not do for a poet on the threshold of his career to develop a shell of indifference. Scratches of social contact should not be confused with the blast of random destruction. In the castle grounds all I had to do was walk with a measured tread and a detached but attentive expression on my face.

'A young gardener with a donkey and cart was spreading peat and manure around the base of shrubs bordering one of the walks parallel with the lake. He had red hair and a freckled face. He reminded me of Frankie. Was Frankie Irish, after all, and not Jewish? Who now could ever tell me, and did it matter? Wars were fought to find an answer to such elusive questions; with swords and guns chasing shades and apparitions and fool's fire through the mud and into the quicksands of oblivion. He stopped work to straighten his back and to inquire after my health. English was attractive with such an accent. And he was so cordial. I could only respond in kind. His name was Malachy. He liked his work. He was twenty-three next birthday and he didn't have the faintest desire to leave the shore of Lough Neagh ever.

' "It's too big for me as it is, I can tell you."

'As far as conscription was concerned he hoped to God it would never be imposed on Ireland.

' "Now that's something I often ask myself," he said.

185

"Why should one lot of people always be so damned keen to impose their will on another? You can't call it human frailty, can you? Not when it requires such a fearsome show of strength. Did you ever see anything like the human race? If they tried it on, the five provinces would go up in flames. And who wants to see that, for God's sake?"

'It was always pleasant to come across Malachy. He took his work, like everything else, at a leisurely pace. Most of all he liked talking. He had a way of scrutinizing plants like a lord of the manor so that they would grow better in the warmth of his benign interest. He knew more about politics than I did. He used to pass the time of day with a genial Mr Birrell who had been a frequent guest at the castle before he gave up his job and went back to London. A very genial man he was, according to Malachy, very kindly and very fond of a joke. My silence saved me from betraying I had no idea he was talking about a man who had been Chief Secretary for Ireland for nine years. Neither my uncle Gwilym nor my grandmother nor Owen Guest nor Frankie had ever so much as mentioned the man's name. Was this a measure of my political ignorance?

'Malachy Ryan would be the end of it. He worked more seriously on his parents' smallholding. To the castle he went for a bit of money and a rest. These people were generosity incarnate. On that little farm I again tasted home-cured ham and eggs and soda-bread and cakes of the kind Auntie Bessie made. This was an improvement on home because of the palsied pleasure that shook Mrs Ryan's arm each time she saw me. I was like someone, she insisted. Her sister's son who got himself killed in this awful war. And Mr Ryan blew out clouds of shag tobacco smoke and said the woman was absolutely right and wasn't I Welsh and shouldn't a Celt look like a Celt? It was all warmth and welcome.

'They were Catholics and Sinn Feinners. About Ireland's complex and troubled history they were ready to tell me anything I cared to know. Here the textbook heroes of English schooling were turned inside out. Walter Raleigh, Edmund Spenser, Essex, Cromwell, William Pitt, Lord Palmerston, were far worse villains than the Kaiser. Doses of indignation speeded my recovery. A doctor used to call,

186

for Mrs Ryan's palsy. He was paid in butter and eggs. He was also called Ryan and a distant relative. He took a kindly interest in my health. He was critical of Lloyd George.

' "Wasn't he the man who tempted Michael Davitt into Wales? A rabid Home Ruler. And where is he now? He serves England and no doubt England pays him well. But does that mean young Welsh lads like you have to be tossed into the fire? Have you asked yourself that question?" '

X

'Men in our hut are being given medical boards before being bundled off to France. The tempo of grumbling quickens. There is unease and foreboding throughout the camp. The news is awful. The Germans are sweeping all before them and look set to occupy Amiens. Everywhere the clouds are low. I shelter in an abandoned bower between the garden and the trees. I pull at withered tendrils of vine wound around the pillars like pieces of discoloured string. This is where Tasker Thomas finds me. He is longing to be cheerful and friendly. I blurt out the new convictions I have acquired from Dr Ryan.

' "This is England's war," I said. "And nobody else's. They don't call it the English Empire. They call it the British Empire. That gives them a better chance to beat off the German challenge to her hegemony of world trade. It's as simple as that."

'The padre shook his head. "We've got to beware of nationalism," he said. "It's the root cause of war. And war is the greatest of all evils."

' "What about English nationalism?" I said. "That's what imperialism is when you get to the bottom of it. From one end of the globe to the other. Lords of the earth. Best in the world. Rampant nationalism."

'The padre was amused. He slapped me on the back. "There speaks a poet," he said. "A real poet. And a true Welsh poet sings to his own people." He was taking me too lightly. "Do you know what I wanted to be when I was your age?" His shoulders signalled that he was about to say

187

something comic. "An actor in English! Oh yes. The West End stage in London. Nothing less. I was mad about it. My heroes had names like Granville Barker and Forbes Robertson and Beerbohm Tree. So much more glamorous than O.M. Edwards or Llewelyn Williams or even David Lloyd George. Can you inagine it? An awkward lump like me on the West End stage? My father put a stop to it. 'Tasker,' he said. 'If you can't think of anything better to do with your life, I'll give you the fare to Australia.' "

'He swayed from one side to the other, overcome with rollicking laughter. For my part I couldn't see what was so funny. It had nothing to do with my immediate crisis. My medical was due in four days. If I was passed I would be on my way back to the end of the world.

' "I'm not going back," I said.

'He had stopped laughing. He gave me all his compassionate attention.

' "I'd rather put a bullet through my brain," I said. That was something I had not thought of doing before I said it. I wanted him to understand my desperation. "If my name is on the Draft." He was some kind of an officer. Could I venture to speak freely? He was a fellow countryman. We spoke the same language. "I'll slip down the Irish pipeline." It was no less daring to say it than to do it. I became more reckless. "I'm in touch with Sinn Fein," I said.

'Was that poetic licence? Doctor Ryan had said in a roundabout way that the organisation would help genuine deserters. It was no more than a hint. Tasker Thomas was horrified; even more so than I had expected.

' "No," he said. "For God's sake don't do that. That would be a terrible mistake. Put it out of your mind."

' "Why should I?"

'The warmth of his concern made me more bold. I was his own kith and kin. He would never turn me in. And was he the man who would refuse to go to Dublin at Easter if ordered to do so? He was desperately serious. His face didn't look the same without the beam of his smile.

' "You'd be hounded," Tasker said. "A marked man for life. You have a career ahead of you. The law. The legal profession. You'd never get back in."

188

'What did that matter? I had the right to gamble with my own life. The Army had; so why not me? Risk all on one desperate throw. Escape from war and death to another life. The roof of the pergola was leaking. A pool of water was forming on the damp floor behind us. I tried to look unconcerned, debonair even. The padre made a concentrated effort to convince me.

' "The professions are all structures," he said. 'Even mine. For better or for worse. Like the State itself. There is no harm in analyzing it to see how it works. No harm in criticizing it. But if an individual pits himself against it, in direct confrontation, he gets broken to bits. Or at the very least, he's an outlaw for ever."

'Perhaps an "outlaw" was what I should be. In the days of their defiance all our ancestors were outlaws. And they had their own poets to sing their praises. Was this, too, some kind of a Call?

' "You must understand this," Tasker Thomas said. "Take my position. I am tolerated as a nonconformist, shall we say. Even the way I'm talking to you now. The system makes a place for me and my kind and we are allowed to dissent so long as we are not disloyal. That is the essence of the system. If you desert, John Cilydd, you are abandoning any prospect of becoming a responsible citizen, accepted by society and by the State. Do you understand me?"

'I saw and yet I didn't see. All his Christianity would do in the end would be to bow the knee. Confused images of Christ and Caesar and coins of the realm were no help to me at all. Let the medical decide. If they passed me and my name went up on the Draft, I would quietly disappear.

' "What did you say?" Tasker had caught me thinking aloud.

' "I said I'd let the medical decide."

' "Decide what?"

'He was stern and authoritative for my own good. I did not answer.

'In my iron cot in the corner of the Nissen hut I trembled with illicit excitement as I wondered what to do next. At night I dreamt I was at boarding school in England with Owen Guest. We were planning to run away and he made it

189

sound like a thrilling adventure. I was cold when I woke up. The blankets were on the floor.

'I came to an agreement with Malachy. He took it all as a joke and I tried my best to smile. There was a bin in their haybarn. He would leave civilian clothes there in a sack.

' "Down to the last shirt button," he said. "But I'm afraid we can't manage your boots."

'There was a cattle lorry driven by yet another relative that would get me to Cavan. From there I would be spirited to the South-West.

' "And maybe do something useful for the Brotherhood," Malachy said.

'Were the Ryans laughing at me? Did they see me as a solemn creature who took himself too seriously? When he'd taken a bit too much to drink, old Ryan said my nostrils reminded him of a nervous horse he had lost money on at the races at Bally-something-or-other. No doubt my situation was comic; if only it belonged to someone else. I was trapped inside my thin and twitching frame as I tossed and turned in the night attacked by fears and anxieties sleep was powerless to subdue. Would it be so much better than the trenches? Poets in the strict metres were not meant for exile. There would be no audience for me in Limerick or Tipperary. Was I about to commit artistic suicide? By the waters of the Shannon I would sit down and weep. I could never learn to sing in any other language. This was the true meaning of exile: being cut off not so much from the land of your birth but from the people it was your vocation to criticize and praise.

'Three doctors had their heads together. Other men were waiting in a patient line. When an interesting case comes up before them, doctors are not to be hurried. They are the three Fates, not so much three old women spinning, as three clerks holding up papers between impersonal finger and thumb. I had been examined. I pulled my shirt over my head. I retreated to the echoing corridor. There was nothing to do but wait. Who holds the distaff, who draws the thread, who cuts it short?

'Tasker Thomas was signalling to me. His face was beaming. My name wasn't on the list. By what miracle had I

190

failed that medical?

' "Well now, John Cilydd."

'He was rubbing his hands as if matters had been brought to a satisfactory conclusion. He looked so harmless, and yet his prayers could be dangerous. They could collide in space with messages from other powers responsible for the punishment of crimes against the family. Had I not sinned against my grandmother, my uncles, my aunt, my sister my home, my dead parents, my ancestors? . . . Rubbing his hands together like an amateur gambler about to collect his winnings.

' "I shouldn't be telling you this. Very confidential." He was whispering the secret in my ear. "Bonny Scotland," Tasker Thomas said. "You will be sent to a hospital outside Edinburgh. A very good place where they specialize in nervous disorders. That's where you're going, John Cilydd."

'Was I mad? Or was it a new name for cowardice?

'The lake was almost hidden in low cloud. I walked alone through the dripping trees. A depression was settling on my mind that might never lift. No sign of Malachy. I heard footsteps on the gravel behind me. Should I run? Apathy made it difficult to put one foot after the other. There was no poetry in apathy. Tasker caught up with me and walked at my side like a keeper.'

Seven

i

A shaft of sunlight pierced the bookshelves to expose the floor where Hefin Mather's table and cupboards had stood. The motes floated up and down the light, serene and indifferent. I needed him and he was no longer there. He was the one person on earth with whom I could test and tease out all the theories and theses forming in my mind concerning my father's life and work. The empty space that confronted me was as painful as an absence of meaning. The intuitive insights, the hypotheses, the emergent structures that had goaded me to leave the seclusion of the manse at Rhyd-y-Groes and seek out this subterranean soothsayer, disintegrated on the spot into particles of floating dust.

My father had survived that war to provide me with my existence. This was a statistic. His survival was a commonplace fact. It was also a miracle. He knew this. How does a miracle disguise itself as a commonplace event? It becomes a small-town solicitor and secretes itself in the elegant detachment of polished verses about birds and beasts and flowers and an underground reservoir of unfinished and unpublished fragments. I needed to know from an objective specialist like Mather whether or not the modulations of his prosody could ever mirror the rawness of his experience, the shock of his survival. Had he suppressed self-expression in the interests of perpetuating the harmonies of the traditional metres that purified and exalted the language of our tribe? Was this a destiny thrust upon him? By the same hand that plucked the brand from the fire?

I found Hefin Mather in an isolated room at the top of an

awkward stair. His name had been freshly painted on the door. The library was being reorganized and enlarged. He was pleased that I had sought him out. Books, pamphlets, manuscripts in the old language reached him by means of a groaning dumb-waiter that he would be delighted to demonstrate. He said he had been elevated if not promoted, and that there was quite a difference between delving in a burrow and perching in an eyrie. The change of habitat had a marked effect on his behaviour. He spoke more loudly because there was no one to overhear him. He was more prepared to pass sweeping remarks and laugh at them.

'I am the last indirect beneficiary of our university's white-hot technological revolution,' he said. 'A false fruit if ever there was one. Still, these are stirring times, Mr Peredur More. There's a tang of change in the air. The mood of protest is moving towards a climax.'

Up here he would be unremittingly jolly. From the casement windows he had a squared-paper view of the slate roofs of the lower town. He was equipped with a new electric kettle and he was able to make tea or instant coffee with an hospitable flourish. He had more room for heaps of uncatalogued books, magazines and pamphlets to grow. He had a control of his immediate evironment that made him appear self-sufficient.

'If it wouldn't be tempting fate, I would go as far as to say the tide had turned,' he said. 'The tide in the affairs of Wales, shall we say. The centuries look down on this new generation and smile with approval.'

He allowed himself an eloquent gesture. I was his ideal audience; safely on the same side. He was sparing in the use of my name as a mode of address. He always reined himself in before reaching 'Peredur'. 'Mr Peredur More,' was nicely ironic. There were still transitions to be made. We both adhered to the polite distances required by ancestral courtesies. It was my prerogative to insist that he called me 'Peredur' and at the first opportunity I would do so. The same excessive delicacy governed our treatment of my father's papers. How much had he read and what opinions had he formed and how frank could he be in expressing them? The steam from his electric kettle on the floor misted

193

his spectacles. He took them off to wipe them. His eyes looked flat and unfocused in his naked face.

'I wouldn't claim to be a man of action,' he said. 'But I like to imagine I can read the times and the seasons. I see it all as a mythical confrontation. Between the authentic myth and the false myth. Between true poetry and the pomp and circumstances of propaganda. An age old confrontation, Mr Peredur More, between the panoply and might of the oppressor and the praise-poetry of the oppressed. David and Goliath. The remnant of ancient resistance and the leviathan state. With subtle variations. Think of a Welsh socialist riding in a golden coach with the helpless captive figure of the monarchical establishment – and both protected and escorted by the combined might of arms and propaganda of the centralized state. What else can it be except a confrontation between the exercise of power for its own sake and the authentic note of a people's poetry?'

He buttoned up his new tweed jacket and looked pleased with himself. I was pleased for him. It was pleasant for the breath of eloquence to make itself felt on a tongue that had long been subdued and silent. On the small area of wall not covered by bookshelves and glass-fronted cupboards, he had put up a framed sepia photograph of a former librarian who had been noted for his plain speaking. The tutelar of the place. A stalwart expositor of seventeenth-century Welsh dissent. Supervisor of Hefin Mather's first research work. His mentor and his hero. The model of his new manner?

'It was your father's generation that did it, you know,' Mather said. 'Your father and his friends. No doubt about that. They revived the national spirit by returning to the source: the essential poetic vision. It seemed poor politics at the time. It didn't win votes. But now, Peredur More, now it will bear fruit. The people will awaken. The tide of protest will bring back that degree of freedom without which no nation can survive.'

He handed me a mug of tea and winked. I was obliged to smile. He was singing the right song, only it was slightly out of tune. Or perhaps I had not adjusted myself to the change in his status. I could barely recognize that first arbiter between my father's shade and me. That gloom between the

194

library stacks was a more fitting token of the mouth of Avernus.

'Mind you, one has to be careful,' he said. He blew on his mug of tea to cool it. 'There's a very odd character ensconced at the back of Oliver Simons's office. Seems to have very little to do all day. Except poke about in the students' records in Registry.' He winked again. His habitual conspiratorial manner was reasserting itself. 'Simons calls him an accountant and murmurs letters like UGC and DES. The man's a Cockney, anyway. A suburban Londoner, to be more exact. And he's got feet like a policeman.' Mather leaned closer to speak in more confidential tones. 'SB,' he said. 'Rumour has it that he's from the Special Branch of the Metropolitan Police.'

Gossip, no doubt, was a relief to his cloistered existence. The fact that a man looks secretive does not mean that he can keep a secret. I should inform myself in greater detail about Hefin Mather's background. He had a home to go to and a wife who prepared the sandwiches he nibbled. More than that I knew nothing.

'There's a lot of writing about your family going on these days,' he said. 'In one way or another.'

He knew a great deal more about me. If there was gossip in circulation I did not want my father's lost papers to be any part of it. If Mather's tongue was loosened there was no knowing how much information had already been released. I was, of course, in his debt. He had more control of me than I had of him. Half the books on the linoleum floor were open. Neither he nor I could move easily in the confined space without treading on them.

'I don't know if you know Gareth Hopkin,' he said.

I shook my head. The name had a familiar ring about it. Redolent, somehow, of South Wales valleys and rugby fifteens and transfer fees to rugby league. Hefin stretched back in his mahogany swivel chair. Like the room, the chair had probably belonged to the tutelar whose portrait hung in solitary solemnity on the wall.

'It seems his sister does your mother's hair. She also sings. A valleys nightingale.'

He was the host. I was the visitor and intruder in

195

unfamiliar surroundings. I had no tenure here as he had. I was in his debt. Was he now about to exact some form of payment?

'He's very keen to meet you,' Mather said. 'I said I'd pass the message on.'

I was not at all keen to meet him. For some reason I saw his sister's large feet in their court shoes moving reverently around my mother as she put the finishing touches to a blatantly artificial coiffure.

'He's writing some kind of history about Wales and the Spanish Civil War. He's been at it for years. A chequered history, I'd call it. Originally conceived as his passport to academic respectability. He was trapped in a Sec. Mod. for years. His wife died, poor chap. Then this sister of his came up to keep house for him. Then he got into the Teachers' Training College. A sort of halfway house he calls it – halfway to what I don't exactly know. In any case he's renewed his attack on his thesis. He's researching the life and times of a communist agitator called Penry Lewis. Pen Lewis. Quite a hero. Gave his life to the cause in Spain. As far as I can make out, a close friend of your father's. That's what he wants to talk to you about.'

I tried not to look embarrassed. As far as close friendship was concerned, this Pen Lewis had been closer, surely, to my mother. He was almost certainly Gwydion's natural father. Why should I say 'almost'? Did I need to protect my mother's reputation even when talking to myself? Voluntary burdens are the heaviest. Hefin Mather was being lofty and magnanimous about my mother's hairdresser's brother. What an artificial and absurd order of precedence. My mother's head exists in order to provide Maud Hopkin's hands with something to do when not looking after her brother.

'Not a bad chap,' Hefin Mather said. 'He's got a bee in his bonnet about being working class. As a matter of fact his father was a local government official and his mother kept a corner shop in Aberdare. We have arguments, you know. Quite interesting arguments. If you dropped in here around eleven o'clock on a Tuesday or possibly a Friday morning you could meet him. That is, if you wanted to.'

196

Silence was my best defensive weapon. It would squeeze more information out of Mather and oblige him to clarify his own motivation. It was surely more than an urge to enhance a reputation for doing academic favours. Librarians liked to be thanked for their helpfulness and unfailing courtesies and indispensable cooperation.

'He's a bit gone on Gramsci,' Mather said. ' "Gramsci said this" and "Gramsci said that". That's understandable for a communist trying to shake off the shackles of Lenin and Stalin. But I tell him he's got it all back to front. The language and the nation take precedence over class every time. Culture cuts deeper than economics, I say. Iron replaced stone for religious rather than economic reasons, I say. And all forms of culture are techniques of perpetuating the existence of the tribe, I say. And then he accuses me of being racist! Proper ding-dong arguments we have up here. You ought to hear us at it.'

My response was not enthusiastic. My concern was my father and his fate. I had no wish to dissipate my energies in fruitless disputation with a pair of nondescript academics. Mather was more perceptive than I realized. He had divined the direction my thoughts were taking.

'Your father was caught up in the same debate,' he said. 'I think that is what interests Gareth Hopkin. Like so many in the thirties your father was torn between the socialist vision and the processes of national regeneration in Wales. My view is that these two movements were artificially polarized by the massive worldwide power struggle of the Second World War. They are not necessarily incompatible. And I think it is only a matter of time before Hopkin discovers chapter and verse in Gramsci that will permit him to accept this analysis.'

Mather slapped the palm of his hand on an open book and burst out laughing. He no longer contented himself with a quiet giggle. I was impressed by the transformation. And by the representation of my father as a figure straddled across an ideological abyss. Not a comfortable position for anyone. For a poet with one skin less than an ordinary person, a Promethean torture.

I just wished Gareth Hopkin would leave. The rumble of his resonant voice and his unexpected good looks were agreeable enough at first. He was recognizably Maud Hopkin's brother, but altogether better looking. So much so that he was inclined to glance at himself as he paced past the only large mirror in the manse. His nose was as aquiline as hers was beaky; her diffidence was obliterated by his sonorous confidence. His raven curls were touched with tasteful grey at the temples while his face was becomingly lined by the sadness of losing his wife at such an early age. He wore expensive clothes with that touch of flamboyance which one tended to expect from the valleys. There was a thick gold ring on his little finger that he enjoyed turning.

'Her credentials,' he said. 'Impeccable.' He had been sucked into my mother's myth-making apparatus. He stared at me without blinking. Not a fly could land on him without his knowing it. 'Labour lads and Labour lords,' he said. 'They all look up to her. Title seems to help somehow. A touch of glamour. Funny how the comrades seem to love it.'

The last thing I would allow him to browse around in would be my father's papers. He kept up the pressure. His aquiline nose rooted about in the twilight. I refrained from switching on the light in the hope that nightfall would make him conscious of the passage of time. I was expecting Wenna. I would appreciate the time to prepare myself both physically and mentally for her visit. I might even shave and certainly wash under my armpits. I would like to meditate on the marvel of her existence and the greater marvel of her coming to me. This restless creature Hopkin was convinced I was withholding something of value. That was true enough. But I resented the rucking and shoving and the elbowing assiduity of a mud-spattered forward that his peer group down there exalted as a major virtue. I held my ground. I knew Hefin Mather would have been too mindful of his own exposed position in the library to blurt out the whole truth. But he had been unable to resist dropping hints.

'A remarkable woman, your mother,' Hopkin said. 'A remarkable story.'

He expected me to be flattered by parroting this chorus. I was merely relieved. It meant he was still safely on the outside. So far he had not wormed himself sufficiently into Amy's confidence to discover anything of real significance about her relationship with my father.

'I mean there was an alliance there, wasn't there? Pen Lewis and John Cilydd More. Wasn't there?'

My father and Pen Lewis had collaborated in Aid for Spain campaigns. I told him that. He knew it already. He continued to harass me with penetrating stares as though he suspected me of concealing vital information.

'I think there was a pact, you know,' he said. 'I'm pretty sure of it. Not that I have anything in writing. They couldn't both go. Pen was the one without family responsibilities. So he slipped off. Caught a bus at the bottom of the road and went off to fight. Never to come back.'

I had agreed to see him to oblige Hefin Mather who was my benefactor. Was this chap trying to wear me down by delaying his departure? Two more minutes and I would rise to my feet and tell him he had overstayed his welcome. When Wenna came to the manse on her bicycle it was always after dark. She hid her bicycle in the old washhouse behind the chapel. I had had a copy made of the key of the front door and it was my intention to give it to her this evening. There were things that were better kept secret, she said, and I was ready to agree with her. It accorded with my nature. And yet in her case I would have been happy to announce our relationship from every rooftop in the village.

'They were heroes. Legendary heroes,' Gareth Hopkin was saying. 'They were men prepared to give their lives for a noble cause. We must never forget that.'

He was expecting visible signs of agreement like a vote of confidence. The rumbling sonority of his miner's institute voice was like a licence to lecture and lead. It was exactly the exhortatory pulpit tradition from which my father had shied away. I considered discussing the phenomenon with Hefin Mather. I concluded that too much detachment was an inappropriate luxury. Today the struggle – the urgency of revolutionary commitment.

'I'll be off then,' he said.

I jumped to my feet with such alacrity that he smiled. Up to that moment my responses had been so guarded. Now, however briefly, he had caught me out. My apology was ineffective.

'I have a great deal to see to,' I said.

'I'm sorry to have taken your time . . .' Huffed as he was he did not fail to glance in the mirror when I switched on the light. 'There's a lot to be done,' he said. 'People haven't really begun to understand that period, you know. Maybe it's still too close to us. There was so much idealism around. In those twenty years between the two wars. Idealism rampant. The new intelligentsia, instead of providing the class from which they sprang – the *gwerin*, the working class – with organic systems of values, let themselves be harnessed – hooked – by idealism, to give the hegemony of the bourgeoisie in Wales an extended lease of life. Do you follow me?'

His head thrust towards me as we stood outside the front door of the manse. I understood him but I had no intention of following him. It was chilly outside. I had a reasonable excuse to retreat to the shelter of the doorway. I watched his departure. The car lights switched on and Hopkin reversed with great caution between the overgrown bushes. It was startling to hear Wenna's voice murmur behind me.

'I thought that man was never going to go,' she said.

She had come in through the back door while Hopkin and I were still in the house. She wore a leather belt to keep her long black cloak together. Underneath she wore a mini skirt of the same material. I was entranced by her presence. I wanted to pay her lavish compliments: about her beauty, the way she walked, her hair, her dark blue eyes. She could have been a mannequin, I wanted to tell her. She had no need of compliments. It was I that yearned to express them. She prowled about the kitchen looking for something to eat. I stared at the width of her stride as though I were measuring it.

'I like this place,' she said. I don't know whether she spoke more deliberately because she could see I hung on her every word. 'Great hide-out,' she said. 'There's a big difference between a "hide-out" and a "safe house." '

She was no more than a girl. Not twenty-one yet. Almost nine years my junior. Yet she was initiating me to the ways of a world of which I was absurdly ignorant. When she spoke of '68 it seemed a place that I myself had never visited. She often smiled as she restrained herself from asking where I had been. Where, indeed, had I been? Licking my wounds in Redbatch. Absorbed in the petty injustices of an alien academic life.

'What did he want?' Wenna's mouth was full and she still continued to look elegant and beautiful. Her gesture with a piece of crudely buttered sliced loaf was as graceful as the movement of a swan's neck. Her fingers holding the bread belonged to the birth of Venus. She had begun to laugh. 'Do you know what my mother calls him? Hop-y-deri-dando.'

Because she accented the first syllable and was so amused, I laughed as heartily as I could, although I failed to make any real connection beween the nonsense line and the man who had just left me. Mothers and daughters who understood each other laughed easily at all sorts of things that baffled other people.

'He came courting,' Wenna said. 'A frog he would a-wooing go . . .' She was amused by the startled expression on my face. 'My mother was sorry for him. I don't think it crossed her mind in the first instance that Hop-y-deri was after her. But then it went from bad to worse. He transferred his intentions from the mother to the daughter.'

I was instantly jealous. The creature was handsome, even Byronic in his own rather bombastic valleys way. The kind of man many women would go for. The kind of man who, in any courtship race or ritual, was certain to carry off the prize. What exactly was the nature of Wenna's laughter? Was it triumph at having captivated a man twice her own age? She was smiling in a tantalizing way and looking at me from the corners of her eyes.

'A male chauvinist of the worst kind.' I was so relieved to hear the soft condemnation. 'All he wanted was someone to boss in bed as well as in the kitchen and the classroom.'

Mother and daughter had amused themselves at the

courting man's expense. It satisfied me to learn how easily their combined wiles anticipated every move the pedagogic marxist could make. They had been proof against all his tactical manoeuvres. Nothing had happened. Wenna took a swig of milk from the bottle in the fridge.

'I thought I'd spend the night,' she said. 'Is that all right with you?' She held out the milk bottle, asking my leave to drink out of it having already done so. The goddess had come to me in a shower of gold milktops. I was doing cartwheels in the sand dunes, defying gravity, laughing at the sky. I had only to stretch out my arms and I would become immortal.

I didn't care how much she laughed at me. She could teach me to laugh at myself. The freedom we found in each other could take over the universe. Should we eat first or go straight to bed? Like unarmed guerrillas or runaway children we made a rough supper in the kitchen. We transformed the drab, distempered walls into an outlaws's cave in the depth of the forest. The marvel was that Wenna enjoyed it as much as I did. The bedroom was ice-cold and there were no curtains at the window. We hugged each other and looked at the stars. I saw the starlight in her eyes, and the dark outline of the houses in the village street that looked like a geological formation. The world was our garden. Our conversation flowed through it like a warm stream in which we could immerse at will. Together we created it.

'You came back looking for a people,' Wenna said. 'And you found the language shaming them into existence. What's this chapel called?'

'Horeb,' I said.

'Well, there you are. "Thou shalt smite the rock, and there shall come water out of it, that the people may drink and think." Let the people drink.'We managed to black out most of the window with a blanket. We lit a candle and dragged furniture about as if we were building barricades.

'Back to basics,' Wenna said. 'Down with three-piece suites.'

We went to bed together fully clothed. In the warmth we created between us we took our time to peel off our clothes.

She was so soft and kind to me, it was beyond good fortune. Life had become a succession of miracles. Whatever wishes she had, it was my privilege to fulfil them. And she murmured the same to me.

'We suit each other, don't we?' she said. 'You must come inside me.'

From words to incoherence, from the cold to sweat that glued our bodies together. Wenna put on her cloak and went to peep through the blanket at the stars. There seemed a message in everything she did. To catch a glimpse of her nakedness in the candlelight was the world's original marvel. I couldn't lose her or live without her. She had become my life and I was committed to her as to no other person on earth. All I wanted was to ask her to marry me. I couldn't fathom why it should be such an awkward question to ask. She had to know how much I loved her. Our heads were on the same pillow. Our bodies were physically pliant, gentle and understanding. There was no secret in my entire life I would not gladly reveal to her. Why should I be afraid of asking, and muffle my voice in the pillow?

'Wenna. Will you marry me?'

She heard me. I felt her stiffen. This was different from the easy flow of confidence and disclosure. It imposed a silence between us that had not existed before. As if she had slipped away from me, or some generation gap of which I had been unaware had opened in the bed between us. This was a generation that behaved according to its own new light and cared nothing for convention or commendation or approval. At college I had seen such young women all around me. But Wenna was different. She was unique and I never wanted to lose her. I could only ask her the same question again, more distinctly.

'Marry me.'

She had stiffened to stop herself laughing. My distress forced me to sit up. She pulled me down again and covered me with maternal care.

'What about poor Sven?' she said. She was stroking my head to soothe me.

'Who the hell is Sven?'

I knew it was a petulant outburst. Whoever he was I didn't

want him to exist. It allowed her to laugh outright. Sven. Sven. What kind of a bloody name was that? I just restrained myself from saying it.

'We were lovers.' The cool statement was like a knife in my side. She held me close to her. 'Listen. In Paris. Our light-headed lot were on our way to a pop concert. Things were happening in the streets. We were watching from the terrace of a café on the Boul Mich. Kids from Wales. Trembling with excitement. You can just imagine. Then suddenly this blonde boy was sitting right in the middle of us and talking as though he had known us all his life. Terrible French. The other girls pushed me next to him. A wild-looking lot of riot police swept down the street. They were looking for Sven. That's how I met him.'

'You loved him.'

That's all I could think about. Her copulating with this blonde stranger. The *événements* or whatever they call them could not have been further from my thoughts. I was being scorched by jealousy. My skin burnt under the touch of her hands.

'For a whole week,' she said. 'Ten days to be exact.'

'Have you seen him since?' My life hung on her answer.

'We wrote. Every day. And then less often. Now he's in prison. In some awful German town.'

'Will you go to him? When he comes out?'

She was shaking her head. That in itself was some measure of relief. 'I'm not going to make the same mistake as my mother,' she said. 'His world is not mine. It was an experience. A stretching experience. For that one must be grateful.'

This was to distance herself from my possessive desire for marriage. That I could understand, but not accept. Did she want to distance herself from me? I was ready to argue with her until daybreak.

'You go to chapel,' I said. 'You play the organ. You even go to Sunday School.'

I thought of the people who idolized her. Members of my extra-mural class who said what a good girl she was. Her mother. Mr and Mrs Lloyd Tai Hirion. When she was at home she was an ornament of local life. The dutiful daughter

204

who waited hand and foot on a mother who had been treated rather badly by fate or this, that and the other.

'That's my cover,' Wenna said. 'Now you know.'

How was it possible to experience so much elation and dejection within such a short space of time. Did that mean only the numb and bloodless were qualified to pass judgement?

'No self-respecting revolutionary can get by without a cover,' she said.

My love for her filled me with foreboding. Did she enjoy the capacity to gamble light-heartedly with her own life? Or was she still a child playing dangerous games? In either case my concern for her could only grow. Love was a grim commitment.

'Now look how much I'm telling you,' she said. 'I'm your hostage. That's much better than being your wife.' It was agonizingly beautiful that she was prepared to comfort me. She whispered in my ear. 'I'll be your cover,' she said. 'And you can be mine. We'll never be far away from each other. Can you think of a better way of threading yourself through the labyrinth of living?'

iii

The sky was as grey as the castle walls. I was close enough to the massive dressed stones to touch them. One of the speakers had said they were cemented into place by centuries of immutable sovereignty and oppression. This was a protest meeting and there were unlimited opportunities for anger and indignation. But the mood of the thousands assembled between the castle and the old-fashioned harbour was festive and cheerful. As I struggled to attain a higher perch on the slanting foundation of the south wall of the castle, I could see the youth and innocence of so many upturned faces and it moved me as innocence *en masse* always does. Young men with long hair and guitars provided protest songs through crackling microphones. In spite of the chill everyone was amazingly patient. Impassioned speeches were sporadic but loudly applauded. Organization was

205

minimal; students carried numerous banners, all rickety and homemade. Rousing choruses were taken up with roaring enthusiasm, repeated and then dropped while everyone wondered what would happen next. It was as good-humoured as a rugby international where the result was a foregone conclusion, and as casual as a pop concert. I wanted to be part of it. It was for this as much as anything else that I had come back.

I could see no sign of Wenna. Her absence was even more disturbing than her presence. In so short a time I had come to depend on her like an addict on a drug. My existence was suspended from hers. We had agreed to meet at this corner. There was no sign of her.

Sleeping together was an uneasy ecstasy. The last time, I woke and my hand reached out for the space where she had been lying. There was a candle burning low on the floor. A memory of a single yellow light reflected in a hotel dressing-table mirror came flooding back and the dry warmth of a hotel bedroom and my mother's large bed empty. I found Wenna squatting on the floor of the dining-room reading my father's notebooks. She had a blanket over her shoulders and her cloak underneath it. She looked childlike and vulnerable and I was filled with love and affection for her. She made a gesture of despair towards my father's papers on the floor and tightened the blanket around her shoulders.

'They were looking for a people that didn't exist,' she said. 'A country that wasn't there.'

I understood what she meant. There was something pathetic about my father and his friends. Pathetic and noble. The classic pathos and nobility of the lost cause. That was what she meant. We understood each other so well. Our conversation bound us together more closely even than our lovemaking. It was this flow that embraced us both with equal warmth. She shivered with the cold and I led her back to bed.

'They were so naive,' she said. 'So ignorant of the true nature of power. It never seems to have occurred to them in the context of their own desperate situation that the armed struggle was the only way to carry a paralyzed political process forward.'

I admired her so much. It was astonishing that she could be

206

so intelligent and so beautiful and even more remarkable that I was the person chosen to whom she could say anything. The frankness between us was like sunlight. She spoke with affectionate contempt of her mother's way of life.

'It's understandable, bless her. That she should wrap all that activity around her. The school, the chapel, Plaid Cymru, Yr Urdd. Her Welsh way of life. One good cause after another. She made that one great romantic mistake when she was young. Making love to a prisoner of war. A handsome young man carrying a hair comb instead of a gun in his dyed brown battle-dress. And here I am. The result. Devoting herself to my upbringing. And all the time the seeds of revolution springing up inside me.'

She was shaking with laughter under the bedclothes. I was entranced by her: by everything she said, everything she did. She was comic about her father and her Italian relatives, and even more contemptuous of their way of life.

'My great-aunts in Lucca live as if Garibaldi never landed,' she said. 'The atmosphere of that house. Stifling. Mothballs and lavender. And the quiet bickering and backbiting that goes on at the factory between the two factions – my father's two brothers. The only time they are happy is when they are dining in public. On a warm summer night with Chinese lanterns in the trees and good food on the tables. That's what my father ran away from. Into his own cage. Blackboards. Chalk dust. Irregular verbs.'

I could only marvel at her maturity and wisdom. Was it possible that this slip of a girl lying naked in the bed alongside me was a natural leader? The incarnation of a cause? Where is she now? She should have been here. To give the untidy occasion a cutting edge: liberty leading the people. I scanned the faces behind me on the edge of the crowd. I saw Hefin Mather with Gareth Hopkin. They both stood a little apart from the mass: a pair of detached but benevolent sympathizers with the cause. Hefin had seen me. He was grinning and beckoning. Even at a distance I could see he was seizing the chance to bring Hopkin and myself together and create an encounter. It was impossible to pretend I had not seen them. Also, Wenna's account of

Hopkin paying court first to her mother and then to herself inclined me to want to examine the fellow in a fresh light. Now Hefin was making a sequence of strange notions like the half-concealed gestures of a would-be tick-tack man at a race meeting. When I joined them he put first one finger and then another to his lips.

'Can you see them?' he said. 'Can't you see them? I can see them.'

Had he been less cheerful he could have been Orestes talking about the Kindly Ones. Hopkin had exiled his hands to the depth of the pockets of his black duffle coat. Everything about his stance demonstrated he was there as spectator, not a participant.

'Special Branch men with cameras.' Hefin gave me the information in strictest confidence. 'See that chap over there?' He nodded in the direction of a bulky individual about my own age, bareheaded with auburn curls stirring in the breeze from the open sea. 'I told you about him,' Hefin said. 'In Oliver Simons's office. Sitting there all day going through students' records. That's him. Look at his feet. Couldn't be anything else but a policeman.'

'Child's play.' Gareth Hopkin made emphatic comment. 'That's what it all is. The investiture included. Irrelevant. Of no consequence whatsoever.' The sonority of his voice gave added weight to the decision. It was his custom to make pronouncements that the world would be well advised to listen to.

'The popular will,' Hefin Mather said. He was issuing a challenge. His head jerked up and the glint on his spectacles reproduced the roguish academic twinkle in his eye. 'The people searching for authentic cultural forms,' he said.

Hopkin was not prepared to take such matters lightly. He took himself and his ideas seriously. I respected him for that. I was inclined that way myself. His interest in Morfydd and Wenna Ferrario showed at least that he was a man of taste and some discrimination. He stood before me now, both as a model and a warning. He was a serious historian well-equipped for a responsible job; he was also a self-absorbed chauvinist unaware of his own excessive partiality to the nexus of male power. Wenna had exposed this weakness in his character with such ease. I had to be on constant guard not to exhibit comparable faults in my own behaviour.

'Three weeks,' Hopkin said. He raised three fingers of a gloved hand. 'That's all they'll need. By way of a publicity barrage. Three weeks and you'll have ninety per cent of the population out on the streets singing "God bless the Prince of Wales".'

An orator was spelling out defiance and whipping up a more determined response. He challenged the crowd with his questions and won a thunderous applause.

'It's warming up,' Hefin Mather said.

Gareth Hopkin shook his head mournfully. He refused to get carried away. 'They won't get far against the telly and the Tory press,' he said. 'Three weeks. That's all they'll need.'

'That's pessimism,' Hefin said. 'And it goes against ninety per cent of your Gramsci and your Goldman and your Adorno. This is affirmative art, man. It's bound to win through in the end.'

Gareth Hopkin's mouth curved downwards. His handsome face as he shook his head was like a mask of doom. I wanted to leave them to go in search of Wenna. She knew about the cameras taking pictures of the faces in the crowd. Hefin Mather held on to my arm. He seemed to be seeking my approval.

'Do you know what I've found out?'

Gareth Hopkin had moved away a few paces as if he had wished to detach himself from our commitment to the protest rally. I was inclined to press him on the subject of working-class revolt. Would nothing less than a general strike fit in with his critical theory? And when the barricades went up, on which side would he be and what would he be holding in both hands? Why did his theory allow him so little sympathy for this struggle for cultural survival? Why should marxist and fascist theoreticians alike use 'separatism' and 'localism' as terms of abuse? I knew why and I was ready to dance on the tarmac under our feet to accompany my comprehensive answer. Because they were both techniques of centralized power and could not bear the notion of people enjoying the authentic freedom of self-government. Hopkin had his back turned to us. Hefin Mather was urgently seeking my attention. He had made a discovery. In his academic way of life that was a major event.

'Tasker Thomas is still alive,' he said. 'Isn't that amazing?'

It was and it wasn't. The man who stood in the headlights of my father's car. Being alive at all was amazing. That haunting, beatific smile in the white light. Statistics show that more and more people are surviving well into their eighties. Living, to me, is a great wonder. Was he still smiling? This is not a zone of my experience where I could encourage Hefin Mather to trespass.

'He's in some kind of home for retired ministers. Off the promenade at Llandrillo.'

Momentarily I saw them in bow windows looking out to sea: rows of old men in clerical collars. Hefin Mather was waiting for my response. I was ungenerous in not thanking him for the information. If I went to see Tasker Thomas I would not want Mather with me inhibiting my inquiries. Gareth Hopkin was giving us his attention.

'You two want to come for a coffee?'

I looked up. The light picked out the lens of a camera in an embrasure of the castle walls. It was a change from molten pitch or poisoned arrows. Further discussion with Hopkin and Mather might not be unwelcome, if only to clarify my own position. Are the values and aspirations of these young people determined by their social class or by their perception of their national identity? If I could frame the question with the proper aerodynamic qualities it would penetrate the heart of Hopkin's ideological defences. The rally was forming up for a march through the walled town, led by a local silver band. Should we join it? Gareth Hopkin was turning down his mouth again and shaking his head.

'They are making it easier for the police to photograph them,' he said.

Hefin Mather was rubbing his hands to show he was feeling chilly. He put his suggestion to both of us in turn. 'What about Bobby Bobs?' he said. 'They've got nice coffee and cakes.'

A brief vision of Hefin Mather's paradise: a café corner

table under a starched white cloth, cups of milky coffee, animated discussion, a plate of fancy cakes. Bobby Bobs, officially Robert Roberts, was one of his haunts. I had nothing better to do, unless I joined the march. There were buses parked between the fountain and the war memorial. To pass between them was a short cut that would avoid the traffic and the crowds and lead us to the welcoming windows of Bobby Bobs. Wenna descended from a bus in front of our eyes. If she saw me or my companions she made no sign. We watched her cross the square and enter a dingy-looking travel agency. She was fashionably dressed in a combination of reds I had not see her wear before. The long scarf was attached to the collar of her coat. The small cap on the crown of her head was the same colour. She did not look at all like a student. She was at her most italianate. I wanted to murmur again to someone about Piero della Francesca or Raphael or Pollaiuolo or any Renaissance name. I had the right to boast about our special relationship.

'You want to watch out for that one.'

Gareth Hopkin's voice reverberated close to my ear. A bus engine was switched on. The length of the vehicle trembled on our right. He had been sharp enough to detect my interest in the girl. It mirrored something he himself had felt. What we had in common was a desire to marry her. I longed to laugh. The noise of the bus made me raise my voice. I looked him in the eye and kept a straight face.

'Why?' I asked. 'Is she dangerous?'

iv

The elderly inmate sat as immobile as a carved Buddha within a few feet of the television set. The picture on the large screen needed readjusting. It was a schools' programme. I could see the flickering image of a lecturer shaking a piece of chalk in his hand like a dice and his mouth contorting without any sound emerging that I could hear. Outside the sun was shining brilliantly and orderly rows of daffodils drew attention to themselves in the flower beds in front of the residential home for retired ministers. The

211

matron invited me to sit on a worn settee with uneven springs. A scent of furniture polish was being overpowered by the odour of boiled cabbage wafting down the corridor from the kitchen. The matron was very much in charge. She tapped the solid shoulder of the television watcher. His body bulged inside his clerical grey suit. There seemed some indefinable correspondence between the folds of fat on his nape and the thickness of the frame of the black spectacles that lent a grave sobriety to the bald, spherical head. The matron called out in a loud voice.

'Mr Griffiths! It's such a lovely day. Why don't you go out for a walk?'

He waved her away with an imperious gesture. She smiled in my direction to show it was the response she expected.

'Mr Griffiths's son has a very important job in the BBC in London,' she said without lowering her voice. 'He feels it's his duty to keep an eye on things.' She moved about the room picking up magazines and journals. She was broad-built but active, a vessel determined to sail on an even keel. 'Otherwise he's a very good boy,' she said. 'You have to keep your sense of humour. Did you see Dr Dylan standing in the passage?'

I had seen an unusually thin cleric with a turnip-watch in his hand apparently checking the time with the grandfather clock, which sent out a tick like a leaden tread along the corridor.

'A most brilliant man,' the matron said. 'So they tell me. But bitterly disappointed. His congregation never appreciated him. There were machinations among the deacons and the presbytery to get him to retire before his time. He's been with us for years. He's expecting the end of the world. He doesn't know the day, but he's quite definite it will be three o'clock in the afternoon. That's why he's always so fussy about the correct time. As I say, it's all right so long as you hang on to your sense of humour. Are you related to the Reverend Tasker?'

I shook my head. 'He was a friend of the family,' I said.

The matron showed she would appreciate more information.

'He baptized me,' I said. 'And, I think, my brothers as well. I'm not sure. I shall have to ask him.'

212

The way she looked at me suggested that she was wondering why none of us had ever visited him before. I felt I had told her enough. I studied the series of glum engravings of biblical subjects in their uniform brown wooden frames and the pattern of faded green singing birds peeping out of the trellised leaves on the wallpaper. There were obvious financial restrictions, but the place was clean and well run. The exchange of information had come to an end. She had many duties to attend to. She gave me to understand that elderly clerics in spite of their lifelong apprenticeship to virtue were even more helpless than males in general. The matron looked at Mr Griffiths in front of the television set.

'It's amazing,' she said. 'He never falls asleep in front of it. When the others want to watch a programme, he trots off to his room.'

A group of retired ministers were clapping their gloved hands at the front door. They sounded boyishly boisterous as they took turns to wipe their boots on the area of coconut matting on which the word CROESO could still be deciphered. The matron raised her head to smile and call out.

'Mr Thomas! Mr Tasker Thomas! A visitor for you. In here.'

They stood in the doorway, their mouths open. Tasker Thomas's companions were even more curious than he was. He wore an open-necked khaki shirt. His three friends wore clerical collars of varying width. The fact that he did not recognize me intensified their curiosity. They parked their hats on the hatstand in the hall and returned at speed in case my revelations were made in their absence. One of them gave Tasker a gentle shove into the room. He had shrunk inside his large frame. I would have recognized his smile by its width although it could no longer be described as beatific. The fluff of hair he had left was still foxy-red. His shoulders were bent with arthritic old age. This thrust his head forwards so that his eyes caught more light. They were bright with what I took to be distilled intelligence. He had no idea who I was. His welcome was as generalized as sunlight.

'Peredur More,' I said.

He repeated the name more than once, each time giving it greater resonance. When the full truth of my identity dawned

213

on him he turned to share the amazing discovery with his friends. They in turn were happy to be astonished.

'The son of John Cilydd More,' Tasker said. 'A national winner, friends. A splendid poet.'

They all knew about my father. Or claimed they did. One lifted his right hand to require silence while he recited the piece about the hawk descending. The others supported him by repeating the last line.

' "The singing dies",' they said. 'Oh yes, "the singing dies".'

This gave Tasker Thomas the time he needed to warm up his powers of recall. His finger trembled as he pointed at me.

'I baptized this young man.' He was pleased to inform his friends. 'And I'll tell you something else. I baptized him on the coffin of dear old Nathan Harris. Do you remember Nathan Harris?'

It was fairly clear they didn't. Not that they were unwilling to make the effort. They frowned and nudged each other and demonstrated that they would be grateful if Tasker Thomas would refresh their memory.

'Stricken with arthritis,' Tasker said. 'Worse than anything you could imagine. Yet stalwart and uncomplaining. A pure fountain of the faith.'

'Now then, boys,' the matron said. 'Who would like a cup of tea?'

They all responded positively except Mr Griffiths who did not take his eyes off the television screen. The thin Dr Dylan had wandered in, momentarily relieved since it was past three o'clock in the afternoon. He stood with his back to the wall watching his colleagues as though he envied their blithe disregard of the doom that had been postponed for only one more day. Tasker had his hand on my shoulder. The others began talking in animated fashion.

'We are a cheerful lot,' he said. 'As you can see for yourself. We are in the world, you see, but not of the world. That's a way of putting it. We were just discussing this investiture business, weren't we, lads?'

He wanted their attention and they gave it. A minister filling his pipe pointed the stem mischievously at Tasker.

'He's very cross,' he said. 'He hasn't had an invitation.'

214

They laughed so much that Mr Griffiths turned around in his chair to express brief but intense disapproval. Tasker was eager to show he shared the joke. But he had a serious point to make.

'I was telling the fellows,' he said. 'These things are always thrust upon us. It's politicians' mummery. And they send in their secret police to mop up the dew left by the spirit of our old saints. Their alien law and order to suppress the spontaneous loyalty of our young people to the loving language and way of life of their ancestors. And do you know who I feel sorry for? The Queen's son. That poor lad Charles. And the politicians dragging him by the hair through their silly circus.'

The minister with a pipe felt his joke was worth trying out again. He pointed his pipe at Tasker.

'Aren't I telling you,' he said. 'He's just jealous because he hasn't had an invitation.'

Tasker was too intensely involved in his train of thought to notice.

'I'm not a republican,' he said. 'At least, I don't think I am. Or have ever been. But a guardian of the faith. Yes. What else are we for? Why were we called? Not to stand idly by while the beasts of corruption trample the white vineyard.'

He had struck a chord. His colleagues responded with approval, to his eloquence and to the sentiment it expressed. I touched his arm to gain his attention.

'Mr Thomas,' I said. 'Could I have a word with you in private?'

His response was immediate, but for my taste over-elaborate. He put a finger to his lips, waved and nodded a private understanding with the matron, bade a temporary farewell to his walking companions and then guided me up the badly lit staircase to his room on the second floor. He threw open the door and waved me in.

'My cell,' he said. 'Not austere enough, of course. Providence and the Old Connexion have been kind to me, towards the end.'

There was hardly room to turn between his bed and the small writing table. The few books were all to do with the scriptures. There was a Greek New Testament on the locker and a chamber-pot under the bed.

'How much does a man need?' Tasker said. 'Look at my magnificent view.'

He stood by the window attempting to straighten his arthritic back and inviting me to contemplate the sea. The shadow of a cloud moving over the restless surface enlarged the vastness of the waters. Just looking at it made Tasker exultant. He raised his arm in an oratorical gesture.

' "Love like the sea",' he said. ' "Mercy like the ocean". It's there all the time and yet for years, you know, I never saw it. I was just telling the fellows as we walked along the promenade. Confessing, you could call it. When I was young, I thought "the Call" meant a call to carry the world's wounds in my own weak person. With His help, of course. But I was wrong. Wrong.' He was staring at me, imploring me to understand. 'I could have been doing more harm than good. That's what troubles me. We were asking each other cruel questions. Indirectly, of course. Did we fail every time? Was the world any better for all our efforts? They're good lads, you know. Hearts of gold. Soft gold, maybe, but gold all the same.'

He was smiling at me with such intensity that I became uncomfortable in the narrow room. It was difficult to formulate the questions I wanted to put to him. How could I say, just out of the blue, Mr Thomas, do you recall standing in the headlights of my father's car by the side of the lake? The old man was absorbed in giving voice to his revelation.

'It was out there all the time,' he said. 'The companion of mankind.' He waved at the sea as a self-evident truth. 'He's out there, whenever you care to look, walking on the water,' Tasker said. 'He's up there holding the sky on his back. He is the god of gods, very god of very god, begotten not made. Do you see what I mean? We can't flourish in this world without that supernatural dimension. Such a simple thing. And it's taken me a whole troubled lifetime to see it.'

There was only one chair to sit on. Tasker sat on the bed. It creaked under him. He called it his bunk. I had a fleeting vision of my father in the corner of the Nissen hut and Padre Thomas sitting on the edge of his iron cot. The same hands

216

folded in the same patient way. The same bones. The mottled skin now fifty years looser, but the same homiletic manner.

'The point is, dear boy, God in Christ did not come to call on the clever and intelligent alone. If that were the case what would happen to the rest of us? It had to be something simple. Like the sea. Simple and all-pervading. Every seashell a holy relic. Every pebble counted.' His eyes began to fill with tears as he contemplated the mystery he had conjured up for himself. He smiled at me. 'So you came back to us,' he said. 'The old language brought you back.' He pointed at me. He wanted to show his religion did not stop him being jolly. 'It's in the marrow of your bones,' he said. 'It holds the deepest secrets of your soul.' Even if it was true I wished he did not look so pleased with himself as he said it. The rays of his benevolent smile irritated my skin. 'Do you know, I think I used almost exactly the same words to your father, all those years ago. Isn't that strange? "It's the core of your being, dear friend," I said. "You can't live or breathe without it." '

'Why did he kill himself?'

At last I got the question out. Tasker Thomas clutched his hands against his chest as if he had suffered an unexpected blow.

'You must have noticed how happy we are here . . . the atmosphere . . .'

Was he begging me to leave him alone? He was silent and troubled. He opened his mouth and spoke at speed like a man who runs out of time and out of breath.

'I was always one for a community. A brotherhood. In one form or another. We were going to rebuild the old monastery on Saint's Island. An International Peace Centre. Your father drew up the deeds. Great visions we had. Visions and ambitions. There were houses in the valleys. A settlement for the unemployed. There were camps. There were houses in the slums. In the docks. And now here I am. A community of old men. Like Simeon we are – ready to depart in peace. I was never more at peace.'

He was pleading openly to be left alone.

'Did she drive him to it?'

217

I couldn't stop myself asking the question. If he was so keen on honesty and purity it was his duty to help me. Tears began to run down his cheeks. Old men cry easily.

'You mustn't blame your mother,' he said. 'You mustn't. I remember her as a young woman. She was like the springtime of the world. And that wonderful man Val Gwyn dying in the sanatorium. It broke her heart.'

'He killed himself,' I said. 'Was it because of her?'

He looked at the palms of his hands. He did not have the strength to struggle to his feet. 'You should leave me alone.' His head was lowered. He mumbled so that I could barely make out what he was saying. 'Why should you break in like this on my peace? When these old bones are learning to pray properly. For the first time.' He looked up, determined to face his accuser. 'He had a despair of the world,' he said. 'And perhaps of himself. I understood that. It could have been an accident. Perhaps the war caught up with him. It comes unexpectedly. Just like you coming here. At the moment you least expect it. You turn around and there it is. On the street or in the corner of the room. The shadow that brings you the guilt of a lifetime. Like a savings account, with its hand out, insisting that you take it.'

It wasn't really much use talking to him. Buried in his own fantasies. The only decent thing was to leave him alone. I rose to my feet.

'My mother never comes to see you?'

I couldn't resist a last question. The old man had recovered quickly.

'She thinks I'm a bit of a fool,' he said. 'I suppose most people do. She could be right, of course. I always had a great respect for her opinion.'

He held out his hand. He wanted me to pull him up on his feet. I was surprised how light he was.

'I have one secret,' he said. He was all smiles and confidence again. 'I know so little,' he said. 'What I do know is not worth knowing. But I can tell you this. Your father was a secret giver. More than your mother – bless her – ever knew.'

The word 'giver' seemed inappropriate. The image of our father we shared, Bedwyr, Gwydion and I, perhaps imposed

218

on our impressionable, childish minds by my mother, was that of a mean man who verged on being a miser.

'He drew up the deeds of this place,' Tasker Thomas said. 'And settled a decent sum of money on it, unbeliever as he was. Now there's something for you to be proud of, Peredur. I give you my secret. I wouldn't want to take it with me to the grave.'

v

The cliff road was formed by cutting away the limestone rock. We parked high above the sea so that we could look sheer down into the glittering water. Wenna had an old guidebook in her hands. She amused herself by reading out passages of pictorial prose.

' "These variations of altitude add greatly to the scenic beauty of the drive", Professor More!' She wanted the best possible view of the pier. ' "Rapidly climbs . . . continuing our course, we come to the best viewpoint . . ." There it is! Isn't it a beauty!'

I couldn't entirely account for her high spirits, but I was eager to share them. The pier was impressive, stretching into the deep blue sea for a distance of half a mile. Seen from this height, it was a model of daring human ingenuity, challenging the awesome extent of the sea. At the pierhead was a landing stage and concrete pavilion. On the deck of the pier people were no bigger than ants.

'Things haven't changed all that much,' Wenna said. 'Listen to this. "Steamboat passengers can land and embark at any state of the tide . . . and the concert pavilion has sitting accommodation for two thousand persons . . . The Right Honourable D. Lloyd George in the course of a speech during the late war said "Your air is a great pick-me-up. However depressed one may feel physically, I shall go back reinvigorated for the great task which confronts my colleagues and myself . . ." Wasn't that nice for him? Oh, and just listen to this. Carmen Sylva, Queen of Roumania no less: ". . .That my health has been so won-derfully restored is due to your climate and surroundings

219

which can only be compared to Italy . . ." So now you know, Professor More. Shall we go down and be invigorated?'

The bay was beautiful. It curved with the precision of a saucer's rim between the two massive limestone headlands. It was the first warm day of the year. There were early visitors on the promenade and family groups scattered about the shore already digging themselves in. As we left the car, a moment from childhood surfaced in my mind. I took hold of Wenna's arm. I wanted to tell her about it. On that very spot at the bottom of the flight of shallow steps that separated the promenade from the sand I had looked up from building a sandcastle to see a seaside photographer creep up on my mother and the man she was talking to. Who was he? And why was she so angry with the photographer?

Wenna looked at me and waited for me to be more specific about the incident. How could I interpret its true significance without unravelling before her eyes the lurid complexities of my childhood relationship with my mother? Why was the man so angry and why did my mother turn away from him so abruptly and look at me as if she needed my help? Wenna's patience gave out. She pulled off her red cardigan and handed it to me with her new Japanese camera. Underneath she wore a tight-fitting black polo-necked sweater.

'Come on,' she said. 'You can take my picture.'

The tide was as far out as it would ever go on this north shore. Wenna kicked off her shoes so that she could dance along the wet margin of the sea. Children stopped making moated sandcastles as her naked feet flew past. I trotted after her and she mocked my slowness by singing lines from a hymn about throwing away crutches and setting our feet free. Free she certainly was. She could circle like a seagull under the blue sky. This was April and she was the appointed guardian of my heaven's gate. On such a day as this in early spring there could not be anything more beautiful. I followed her to the pillars that held up the iron pier that had so much taken her fancy.

'Are you ready?'

She called out to me. It wasn't the picture of enchantment

I wanted to take. Whatever I took of this seascape needed her as the focal point. The picture would record this day as ours and no one else's – capture an incomparable moment, a unique fragment to reflect the beauty of creation that belonged exclusively to us. I shook my head and pointed out the black hood of shadow cast by the pier on the bright sand. She threw up both her arms and sounded cross.

'There's a flash on that thing! Just you shoot in the direction I point when I say "shoot".'

I could only do exactly what she told me. People watching at a distance would assume I was taking her picture. Every time she pointed and called out, her back was turned to the camera. This seemed absurd. She brushed my protestations aside.

'Do exactly as I tell you,' she said. 'Just shoot in the direction I point when I say "shoot".'

She danced about among the iron pillars and struts. It was an imposing structure as solid and unbending as the tide was restless, even on this calm day. Wenna pointed at the girders carrying the deck above our heads and I photographed them. She called out something about the elevation and the crest of the highest wave exerting intense pressure on the surroundings. She was disappointed when I called out that the film was finished. We left the shadow of the pier to sit in the sun.

'We could hire a boat,' she said. 'There are caves, you know, in the headlands. Did you know that? I would like to examine them. Not today perhaps. Some other time. When we can make proper arrangements. Will you come with me?'

'Of course I will,' I said. I was so totally in love with her it delighted me beyond words to agree with anything she chose to say.

'Do you know what I think, Professor More?'

She had taken it into her head lately to address me in this way. It didn't give me any pleasure, but if it amused her I suffered it gladly.

'If you don't blow a hole through the wall of history, it will bury you alive.' She pointed out to sea and the way it spread implacably to the horizon. 'A speedboat. A wet suit. A couple of limpet mines. And a lot of guts. That's all you'd need.'

221

'To do what?'

'Blow up the royal yacht,' she said. 'What else?'

It was hard to know how to react. Should I assume she was joking? Her manner was too thoughtful for that.

'It's the kind of thing you would get an Iron Cross or a VC for,' she said. 'Provided you were on the right side, of course.'

Now she was smiling, so I could laugh.

'There was a chap my father knew. His best friend at school. Devoted to Mussolini. He went into Bastia Harbour in some kind of midget submarine to blow up a French warship. He got caught like a fish in a steel net. When they pulled him up he was dead. Suffocated. It's no joke being a hero.'

I never imagined it was. And it had never occurred to me to blow up the royal yacht. Were we on the same side or was I bound to her simply by physical attraction? I believed the extra-mural class at Pantgwyn had justified its existence by bringing us together. She was the essence of what I had come back looking for. So what were these prisoner-of-war yarns and why tell them to me? Did I remind her of her father? Had she been closer to him than I had been given to understand? She and her mother were always nice about him in a pitying sort of way. I had imagined a weak, vacillating man who couldn't stand the Welsh climate, who never knew which side he was on in public or in family politics, who lurked in his classroom in a Roman suburb, a man among boys, and drove nervously in the noisy Roman traffic, a boy among men; not a friend of solitary heroes intent on blowing up warships and royal yachts.

'How am I to tell whether I can trust you?' she said.

She was pushing her slim fingers through the damp sand. It was exactly the kind of question I should have been asking her. I took hold of her hand. It felt small and cold and delicate.

'I would give my life for you,' I said.

I meant it. It didn't seem to be what she wanted to hear. She freed her hand to point at the pier.

'We are going to blow that up,' she said. 'A much easier target. And there would be no need for anyone to get hurt.'

222

My left leg began to tremble in a way I couldn't control. I had to shift on the sand so that Wenna should not see it. She was serious. I was involved whether I liked it or not.

'This is a propaganda war,' Wenna said. 'We don't mean to kill anybody. What we've got to do is influence public opinion.' She was talking to me seriously and gently. She had spotted how nervous I was. 'If we do nothing,' she said, 'history will bury us.'

She jumped to her feet, capable of any exertion. Were there only nine years between us? I was weighed down into the sand by fear and despair. I was all for protest. I was a dissenter by upbringing and inclination and by philosophical conviction. A bombing campaign was armed resistance. I wasn't trained for it. To partake in it would bring down the entire superstructure of law and order on my defenceless head. My skull wouldn't stand it. I would become an exposed victim of the might of the modern repressive state. Had this girl any idea what she was doing and demanding? This was the way infatuation evaporated, like a soap bubble.

'Are you coming?'

She was smiling at me. In a way, a beautiful stranger. If those photographs were developed I would only see her back. I had slept with her, made love to her, swum with her for hours on end in the same warm stream of conversation, and the sum total of my carnal and spiritual knowledge was nil. She led the way to the car without bothering to look back to see if I was following. When we were seated in the Triumph Herald, her chin slumped despondently on her chest and my love for her came flooding back. She was like a pretty child who had suffered a disappointment at a party.

'It's not intellectuals we need,' she said. 'Especially Welsh intellectuals. They can talk themselves out of any form of action.'

A necessary minimum of courage returned with my affection for her.

'Right, Commandant,' I said. 'Where next?'

This didn't really cheer her up.

'You need simple working men,' she said. 'Unsophisticated. Hard. Dedicated. Thick skins. Intuitive. Uneducated. Not college kids or college lecturers. Men who can handle

223

things. Gelignite. Detonators. Handle them like screw-drivers and hammers.'

We both looked at the softness of my hands. I felt apologetic.

'And I'm left-handed,' I said. 'The manual dexterity of a duck.'

I was hoping she would laugh. She didn't.

'You are the only cell I've got,' she said. She was desperate with disappointment. 'What kind of a country will it ever be, if nobody is willing to die for it?'

This could only mean that she was willing. My response was a thrilling sense of commitment both to the girl and what she wanted to stand for. It was a deeper commitment than marriage and it would transform my fright into some kind of substitute for courage.

It had been my intention some time during the day to take Wenna to the retired ministers' home to meet Tasker Thomas. Her presence, I imagined, would brighten up those grey lives. There was also the possibility that the old man who had such a concern for the well-being of my parents might pass on the equivalent of a blessing on our precarious alliance. I might even have cherished some illusion of her being influenced by his transparent goodness to consider marriage to me more seriously.

'Wenna,' I said. 'Shall we go and visit the old minister who was my father's friend? Old Tasker Thomas.'

She shook her head.

'I just thought . . .'

I couldn't tell her exactly what I thought. The strength of her positive convictions was so great it withered any form of tentative speculation that dared to make itself manifest. She was firm and decisive.

'You've got to shake it off,' she said. 'You can't go on being oppressed by the past. All these shreds and tatters. If you want to make a fresh start, if you want to change the course of history, you've got to find the strength in yourself and in this day and age to impose a new law and a new order on this mess that surrounds us. How can you hope to make a fresh start with so many chains around your feet?'

I was impressed. The girl was an oracle. She was qualified

to impose tests and even destinies on creatures like me she had selected for close attention. I had a brief vision of social change and even civilizations as molten substances whose course can only be changed by the rocklike will and determination of rare individuals. Could this girl be one of the chosen?

'All those relics and fragments and papers of your father's. You should burn them.'

She was looking at me straight in the eye, her fingers running upwards through her hair transforming those tresses into black scourges as repulsive as a gorgon's head. I became so deathly pale and silent I think she realized she had gone too far.

'What will you do with them?' she said. 'What are they good for?' She was losing her ascendancy over me. Talking like a silly girl. 'Edit them nicely and bring out a limited edition for the cognoscenti, all two dozen of them? And what is it in the end? Another record of failure. Haven't we got enough of those already? All those high hopes that come to nothing. All those evaporating visions. Is that the kind of world we have to perpetuate?'

I remained stubbornly silent.

'Haven't you had enough of lost causes?' she continued. 'I know I have. Picking at the dry scabs of old failures. That's no way to create a new society. Why don't you say something?'

'You sound just like my mother,' I said.

It was the most hurtful thing I could think of saying. I wanted to sound bitter. Wenna just clapped her hands and laughed.

'Good boy,' she said. 'It was just a test. I didn't mean it. Not literally. I just want to detach you from your obsession with it. That's all. For your own good, Peredur.'

It wasn't her place to patronize me. Or to test me either, if it came to that.

'We've got to be more desperate,' she said. 'History can't be sorted out by people just being nice to each other.'

She was looking for my hand to take hold of it. How could I resist her? We drove to the end of the promenade where there were less people. I was willing to hold hands for ever

225

so that we could go on talking and come to a better understanding. She insisted that in order to create new states of mind you had to destroy not just for the sake of destruction but in order to uncover new and stronger sources of indigenous power.

'You can't have a new society among a people who want their lives controlled by an invisible deity that lives underground somewhere in London.'

We laughed at that together as if she had made a wonderfully witty observation. She was so beautiful and persuasive.

'There they are!' I said. 'Just look.'

Tasker Thomas and several of his friends were taking their morning stroll. He was the only one bareheaded. In the middle of so many clerical figures holding on to their hats he looked like the fragile ghost of an open air fanatic, a dried leaf skipping ahead of the breeze.

'There they go,' I said. 'Stout nationalists all. Christian soldiers on the march, talking away for all they are worth.'

Wenna was not amused. 'Oh God. What use would they be to anybody?'

'Voters,' I said. 'Statistics show that the old-age vote will be of increasing importance in the next few decades.'

' "The sickly smile out begging votes",' she said. 'Listen. Will you drive to the town centre, go into the biggest store and buy two alarm clocks?'

She was putting me to the test again. The process delighted her. I should be pleased to bring that smile to her face. The orphan of two cultures and the heiress of neither. She needed my love and attention. All the same, it would not do to be too slavishly obedient.

'What for?'

'To twist the dragon's tail,' she said. To humour me she embarked on a more detailed explanation. 'Any alarm clock will do,' Wenna said. 'You take off the glass that covers the clock face and drill a hole in it. Take off the minute hand and rub the paint off the hour hand to make a good connection. Insert the positive wire through the hole in the glass and tape it in. Connect the negative wire to the winding lever. From the battery run the negative wire to the detonator in the geli. And wait for the hour hand to move round and touch the wire and . . . bing-bang.'

'Who taught you all this?'

She seemed so certain of her procedures.

'Sven,' she said. 'Poor old Sven. Who else?'

The assertion had the weight of lead in the pit of my stomach. The mystery and power of the girl were too much for me. And yet to attempt to disentangle myself from her mystery and her machinations would be a betrayal of the love that bound me to her.

'Will you go?' She was talking to me so quietly. 'Two alarm clocks. Woolworth's will do. Say they're for Tasker Thomas and his brotherhood, if anybody asks. To wake them up.'

She was teasing me. It made me out to be a nervous coward. There was no need to feel guilt as I walked up to the appropriate counter. They were there, rows of clock faces, begging to be bought.

vi

Wenna's mother raised her hands to form a halter on either side of her head. I noticed how much plumper her fingers were than Wenna's.

'It's the world we create for ourselves in here. Isn't that so, Mr More?'

This was her tea-table and not my extra-mural class. She persisted in confining me to the role of tutor. Either she did not know or did not choose to know that I was her daughter's lover. What excuse, if any, did Wenna make when she spent the night with me at the manse? Mrs Ferrario laid out topics for discussion like varied plates of bread and butter, cakes and scones between us. I was to understand she was a woman of the widest intellectual interests. The interior of her skull was even more lavishly furnished than the rooms of her house. I could see the flower-arranging, the harp in the corner of the drawing-room, the Welsh language women's magazines and publications, the slightly damaged antiques. Her green

227

fingers made the small garden flourish. There were rows of exotic tea canisters in the kitchen, and on this table beween us the stifling comfort of an array of homemade cakes. I could never possibly be expected to try them all. I had expected Wenna to be here. This was the occasion when we should be together taking her mother into our confidence. Did Morfydd Ferrario have any idea what her daughter was up to? I saw little prospect of help from this comfortable corner. The woman was perversely oblivious to my desperate condition.

'I'm a little shy of trotting out my pet ideas in the class,' Morfydd said. 'They might sound silly. Naïve and eccentric. And that old Manchester electrical engineer would be down on me like a ton of bricks. Making me out to be a foolish and ignorant woman. But I feel steady and certain inside my own territory, Mr More. Did I tell you my family have farmed their land here in unbroken succession for three and half centuries? The Pritchards of Penybryn.' She expected me to look impressed. 'But of course it all goes back much much further than that,' she said. 'That is the point I am trying to make. It's all in here.'

Her hands had gone up again. I should view them with a certain affection. They had nursed Wenna, brought her up. Where was the girl at this moment? I was here at her behest. The mother was supposed to be out, preparing the tea for some children's eisteddfod. Instead she was sitting here, my hostess giving vent to her theories about identity and nationality. Listening with polite attention was a strain. Mrs Ferrario's hands pressed inwards on her head without disturbing the arrangement of her hair. A flush rising from her neck suggested she was in the menopause. It was necessary to be sympathetic and attentive so that the balance of her emotions should not be disturbed.

'Our cultural inheritance is the source and the seed ground of our identity,' she said. 'And in my case, Mr More, and since we are alone I can be quite frank about this, it is an unbroken connection that goes back to the Age of the Saints.'

I had to make some indication of sharing her pleasure, her triumphant delight in her ancestry.

'The continuity of the thing, Mr More,' she said. 'Do you know we had one field called Llys Rhodri? There was a ruin there that archaeologists used to come and excavate. But the corner that gave me a special thrill even when I was a little girl was the spring that never dried up. In Cae Ffynon. Alongside the old house. And do you know what it was called? You would hardly credit it. *Ffynon Gybi*. And that takes you straight back to the sixth century. Isn't that remarkable? I played in it as a child. I was baptized in the same fountain as a sixth-century saint.' She contemplated this awesome fact with an open mouth before patting her chest and bursting into laughter. 'So you see how important I am,' she said. 'Goodness, isn't it hot in here?'

She shifted her chair further from the fire. It was as well that I learnt as much as there was to know about Wenna's family. Her mother should be well disposed towards a suitor for her daughter's hand. She had to be an ally in my longterm strategy. Sooner or later I would win the girl, persuade her to marry me. History may not repeat itself; the species has no other alternative.

'Farmers and doctors.' More information was forth-coming. 'That's what we've been, Mr More, for at least three centuries. No poets, I'm afraid. A down-to-earth lot. That's what I wanted myself. Medicine. But my brother came first. So I had to stay home to help on the farm. Help to pay for his training, you could say. I didn't begrudge it. Girls took second place in those days. And, of course, there was a war on. And along came Giuso. So gentle and so handsome. Not a bit like me!' She was laughing again. 'Poor fellow. I think I must have made him marry me. In the teeth of opposition, I can tell you. It's possible, you know, I was subconsciously avenging myself against my parents for not letting me study medicine. I was so keen on it, you've no idea. Given half a chance and I would be operating on the animals. I had this dream, you know, of being the first woman surgeon in my family. Poor Giuso. He had a lot to put up with. In the end I settled for teaching and he went back to his Italian sun. My other brother farms the old home. He's got four children so there's little hope for an inheritance for my Wenna in that direction. Never mind. So

229

long as the old breed flourishes. We shan't die out just yet.'

That was something she expected me to be pleased about. Of course, I was. We natives were on a demographic hiding to nothing. Alarm bells should be ringing from one end of the country to the other. Trumpets sounding. Bombs going off . . .? Where was the girl?

'Mrs Ferrario.' I made an effort to sound calm. 'Wenna said there would be a meeting.'

She could have guessed how passionately I was in love with her daughter simply by the way I uttered her name. She gave no sign. This was a time of increasing political activity. Perhaps she thought I was like Gareth Hopkin, a besotted academic, much too old for her daughter. She was trying to spare my feelings. She leant across the table to speak in a low, intense voice.

'Our cause is just,' she said.

What exactly did that mean? How much did she know? Was she being discreet to spare my feelings or to sense how much I knew?

'She's with El,' Mrs Ferrario said. 'Elwyn Garmon. You know El. At the Nant Garage.'

I knew him by sight. A hulking chap in greasy overalls who hauled himself out of the inspection pit in a ramshackle corrugated iron shed between the road and the river to serve the passing motorist from the only pump that was working. The other pump was like a rusty monument to the 1920s. 'One of us' I never doubted, and extremely surly towards me on the rare occasions I had stopped there for petrol. Mrs Ferrario let me into a secret.

'He's building a car for her,' she said. 'You may as well say that. It's basically a Ford, he tells me, and he's hunting the countryside for the last bit to put in it. I pay for the parts and old El does the labour in his spare time.'

This was something else Wenna had never mentioned. I wondered if 'old El' could also supply alarm clocks. Mrs Ferrario put up her hand to half cover her mouth, as though to show she disapproved of what she would say next.

'Beauty and the Beast,' she murmured. 'Which isn't a very nice thing to say. But he'd do anything for her. Of course, she never takes advantage. It's quite a rule with us. "Never

230

put yourself in the position of begging favours." '

She trotted the line out like a family proverb. She had no idea how ominously complacent it sounded to me. If the mother practised self-deception with such ease there was no reason why her daughter could not excel in the same flexible artifice. They probably used the same ready-reckoner of male gullibility. Where did I register on the scale? Above or below Gareth Hop-y-deri-dando, or Elwyn Garmon, the soft-hearted monster who lurked in a greasy lair called Nant Garage? To conceal my nervous apprehension I accepted a piece of lemon sponge I didn't really want.

'He looks rough,' Mrs Ferrario said. 'But he's one of the pure in heart, our El.'

'Our' El? I could not allow primeval jealousy to sour my view of the world. Where was the girl? It was her I should be talking to with a sharper degree of frankness. This guarded exchange with her mother would get me nowhere. I should make my excuses and speed off to that garage. Every moment trapped in this over-decorated room was time wasted. Always there were crises threatening like substances capable of exerting sudden and untoward pressure on the bounds of my existence. I was suffering dreams of uncontrolled violence. The girl should be beside me every night so that at least I knew where she was. There was an explosion in my dream last night. I stood in the middle of a road the colour of blood unable to decide whether the fragments were flying apart or flying together. On a page of the Children's Encyclopedia the sun started bleeding. There was my mother's head under the hairdryer with no body under it, repeating like a pirate's parrot 'A little knowledge is a dangerous thing. A little knowledge is a dangerous thing'.

'I worry about her you know.'

I looked at the flush rising like a temperature in her neck. We were here to worry together. We both knew too much and too little.

'There are some very rough types that foregather in the back of Elwyn's garage,' she said. 'Some very common types. Not that I'm a snob. Snobbery is no part of our way of life, is it? I can't help asking myself, why should they attach themselves to our cause? Are their motives pure?'

231

I felt she was preparing to be frank with me. It seemed a great effort.

'Do you know Cled Syd? And Roli Mike?'

I shook my head. She was discouraged.

'Why should you. I could never do anything with them in school. Dragged up, not brought up. They are absolutely wild. Now what I'm asking is this. To change the way things are, to what lengths do we have to go? You can talk about revolution . . . what kind of people do you have to consort with to make one? That's my point really.' She leaned over a plate of cakes to offer me a share of piercing sincerity. 'I don't want to be personal,' she said. 'But take your first name, for example. I don't remember the details, but you can't recover the Holy Grail or redeem the wasteland or whatever it was by foul means can you? We are so small in number. You could say we are obliged to be pure in heart. To change things, to what lengths do we have to go? That's what worries me.'

It worried me too. She was worried stiff about the girl. And so was I. She was feeling her way to enlisting my help in keeping an eye on her. Her difficulty, like mine, was finding the correct form of words for an effective concordat between us. The girl at this very moment could be in bad company plotting and conspiring . . . if those were the appropriate words. How could we express it to our mutual satisfaction when we were so uncertain of where we stood themselves? As my mother would say, there was always more to conceal than reveal. Reserve all news.

We were startled by a tap on the window. Morfydd put her hand on her chest. She said it sounded like the beak of a bird of ill omen. There was a noise in the road of a motorcar without a proper silencer on its exhaust. Wenna's face appeared. The oil and grease on her cheeks and the grin of triumph made her look like a naughty child in a school pantomine. Her hair was hidden by a dirty peaked cap several sizes too big for her. It made clear the square, determined jaw I had noticed the first time I clapped eyes on her. The strength of character lurking under the playful exterior went back centuries, like original sin. The dark blue pupils of her eyes were enlarged. Was she perhaps a witch?

232

Wenna was at the back door removing her wellington boots before she came in. She placed a hand on her mother's shoulder to keep her balance.

'Look at him,' she said.

She wanted her mother and myself to admire Elwyn Garmon sitting at the wheel of a ramshackle car of his own making. His greasy curls hung over his eyes. His hands looked enormous on the small steering wheel. She wanted Elwyn Garmon to come in the house and enjoy her mother's cakes. She was busy telling everyone what to do and we were all making corresponding gestures of reluctance as we willingly obeyed her.

'He's a genius.'

It was also obligatory to agree with her pronouncements.

'A man who can use his hands. He made it himself. Alone and unaided. Mam! All he needs is a little cheque to pay for a differential or whatever you call it and then my car will be on the road within a week! Isn't that wonderful? Fill him with cakes, Mam. And gallons of hot tea.'

Adding to the spontaneous gaiety of the occasion, an Austin 35 drove around the corner cutting off the escape that Elwyn Garmon appeared inclined to make. Mrs Lloyd Tai Hirion threw up her hands in mock horror at the prospect of collision. She was able to escort the giant to the back door. She showed that she was aware of the comic difference in their size and appearance. Mrs Lloyd was wearing one of her ornate hats as part of her array for one of the cultural activities that played such a part in the lives of the militant ladies of Carreg Wen, Pant Gwyn and Rhyd-y-Groes. Under a deceptively tranquil surface this whole area of green hills and villages concealed hives of social and cultural activity. Even Elwyn Garmon was laughing now, caught up in the gusts of mutual understanding generated by these three women. He shared with them a depth of communal experience. I was the only outsider. In the midst of the chatter and laughter in the kitchen I felt Wenna take my hand.

'You come with me,' she said.

I followed her halfway up the stairs. Her hair hung down over her face as she turned to smile at my hesitation.

'Never mind about him,' she said. 'You can come and scrub my back.'

I had never been in her bedroom before. It belonged to a schoolgirl. There were dolls in ethnic costumes still standing in their cellophane cylinders on the mantlepiece. On the wall a colour reproduction of a Degas dancer hung alongside a French poster of Che Guevara. In a moment of theatrical extravagance her mother had erected a silk half-canopy above her only daughter's single bed. There was a framed photograph on the desk where she used to do her homework. An enlarged snapshot of a blonde young man in bathing shorts grinning at the camera on an anonymous beach.

'I'm dying for a pee,' Wenna said. 'That Nant garage is a corrugated shack from the stone age. You can't get near the w.c. without shifting a ton of spare parts. You just sit there like a good boy.'

The photograph had to be Sven. The inevitable Sven. Strength through joy on a north German beach. I examined the photo in a trance of hatred. She had gone to the trouble of getting it blown up and framed. He was the hero of her heart. The immutable icon, venerated all the more for being unavailable. I could hear the water running noisily in her bath. Downstairs the chatter of ladies rose and fell. I could imagine El Garmon's large hands clearing the plates of cakes and scones and their admiration of his appetite. Wenna called my name. She was already in the soapy bath. Her black hair was tied up in a way that made her face unfamiliar. I stood staring down at her.

'It's only me,' she said. 'Better lock the door.'

I took off my jacket and rolled up my sleeves before sinking to my knees. I would bathe her with the tenderness and care of a parent to begin with. Under the influence of my hands sliding over her skin the phases of her development would follow in smooth succession. She was so relaxed she began to purr like a kitten as I stroked her until she opened her eyes and reached out her wet arms to pull me down towards her. While she was doing this, her mother called out from the bottom of the stairs.

'Wenna! Elwyn is leaving now.'

234

I sank in a nervous heap on the bathroom floor. Wenna's voice echoed above me. How could it not reverberate with sexual tension?

'Did you give him a cheque?'

'I couldn't persuade him to eat any more.'

Wenna spoke even more loudly. 'I said, did you give him a cheque?'

These exchanges went on over my head. There were differing degrees of excitement in both their voices. I was the intruder on the bathroom floor. The harmless presence of a male tolerated like a domestic pet.

Wenna stood up in the bath, a soapy Venus rising from the waves. When Time mutilated the earth, this stepped out of the foam, sensuous and dangerous. Drying her with a large towel was like an amorous intrigue. The people downstairs could never know how avidly I was covering her body with kisses. This wasn't the purer higher love I believed we aspired to. It was pagan worship. She lifted my head and brought me to my feet. She led me with quiet decorum to her bedroom, touching her lips with her finger and not laughing until we were lying on her bed.

Beneath us I could hear Mrs Lloyd and Mrs Ferrario still engaged in animated conversation. Wenna was amused and excited by her own daring. She took charge of me and I was her willing slave. While I lay rigid and disciplined under her, her mother called out again to announce that she and Mrs Lloyd were leaving for their meeting and that she was locking the back door. The fact that she made no mention of me could only mean she accepted me as her daughter's lover. This occasion, in its own intoxicating pagan way, was a form of marriage. Once the door was locked I could worship her as long as I liked in the original temple dedicated to her well-being. Whatever we wanted from each other we could take until we were exhausted and hungry.

Downstairs, without the mother, it seemed a different place. Homely but still exciting. Wenna ate what was left of the homemade cakes. With her mouth full she pointed at me and her dressing-gown slipped apart.

'Do you know what I would like?'

I had to give her anything she asked for.

'To meet your mother.'

She was smiling so I assumed she was making a joke.

'Explore the old bitch. See what makes her tick. Wasn't there a German general who kept a picture of his opposite number in his caravan to stare at and guess his next move. Or was it the other way round? It's a very close relationship, isn't it? Between mortal enemies.'

She was rubbing her chin on her knee. She was like a child pondering the mysteries of ancient history. If she married me she would have to meet my mother. Should I say that or would it put her off the notion even more? Why should she regard domestic bliss with so much contempt? If she met Sian and Bedwyr that would improve matters. They would be visiting my mother very soon. Bedwyr had work to do on the Hall. Meeting Sian would make all the difference.

'You could take me inside that stately home,' Wenna was saying. 'I'd like that. Spy out the land. Study enemy territory.'

I was uneasy because I couldn't think of a quick and convenient way to comply with this wish. Did she really want to meet my mother? I tried not to look suspicious or appear to be harbouring unworthy thoughts, wondering yet again what my goddess was up to. Aphrodite in a dressing gown. She was notoriously capricious and yet she had to be propitiated. I demonstrated a sudden inspiration.

'Sian,' I said. 'My sister-in-law. They'll be coming here next week. I don't know whether they'll stay in the Hall or up at my mother's place. In any case I'd like you to meet her.'

Wenna looked sceptical.

'She's "one of us" as your mother would say,' I said.

'Is she?' Wenna was unimpressed.

'Apart from you,' I said, 'I suppose she's the woman I most admire. My brother Bedwyr is a very lucky chap. Almost as lucky as I am.'

She guessed I was about to attempt to sing the virtues of the married state. Sian was wonderful with those children. They responded to her. The richness of that home life had to be seen to be believed. There was no earthly reason why Wenna and I should not wend our way hand in hand through the garden of matrimony into the promised land of our own lineage.

'I don't want marriage and I don't want kids,' she said. 'Not yet anyway. Certainly not yet. I must find out how far I can go. Does that displease you?'

I steeled myself to conceal my disappointment. There was only one thing I could say.

'I love you for yourself alone,' I said.

It was true. The rest was concept. My hands were able to wander over her skin with the blind ecstasy that blocks out every doubt and hesitation. She rewarded me now with an embrace that was momentary immortality. Later she had a childhood reminiscence that I could listen to and cherish.

'We used to climb that wall,' she said. 'Very daring. And see the big house in the distance. Brangor Hall. We thought a monster lived inside it. We did, honestly. It would be fun, wouldn't it, if you could take me inside?'

vii

An urgent message from my mother. She wanted, very much wanted, to see me. I could barely suppress my excitement. This was the call I had been waiting for. The route by which it reached me confirmed that.

'You've just missed him,' Hefin Mather said.

So much happening at once. His eyes glistened with the elation of a supporter of the winning side. His room at the top of the old library tower was far above the dust of the arena, but the reports came pouring in.

'Sit-ins and hunger strikes,' Hefin Mather said. 'Protest marches. It's spreading. Gareth Hopkin is very worried. His students in the Training College are getting out of hand.' He giggled cheerfully. 'The thing is, there's a safe Labour seat coming vacant and he wants it to drop like a ripe apple into his lap.'

The appointed emissary from my mother: the great Hopkin, expert on the Spanish Civil War, a stalwart and charismatic neo-marxist whose baritone could reverberate the length of any public hall. Miss Maude Hopkin had first

237

learnt the words of the aria and clasped the message to her bosom. The throne under the hairdryer had served as a royal confessional.

'You might have passed him on the stairs. With a worried look on his face. Your mother wants to see you. Very urgently.'

Mather was more alive than I had ever seen him – crackling with static curiosity. His room in the tower was humming with the present as well as the past. His observation post was immune from harm and still at the heart of an intelligence network.

'The young people are showing the way,' Hefin said. 'God bless them. Gareth Hopkin doesn't like it. He's supposed to lead and they are supposed to follow.'

My mother had realized at last that I was up to something. She was worried about the hoard of my father's papers she had never seen. She knew about them. Gwydion had light-heartedly broken his promise to me not to mention them to her. That was good. In whatever way it had leaked out, it reached her as a threat. The hairdresser had whispered in her ear. Mather had indulged in one academic nod and wink too many. How could he resist showing off to Gareth Hopkin how much he knew? It didn't matter. The threat had arrived out of a time of tension; and now the sooner the better our confrontation should take place.

A brief note posted to the manse at Rhyd-y-Groes would have reached me with far less delay. She was clinging to the fiction that Lady Brangor had no idea where exactly her youngest son was living or what exactly he was up to. He was a highly-strung obsessional creature, a solitary who nurtured obscure concerns in obscure corners, and dabbled in sedition; so unlike her Bedwyr who designed modern buildings to stand in the sun, or her Gwydion who brought life and colour into the drab parlours of the people. Fictions were essential to her well-being. She secreted them with the industry and enthusiasm of a colony of polyps decorating their chosen habitat with a continous sheet of pink tissue – all to protect Lady Brangor from her own past. It separated her from Amy Parry as effectively as the estate wall separated Brangor Park from the public highway.

238

I drove up to those wrought-iron gates with caution. The twin lodges built of blocks of local granite stood silent and empty on either side. The moment had come to recapture my original vision; I needed to be recharged with the force that drove me to resign a safe job and return to my own country. The fact that I was miserable at Redbatch and judged my career there to lack meaning and purpose was no longer relevant. Neither was the humiliation of being turned down for a position on my home ground for which I was more than well qualified. This was the place where a new creative atmosphere could be generated. This bright morning, as I pushed open those heavy gates, the whole issue hung in the balance. My hands tingled as I grasped the wrought-iron bars. The middle way is always the most difficult. Wenna was young and impetuous. My mother was old and encrusted with illusions of a lifetime that glittered like the too many rings she wore on her fingers. If I were positive and careful, in me the two forces could meet. Not be reconciled; that would be too idealistic. Bent by my will to those forms of restraint that would make it possible for them to co-exist for the greater benefit of a way of life under siege. My concept of cultural ecology was valid. The difficulty was putting it into practice.

This was the place. The beech trees were in bud. Their strength was fed by the soil of centuries. The park was surrounded by rising mounds and sloping hills. Most of the area had been in continous cultivation for at least five thousand years. It had been beautiful since the first dawn of an infant world. It had know every twist and turn of social organization that humanity had thrown up in its never-ending struggle for survival. Here the seasons came and went with a calm regularity related to the stars in the heavens. Brangor Hall, that grey monument to a British imperial past, was merely the latest and perhaps the least in a succession of aspirations that went back to the cromlech on the southern edge of the park beyond the avenue of trees that my brother Bedwyr said needed drastic surgery.

I would go there first. Sit on the sloping capstone and work out my strategy. When we came face to face there would be claim and counter-claim. She was his widow. I was

239

his youngest son. She would point out that Bedwyr's claim was stronger. But why talk of claim and counter-claim when the whole cache had languished in ignominious oblivion in a disused outside lavatory for so many years? How in any case had they landed there alongside those First World War copies of the *Illustrated London News?* She wouldn't know. She, the widow, was too intent on scaling the social heights to bother about the detritus dislodged by her scrambling feet. Perhaps the papers had been kept in his office. Removed thence by his secretary loyal to some vow even after his death. Had he ordered her to destroy them and had she been unable to bring herself to carry out the order? Miss Price. I remembered her faintly. Dedicated to my father, devoted to his sister's memory, an enemy of my mother. Was she still alive? I should find her.

This might account for my mother's anxiety. She imagined I knew too much. This hoard had survived when she had gone about burning everything she could lay her hands on: all the incriminating evidence that proved she had driven my father to his death. She thought she was getting away with it. The years had rolled by. Her prestige and wealth had accumulated like protective walls. And all the while, the truth was waiting. More to conceal than reveal. Reserve all news. Not suicide. An unfortunate accident. The birds in the woods were singing their nesting songs. Every spring that came was a renewal of a whole world where nothing could be hidden.

I saw the little car in which she drove around the estate parked on the edge of the drive. The door hung open. It was somehow typical that she had not bothered to close it. A sign of her presence and her sovereignty. She would open it in a hurry and rush out to check on any detail she found out of place. There was so much to keep an eye on, all the year round. Whatever their origins a place like this moulded any man or woman into a proprietorial shape. The best manure is always the farmer's foot. Where the vines are, thin them out with bent fingers; weave hedges, keep out the cattle, clear the brambles, trim the trees.

Near the cromlech I saw my mother confront the three

240

Huskie women. She was wearing an ancient grey raincoat that reached to her ankles. I could tell by the way her left fist thrust into her waist that she was angry. May and Rose Huskie shielded their mongoloid sister Milly who shifted about behind them looking smug under their protection. Milly had a blue ribbon in her thin hair. She had to be pushing forty but she wore the clothes of a junior schoolgirl. Her white plimsoles were stained brown and green with earth and moss. I could hear my mother's voice quite clearly in the still morning air.

'It's got to stop,' she was saying. 'And I hold you both responsible.'

May Huskie was still trying to take the matter lightly. She was a powerfully built woman in her brown tweed and open-necked white silk blouse. Her sister Rose looked miserable and apprehensive. May was relying on her long-standing friendship with my mother. She had been part of her loyal bodyguard for so many years; she had a right to speak out and defend herself.

'It's only a heap of old stones,' May Huskie said. Her own adenoidal Liverpudlian delivery made the words a mimetic reproduction of the objects they represented. 'I mean, they're not sacred, are they? Pagan things. I mean, the poor little girl is only playing.'

'Is that what you call it?' My mother was angry. 'I tell you, it's got to stop. She is not allowed in the cromlech or the tower unless one of you is with her. Is that clear? I will not have her wandering about the park like a wild animal any more. Is that clear?'

She was demanding an obedient response. These women depended on her. They lived rent-free in one of the garden cottages. A grace and favour reward for past services, no doubt, and, as I guessed, an irksome dependency on both sides. May Huskie had spotted my approach. It offered a welcome relief. I was never her favourite. That position was reserved for Gwydion. They didn't even mind when he treated them with affectionate contempt. He was something they could see on television. To Milly he was virtually a sacred being. May nodded vigorously in my direction.

241

'You've got a visitor,' she said.

My mother turned her back on them and advanced on me. I could see she was in militant mood. She spoke loudly in the language the Huskies could not understand although May and Rose had spent most of their adult lives in Wales.

'That girl is getting totally out of hand,' my mother said. 'I've had the cromlech nicely cleared and she's using it as a public convenience. I've actually seen her at it. With my own eyes!'

She laughed suddenly at her own indignation and an ancient longing to be closer to her welled up inside me. When she put her mind to it she could manipulate me even more skilfully than Gwydion could. I had to remember how she had cherished these Huskies when they were of use to her. Now they were in the way she rejected them with a forcefulness that verged on racial discrimination. I watched the three Huskie women trekking homewards down the slope like refugees returning to a transit camp.

'She's getting worse, I'm afraid,' my mother said. 'But those two have nothing else to do all day except look after her. And write letters to Frank. You knew he was in prison?'

This was their brother. A shifty house-agent. Connie Clayton claimed to have caught him pinching Meissen china from the butler's pantry. When Connie was alive there was an uneasy balance of power among the staff of Brangor Hall, as it were between Celt and Saxon dependants. Now it was one-sided and unsatisfactory. Connie was dead and most of the house had been closed up. My mother had retired to the one-storey house on the slope that Bedwyr had designed for her. There wasn't all that much for the Huskies to do. They had outlived their usefulness. Now they were in the way of whatever grandiose plans my mother had in mind for the place. Like all politicians, and even more politicians manqué, she was ruthless.

We walked back in silence to her car. I was engaged in keeping my thoughts in order and my feelings in check. I was not disposed to make overtures that would leave me unprotected against one of her emotional sorties. She leaned on the open door of her little car and looked at me with engaging frankness.

242

'Peredur,' she said. 'Let's not sink into a pattern of antagonism, shall we? I've got a lot I want to talk to you about.'

Her smile was imbued with unforced affection. My difficulty was to reserve my position without appearing churlish. Like my father, as I imagined, I was an abiding disappointment to her. Such effortless charm needed to be reflected back like an image in a burnished mirror. The middle-aged woman who leaned on the door of her little car was so closely akin to the golden-haired girl. Whatever time had whittled away the spontaneity was as fresh as ever.

'I just hope you don't think I had anything to do with your not getting that job you were after.'

I couldn't help myself blushing. She had reached the sore spot with unerring accuracy. She knew me. She knew my weaknesses. Out of the few words and phrases Gwydion let fall like amusing asides or references to my more comic aspects, she could build a comprehensive account of my emotional condition. I resented it.

'I was furious,' she said. 'Devastated wouldn't be too strong a word. I wanted you near me. For very good practical reasons, apart from anything personal.'

Like she wanted me with her on that train journey or in that London restaurant near the sacred House of Commons where Mr Everett could cover her hand with his.

'I found out afterwards what happened,' she said. 'I made it my business to. Lord Mared told me himself. He was very impressed with you. It was those two old dinosaurs on the committee. I don't know whether you noticed them. The old woman choking with pearls. And the old man with a face like a grandfather clock. They were adamant. Wouldn't have you at any price. And the academics just caved in. Mared said it was pathetic. There wasn't much he could do, he said. They were convinced that you were anti-English. That's all there was to it.'

She was telling the truth. I had to accept it. As an explanation it had its own residual satisfaction. Dilkes's disparaging attitude to Welsh never came up. Hardly a martyr's crown for me. Just the whiff of hidden persecution, enough to put my integrity to a reassuring test. She was still smiling at me.

243

'Shall we take a look at the tower?' she said. 'There's ivy that has to come off. Will you come with me?'

I had to admit it was pleasant to walk in the park with her. The spring sunlight in itself was a source of reconciliation. A pheasant squatting in tufts of grass shot up on whirring wings at our approach and squawked out its harsh alarm call.

'It brought something back to me,' my mother said. 'The whole business. It reminded me of the way Val Gwyn was led to believe he would be given the wardenship of the adult college at Plas Iscoed. It was snatched away from him at the last moment. I was devastated. I was given to understand it was all my fault.'

Her voice was soft and elegiac. It was a mood I could easily enter as we approached the tower. Here, too, proud Ilium had fallen. Under the same sky the gods of history had overthrown a guiltless race.

'He was the man your father and I loved. He was the one from whom we both expected so much. For me, he was my first love and my leader. Losing him, we thought we'd lost everything. Perhaps we had.'

She stopped to look back at the view of the Hall. From the rear it was a more pleasing group of buildings. We couldn't see the pretentious Gothic facade. My mother was dramatizing herself and her life history. Approaching the threshold of old age? I should not begrudge her such indulgence. If I was making a case against her it should not be constructed out of mean shreds of animosity.

'You must never think I've forgotten him. Or Enid. Or those early ideals we fought for. You must never think that.' She knew that was precisely what I did think. 'Days like this, days of spring, bring it all back to me. Brings them back. I don't need to dream about them. They are here with me. Not ghosts either. Vivid presences. She raised her arm and seemed to grow taller as she pointed down the slope towards the Hall. 'I was the born extremist,' she said. 'Even more than Pen. His extremism was born out of marxist philosophy. Mine was born out of my nature. I suppose that's how I still am. For better or for worse. Probably for worse. We had our beliefs then. Our credo. Clear like running water. Val was our Gandhi, if you can imagine it.

Non-violent nationalism and our own brand of socialism and working all out against exploitation and pauperization. Those words. We used them all the time. Day and night. When I found out the Prime Minister and the Home Secretary were meeting in Plas Iscoed to discuss unemployment and the war in Spain, we had the nerve to march right up to the the front door with petitions. Twice. The first time we got as far as the front door because I knew the way. The second time a mixed force of local police and London detectives poured down on us out of the trees armed with truncheons and sticks. I thought they were going to beat us to death. Val was ill. He had TB. He couldn't get away. They beat him on the ground. I'll never forget that. Or forgive it. Or forgive myself.'

She insisted that I looked at her. I saw the blue pupils of her eyes like pools of honesty.

'It's not so much what we say as what we do,' she said.

She was working towards an agreement with me. It was still negotiaton. I had to be positive. If she knew about my father's papers in my possession, the knowledge did not seem capable of bringing much pressure to bear on her. She had such little curiosity about them.

'Does your father write about Val?'

This was an admission. I seized on it. She knew about the papers. They might give me some leverage after all. By pressure rather than persuasion I would force her to put this place to better use. She was a formidable opponent. All this about Val Gwyn was more than an exercise in nostalgia. It was calculated to weaken my resistance to what she had in mind for me.

'He used to say he would write a memoir. Even a biography of Val. And publish Enid's letters. Maybe both together. He never did.'

And whose fault was that? I was tempted but I did not say it. She probably knew I was thinking it anyway. She punched me in the arm and began to laugh.

'Now you listen to me, young man,' she said. 'I know what's going on. Protests galore. And I don't mind. What you've got to understand, what you've got to learn, is how to contain a situation. And I don't mean "playing along". I mean containing the situation. That is the essence of politics. That's about all I've learnt all these years.'

We stood in the shadow of the tower. My mother took hold of a thick ivy stem and shook it. She showed me how far the twisted roots sank into the soil. This was something else that Bedwyr had to supervise. There was so little time if even a fraction of the plans that teemed in her brain should ever come to fruition.

'Let me prove you wrong.'

She placed a firm hand on my shoulder. We were not mother and son so much as two political activists. One experienced, one amateur. She wanted me to collaborate with her: to negotiate, strike a balance, accept a proportionate measure of her policy in return for her support for so much of mine, politics being the art of the possible. She had a vitality that never gave up. Was I obliged to admire it?

'You can only put in as much as the situation can hold,' my mother said. 'You can only advance as far as the majority of the people will allow you to advance. Now in the majority of the Welsh, alas, there is still a residue of ancient royalism mixed with the servility of centuries. You have to work inside that framework as well as attack it from the outside. Now all I claim for what I am doing here is that we must impose on the establishment as much Welshness and as much social and economic devolution as the situation will bear. As a simple example. If the prince has a Welsh home, if he speaks Welsh, has a Welsh family even, or at least has a concern and a responsibility for the totality of Welshness that is the well-being of Wales, then we shall have contained the situation. If this place is conspicuously on the side of Welshness – and that's where you could play an important part – we may even convert yet another miserable historic defeat into a pyrrhic victory. Do you see what I'm getting at?'

It was possible to see it as the dream of a woman longing for the best of both worlds. As an analysis of present conditions and motivations it was inadequate. Why should the government or the monarchy or the institutions of an alien state care about the life and death of a small nationality

246

they happened to govern? How loudly did we need to rattle our chains?

'Don't you agree with me?'

She could see no reason why I shouldn't. Gwydion was so like her. She wanted her Brangor Hall to be important because she herself longed to be important. First you act and then you find all the reasons you can dig out to justify what you have done and intend to persist in doing.

'No,' I said.

'Why not? Why not?'

There was no point in going into detail or in being unpleasantly personal.

'You can't build a sound argument on a false premise,' I said.

I was rather pleased with the proposition. It was difficult to refute and it kept our discussion on a level of rationality. My mother was smiling at me. My response disappointed but it was not far from what she had anticipated.

'Oh dear,' she said. 'You are much too clever for me. A false premise. I thought life was a bit of a false premise in the first place.'

She took my arm on the pretext that I could support her progress down the slope from the tower. She was willing a greater intimacy between us. It had happened so many times before. My defences would be lowered and then in some way or other she would take advantage of me. While her arm was in mine there was the sharp realization of the misery and mock splendour of a relationship from which there would never be an escape. We were bound together. I was conceived when she didn't want me to come into existence. My life originated in hers and existed to torment her until she was able to torment me. It would continue for ever throughout circular phases of existence for which this day and age were no more than imperfect rehearsals. I wanted to call her by her first name.

'Amy, there's a poem about you carrying a flag. Did you know that? Very romantic. A young girl with golden hair carrying a flag.'

She laughed and squeezed my arm. 'My dear boy,' she said. 'I'm still carrying it.'

247

'What shall I do with them?'

She knew I was talking about my father's papers. It amazed me that she didn't seem to care. Not that there was much in them to condemn her. Perhaps the condemnation was mostly in my mind as I went through them. The poorest things there were the early pieces that idealized her. Like the poem about the girl with a flag reaching the top of a hill.

'I really don't mind,' my mother said. 'You look after them as best you can. I suppose you could be described as his spiritual heir. Poor old thing.'

Did she mean me or my father?

Eight

i

'The practice of poetry is more than therapy. It should do more than heal my bruised understanding of the nature of existence. My sister Nanw treasures a glass swan she imagines Owen Guest gave her as a token of his devotion. He will never return to deprive her of this fond illusion. I have a mother-of-pearl penknife he left behind in his desk in the office. It runs between my fingers as I try to concentrate on tort and conveyancing and wait for the world to be born again. The education of a poet is carried on in secret. I need to acquire that key to the splendour of utterance capable of celebrating noble behaviour, high aspirations, deep understanding. Who is there to help me? These things cannot be raked out of the ashes of last week's fire in the cast-iron grate of a solicitor's clerk's office.

'My uncle Gwilym considers himself a poet. What he writes makes my skin prickle with embarrassment. A poet needs a new world to inhabit. When my uncle Gwilym prattles knowingly about Lloyd George and Asquith it is worse than the stale sweat that seeps like prejudice from the layers of wool and tweed that he wears. I cannot bear to read that turgid mixture of narrow-minded bigotry and received opinion that issues forth weekly in his column in the *Glaslyn Herald*. It is worse than my discomforting recollection of studying those war maps cut out of Northcliffe newspapers and stuck all over the inside wall of his dingy office; and those blush-making boasts about being related to the Prime Minister of England within the ninth degree. To think he was once my mentor. Poetry has nothing to do with a penny-a-liner who insists on bardic status because of a certain facility in the strict metres. It has everything to do with discovering a new and better world to celebrate.

'The word "Disestablishment" leaves a bad taste on my tongue. In the compartment of our stopping train I listen to my uncle Gwilym and a pair of kindred spirits in starched cut-away collars and bowler hats use it with smug satisfaction. The two incline their torsos towards my uncle trying to work out how much respectful attention is due to a columnist with minor druidical status. "Disestablishment" rustles between them as though that irrelevant issue from a world that came to an end in 1914 was a great victory of their own making. These are the types who used to chatter about "our boys", lining the pavements to cheer the young marching off, reading casualty lists like fat-stock prices. What a nice, neat and painless process "Disestablishment" had been, while all the rest of the world was racked with war, famine and revolution. They fill their pipes, the compartment fills with shag tobacco smoke and my uncle Gwilym assures his eager listeners that Home Rule is the logical next step and will not be long in coming since the greatest ever Welshman, living or dead, is at the imperial helm. Under the waxed ends of his moustache my uncle's mouth is embalmed in a beatific smile. That name so famous it rings around the world and reduces my uncle to a paralysis of uncritical adulation.

'There are posters all over the seaside town. A great wooden pavilion has become a place of pilgrimage. It stands above the streets, like an ancient temple, facing the sea, and the faithful wend their way on foot towards it, passing through the gorse and the heather of the heath with raincoats over their arms. My uncle has stuck a green delegate badge on my lapel. I am an ex-serviceman masquerading as a representative of the Glaslyn Young Liberal Association. Shortly I shall see for myself the staring eyes of mass hysteria, the feet poised to stamp on the pavilion floor, the rows of clapping hands, the throats barely containing the ecstatic roar that will be released as the side door opens like a pre-arranged signal and the white-haired sorcerer appears.

250

'A portly cleric in a silk hat and frock coat had paused on the hill road to get his breath back. In no time my uncle Gwilym engaged him in animated discourse. I assume the cleric put up with it in the expectation of reading his name in the next issue of the *Glaslyn Herald*. He has but to nod his Roman head and my uncle will attribute his own spasm of enthusiasm to an exalted ecclesiastical source.

' " 'Home Rule all round'! Just like the old days. The P.M. will re-discover the enthusiasm of youth! *Cymru Fydd Redivivus*, archdeacon? Now this time, this time he has the power and the strength to carry the stone to the wall."

'Ink eloquence. I could already see the phrases floating like sea wrack when the *Glaslyn Herald* docked on next week's tide. I heard him mutter to himself the names of important personages we would see on the platform. The cruel years had never been. My uncle was back in the Arcadia of his youth. His Welsh millenium was due to start with the new century. No power on earth could halt the progress of a movement led by such a galaxy of talent.

'And there they were. Faded versions of these legendary figures were already seated in their places on the platform. My uncle was eager to point each one out and trace the outline of their former glory. I saw them stuffed and lifeless, lay figures in a political puppet-show, controlled by a distant hand in 10 Downing Street. He would never turn up here himself. He didn't need to. They had already started singing. Some satrap or other would stand up and toss vague but florid promises across the void between the platform and the people. I was repelled by the easy emotionalism of the singing. Did we have to be so gullible? On the excuse that I needed a cigarette I went outside. I sat on a low wall turning my back on the concourse of people and stared across the gorse and heather over the rooftops, to the expanse of open sea. We had enough legends about neglect and folly to fill cities and cathedrals under the sea. They did nothing to save us from the reality of present illusions and ineptitudes.

'Tasker Thomas tapped me on the shoulder. He appeared as unexpectedly as a genie out of a bottle. There he was. Inside a copious trench-coat, wearing an open-necked shirt and that bronze tint on his skin as if he spent more time than

251

most men with his face tilted towards the sun. A natural worshipper. He was grinning down at me like a benediction.

' "John Cilydd," he said. His voice vibrated with affection. "I am so glad to see you."

'I was pleased to see him. A living illustration of the cult of the open air and the virtues of tramping across the hills and through trackless forests. He was carrying a load of crudely printed pamphlets in Welsh and English. The words "Versailles" and "Reparations" were visible in smudged capitals. It would not be long before he commandeered my help in distributing them. He was set on his relentless course of doing good. Once he had satisfied himself that I was on the way to becoming a fully qualified solicitor, he launched himself on an excited discourse about sowing dragon's teeth and about the iniquities of the Versailles Peace Treaty.

' "Three million Austrians incorporated into Czechoslovakia, my boy," he said. "Two million Germans passing under the Polish yoke. One hundred and forty thousand milking cows expropriated by France while millions of German babies go without milk."

'Armed to the teeth with statistics. Versed in the refinements of Westminster politics. Lloyd George was the prisoner of the Tories in his coalition. An odd mixture. To be such a conspicuous candidate for sainthood and take so much delight in his fleeting intimacies with the rich and the powerful. It appeared that notable English Christian men like Sir Samuel Hoare and Lord Halifax's eldest son had dispatched a fatal telegram to our Welsh Arthurian hero urging him to rein in his inclination towards magnanimity. The same rule was to apply in dealings with the Irish, the miners, the Indians, and a whole range of lesser breeds without the law.

'Tasker swivelled a thumb in the direction of the pavilion. Another hymn was reaching a deafening climax.

' "I don't think he'll turn up."

'His inside knowledge of the Prime Minister's movements made him look weighty and worldly. Smartened up and divested of his odour of sanctity he could have slipped easily into the ranks of the great man's retinue at one of those continental conferences that occurred like feast days on our

252

contemporary calendars.

' "I had a word with Iscoed."

'I was being taken into his confidence. Lord Iscoed the coal owner. One of the names he dropped as we walked along the shores of Lough Neagh. Tasker was chuckling.

' "Not that he wanted to speak to me. Or be seen speaking to me. But I got him to admit that Reparations were the greatest single threat to the well-being of the South Wales coalfield. He's torn, poor fellow."

'Tasker brought his head closer to mine. I could smell the onions on his breath. The spirit of camping and cooking.

' "I speak to him quite freely. Our two families are connected by marriage, you see. And, I wouldn't want this to go any further, I was engaged to his sister in the summer of 1912. Not a good idea. Amazing how long ago it seems."

'The singing in the pavilion was interrupted by a rousing cheer. Politics was like football. Our team had taken the field. Perhaps the great man had appeared. Tasker's broad face tilted to the sky. Had the sorcerer turned up after all? Such a sudden reversal of the course of events required an explanation. Anything could happen. The course of history was not predetermined or preordained. The gods could lean out of the sky and alter course with a touch of the finger. Tasker urged me to follow in his wake. He shifted about with surprising aggression, peering over people's heads until he had acquired a piece of territory for us both on the wooden floor.

'A man of consequence was addressing the mass meeting. D. Lloyd George was nowhere to be seen and yet his style hovered like a presence over the platform. The colonel in uniform with black hair plastered close to his balding head and a fierce black moustache was doing his best to exercise eloquence. He glared at the meeting to exemplify righteous indignation.

' "It's only Iscoed."

'Tasker whispered his disappointment in my ear. The miraculous appearance had not taken place. The ruling magician was absent. One of his minions spoke in his place. Lord Iscoed raised an oratorical fist.

' "I'll be frank with you."

253

'He was about to make a daring assertion.

' "In my opinion Mr Lloyd George is at fault. And I shall tell him so next time I see him. To his face!"

'There was a rousing cheer to applaud his courage. He had given vent to the mood of frustration and his reward was the music of popular support. He flourished under it like a green tree in a shower. Now he could reach out to notes of eulogy and together they could renew pledges of devotion like married lovers after the briefest of tiffs.

' "We know he was the architect of the victory in the greatest war the world has ever seen . . ." Lord Iscoed's chest expanded inside his colonel's tunic which was tight for him. "We know he is one of us and we know he will rank among the immortals of world history and we know he will be the chief architect of a lasting peace . . ." Lord Iscoed's eyes were bulging in his head in a do-or-die attempt to meet the challenge of the moment and match the oratorical magic of his absent master. "As I say, he is one of us! And we have a natural right to praise him and even bask in the reflected glory of his matchless achievements. And by the same token, friends and fellow countrymen, we have an inalienable right to remind him of the land of his birth, and of the dreams of his youth! He has given freedom and self-determination to Bohemia, to Poland, to the Baltic States. He has set free the captive nations of this earth. Let us appeal to him, from this historic conference on his native soil, in his own good time, to consider the just claims of his homeland, and to renew his pledge of old to create a national parliament for Wales, supreme in all matters relating to native government, loyal to the British crown and democratically elected by the adult manhood and womanhood of our ancient land."

'His eloquence was running out of steam and I knew why. Like my uncles Gwilym and Simon, like the middle-aged cohorts of the Liberal Party from one end of Wales to the other, what Lord Iscoed and this great audience wanted was some colourful cardboard to camouflage inertia and infinite postponement. They didn't want the dangers or even the discomforts entailed in gaining what they so vociferously demanded. They wanted Home Rule as a first prize in a

254

celestial eisteddfod awarded for virtue and brilliance, compliance and good behaviour, in equal measure. How right the Irish were. Our favourite son would stay in power only as long as he was capable of carrying out English imperial policies. They all knew it. What force could ever impinge on the oceanic store of wishful thinking that surrounded me in this pavilion?

'The force arrived even as I yearned to feel it. On the platform a tall young man was demanding the right to address the meeting. He understood the procedures. A resolution was in the making. Delegates had the right to speak. Tasker knew him. Tasker knew everybody. He was able to give me an outline of the young man's credentials. Some sort of liaison officer with the French forces in the Rhineland. Val Gwyn. Tasker was capable of tracing the main lines of the man's Pembrokeshire ancestry. He was handsome. He could have passed for an American film star. A lock of black hair kept falling over his forehead as though he were in the middle of rescuing some damsel or other from a villain on the opposite side of the screen. His voice wasn't as loud as it should have been. This wasn't a cinema with a piano thumping away. He had a steely command of himself. His thin fists were clenched. His mind was clear and his precise utterance demanded attention.

' "We are not here to present the Prime Minister with a blank cheque. There are things happening in Ireland that are a disgrace. If we have any pride at all the first thing we should do is disassociate ourselves from the atrocities that are being committed in our name."

'My heart began to beat faster. He was a Daniel to walk into such a dusty den of ageing and yet still dangerous lions. I was already on his side. The audience were ready to enjoy a platform clash. They had travelled far in the hope of seeing and hearing the great man himself. At least a first-class row would give them something to take back home. The old lions were stirring in the back. A pack of place men and office seekers, collectors of dubious honours; effective agents of their own brand of stifling complacency and inertia. I longed for Val Gwyn to shake them up.

' "He may not be here in the flesh . . ." Val was

determined to have his say. "But you can see for yourselves that he is well represented by his angels and ministers of grace. So if this meeting has a message for the master, and I believe it has, there is an army of errand boys on this platform waiting to deliver it."

'There was visible unrest behind him. A white-haired nonconformist minister in black shook his fist and tried to rise to his feet. A less explosive colleague pulled him back by his coat-tails.

' "I propose . . ." Val Gwyn had to repeat the formula several times. Opposition from the floor was making itself felt in gusts of growls and boos " . . . That this conference pledges to work by direct and independent action to secure for our people the institutions of nationhood. It pledges itself to summon the people of Wales to a national convention that will create a new and independent political party for Wales . . ."

'Noises of objection and disagreement were far louder than any sound of support. I could see the smile of contentment spread on the chairman's cunning old face. He even turned to the elders to reassure them that the moment of danger had passed. Val Gwyn had no idea what was going on behind him. They were giving him all the rope that was needed to have him and his proposals twisting in the breeze.

' "We propose, in all seriousness, a non-violent citizen's army. To train themselves in self-discipline and self-sacrifice. This is the road to follow. If we learn to exercise the weapon of non-violence, we could become as effective as Mr Gandhi's Congress Party in India."

'Opposition, raucous ridicule, spread to every corner of the hall. He had gone too far too soon. Someone near me yelled out, "Get back to Ireland or whatever hole you crept out of." Val Gwyn tried to speak, but the conference had decided not to take him seriously. The chairman seemed to be enjoying the noise. Val stood his ground. I heard his shrill shout and I saw his face flush with effort.

' "What kind of a people are we? To be constantly fobbed off and hoodwinked!"

'I feared for him. He was in physical danger. Each time he tried to speak there was a greater threat in the roar of

256

response. At a signal from the chairman a dapper little musician in morning dress with a flower in his buttonhole and his hair dressed in a flowing style like a personal tribute to the absent leader, stepped forward to raise his order paper like a baton and lead the conference in a spirited rendering of an ambiguous patriotic hymn which appealed to the Almighty to remember our homeland without being too specific as to its exact whereabouts. Tasker nudged me and tried to say something. It was about Val Gwyn's inexperience and inability to control an audience. It was true but I was in no mood to be critical. For me he was already a hero. My mind was already made up. This was the kind of leader I had been looking for.

'I found him leaning against the wall of the public lavatories at the back of the pavilion. He looked to me as if he was going to be sick. His arms were folded tightly. He was shivering. Closer to, he looked more frail than when he stood alone on the platform. I became suddenly shy myself. I wanted to express my admiration. It was so intense, speaking was like a declaration of love.

' "You were great." I managed to say that. And add, "Splendid. Splendid."

'I could see how much the effort had cost him. He was a man not driven by personal ambition and without any taste for politics in the vulgar sense. He was possessed with desperate affection for a country, for a nation he could see sick and dying. He was shaking his head. Finding fault with himself.

' "I handled them badly," he said.

'This was true. But I wasn't willing to hear him criticise himself. I wanted him to know I shared all his convictions. If he wanted me I would support him.

' "I went about things entirely the wrong way."

' "You bore witness," I said. "Once that's been done, things can never be the same again."

' "Do you think so?" he said. He was consoled. He smiled at me and it was like the sun coming out. "We've got to start somewhere," he said. "I suppose that's true."

'We were able to laugh together. We were comrades.'

257

'The old man was a fixture on the hump bridge. His arthritis and his thick clothes shaped him into a gargoyle ostensibly staring down at the river reading its fluidity like fleeting messages concerning the meaning of existence. He had noted my presence and surmised my purpose. Shadowed by the rim of his battered hat, his eyes could swivel from left to right to take account of goings on in the village with the intensity of an augur seeking signs of larger events: assemblies of clouds, the feeding habits in the hen-run on the river bank, the movements of his neighbours, the arrival of a stranger.

'All I was up to was the purchase of a second-hand motorbike. It was advantage enough for me. The machine sat on its rear stand at the back of a barn-like garage with half its wall open to the sky and the weather. It was covered with a tarpaulin like a new invention awaiting the official unveiling ceremony. The owner of the garage was squatting in his tiny office engrossed in paper work. The mechanic attended to me. But the owner kept an eye on our transaction by lowering his head to peer through a half-moon of clear glass in his frosted window. I was in the mood for perpetual motion. With this machine I could speed over roads to delectable destinations like the river bounding over rocks and pebbles. Yet I stared at the bike as sternly as I could. My ignorance of machines should not interfere with primeval commercial practice.

' "You may as well say it's brand new," the mechanic said. "You may as well say that."

'He was a farm labourer who had learned about bikes and engines in the Army. He and I had seen the inside of the same camp at Rouen. He was throwing in a leather coat and goggles with the bike – left behind by the previous owner. I glimpsed the proprietor's face in the half-moon of clear glass; he was like a predatory bird peering out of its nest. His white hair was brushed back in streamlined fashion. He was an agent of speed and modernity.

' "It's got the power, see," the mechanic said. "And the glory. You wouldn't get a bike like that new under fifty pound."

'He knew he was being monitored by the bird of prey on his nest of invoices. So did I. So did the old man on the bridge. Such complexities of perspective were worth a poem. Would it be about the bird or the bike?

' "There was an accident, wasn't there?"

'My tone was all innocent inquiry. The mechanic winked at me. He seemed to admire my performance.

' "It wasn't the machine's fault," he said. "You can't blame the machine. You're a lawyer, so you'd know about that."

'I desired the bike. I could have enquired more loudly about any shortcomings of workmanship. There was talk in vague terms about guarantees. Worth nothing I knew. My best safeguard was to lower the price.

' "Twenty pounds would be a fair price. Under the circs," the mechanic said.

'I cut that one off as quickly as I could. "Fifteen," I said. "That's my limit."

So there they were. The mechanic anxious to please his master and the bird of prey in his litter of bills and bones. The dream took over. With Val on the pillion, we would roar off the boat at St Malo and penetrate deep into Brittany and into a France well away from those dread trenches and burial grounds. As far south as Correze and that fine castle of Turenne on its mountain-top and all those legendary sites invested with additional meaning and magic because they had been illuminated with Val's presence. There was a sweet urgency in the mode of travel because there was so much to examine: into the cool of a cathedral and out into the brilliant sunshine to drink coffee under an awning, and be back in time for the Grand Pardon at Sainte Anne-la-Palud. We would touch our nonconformist hats with respect at Madame the Virgin and not forget the Trinity. The man in the cubby-hole should realize the exalted nature of our pilgrimage: proceed three times around the church on your knees. Val knows so much about Brittany. The purpose of poetry is to recreate worlds.

'The white bird-head in the office nodded. The bike was mine! The mechanic wheeled it towards the petrol pump. He swung the handle of the pump with sacerdotal pleasure.

' "It's got power, Mr More," he said. "And that's what a bike needs. Power, you see. Plenty of power."

'I struggled into the stiff leather coat and put the goggles over my eyes. The world was circumscribed. The machine would make the hedgerows move and roll up the landscape like a magic carpet. I would straddle the distance between desire and reality: accelerate arrival and departure, command my own means of escape and unheralded return.

'It wouldn't start. The mechanic joked that it had been standing so long it had stiffened and grown cold. I saw the bike hidden under sacks in the back of the garage until memory of the accident faded and the mechanic had found time to repair it. Should I demand my money back? The mechanic was laughing.

' "It's nothing," he said. "I'll give you a push. Over the bridge and then down the other side. That's all it needs. It won't let you down. I promise."

'The old man had moved to the middle of the bridge balancing himself on his thick walking stick, his feet wide apart, a stone carving miraculously transposed.

' "I'm supposed to know you."

'He was chewing tobacco and spoke with the confidence of a man on whom old age had conferred the right to say what he liked to anybody. The mechanic gave a good-humoured yell.

' "Get out of the way, Enoch! You're holding up the traffic."

'The old man was not to be set to one side.

' "Talking about the war, were you?"

'He addressed his question to me. The mechanic was a ruffian incapable of discourse.

' "That's over now," the mechanic said. "We want to forget about it."

'Enoch's legs were in solid position. He could venture to raise his stick to point at the motorcycle.

' "It won't be over for long with those things about," he said. "That's the machine that killed Teddy Ty'n Rhos."

' "*Duw annwyl*," the mechanic said. "Is it your intention to put a curse on my business?"

' "He went down the road like a bullet," the old man said. "Said he learnt to ride one in the army. His skull cracked against the stone wall like an eggshell. The bike was a mess too."

'The mechanic's face flushed. "Don't tell lies, Enoch Jones. That wasn't the same bike at all."

' "You are a lawyer, John Cilydd More. And your grandmother has got sense. Which is the fault on this earth? The man or the machine?"

'This was Enoch Jones. Reputed to know several hundred folk songs. Should I ask him to sing? I was sure he would respond. The day was as bright as ever. I wondered how old he was and how he had accumulated his repertoire. Songs that went back centuries.

' "It's bad enough to have you perched all day on this bridge plotting harm to my business," the mechanic said. "You can't plant yourself in the highway, Enoch Jones. You've no right to do that."

' "God doesn't like those things!"

'He meant motorbikes. This is how folk songs were born. The peasant's response to change. Or at least to painful experiences like love and death and hardship and earning a living. Something to think about while I was sailing along and my magic steed was eliminating the difference between up and down. Wheels were words that could alter our picture of the world. The mechanic was roused.

' "What right have you got to pronounce what God likes or doesn't like, Enoch Jones? No more than a hen or a heifer."

'The old man was ready to bask in the mechanic's abuse.

' "I can tell you why, cub," he said. "Because those things you fiddle with are inventions of the devil. So He would be obliged to hate them, wouldn't He? *Mene, mene, tekel*. If you weren't so stupid, you would read it on the wall."

'This was it! The subject for my crown poem. I tingled with excitement. It would be this bike. A gift horse not to be looked at in the mouth. A winged horse sprung from the blood of Medusa. I had to dare to ride it. Great poems are

261

not born from small ambition. This sooth-sayer on the bridge was sent to inspire me. All around us were the sounds of nature mingling easily with the modulations of the river flowing under the bridge and of this machine for eating the future. The themes were there for my verse to clarify. Experiences lay in wait for the companionship that would develop between me and my trusty machine. A good morning's work. I have bought a friendship and I have caught, captured, conjured up a proper subject. The magic of the machine. The Pegasus that will carry me from the old world to the new. Enoch Jones gyrates his stick above the dust as if he contemplates writing in it. He can see the grin on my face. He shuffles like a crab to one side.

' "If you want to ride off to perdition, young man, don't let me stand in your way."

'The mechanic has made adjustments. I kick and the engine roars into life. The music of freedom. I can go where I like.'

iii

'I stood up in the open tourer to take a look at the two girls through the binoculars. Even at a distance they were beautiful. Beautiful Amy and perhaps less beautiful Enid. And both no less beautiful for being besotted with Val and following him so eagerly up the slope to the ancient ruin. He spoke to them with such gravity as if they understood everything he said. Perhaps they did. They were certainly ready to agree with him before he opened his mouth. And when he had finished, his smile was so like a benediction I could see them kneel side by side to receive it.

'The binoculars belong to Enid's brother Emrys. I suppose I put up with him for the sake of his sweet sister Enid. He is so absorbed in his career prospects he takes his briefcase to bed with him. He is bent on being important. He is envious of Val. These German field-glasses he claims to have taken off the body of a German officer. He has deliberately kept me back now so that I should not follow up the slope too closely on Val's heels. He has a twelve-bore

262

gun and he has the nerve to expect me and his younger brother Ifor to act as his beaters. He wants game and he wants attention. If he shoots a pheasant or even a rabbit he will drop it at Amy's feet. He believes attention is the first step to affection. I dont see how he can avoid observing the devotion of both girls to Val Gwyn. That doesn't deter him. His will to succeed exceeds his sensibility by a ratio of at least one hundred to one.

' "Look at the fellow," Emrys said. "What does he think he's up to?"

'Val had emerged from rocks and gorse bushes to face a limestone cliff. He intended to climb it. How the man drives himself. He is always complaining of too little time and so much to do. Nothing less than change the course of history, ha, ha, says Emrys. Save a nation from premature extinction, say I. That sort of thing. He was determined to climb. His arms and legs spread out against the rock face looked spider-thin. He doesn't eat enough. He doesn't sleep enough. Ideas drive him on. They gnaw at his entrails. Is that what vision means?

' "Showing off!"

'I heard Emrys snorting behind me. I did not turn around. His German field-glasses are like a millstone around my neck. In the back of the tourer he has two golf bags: one for clubs and one for his fishing tackle. A great one for "belongings", our Emrys. I made a quiet joke about the impossibility of hunting, shooting, fishing and playing golf all at one and the same time, but he affected not to hear. He can't make his mind up whether to climb in the Civil Service, the Colonial Service, or Educational Administration. He ponders these problems aloud as though the future of civilization depended on his decision. And he condemns Val for attempting to climb that limestone cliff. I don't see why I should be bored by him. I take a last look at the girls before setting out to join them. I, too, long to hear what Val will have to say.

'They scramble around the slope on hands and knees in an effort to reach the top before Val climbs the cliff. They look back and wave as if they know they are under observation. They begin an uphill race for a path through a plantation of

263

fir trees. Close to each other, laughing and shouting, they attack the slope. They are little more than children and all the more beautiful for that. It's a race for the first to reach him and greet him. I must not be jealous. I have no right to be. One day Val will be a great man and they will know then how right they were to love and admire him. Enid overcomes her laughter with a burst of energy. Just as she is about to set her foot on the narrow path, Amy reaches out and grasps the hem of her skirt. In helping herself forward, she pulls Enid back and takes the lead herself in an undeclared contest. Enid has fallen. Amy returns to help her back to her feet and dust her down. They half embrace and shake with laughter before struggling on hand in hand through the trees. Seen from this distance their friendship is moving and beautiful.

' "Come on, you two. Come on then," Emrys said.

'He was ready to go shooting. He aimed his gun at all points of the compass. I was glad to walk away from them. His brother Ifor is a nice enough fellow, but noisy and too much under his elder brother's thumb. He listens to him as to an oracle. He is capable of being fascinated by such topics as whether the Civil Service or the Colonial Service offers the better prospects of rapid advancement. Where is a bright young man more likely to be overlooked: in Streatham or Ibadan? Which is the shortest route to the membership of exclusive London clubs? These are the questions about which Emrys ruminates and ponders in his heart.

'The ruins are impressive at close quarters. The walls are shattered heaps of stone and the one tower that remains standing is held together by a mass of ivy and too dangerous to climb. I am out of breath. Val is striding about or standing stock still with the intense preoccupation of a scientist examining some unique specimen. It is all sacred to him. Every hill and every valley. The land around us is a living thing; from the leafy hollow to the bare hillside, the earth turns its face to the seasons. It is ready to be bruised by the heel of history and restored by the care and affection of hands in league with the elements; the toughness of skin and bone, the modulation of the chill wind, the warmth of the water brooks. Eastwards a long, uneven and yet fertile

264

plateau is rimmed with a range of billowing low hills. South-west of us a rich valley lies relaxed and secure as a sleeping form between bare hills with its green arms flung out in the shallow gaps.

'Enid has found a spur on the north side of the ruin that gives her an uninterrupted view of a vast, shimmering sea. She stands still, her arms folded, an exalted expression on her face. Amy is watching Val, curious that he should appear to see so much in stones, bare earth, coarse grass and sheep droppings. Her presence illuminates the place. The breeze plays with the hem of her frock and as she stands against it she becomes a candidate for deification, the model of a mythological goddess. The radiance of her person inherits the earth. Enid is more aware of the spirit of the place. She is the one prepared to pour the soil of respect over the stones. She wants Val to tell them everything about them. He is very ready to oblige.

'The place where we stand was a centre of resistance. Time and again when the movement of Teutonic peoples threatened the last outposts of Romano-British culture with devastation, the whole country rose against the invader. A victory on this very hill against the Normans was the crowning glory of a revival of the fortunes of the House of Cunedda.

' "When was that?" Amy said. Her curiosity had been roused by Val's eloquence and Enid's enthusiastic response.

"1094." he said.

'He enunciated the date so solemnly, she laughed.

' "Quite a time ago," she said.

'He was amused by her scepticism. Enid was less patient.

' "Because of the victory," she said; "and only because of that, we are able to stand here now and call this country our own in our own language."

'Amy was ready to tease. She looked at her friend in mock-innocence.

' "I thought you weren't keen on battles and all that sort of thing, Enid Prydderch," she said.

'My fate is to desire two women and have no title to either. They both prefer Val, as I do myself. I have become as painfully self-aware, and as self-conscious, as this age in

265

which we live. In the peace of a world under sedation, I watch myself float between the soil and the sky. The dislocated imagination indulges in choices which are no choice at all – a condition made worse by being bilingual. To have always two tongues you need two faces. Emrys, the great huntsman, firing away at nothing in the woods below us, airily declares that having two languages at your beck and call is better than having merely one. It is easy for him to talk. There is never any danger of poetic impulse threatening the pedestrian beat of his ambitious heart. Words for him in whatever language are rungs to assemble into a ladder. To achieve the forms of poetic utterance that approach the sublime, you have to be possessed with one language to the exclusion of all others. You allow it to take control of your being so that it can speak with authority through your experience. But what experience of mine can have any permanent value when I am so lacking in conviction; shifted about like a fallen leaf by any wind of opinion that blows? That is why Val is so important to me. The strength of his convictions structures my condition. He provides me with "reasons of being" in a world of post-war confusion. Without his strength I would be a coward. Without his capacity for joy I would sink in my own quicksand of sadness. Without him I am a spineless and fearful creature, plagued with doubt and hobbled with uncertainty. He gives me the strength I need to harness the invisible power of song.

'He is lecturing the girls. He has a way of leaning forward that makes the individuals he is addressing feel unique and important. His voice is soft and husky. More effective at close quarters than on a platform. Amy, too, has fallen under the spell of his sincerity and confidence.

' "The Great War has blown a great hole through the armour-plated complacency of the nonconformity in which we were brought up. Wouldn't you agree?"

'Both girls agreed. Amy does not need to refer to Enid's expressive face to establish her own reaction. She sustains a look of stern concentration that has its own charm.

' "Now this is very serious. A major crisis, because for us the church is native, but the state is alien. We have no control over the state. If the church is crumbling from within, who can protect us from the tidal wave of the new barbarism?"

'He goes on like this at length. Until the girls can no longer bear the intensity of his vision. They both shudder and then laugh to camouflage their embarrassment. He extends his hands towards them.

' "It binds us to each other and it binds us to the past. A language is the accumulated deposit of attempts at civilized living that have gone on for thousands of years. It is more than the legacy of Arthur. If we have any honour left in our hearts and minds, have we any choice except to defend it?"

'They were infected with his excitement and so was I. We heard the motor-horn of the tourer being squeezed and we all burst out laughing. Val said Ifor was a Roland who would never refuse to blow his horn and both girls laughed even louder, although Amy had no idea what he meant. She squeezed Enid's hands and suddenly let them drop.

' "I'm going to be first back anyway," she said.

'She started down, looking back to challenge Enid to another race. They were filled with joy and delighted to find a way of releasing it. Amy led the way down the path. Enid plunged down in pursuit. Val and I watched them until they disappeared behind tall gorse bushes. Only their laughter was to be heard as they sped through the trees. He, too, began to run, leaping down the slope between the limestone cliff and the path with reckless surefootedness. I had to follow him as best I could. He overtook the girls. The brothers in the car were standing up to watch the race. Emrys abandoned his gun and snatched the binoculars from Ifor. When I emerged from the trees, the girls were halfway across the rough field. Enid gained on Amy. Amy caught her foot in a tuft of coarse grass, lost her balance, and tumbled to the ground. Enid flew on, unable to stop herself and unaware of what had happened to Amy. I was there to stand over her as she panted on the ground, ready to help her to her feet. She had difficulty in speaking. I knelt down.

' "Winded," she said at last.

' "You haven't done anything to your ankle?"

'I felt it with great tenderness. She seemed so young and

267

helpless as well as beautiful. She took my hand when I offered it. She allowed me to support her with my arm. If she accepted my help, she might accept me. I had visions of riding out on my motorbike to visit her in her home at Llanelw. I knew she lived with her uncle and aunt in cramped conditions in a workman's terrace house in the seaside town. The uncle was difficult. He was lame. He had failed as a smallholder and had an unsatisfactory job in a bus depot. I could arrive there on the offchance. This would put my motorbike to good use. And spirit her away on my pillion. Nothing could be more wonderful. Rescue her for at least a day out. I wanted to tell her how valuable she was and how I did not want any harm to come to her.

' "He's brilliant, isn't he?"

'She was talking about Val. I wanted her to lean more heavily on me. Val and Enid had reached the car. This was how we should be paired. Amy was looking at the car and straining to hear what was being said. Emrys had jumped out to open the rear door with his twelve-bore gun on his shoulder and a great show of mock military efficiency.

' "Even Emrys admits it," Amy said.

What she meant was that Val was more than brilliant. A leader. We had to have a leader. That was true enough. Like the children of Israel in the desert. All the countries of Europe seemed to be aware of this need after the Great War. The need for a new leader. What this girl needed was someone like me to protect and guide her. All her weight was on my arm. I had to be extra thoughtful and concerned.

' "We are suffering from hero-worship," she said. "Did you know that?"

'It was such a shrewd remark from such virginal lips that I blushed. She saw my cheeks grow red and she laughed.

' "You are a natural hero-worshipper, John Cilydd," she said. "I think I like that. It shows what a nice person you are. I'm not. Not a bit, really. Isn't that awful."

'We were friendly and alone together.

' "You're a poet," she said. "You understand things. That's wonderful."

'She tested her ankle. There was nothing really wrong with it. There was no reason why she should continue to rely

268

on my support. With childlike abruptness, she broke away from me and ran back to the car. I could hardly stand as she left me, dizzy as I was with a vertigo that seemed like falling in love.'

iv

'Through the windscreen all I can see is the prison wall. Is he determined to be a martyr? The oblique sunlight is counting the stones. So much labour gone into building that twenty-foot wall. On this side is the wide street down which the traffic flows. Inside they can hear the clang of the trams as they trundle past carrying the workers on the early shift down to the steel works and the coke ovens between the slums and the mudflats. This wall represents the power of the state. It is a more permanent construction than any building in this area, including the Mission Hall built with the profits of the most successful local shipowner, with his coaling stations like pock-marks around the globe and his unswerving devotion to his Methodist Connexion.

'His Majesty's Prison. There is a certain sonority in the phrase. They don't want Val in there. Why should he insist? I know the reason and I resent it because it shows me in a paler light than I would wish to see myself. This man constructs himself into some heroic ideal. He is in full command and prepared to sacrifice all he has – even the delectable Amy, my young wife's best friend. I am not sure whether Amy appreciates the extent of his purpose and dedication, but I know that Enid does. Hence my submerged resentment; hence my jealousy which I protest is purely theoretical. But I feel it as I watch those pretty heads move closer together in their concern for this suffering hero.

'They are too young to detect the artificial element in his will to sacrifice. These acts of will. He steps out of his comfortable bourgeois academic groove to share the suffering of the stricken Welsh working class as if his long body would be some sort of bridge to link them to their own past and preserve them from the helplessness and alienation that go with poverty and unemployment. In an age as

269

self-conscious as ours this is an absurd quixotic attempt to intervene in the process of historical necessity which has usurped the government our pious immediate ancestors assumed belonged to a divine will. I know all this. Painful lessons learnt in my own experience. And yet here I am again. Waiting for his release. Waiting to ferry him to whatever meetings he wants to attend, from an emergency conference in Porthcawl to a protest outside the City Hall, from the Settlement to the soapbox on the street corner.

'This is not my vocation. Enid knows that. I, too, in my small fashion am making a sacrifice. She knows that I am a dedicated artist and she knows that if it ever came to a choice I should let my country down, betray it even, in order to feed my art. She also knows that the language binds us together so inescapably such an option could never be mine. She calls this a tragic joke and she is prepared to laugh about it. She is prepared to laugh about anything. When she writes to me there is usually an undercurrent of her own hilarity in all her letters. "Dearest C. These are our mountains. There is only one language that can open their mouths to echo the song of the sky . . . Dearest C. We must never allow Death to become an accident . . . When that happens the state will take over the material debris and exchange sanitation for salvation . . . Our hesitations should always be the outcome of a certainty that is rooted in the belief that an unbreakable bond exists between what we call Love and the Will that created the universe and I can hear you saying believe that and you can believe anything even as I write it, Sionyn . . ."

'I told her she should write to Val, not to me. She laughs again as if I had made a joke. Exasperating and still lovable. She has chosen to marry me, to sacrifice herself, her own brilliant career, as her family must have insisted *fortissimo* – her father, her mother, her brothers, her great-uncle, her HMI aunt – what a chorus – in order to support me in my impossible task of making mountains sing. "Dearest C. Our world will be something we weave out of words well beyond the burning eyes of disapproval that now make Ivydene such an uncomfortable house to live in. There is a sagging of the skin in the corner of my mother's eyes for which I feel responsible. The communication between us was never

270

good. Now it is turned into reproach and blame. This makes me resentful as well as guilty. By loving you I have robbed her of something she believed should have been hers. It is time to leave . . ." How could I not adore a girl who has given up everything for me?

'And yet she expects me to accept that my artistic ambition is lower in any scale of values that we can share and use than Val Gwyn's dedication and self-sacrifice. This is what we say aloud to each other in daily variations of reassurance: there is no good life to compare with right conduct. Val commands our allegiance on the basis of heroic goodness as much as the force of intellectual argument. We are agreed about this. And yet, as I alone know, at the bottom of my consciousness, in the dangerous half light, lurk reservations. These dregs that make me jealous.

'I am here waiting for his release. Not for the first time. I have paid the fine the magistrates have imposed upon him for yet another puny act of defiance against the power of the state. It's a stupid game that might go on for ever. He refuses to pay and they put him in prison. With my money and my knowledge of the law of England, I bail him out. The state is immortal. It decides where you live and where you'll be buried. It punishes disobedience and deviation with the utmost rigour, as the phrase goes. It is in charge of the furnace and the graveyard: it disciplines the flames and counts the worms. It goes on for ever. Individuals who feed on pride are allowed to gain brief glory in its service before the wheel turns and they are crushed or thrust aside. What can this son of a Pembrokeshire widow do except bang his head against that prison wall? A revolutionary is an individual who wishes to kill the state. You can't kill a wall. In any case Val isn't a genuine revolutionary. He's just a martyr dedicated to sacrificing himself.

'And yet I am jealous. I consider syphoning off this bone-burning emotion into a work of art. Using it like engraver's acid. And as a source of inspiration. Suppose Desdemona were jealous of Othello; the roles reversed? I mentioned the notion to Enid. As usual she was enthusiastic. That was enough to cause the idea to evaporate like cigarette smoke. I have no model for a jealous woman.

271

Enid is incapable of jealousy. She understood my earlier infatuation with Amy and condoned it. She is like Val. She will never tire of the promise of the kingdom that is to come. Both natural believers. Superior beings. Seeing in others unfailing mirrors of their own goodness. Impossible people.

'I watch Amy with increasing suspicion. I can't believe she is as devoted to Val as Enid is to me. Val admires her because she stands on her own feet and makes a cult of feminine independence. He loves her appetite for action. She has a way of clenching her fist and flashing her eyes that makes him laugh with delight.

' "I'd rather die on the barricades than live a life of remorse."

'When did she say that? Her voice echoed now in my ear. Was it a student's debate; no more than that? It was her spirit that alarmed me. The spirit that throws bricks through windows and stirs peoples to action.

' "You must act. You have to."

'This was her again, in search of a cause more elevated than stopping Sunday golf. Enid says she has a natural delight in the processes of living that nothing will ever impair. Enid says that is why it is always a pleasure to be with her. Even to quarrel with her. I am not so certain about that. Enid says that "natural" is Amy's favourite word. She loves to hear her use it. It embraces farms, animals, fields, open skies, the great cycle of the seasons, appetites, cleanliness, common sense, and keeping things as simple and as unambiguous as possible. Very nice, of course, to imagine that the grinding poverty of that smallholding in the hills has taught her something; but I doubt it.

'It is Val who roams the shattered world of Wales like an Arthurian knight in a storm, looking for people to rescue and causes to espouse. Amy is more in search of adventure. I can never believe her motivation is as pure as his. She is a pagan if ever I saw one: a force of nature. She can hardly begin to comprehend the urge to self-sacrifice that drives the man she loves or believes she loves. Enid says that does not matter. I think it does, because my punishment is that in spite of my scepticism, I am compelled to follow him. I need him. I need him far more than Amy does. That is why I am

272

sitting here leaning on a steering wheel and staring at prison stones. He gives shape to my existence. He reduces the embarrassment of choice. He imposes unflinching courses of action. They irritate because they are never at one with my artistic purpose and ambition. Why should I have to say 'no' to selfish passions that could transform pedestrian lines with their incandescence? Why must I suppress so many enticing forms of disobedience?

'He is no bigger than a boy outside the massive prison doors. They are well calculated to intimidate. He has a brown paper parcel under his arm. There are patches of dust on his navy-blue suit. How thin he is. He smiles and waves when he sees me. My heart melts. This is early morning and a pale trace of the moon still hangs in the sky. His shadow follows behind him. He needs a good meal; he needs a decent rest.

' "Have you got a cigarette?"

'I want him to take me for granted. I offer him a Gold Flake. He inhales, closing his eyes with gratitude. He is powered by a force as distant and as beautiful as the last star I saw vanish with the sunrise. I want him to choose me as his companion for any journey he wishes to make. I must also scold him as a good wife would do.

' "You don't have to, Val." I can hear myself saying it. Like a tired priest listening to the echoes of his own early morning litany. "Stand on soapboxes on street corners. Bursting your lungs out. You don't have to."

'Of course he has to. Nothing less will do. He has to wear himself out in the absurd exercise of building a national movement out of peaceful persuasion, example, and something called "love". He knows perfectly well that there has never been a state of any shape or form in the history of this world that was not founded on bloodshed, not given its shape by violence and maintained by the cohorts of brute force in fancy dress. How can we ever be different? Wales of the singing festivals and white gloves. The valley marxists are right to laugh at us. Home rule for charabancs and Sunday School trips. Self-government for children's eisteddfodau. He sits in my car as if smoking a cigarette in the passenger seat were the height of leisured luxury. There

273

is nothing I can do except stand or fall alongside him. That's all it amounts to.

'His character is as rugged and enduring as the blue stones of the Preselau. I can only describe him in atavistic terms as if singing his praises were my vocation. There is the mystery and magic of the first book of the Mabinogi about him. He is a prince capable of changing places with the king of the Otherworld for a year and a day and sleeping with the queen in the king's shape without touching her, in the name of an honour that is tantamount to a higher form of love. There has to be an ideal and it is the purpose of poets in our language to proclaim it. This man is open-handed and is entitled to respect by right of the lineage of the virtues he practises: easy with people, flexible, charming; rigid and unbending in matters of principle; ready to spare others, never sparing himself; dedicated to the defence of the defenceless; honest to the point of his own undoing; an authority on the past, designing a better future. What better lamp to follow in the gathering dark? A flame to keep the cold at bay. Without this new form of leadership, this new style of politics, the human race is doomed. This is the conviction I am obliged to cling to, however absurd the activities in which I get involved.

'We picketed the morning session of the South Wales Miners' Federation emergency conference. We were about as much use as the seagulls perching on the rails of the promenade and the roof of the hall.

' "What's this, mun? I can't read the bloody thing, can I?"

'The young miner spoke to me from one corner of his mouth with the stump of a cigarette in the other. He stuffed the leaflet back into my hands and shuffled on in the press of men making their way into the picture palace for the meeting. The older men were more willing to take our leaflet. Some of them anyway. They dropped them underfoot so that the pink sheets littered the steps into the building. Strong simple language indeed. They spelt out a message that was no news to them in any language. They knew better than we did that there were more unemployed in Wales than anywhere else in the four countries of the United Kingdom. They knew that our industries were dying

274

and our young people emigrating in droves. And that more people died of tuberculosis in Wales than in any other country in Europe and that the percentage of people speaking our native language was now down to thirty-six per cent and that one form of consumption and decay fed the other. They knew all these facts and many more, but their remedies were not ours. They rejected self-help as well as self-government. They turned their backs on any form of home rule, to rely on eloquence and Westminster party politics. They believed with pentecostal fervour that socialism would blow like a winnowing wind through the cobwebbed corridors of power and that at the end of the struggle a door would open on a brave new world.

'We found a bench near the weather kiosk on the promenade where we could eat our chips out of a greasy bag wrapped in old newspaper. Val said there wasn't time for a proper meal. There was canvassing to be done for a local election. There was the committee on the children's summer camp. The evening class and the choir rehearsal were cancelled because of the Means Test Rally. There would be the ritual evening competition on the soapboxes between the red dragon and the red flag. Val had a line of argument he was eager to clarify by outlining it to me. He let his chips go cold as he made a case for the wider use of English in propaganda among the unemployed.

' "Funny logic," I said.

' "What do you mean?" He was impatient with the interruption.

' "You save the language by abandoning it," I said. "A quick way to defeat our own ends."

' "They are there," Val said. "Waiting for a new vision. Economics is what matters now. You can't talk about anything else to people with empty bellies. It's got to be clear. It's got to be simple. There's a battle going on since the war between the banks and industry in England. It's as simple as that. That's at the bottom of all our troubles. And the government always comes down on the side of the banks. Why? Simple. Because the Empire they worship is in essence a financial empire and our unemployment is a direct consequence of imperial financial policy. Does that make sense?"

275

'I wanted to hear about his days in prison. Last time he shared a cell with a burglar who used to be a private in the Indian Army. He was robbing a golf-clubhouse at four o'clock on a Sunday morning and his sack was so full he telephoned for a taxi. As luck had it the taxi driver was a policeman's brother who drove him straight to the nearest police station. I loved to hear these stories and see Val relax as he told them. There is no time now. There is never enough time. The fate of the world hangs on the use of every second. He has no cunning. (How can you begin to be a politician without cunning?) Only energy and conviction. Should I ask him if he had seen the ex-public schoolboy who posed as an impecunious viscount and sold bogus shares to ageing clergymen in rural rectories and life insurance to their wives and daughters? No time for that either. He wanted a detailed report on a paper given at our weekend school on the degrees of flexibility in the relationship between local authorities in Wales and the central government in London. I had taken notes and I was obliged to read them out. A posse of six beach donkeys hitched together led by a morose-looking gypsy woman in black costume and a straw hat, trotted past close to our feet. Val took no notice. He was absorbed in working out a blueprint for economic collaboration between local authorities in Wales. I refrained from making any frivolous comparison between the donkeys and county councillors.

'We only had time for a cup of cocoa at the Settlement before sallying forth to a rally on the Means Test. And after that, on the usual street corner, he made use of the megaphone for an extra meeting. There were hungry sheep left after the rally looking up with their mouths open and still longing to be fed.

' "A nation as a basis of social life, my friends, needs to be small enough to cherish and yet large enough to afford men and women, families and communities, unions and societies, a fullness of life within itself. In this way, the European way, the lives of nations should relate one to another. On this basis, political and economic unity should be the priority for European politics in this century. This is what international-ism means!"

'His voice is hoarse but he ploughs on. They are ready to feed on words since there is little else to eat. The little communist leader called Wes Hicks is also hoarse. His spectacles have been repaired with bright beads of solder. A yellow quiff of hair escapes from the peak of his cap. He, too, is armed with a megaphone. The crowd enjoy the dialectical rivalry between the two absurdly hoarse voices.

' "Petty-bourgeois idealism. That's all you've got, comrade. Long live the proletariat!" He was disappointed with the ragged cheer. "Social fascism!" Wes Hicks tried his best to inject more venom into his hoarse utterance. "That's what you're listening to, comrades! That's not the voice of the working class. I can tell you that much for a start. What you are hearing over there is petty-bourgeois social fascism."

'A voice piped up from the ragged crowd.

' "What's that then, Wes?"

'It was a genuine, innocent, enquiry. But the laughter it caused infuriated Wes Hicks. He pulled off his cap and stamped on it.

' "How you do dant me, you ignorant bugger."

'There was more laughter. The crowd's concentration was broken. It was time to sing. "Sospan Fach" would hardly be appropriate. "Bread of Heaven" too ironic. Through the megaphone Val offered to sing the Internationale in French if the crowd joined in afterwards on "Hen Wlad fy Nhadau". It was a fair offer and a noble effort. Val reached the last line "le genre humain" before he was overtaken with a coughing fit. I supported him as he stepped off the soapbox. They were still singing as he sat down on the wall and clamped his handkerchief on his mouth. When the spasm was over he opened the white handkerchief. It was spattered with bright spots of blood.

' "Well, look at that." He sounded quietly surprised. "Just look at that," he repeated.'

v

'What constitutes a stranger? A face in the crowd that flows over London Bridge? A chance encounter on the road from

277

Jericho to Jerusalem? I wanted to show the American girl Enid's letters. Some of them at any rate. Like a mendicant selling sacred relics. Hetty would have responded to that crystalline idealism and concern. "Dearest C. I stand outside the doors of their respective bedrooms and say to myself I am the child of a peculiar marriage, therefore I am peculiar. No. I am not. I refuse to admit it. I wish to be typical. I cultivate a passion for the truth and that is not peculiar. This is an essential human quality. It has to be, Sionyn, otherwise it is a poor lookout for the human race . . . We used to look to you and to Val, Amy and I, as our spiritual directors, and I think we were right . . . There has to be an heroic ideal and a link with the heroic past if there is to be meaning and inevitability to actions which make possible a worthier future . . . It is true that our fate is a great mystery. We can say that Hell and evil separate us from the will of God and from such simple exercises as the daily effort of cleansing whatever source of goodness is able to persist in souls shrinking with selfishness . . ." She was never afraid of preaching, my Enid. "Of course, hell and evil exist, otherwise (yet another otherwise) we would not be separated from each other . . ."

'And so must I thank the will of God that we are now separated from each other for ever and ever, amen? She lies rotting in the cold graveyard and I maintain a precarious hold on my sanity by practising company law in a London office, attending meetings of the Socialist Lawyers Society and chamber concerts and English poetry readings and talking to Hetty; or more accurately to Hetty Remington, Margot Grosmont and her cheerful cousin Nigel, and our Eddie Meredith successfully disguised as a past-President of the Mermaid Society and a left-wing expert in the art of speaking Elizabethan blank verse. I would like to show Hetty some of Enid's letters. No one else. She is the only one who might understand and even throw light on things hidden in the darkness of the blind abyss. But I don't. I can't. I would have to translate them and no one knows better than I how the poetry gets lost in translation. Probably I have more devious reasons for suppressing this desire to share Enid's letters with an American stranger.

278

They don't always show me or my relationship with my late espoused saint and girl-wife in the best possible light. As things are, in their most sympathetic moments, Hetty and Margot see me like a stained-glass window suffused with the dim religious light of my sorrow. They can only guess at what a wonder my young wife, the living Enid, was. They have my melancholy visage as pale evidence of the glory gone for ever from the earth. Furthermore, I am a poet in a language they cannot understand, obliged to labour in a boring city office as well as carry the burden of irreparable loss. There is no enchantment to compare with unfathomable numbers. Their attention brings me solace. It is a relief from the self-loathing that is liable to sweep over me when I sit alone in my lodgings in Camden Town.

'Hetty Remington. Her father's uncle made those celebrated paintings of the Wild West and the freedom of Indians and cowboys in the saddle. I think she would have liked to be a female Walt Whitman, emerging fully grown from the foam and water of the democratic masses. To sing the song of companionship and a programme of chants! When she is roused her back straightens like an exclamation mark. Hetty! Her wealth weighs her down and her expensive education obliges her to consider the entire human race as potential sisters and brothers. I feel closest to her among this generation from Oxford, younger than myself, who have brought the balm of their impulsive generosity to soothe my wounded spirit. I am the stranger but they have made me welcome. I need to be grateful and most of all to her.

'Margot is tougher. She has the authoritarian English proconsular manner of her family. At first I resented her polite bossiness. Now I am more inclined to respect her forthright honesty. It reminds me of Val. Anything that reminds me of his integrity brings a lump to my throat. I shut my eyes and I see him lying like an alabaster effigy in that sanatorium bed and outside the window the smoke rising from burning leaves in the still autumn air. I am a fugitive from an accumulation of native sorrow, capable at any moment of being strangled with self-pity. This is why it is so essential I should address myself to immediate and urgent problems whether commercial or political. Margot is there to nudge me; to activate a conscience that is in danger of falling asleep from overwork and exhaustion.

' "You can move Left or Right," says Margot in that ringing accent that for generations has governed colonies and commanded the attention of the House. "What you cannot do today is stand still."

'It sounded profound when she said it. I heard the ground tremble with the tramp of marching feet: left, right, left, right, left, right. Whatever direction the politics dictated, the outcome that threatened was hideous war. This was something I knew more than she did. I had buried heroes in a world these charming young people could not inhabit or imagine – those distant ghosts who once governed my existence. How could there in my lifetime be a second visitation of indiscriminate carnage? How could we allow it?

' "If you are chosen you should go," Margot said. "It's as simple as that."

'I was inclined to agree with her. The situation in Vienna was terrible. The Social Democrats were desperate and in need of legal help. The fact that I spoke no German was an obstacle that had to be overcome. There was an urgent demand for lawyers with socialist sympathies from all over Europe to attend those trials and make at least the appearance of justice possible. What justice can emerge when an army can use machine guns and even field guns to clear the streets of a city? Everywhere regimes are springing into being supported by fear and bayonets; everywhere there are restrictions on liberty and the persecution of the innocent: systems of spies and informers, networks of concentration camps and families in thrall to the power of the omnipotent state. The whole of Europe seems to be sliding slowly down into a morass worse than the outburst of suicidal madness that shattered the peace of 1914. The pestilence confined in those four years to the trenches will spread now to every corner of the continent.

' "If that's what you think," Margot said. "You have to do something about it."

'It might be better for the world if all problems of government were left to uncomplicated souls like Margot. She told her blithe cousin Nigel exactly what to do . Under her direction he would join the Communist Party instead of driving his taxi in every capital in Europe. Margot thinks he ought to chauffeur a small complement of British lawyers in his taxi from one of the channel ports to the gates of Vienna. He is very taken with the idea. He says it is a neat solution to his private dilemma.

'We roll along the Embankment in his beloved taxi. It is agreeable to share their youthful high spirits. This is a London that banishes dull care from its streets. Not a bad place to be when the sun sets behind the black chimneys of the power station and the tugs hoot as they fuss through the rosy waters of the painted river. In Markham Square dwells a painter engaged in a sequence of surrealist portraits of Margot's family tree. It amuses her. On the floor beneath a philosopher pursues his investigations in an empty, carpetless room and quarrels every evening with a piano-playing Pole. The daughter of a pacifist peer gives frequent parties in her flat on the ground floor. Hetty waxes Whitmanesque and urges me to clap my hands at the infinite variety of the world. "Living beings," she said. "Identities now doubtless near us in the air that we know not of . . ." Then she blushes at her own enthusiasm and subsides into silence, her long back bending into a question mark.

'Eddie Meredith insists that Hetty is in love with me. I take this as yet another expression of his predilection for making mischief. He has an image of himself as irresistibly naughty boy, all black curls and roguish dimples. He affects to be more drunk than he can possibly be in reality in order to allow his tongue more freedom. The workhouse master's son who dreams of himself as a great playwright and actor. He is more likely to eke out a living as a gossip columnist. I have told him as much. He chooses to ignore my frankness.

' "She has plans for you," Eddie whispers in my ear in the corner of the saloon bar. "I've told her what a great genius you are in our native tongue. She wants to set you free from the strait-jacket of the strict metres. Some day you'll thank me for it."

'He does his best to pollute our relationship. Hetty is someone I can talk to. She has an understanding that is honest and unpretentious. We are interested in the same things. If she would have me accompany her on a tour of Provence and Savoy why should I refuse the invitation? She has thought long and hard whether or not I should attend the trials at Vienna. In spite of the strength of Margot's character and my own altruistic motives it was Hetty's view that I should not go. She had a better suggestion to make. I should take a sabbatical term, as she called it, in an old farmhouse her mother owned in sight of the Pont du Gard. There was a family there who could look after me. If I liked I could take my sister and my little son Bedwyr. It was a tempting offer. I don't know what absurd old-maidish caution prevented me from taking it.

'She has a mistaken image of me as a man who suffers in silence, worrying too much about the state of his native land. As tactfully as she knows how, she talks of the obligation of a poet to explore his own selfhood (as if I ever did anything else!) That might do very well for Whitman and his wide open spaces. I don't have the courage to share every atom of myself with any stranger who happens to drop by. I am a dependency. A secretion. How could I ever start anything new? There is a Russian called Igor who sometimes joins us on our social expeditions. The first time I met him he poked me in the ribs and asked me did I know Ernest Jones and had I ever read *Moses and Monotheism*? He has a way of making pronouncements in a Slavonic basso-profundo that gives them an extra resonance. "We are all of us exiles now. You realize that, don't you, More? From now on that will be the natural state of all cultivated people." Margot dismisses him as a reactionary White Russian and blames Nigel for bringing him along. I can't help feeling there is something in what he says. Another of his pronouncements: "The twentieth century is an aborted revolution."

'When Amy turned up I felt guilty and uneasy. It was possible she still blamed me for Enid's death. She was more conscious than I had ever been of differences of class and nationality. On the rare occasions when we were alone together she would say, "They're not the same people as us, are they?" Which was true enough and I may have been too self-absorbed to have noted the difference and taken its details to heart. The way she said it gave a sudden tug to the

282

invisible restraints that still bound us together. She seemed to be saying it would not be easy for us to escape from our common mould. She gave me a photograph she had taken of little Bedwyr as if it were a warrant for my arrest. At what age does it become impossible for a grown man to avoid his responsibilities?

'She had a particular aversion to Margot's family townhouse at Culpepper Place, probably because her aunt's cousin was in service there as housekeeper. She was particularly incensed by the way Lady Violet took advantage of her housekeeper; and even more by the absurd pride that Connie Clayton took in the house and its imperial contents from the Chinese Room to the neo-classical statues in every niche of the orangery. Her barely concealed hostility to the people and the place were overcome by Margot's determination to make Amy her friend. Margot worked at it, I imagined at first, on principle. Amy was such a glowing example of the potential of the working class. In Margot's eyes she became a standard-bearer: a living model for an inspiring painting of proletarian revolt led by a young woman in her prime.

'It was Margot's idea that we should all go out that night to Fralino's. It was to celebrate something and, I suspected, to give Nigel a chance to get closer to Amy before she returned to Wales. It was difficult to be jealous of Nigel and that in itself was a relief. He was such a cheerful chap and so straightforward and well-meaning and it was obvious that Amy could never feel anything for him other than comradely regard. They danced well together. He has the flow and agility that sometimes belongs to a man of solid bulk. He responds to the music with a feline grace that speaks of long practice as well as natural ability. Amy in his arms is strikingly beautiful in a white evening dress with bold sleeves and a frilled skirt hemmed with a blue that harmonizes with the colour of her eyes and fair hair. I had to refrain from staring at her. Hetty was struggling to express her thoughts with precision through the noise and Eddie Meredith's pseudo-inebriated attempts to draw attention to himself.

' "You need it, John Cilydd," she was saying. "Not just the sun and the woods and the vineyards. The voice of

283

another people. Warm as the weather. Every house has a courtyard. They do everything around the big fireplace. Flat-irons. Stew. Pots on an iron hook. Red pea soup. To give you another view of the world, John Cilydd. I'm not saying a deeper view, but a wider one. It seems to me you have to choose. There are other lawyers that can devote themselves to politics. You are a poet. Your poetry should be your contribution to the cause. You can't do both. It isn't humanly possible. You don't mind me saying exactly what I think? If we are going to be of any use to each other we have to be absolutely truthful. Don't you think?"

'It was the quality I most admired in her. The dark pupils of her eyes were like wells of truthfulness. Her sincerity was reassuring. It wouldn't be impossible to marry her; a marriage based on intellectual understanding rather than physical desire. What was wrong with that? It certainly came nearer to any concept of elective affinity than mere animal attraction.

' "That's why I think Vienna isn't really a good idea. For you, I mean. In your case. You have your vocation . . ."

'I listened to her intently and avoided looking at Amy who sat resting with her back to the dance floor. Nigel was steering Margot around in a foxtrot. Hetty was right about my vocation. Being a poet should be a full-time job. She could make that possible for me. Why should I suppress the thought as something mercenary and unworthy? Hetty's dark hair rose in waves from her high forehead. She was not overwhelmingly attractive. She was sympathetic and sincere. Those were rarer qualities than yellow curls or the lure of red lips and blue eyes. A vast woman in a fur-trimmed gold lamé evening dress had loomed up into the space behind Hetty. She was jabbing her finger in Amy's direction and accusing her of staring at her all evening. It was a sudden crisis. An ugly intrusion. She shattered the affinity that Hetty and I were creating for each other. This fat woman was a hostile stranger. Her attack was directed at Amy.

' "Staring at me as if I was dirt. Yes, you were. Who do you think you are?"

'It looked like concentrated hatred. Eddie was sober enough not to take up the opportunity to draw attention to

284

himself. If anyone was called upon to defend Amy it was me. One of the fat stranger's companions persuaded her to return to their table. But our harmony was broken into so many pieces and there was no way it could be put together again. Amy wanted to leave. It was early; only half past nine. She was determined to go. I could do nothing but follow her. In the dimly lit area by the cloakroom counter I saw her eyes fill with tears. She had only come in order to talk to me. She said she had no time at all for the others. She couldn't stand the sound of Eddie Meredith's put-on Oxford accent. She wanted to talk about little Bedwyr, of course. Who else. What else. Before we reached the door my shoulders were bending under the yoke.

'She wanted me to leave her alone. Or so she said. She wanted to cast me into the outer darkness reserved for enemies and strangers. Outside it was pouring with rain. I could not let her go. There is a fate which awaits each one of us and the art of the poet and his exalted consciousness is to know how to embrace it.

' "Go back to your friends," Amy said. "Go on. I'm sure they are much better than anything you could find at home."

'How could I leave her? On such a wet night at this, in the West End, to find her own way home? I took hold of the umbrella so that both her hands were free to raise the hem of her balldress that was being splashed by passing traffic. A moment such as this, disarmed and innocent and unaware, when the light of revelation pierces the darkness that surrounds us. In the corner of an empty café, over coffee and cakes bought as an excuse to be there, she asks me, Amy asks me, whether it had ever occurred to me to ask her to marry me. My entire existence hung by a thread a breath of wind could break. I whispered instead of shouting. The light of revelation was a sword out of a dark sky and it smote me with a rhetorical accuracy beyond anything I myself could ever compare. She was smiling at my confusion and the joy that had transformed my face.'

'In my dream the bass voice of the judge rumbled like thunder around the well of the court. Everyone knew he had made his reputation as a barrister in breach-of-promise cases. Old Mr Caddle and my great-uncle Ezra were galloping along the promenade with reckless abandon so as not to lose a single word that might fall from the judge's juicy lips. It was a performance no cultivated man should allow himself to miss. He could change wigs and positions, sit with the jury, shout from the gallery, stand in the witness box, join the press or the prosecution: anything in fact except conduct the defence. That position was vacant. On the wall above the judge's bench there was a murky painting of a storm at sea that included a sheepdog floating on a royal shield and my father's ship going down. The megaphone outside the courtroom transmitted the summing up to an attentive population of the living and the dead. It hung from the flagpole by a piece of string and for some inexplicable reason I was worried that it might fall before the great exponent of the law had completed his outline of the true nature of marital bliss.

' "If a wife has been unfaithful once, then it stands to reason it cannot be so difficult for her to be unfaithful a second or even a third time . . ."

'It seemed reverberantly true, but I wanted to submit it was false. For that reason I stood in the dock. This was no law at all, of England or anywhere else. My qualifications were disregarded. Worse, they were stripped from me, like my jacket and trousers. I stood, bare-footed, in my shirt which I understood would serve as my shroud. The courtroom was packed with people who never knew Amy. They were queuing up to give evidence against me. My Uncle Simon's earth-caked finger trembled in my direction. Mrs. Klugman collapsed in a heap and was carried out to lie on the pebbles on the beach. The tide lapped at her black dress and button boots. Alice Breeze and Captain Caddle were particularly vicious. They insisted I was the greatest traitor the world had known since Judas Iscariot. Caddle had a gun and pointed it in my direction. He was eager to fire, his finger twitching on the trigger. The judge rebuked him sternly and was distressed to have to remind a man who should know better of the rules of inadmissible evidence.

'All day I wanted to tell Amy about my dream. She was the one person who should know about it. It was her trial, not mine. To what extent could she be held to have betrayed Val Gwyn? No jury on earth would bring a verdict of guilty. Neither would I. Pen Lewis was a different case. He had died a hero's death in Spain and I had accepted the role of father to his son. By some obscure reversal I could not understand, I was expiating their lapse into what my immediate ancestors would certainly have categorized as sin. Aesthetic analysts would assume she had given way to an overwhelming physical attraction. It was a delicate and painful question about which I wouldn't want to question her too closely: to spare my own feelings more than hers. Wars have come and gone, my sister has burnt to death, and Time is engaged in the quiet process of reducing us to creatures of habit. Habit is healthy. Like an insect's nest paper-thin among evergreen leaves, it is easier to survive in it.

'In the late afternoon, she stands in the doorway of my study trying to persuade me to come downstairs and talk to Colonel Rollo Ricks. I know what he is after: a slice of the shoreline and the rough land of Ponciau cliffs for another of his superior holiday developments. What I want to know is what my wife hopes to get out of it. I know she still dreams of lordly things. Dreaming or waking, the courts she frequents are carpeted with her desires. She needs followers and admirers in quantity. Her authority and charm need places and parks to parade through. She needs compensation for the glittering political career my limitations and commitments have denied her. She was telling me it cost nothing to be polite. I should have told her about my dream. We could have discussed its meaning and even laughed together about it: apprehensions easily dispersed. Instead I stretched my jaw forward and spoke in my most forensic manner.

' "Do you think I am prepared to dispose so easily of my patrimony?"

' "Patrimony! Your Uncle Simon's Ponciau. John! How many times have I heard you say you couldn't stand the place.'

'The ghost of her vanished innocence stood behind her. What was she after? Why was she so anxious for this alien to get his hands on the place? Do we assimilate so easily? Three drops of power and wealth and influence and our shapes change. This was the same girl who brought me a flag to wrap around my waist. What was she thirsting for? More power, more wealth, more influence. It was at that moment I conceived the notion of tying up such properties as I had inherited in a complex web of entail. I would confer, assign, transmit responsibilities to my eldest and my youngest in a fixed line of devolution as irreversible as original sin. I would have the sacred places inseparably attached to hereditary successors. What else was my practice in law good for? She could see I was smiling and she could see the lens of my spectacles were still enlarging my suspicions.

' "How many times do I need to tell you, John? We have to change with the times. No one can put the clock back."

'The most unpleasant thing about clichés is their assumption of absolute truth. In a moment she will accuse me of living in the past and I will reply that it is the only safe place to be. Sometimes it feels as though each time either one of us speaks the words that come out are predestined to push us ever further apart. She calls me "John". Enid called me "Sionyn". In the letters which I increasingly treasure it is usually "Dearest C." – not a form of address that would appeal to Amy. "Dearest C. All forms of love as they occur to a creature like me become destructive unless they are provided with adequate creative outlets. So there! I give you fair notice that I am determined to help you in your work . . ." Her words should be a constant presence between us. Yet we rarely speak of her. Her letters are the relics of a saint who has come to mean something different to two opposing camps among her successors.

' "Look. You can hardly call two neat rows of holiday chalets on Ponciau cliffs desecration or mass immigration, can you, John?"

'She is talking English. It isn't mere politeness. The gallant Colonel is downstairs out of earshot. It is to do with the distancing and the cold space that stretches between us: the absence of intimacy and innocence, a diminution of the power to love. "Whom the gods love die young . . ." We should go on loving them. Learn to love more, not less. After the chaos and cruelty and mechanized confusion of war, how else can a little child lead us.

' "You know I sometimes think you won't be really happy, John until they put up a customs post in Chester."

'Had she raised her voice in the hope that the Colonel would hear? What is the difference between a barricade and a customs post? Answer: the young Amy could have mounted a barricade and been willing to die on it instead of suffering a lifetime of remorse. Remorse was no part of her nature. For that at least I could envy her. I did not go downstairs. I moved to the top of the stairs to hear her coping with the awkward situation. It comes easily to her. Besides, all her courtiers, particularly this man Ricks and the Huskies, delight in responding cheerfully to her demands. I am impressed with her poise and the ease with which she holds sway over them.

'She calls me a "culturalist" and herself an "activist". They are convenient terms, she says; easy to use. She does not consider her version of reality and mine are of equal validity. She argues that by definition a desire to live in the past is a confession of impotence and a refusal to face the future. She resists the inalienable right of the past to use us and our powers of recall at its legitimate and permanent dwelling place. She says the state of the world is so awful the tribulations of Wales are hardly worth her energy and attention. "What is any small nation in the post-war world except a chained captive tied to the chariot of one great empire or another . . ." She doesn't have much time for Pendraw either. There are times when I wish I could share her cheerful contempt for the place. My "activist" wife sallies forth to some committee or other where she can exert her influence and on her way subdues the populace with her intimidating smile. Here she has no need to apologize for her "culturalist" husband since he is effectively camouflaged

289

as a native son who long ago won his licence to solitude and poetic sublimation by being a "national winner". Not even bigwigs or busybodies have any jurisdiction over incomplete poetic projects or psychic dreams.

'It was natural that I should take Bedwyr and his best friend Ken Lazarus to the Eisteddfod. Ken was a musician above the average. He sang like an angel. The Eisteddfod, that scene of my small triumphs and disasters, was back in full regalia in spite of death camps and atom bombs. Which is the dream and which is the reality? The ebb and flow of people around the pavilion dressed in pre-war clothes and clutching their clothing coupons: were they aware that they had eaten of the new Tree of Knowledge? Let the poet be crowned and the ceremonial sword be sheathed. Satan has acquired feet and hands and spectacles and stalks the sky like a mushroom cloud pretending to be God. The Eisteddfod field is a garden haunted by the ghosts of those who enjoyed gentle, old-fashioned forms of death. Whom the gods loved . . . With my raincoat over my arm and my programme in my hand I long to believe in the indestructibility of the human soul. Let my Val and my Enid and even Pen Lewis dwell in a state of eternity capable of communicating with each other and keeping my ineffective existence in mind. Out of this inchoate present that surrounds me like an invading army let there be an outpost of eternity where a stricken sensibility may hide for the tick of a second or the petrified moment of a geological aeon.

'Amy is not with us. Eisteddfodau are high on the lengthening list of things she "can't bear" or "can't be bothered with". She is in London visiting Margot who is on leave from her relief work in Helmstadt. There is some talk of Margot being transferred to supervise the work of the Save the Children Fund in Austria. Amy professes an intense interest. I suspect she is keeping her contacts with Transport House in good repair. She has never altogether abandoned her parliamentary ambitions. She allows D.I.Everett to tend the flickering flame of his ancient attachment by remaining on his party headquarters mailing list. How easily she used to laugh about being pestered by his protestations of undying love. The sapphire brooch on a gold chain inside a stiff blue pay-packet and a threat of suicide. Now it was circulars, agenda and furtive notes. If the past meant a little more to her she might discern the irony of it. How she who led me from London by the nose for the sake of my cultural inheritance and my duty to my motherless first-born now seizes on every excuse to dash up to the metropolis, even at the cost of leaving Gwydion and Peredur in the care of alien barbarians like the Huskies. When you are the hub of the wheel, how can you tell when it has come full circle?

'The boy is beautiful. I first saw this when the school choir sang Pergolesi's Stabat Mater. The light from the stained glass window of the school memorial for the Fallen of the First War, fell on his face and gave it the innocent immortality of an Italian renaissance painting. The music issues from his rounded mouth and the shaft of light glitters on his golden curls and domed forehead. It puts me in mind of the love I bore those whom the gods loved and took. Together memory and music are magic. Bedwyr told me that Ken composed music himself, but was shy about it. He played various instruments to improve his skill at composition. His father was our police sergeant and a pillar of the small Baptist church in Pendraw. Ken had a shed behind the Police Station where he practiced. Amy approved of Sergeant Lazarus. She said he was a man of broader interests and sympathies than the average inhabitant of this small-minded town. She could flaunt her contempt for the place and they still admired and even loved her. My concern for an imaginary stronghold of traditional values they treated with the deepest suspicion.

'Sergeant Lazarus permits Ken to come camping with us since he is Bedwyr's best friend and life in the open air will do the boy the world of good. The sergeant was keen on camping himself before the war. Now he knew if he slept out of doors, sciatica would attack his spine and rheumatism gnaw at his joints. He is an agreeable man to talk to. He had an uncle, also a policeman, who collected manuscripts and recorded folk-tales and left his collection to the National Library. He declared himself to be a man interested in what he called "The Things", which meant a wide range of cultural activities that revolved around a cherished language.

'We camp in a meadow upstream from a ruined castle. Two

291

fields away, at the top of the slope, is a barn that was part of a medieval abbey where I can leave the car and extra equipment and where we can shelter if the weather breaks. Clem Cowley Jones has a delicate chest, according to his Aunt Flo. This is nonsense, according to his Aunt Menna, who says Clem is as strong as a horse and far noisier. Those two sisters can never agree about anything. If Menna was over-anxious to oblige Amy, Flo would automatically want to favour me even if she disapproved of my intention, as in the case of our camping expedition. Bedwyr and Ken say that Clem sleeps with his eyes half open. Clem denies this indignantly. The first morning a bullock thrust his head through the flap of the bell tent. Clem said the bullock's face reminded him of their headmaster at morning assembly. Jokes sound better in the open air. Their happiness is a tonic. I listen to them laughing as I fry bacon on a Primus stove and a wren darts into a thorn bush that hasn't been cut since before the war.

'When the sun shines the boys bathe naked in the swirling river pool. Handsome lads on the threshold of puberty. Bright intelligence illuminates the perfection of the bodies of athletic children. Their naked figures restore the world to the unsullied innocence that must have been its original intention. They will be men soon enough but until that happens they seem outside the reach of corruption and death. Their presence endows the entire landscape, from the ruined castle to the flowing river, with a pre-lapsarian simplicity. As I lie on the grass and watch them, the fabric of existence trembles as though some providential finger was holding back the progress of the sun.

'There must have been a moment when I suggested to Ken we should attempt something together and he nodded without saying anything. The quality of his shyness added to his attraction like the plumage of a rare bird. When he spoke I discovered a profundity in whatever he had to say that seemed heaven-sent. He would listen to me as I discoursed on the preoccupations that were closest to my heart. Young as he was he understood perfectly that the practice of art was a way of imposing discipline, order, significant form on the ungovernable torrents of subterranean passion. I could speak to him in poetry and he could understand well enough to set words to music.

'It became necessary to meet not exactly in secret but in places where we would not be disturbed. A friendship like ours in a small town like this could be easily misunderstood. In school, or in our house even, with Bedwyr and Clem, or in the Baptist chapel I could hear him sing or listen to him play. But to converse freely and lay the foundation of collaboration we needed to be alone together.

'I had to escape from the house – to take the path behind the "Western Hydro" unoccupied since the troops left, with paint peeling from every window frame. Through the labyrinth of gorse and across the wasteland I hurry like a man late for an appointment. The wrong path could lead me into marshland caused by choked and neglected draining ditches. The right path led to the sand dunes where we could meet; or, better still, to the deserted foreshore, and half a mile away to the west an isolated rock. The place I favoured for reflection and prolonged contemplation of a landscape I took to be basic to my existence. All around the bay mountains to be reaffirmed with names and under the wet roof of the bay where sailing boats bob on waves like sea-gulls, the mythic cities. This above all I wanted to share with him. A landscape old enough and large enough to contain our mortality. Here I can communicate with those I loved and want to go on living. Here I escape from the despotism of the diurnal round and even cultivate the fragile cotyledons of forgiveness. "Dearest C. . . . All forms of love as they occur . . . My poor mother is so angry these days she can hardly bear even to speak to me. You know, an incapacity to forgive shrivels the soul; and when that happens, love becomes less and less possible . . . I have had a letter from Amy. How I love her. She is so sturdy. Can you love someone just because they are sturdy? She is positive. She demands action. She and Val together will be such a powerful combination. I am certain of it . . ."

'I don't know whether it was one of Clem Cowley Jones's aunts or Ken Lazarus's mother who first approached Amy to whisper their oblique complaint. I felt a certain unease for some days before she spoke. They were mostly love lyrics that we composed together. I could not tell with any degree of accuracy how much the boy understood. He was able to set the words to music. They were simple forms. Without these exercises and the emotions they dealt with what could eternity be except a cold expanse of desolation?

‘ "Is it about me or about him?"

'She was at my desk standing above the folder of white leather in which I secreted the poems I was working on. She would never normally bother to look at them. The pouches inside the folder were stamped in gold leaf: *lettres à répondre* on one side, *lettres répondues* on the other. Val had brought it back from Paris years ago. I treasured the folder more than what it contained. She was looking at me with a cold curiosity that sent my blood into extremities of heat and cold. I watched her fingers bend the chrome spine of my reading lamp until it touched the white folder. Was she turning me into an object of contempt?

‘ "You can hardly go, can you? As it is."

'It was all arranged. Our camping weekend. The smaller boys were coming, too, and one of their friends. Bedwyr and Clem Cowley Jones had undertaken to look after them. Ken and I could work on a more ambitious composition for voices and a small orchestra. It was all arranged. Bedwyr knew about it. It was all in the open. Above-board.

‘ "I had no idea . . ."

‘ "No idea of what?"

'Since the winter we had been sleeping in separate rooms. My cough disturbed her. Then Peredur had some form of bronchitis and she took him into her bed. Then moved his bed into her room. One night when I had been drinking I hammered my fist on her door. I hardly remembered the episode next morning. Why in any case had she locked it? One arrangement led to another and they increased the distance between us; so how could she have any idea? Was I anything more in this house than an awkward piece of furniture? There were new forms of contempt assembling in her eyes. She had made remarks on more than one occasion about people with one skin less than the rest of humanity wandering about looking for sympathy and attention. If I was innocent I was pathetic and ineffective. If I was guilty I

294

was perverted and unclean. Why was she reading these when she said herself she could never be bothered with poems that squealed and squeaked about the suffering and frustration love could cause? I could see by the way she looked at the sheet of paper that she found the love I celebrated was no more than an obscure and unhealthy cult.

' "Of course if this is what you want . . . I hope I'm not narrow minded . . . but there have to be limits."

'And she was going to propose them. I sensed it even before she spoke.

' "If we lived in the country everything would be much easier," she said. "We'd have room to breathe. All of us."

'She had quite forgotton how I had pleaded with her when we were first married that we should live in Cae Golau. She claimed it stank of cats. That it was in an unhealthy spot in a hollow without a view. It was not until my sister's breakdown that I realized the old orchard at Cae Golau had been the scene of her adulterous affair with Pen Lewis. She had no difficulty at all in forgetting her own betrayals. If there was shame in this room it was to be mine, not hers.

' "May Huskie tells me Plas Arthur is coming on the market. It needs doing up, of course. But it's always been a place that attracted me. Such a wonderful position. And really well built. It would be a wonderful place for the boys. I was thinking if you sold Cae Golau and gave Rollo Ricks that piece of Ponciau cliffs he is always going on about, we could easily afford it. What do you think?"

'I was supposed to be relieved that she could sound so warm and friendly; to be grateful that she would accept and even incorporate into our way of life my strange attachment to Ken Lazarus, provided she could entertain her friends as the châtelaine of one of the more impressive houses in the district. Plas Arthur was a delightful spot. It had a southern aspect and a view of the headland and the islets. Sheltered mature gardens where exotic trees and plants could flourish. The smile on her face was a serene reminder of the old days. It was only after I had fathomed the extent of her offer that it began to look Mephistophelian. This was a move on her part to take control of our finances. If I gave way to her now it might make life easier; it would also be an admission of guilt. And a permanent abdication of power. She could see I was shaking my head. And I could see the change in her face as she hardened her heart.

' "Well you can't possibly take them camping, can you? Not after this." She held out the poem like a threat. "Mrs Lazarus would never allow it. And I must say, as a mother I wouldn't blame her." '

vii

'In the cottage hospital I sit at the bedside of a dying man making his will. To give us the illusion of privacy the nurses have drawn a curtain around us as they would have had he been using a bed-pan. He lies still as if he were embalmed in ether. On the curtains there is printed a convoluted pattern of faded leaves and idealized roses like a folk memory of the Garden of Eden. The patient and I are caught up in the design. My hat is on the floor. My briefcase on my knees. This man put to bed like an obedient child is a sepulchral shadow of the quarrelsome hulk I had to defend more than once in the Magistrate's Court on charges of brawling on market days and quarrelling with his neighbours about fallen walls and boundary hedges.

' "What about your wife, Evans?" I said.

'It was clearly something that had not occurred to him. A mournful worn-out wisp of a woman with a goitre, chapped hands and a sack apron. I used to suspect him of knocking her about until his sons grew big enough to put a stop to it.

' "Give her a hundred or two," he said. "And the egg money."

'He had a touching faith in me and my knowledge of the law of the land. The aggression has vanished from his eyes. They long for nothing more now than sympathy and understanding from anybody. I hold the new clauses within two feet of his face so that he can see them at least, if not read them. He never was much of a reader. He has grandchildren and this establishes a trust on their behalf. His eldest son will inherit the farm as he himself had inherited it and this should allow him to depart in peace.

296

'He is dying in orderly fashion, not twitching on brambled barbed-wire. Here my hands are free of blood. There is no ice yet in his eyes. I see no bleeding wounds that need attention. It won't be me shovelling earth over his grinning mouth. I am not here to sing a sick-bed poem or compose his elegy, only to draw up his will. In Llewelyn's army he would have been formidable wielding an axe, an ironpole, a hammer, a two-edged sword. Now he is too weak to hold a pen. His ancestors were mountain folk, a turbulent and contentious lot. He was never afraid of quarrelling. I can't think how far back it would have been that a forefather gave in with a sigh of relief and submitted to the authority of a distant power that gave shape to this will: syllables heavy with force of arms and royal pieties about the will of God. The language of law and order was alien and still is, but it gives this man and his kind the forms of security and continuity a farmer's nature craves for. I could attempt to sing his praises. In his prime, this sepulchral shadow was a notable bass at singing festivals although he never made the big seat in chapel due to his quarrelsome nature. Here is his will and there is his hymn-book. He has chosen the hymns to be sung at his obsequies. The silent invasion that ravaged his physical prowess has nothing to do with upheavals of the spirit. With all his quarrels he never questioned anything. He has no need of uneasy music. What he needs from me is dexterity with the nets and snares of the laws of the land that circumscribe his existence. "Old More will get me off, fair play to a would-be-poet shrivelled up before his time . . . He's an old bugger . . ."

'The fact that I am expert in the traditional metres means nothing to him; my philosophical and political views nothing. Yet he is a type I want to celebrate. A man able to stand on his own land looking at a field or a tree and feel it to be an extension of himself. He and my Uncle Simon and any pen of animals at the mart would understand each other. They are the natives; I am the internal exile. They tolerate me. They know poets in pulpits or on soapboxes are harmless. They are like hymn tunes. They soar and rage before everyone hurries home in time for tea and toast.

'A plump nurse acts as witness. I conduct the ritual with a

solemnity that quells her boisterous manner. There is something to be said for the rigour of the law. She is still enough to transpose into a starched figure in the wall painting of a tomb. I place the fountain pen between the farmer's cold fingers. He barely has the strength to hold it. As the pen scratches the parchment I am pierced with a resolve to impose order on my own existence.

'A man is like a star. He can explode or implode. How many times have I forgiven her? I must set that down. The witness scratches on the parchment. Each time it was more difficult. When her lover was killed I accepted their son as my own. That was forgiveness. The boy resents me. That is natural. He tip-toes on the landing when he passes my study and I estimate the extent of his mother's influence on the pressure of his soles on the carpet and the linoleum. I forgive her for that. When a case is unravelled in sufficient detail most things become understandable. The boy has been in trouble and there have been times when I could believe my chief function in this world is to bail him out. That is no more than a parent's common duty. Her behaviour brought about my sister's death. In my mind lie sheaves of evidence that lead the impartial investigator to that conclusion; except that I am not impartial. It was my blindness, my wishful thinking, my insensitivity, my infatuation with the surface image of Amy, that made me party to my sister's destruction. In such a difficult case, sharing guilt could be classified as a form of forgiveness.

'Tasker Thomas stood in front of my car with his hands up and the light from my headlamps blanching his broad face. Night had fallen on the artificial lake. Was he the man in the moon or a white owl? I wanted to ask my son in the back seat but the boy had too little experience of my voice in humorous mode. Desperation had driven me. The boy was the victim of an outrage and it was right and proper that I should forthwith remove him from the sphere of her evil influence. She was due for punishment. Every child is grateful for being rescued from the wicked witch. To take an innocent boy, my youngest son, and use him as a cover and excuse and travelling companion on her adulterous rendezvous. No one could forgive that.

'Tasker was trembling with spurious authority. This bulky figure from the past helped to establish our marriage and now he felt obliged to put it together as it fell apart. By what authority? Both he and the religion he professed were shot through with fallibility. Who appointed him as God's agent on earth to bury the innocent with biblical protestations about God's will and to patch up the broken pieces of the less worthy and the wicked that providence saw fit to exempt from the slaughter, so that they walk the world and possess it? God had reconciled Himself to a wicked world by a gigantic act of forgiveness. That was the gist of the reverend Tasker T's message and always had been from the battle of the Somme to the invasion of South Korea. History had hardly allowed it to wear all that well in spite of the unwearying smile on his round face. (I must ask him was his homily applicable to conflict outside the official limits of Christendom?)

'It was his solution to everything. His universal cure-all. His vade-mecum. He had taken to wandering the face of the earth as an unpaid peacemaker and little thanks he got for it. He was rubbing his hands now with the prospect of massaging his message into my bruised bones. What could be more pleasurable than dispensing a well-loved remedy among old friends? He was offering his services as mediator so that he could return to the scene of some of his notable spiritual triumphs. He needed to believe he still had talents that could be made use of. Cold wars in the home should be easier to contain.

'The howl from the boy on the backseat brought me back to my senses. Throughout our journey south he had been so silent. Nothing a parent does, however impulsive or irrational, surprises a child. The howl made me shudder. It was sudden thunder from above the clouds in my mind. The heavens opened and the face of the earth crawled with practical problems. There are specific instances when a woman taken in adultery can be put to death. Stoning requires many hands, a knife only one. It would take days, of course, to seek out the precedents in the Law Library. Where were the cases in which the injured party was required to carry out the sentence himself? I spent that night in Tasker's lodgings gnawing at the problem. How could it be done and, like justice, be seen to be done without the violence of the father being visited on the sons unto the third and fourth generation? This was a great historical problem. How can justice be done and the cycle of violence broken? How many war-heads can be poised on the head of a pin? It was only when dawn broke over the wet rooftops and I turned for the last time on that comfortless bed that I arrived at the only possible condition of survival. Natural justice – nature being what it is, and Amy, according to the most sympathetic verdict given long ago by Enid our one true love, being a child of nature – demanded a custodial sentence.

'To establish a form of co-existence I was obliged to go through the motions of reconciliation. Tasker, as usual, did the talking. He was so tactful with both of us. Amy and I faced each other across the room like exhausted enemies reduced to signing an armistice. The assumed headings of agreement were all variants on the theme of what was best for the boys and their future. An underlying protocol, unrecorded, flowed from what was best for Amy. Our front drawing-room smelt of furniture polish. It had ceased to be a place for everyday living. It was reserved for occasions like this. The glass bookcase was locked and never opened, the wallpaper never changed, the pictures never looked at. The boys never came in here. It was most frequented by our cleaning woman like a corner kept in order to receive my coffin.

'In an incautious moment, perhaps when my fist was pounding on her bedroom door, Amy had spoken of divorce. It was an interesting conception. On what grounds? I may have yelled at her. (Or was I more considerate? Was the boy in her bed?) The disgrace of adultery belongs to her, not to me. Between us it was the only subject left to talk about. A dialogue conducted in prolonged silence. Across the table her cold glance might imply that if I were a gentleman I would oblige her by taking the blame. As a lawyer I had to be well acquainted with the intricacies of manufactured evidence. She was untouched by shame or guilt. She saw herself as blameless and unblemished as a statue on a wall.

'In spite of the emotional energy they consumed, these interminable and mostly unspoken dialogues were academic.

Divorce as a convenient substitute for death was not in her immediate interest. It seemed her brilliant career was about to take off again. In our corner of the forest at least, the Left was back in fashion. Our sitting member of parliament had been caught out flirting with the Liberals. His mission in life since the day of his election had been to maintain a balance between the practised inertia of the remnant of the old Liberal hegemony and the restlessness inherent in the Left Amy represented. A convenient number of ex-Liberals had expired and the balance of power on the constituency committee had tilted in the direction of my wife and her allies. The MP had taken to eyeing her activities with an even greater suspicion than mine. Amy could not afford a scandal.

'She was imprisoned as much by her own ambition as by my custodial sentence. It seemed a satisfying form of poetic justice until I noticed that the number of her admirers was steadily on the increase. There was nothing I could do to turn them away. I sat in my study upstairs, unable to write, registering their comings and goings: the doctor, Wilson Thomas, and his vulgar wife; May Huskie, ready to carry out any mission provided she is allowed to play bridge downstairs at least once a week; Soniatawksi, the refugee Pole, who claims to be a count, doesn't want to go home, and longs to share with my wife his expertise in antiques and icons; the secretary of the Golf Club and his wife; the absurd Major Roberts of the Yacht Club, late of the Home Guard; and the inevitable Rollo Ricks. And whoever they care to bring along or Amy cares to invite. This house has become the pivot of a subtle network of enticement and reward rather than a hub of revolution. Amy is at the centre of it all. Her bourgeois friends are untroubled by left-wing views which are no more than a stylish costume designed to add to her attraction. They have long sensed that what matters most to her is the exercise of power, even in the smallest quantities.

'Set this down in so many words. She has no only betrayed me, she has betrayed every single principle Val and Enid stood for, all the values we cherished and believed in. If this wretched country of ours were a nation state she would have been condemned as guilty of treason. So what law can operate in this house? Only her whim prevails. By a sleight of hand I did not even glimpse, she has transferred her sentence to me. The length of my back closes in on the length of my legs and I am closing in on myself like a penknife. The custodian incarcerate. When I hear laughter float up the stair-well, as I often do, I can only assume they are laughing at me.

'Whichever way I enter the house the boys back away from me. You could hardly call that arriving home. This is her most complete triumph. I can watch her with them and still admire the subtlety of her winning ways, still see the magic in her image. The smoothness of her voice and her skin, the quick touch of her finger and the implication of tenderness that goes with it, the expansive understanding of her smile, the sweet reasonableness of her persuasive discourse, the sparkle in her humour and readiness to laugh. She is all colour and sunlight. I live in a grey cloud. How can they not prefer her to me when I so much prefer her to myself? When I am present our meals are often conducted in silence. The boys sit between us. They see how precisely my end of the table is provided with a diet for my supposed ulcer. I do not even eat the same food as they do. Everything that happens in this house serves to distance me from my sons. I am the ogre that lives up the stairs, the most eccentric and least acceptable inhabitant, the oppressive authority who insists on paying all the bills as though he were composing complex odes in twenty-four metres.

'The office has become my refuge. There, at least, poor Miss Price is entirely loyal to me. Why do I say "poor"? Echoing Amy, who long ago decided to pity her. Miss Price has fuzzy hair, an unprepossessing face and her exact age is not generally known. Amy says the woman's teeth need attention and her skin shows that she is suffering from constipation. Miss Price was friendly with my sister Nanw. Her first name is Florence, but I never use it. She wouldn't want me to. As an employee her devotion is total. Amy used to joke that Miss Price nursed a kind of secret passion for me that she could not admit even to herself. All I know is that Miss Price is reliable. She is loyal, and loyalty, in my situation, is a virtue to admire above all others.

'My fountain pen has slipped from the farmer's fingers

making a row of minute blots on the parchment. The fat nurse holds her breath as though some form of desecration had occurred. Would we have to go through the whole ceremony again, draw up another will? The dying man's eyes swivel up searching for forgiveness. I touch his shoulder to allay his anxieties about such trivial blots on his escutcheon and feel bone under his pyjama jacket. Should there be such a thing as a soul, his was on the verge of leaving what was left of his body. Does he already see the world as a blur of phantasmagorical images as I close my briefcase, put on my hat, and proceed with narrow caution down the hospital corridor?

'I need to draw up my own will, a detailed testament for the sake of my sons. An apologia and an apology. There is so much that will be lost in obscurity, so much they need to understand; even, it seems, their own names. It was that man Ricks whom I overheard as I tried to make my way upstairs unobserved, asking Amy, in the most cheerful possible way, why it was she had given her sons such difficult, not to say outlandish names. I didn't hear her reply. It must have been amusing since I heard them both laugh. It is a question she can no longer answer. They are names I gave them each in turn and the boys should know how they relate to something greater than themselves. The names should support them to live through a new age when all the appropriate commandments will be weakened because the myths that sustained them are fading away. The passage of time was little value in itself except to extend the bounds of our bewilderment and the depth of our guilt.

'Amy doesn't often call at the office. She caught me when I was on my knees, with my hat still on, in front of the cupboard where I hide this record. Only Miss Price knows where the key is kept. Amy's voice always reverberates in our office. She seems to raise it even as she climbs up the stairs.

' "John . . . What on earth is it you keep in there?"

'I turned to give her a quiet smile. "The Truth," I said.

'This made her laugh. I could see Miss Price look nervous and worried.

' "What do you know about it?" Amy said. "You can't even tell me the truth when I ask you the time." '

'I watch my sons from the window. On the wasteland between the harbour and the sand dunes a great bonfire is burning. Another fifth of November. A date scheduled to go up in flames. They leap into the dark sky making their own frantic annunciation. They light up a fresh generation of children's faces. They show up the dunes as undulating ramparts against a sea hungry as ever for the land. Lights flicker in the entrenchment. There are no stars visible. I hear the voice of Mr Mackay reassuring Frankie and me about fireworks and God's good intentions. My Peredur is trembling with excitement. Even at this distance I can see the firelight reflected in his eyes. He will grow up to be my son of prophecy. These fires and these figures have to recur in our consciousness or we are doomed to darkness. I should go down and protect him. He is dancing too close to the fire. The children are prancing around the flames in a release of primeval energy that is authentic and joyful; a communing with the original gods as much as an imitation of painted actors on the picture screen imitating painted savages. There cannot be all that many different ways of stamping feet on wet sand, whatever legendary exploits of gods and heroes unwind in their skulls.

'I stand in the bay-window of my study on the second floor of a terrace house that was built in the 1880s to accommodate an anticipated influx of visitors carried here by the steam locomotives of the Great Western Railway and a surge of imperial economic optimism. We inhabit the bricks and mortar of our grandparents' dreams. When you try to tell the time, what could be more accurate than contemporary archaeology? Amy's train is late. The boys couldn't wait to light the fire once darkness had fallen. There was a threat of more rain but now the wind keeps the rain off. The flames of the bonfire are reflected in the windows of the terrace houses and in the long puddles of rainwater on the Embankment Road. Between the terrace and the promenade stands Pendraw's only bomb site. The Town Council is still arguing what to do about it. In the great darkness of the winter solstice the fire burns in optimistic isolation.

'It is better to keep my distance. The older boys are watching. My presence would impose unwanted restraint on the festivities. I have a talent for disrupting ritual occasions. Ken Lazarus is there. Sergeant Lazarus died last year of a heart attack described as massive. After the funeral I made an offer to help pay Ken's fees at an expensive music school. It was the only way I could think of bringing him comfort that would have been socially acceptable. I was told by his mother that he wanted to give up music for philosophy. My interest was quickened. For a few moments it was the only thing in the world I wanted to talk about. But Amy was watching me. And because she was watching, so were the boys. Even Peredur. Lines and threads of restraint. I am obliged to move along the fringes of people's lives, even my own sons'. The only elements I come to grips with are the disputes and entanglements brought to my professional attention in the office and the law courts. Bedwyr is determined to become an architect. His solidity is a source of pride to me. The buildings he designs will not easily fall down. I wish Amy and I could do more to share our pleasure in Bedwyr's youthful gravity and politeness.

'Gwydion prowls around the fire, stirring the smaller children up into fresh frenzies. He would burn down parliaments without any compunction or remorse, especially if he had Frank Huskie alongside to lurk in the shadows and render assistance. Adolescence has taken hold of Gwydion's cherubic face and stretched it artfully to suit a junior fiend ready to add fuel to any contemporary hell threatening to expire through lack of attention. He and Frank are foraging out there, never empty-handed, endlessly resourceful in finding something else to burn. They have also put themselves in charge of the fireworks. Peredur will do anything for Gwydion. Pleasing him is his way of life. I can see that small face so clearly in the firelight: pale, loyal, expectant, so intent. The great Gwydion is opening the box of magic. In Peredur's eyes there is no marvel his brother cannot conjure up. Coloured lights begin to blossom briefly in the sky. They don't satisfy Gwydion. He needs more

305

radical and enduring transformations. He waves his arms about to order more fuel on the sinking fire. A colony of ants could not be more hard at work. The sparks fly upward. Gwydion instructs Peredur to hold a thick firework while Frank Huskie turns his back on the wind to light a match. I bang on the window-pane. The noise of the sea and the wind smothers my warning. I should be down there with them. The blue paper is already lit and glowing like the end of a cigarette. Bedwyr shoves Frank and Gwydion out of the way, snatches the firework from Peredur's hand and hurls it towards the dunes where it spurts, explodes and expires as harmless as a firefly. A brief war is over.

'What future could there be without a "Mab Darogan", a Son of Prophecy? There will be more wars. We are informed that the Americans have the capacity to construct a hydrogen bomb which would be a thousand times as powerful as the atom bomb which dissolved Hiroshima and its inhabitants. This is presented as good news, yet another happy demonstration of earthly powers. Gwydion is armed to the teeth with scientific technology. Who would be responsible for him except some son of prophecy, a deliverer of nations who would have time also for the small and insignificant people of the earth? When the rocks melt in the sun, hair will stop growing. Amy has noted my foreboding and asked whether I shall be writing a poem about it. "I suppose you'll be writing a poem about it?" she said. Her smile was enough to show that such obscenities were outside the comforting confines of the strict metres. Metal instruments were better suited to capture microscopic particles of ash from the atmosphere and subject them to radiochemical analysis. It would have been some consolation to have gone over this problem together. Fissile material was no longer poetic material because this degree of fragmentation undermined all previous known forms of coherent poetry.

'I thought it might amuse her if I wrote to the President of the United States from the office on our new bilingual – headed notepaper as from one public official to another, asking among other things, how, by the sweet light and breath of heaven where the gods are accustomed to take

306

their rest and recreation talking Latin and Greek, did he propose to convince the Russians or anybody else of the value of individual liberty by slaughtering them a million or so at a time? Jove with his thunderbolts was more discriminating. And was he aware of the serious overcrowding that already existed in the Stygian marshes? And how he was putting God (in whom he trusted) in a very awkward position? Fair questions from the all-powerless to the all-powerful.

'Peredur was being chased from the bonfire towards the Embankment Road. It was a new game. He reached the edge of the pavement and stumbled. I saw it happen with the clarity of slow motion. He fell face forward into the largest puddle in the road. He lay there helpless for a protracted moment until Bedwyr reached him and hauled him to his feet as wet as a spaniel. I saw how his face crumbled with bewildered resentment and dismay to have been overtaken by such a mishap at the very pinnacle of his evening's pleasure. I hurried downstairs to switch on the lights and open the front door. At least his home should look bright and welcoming.

' "He'll have to take all his clothes off," Bedwyr said. "He's soaked to the skin. Those puddles are deep enough to bathe in."

'Ken Lazarus hovered on the pavement outside. He didn't come in. Peredur's knees were grazed. When he saw broken lines of blood drops appear, he burst out crying. He wanted his mother. "Where's Mam?" he said each time he gathered back enough air in his lungs. He would not take any comfort from me.

' "The train is late," I said. "She should have been here by now."

'Bedwyr took him up to the bathroom. Across the road the festivities had resumed. Gwydion was marshalling yet more rubbish to throw on the fire. The wind swept his voice across our open front door. I couldn't bring myself to close it while Ken Lazarus stood on the pavement outside. He solved my problem by walking away. I went upstairs and stood in the bathroom doorway. Bedwyr had decided Peredur should have a hot bath. Peredur looked at me reproachfully as though it were my fault that Amy's train was late.'

'It would be gratifying to devise some rational alternative to love. Contemplation is not enough. I can sip my whisky in the bay-window of my pleasant prison on the second floor, sitting in the rocking chair Enid bought and observing shore birds, for example, exploiting the tide in the silted harbour and the light changing for hours on end. Sometimes I discover significant structures in their behaviour and I contrive to incorporate such meaning as is brought to light in short pieces, often in the strict metres. Small poetic exercises bring small satisfaction when they succeed. At the lowest level they pass the time. But as a way of life they are less compelling than an oystercatcher's deft selection and unsealing of stranded shellfish. This is not an art to encompass, compete with, or even minutely reflect nature's teeming prodigality. Therefore, sip whisky, smoke a pipe and attempt to appear urbane.

'Amy scorns my inactivity. I sense it at a glance whenever she spares a moment to look at me. I have my office. It is a satisfying practice as far as it goes. If I worked harder, longer hours at least, I could make it more lucrative. She believes I choose not to and she is probably right and is entitled even to resent it. I divide my time with a certain irritating precision between sanctuaries: my study on the second floor, my office off the High Street and my isolated rock on the foreshore. Not such a bad way of life, if sometimes a little numbing. I can identify with the shore birds, scavenging and beachcombing for poems, scooping up perceptions from the surface of the water, even diving occasionally to the bottom of my consciousness and coming up, my lungs bursting, with painful insights such as the need to discover and sustain and exploit a rational alternative to love.

'Amy did not need persuading that God had departed from our inconsiderable corner of the planet. He had been a little late in leaving, but that was appropriate. It corresponded to our position on the habit-encrusted fringe of a continent itself running out of confidence and creativity; a small people eking out an uncertain existence on the margin of history. As long as His shadow lingered here we went on singing to justify our dwindling importance. Her uncle had been a disappointed lay-preacher; my grandmother a resolute and unbending Presbyterian determined to defy any tide of historical necessity. What Amy and I still had in common, binding us together, I was ready to hope, like a pair of lovers in the second circle of Hell, was our innate scepticism, our inability to trust in absolutes, our reliance on opportunism, our reluctance to hope or believe. I wanted her to accept that by any objective evaluation, at a distance or close up, we were shaped by the same mould of social class and culture.

'This could be a benefaction as well as a burden – sufficient for us to devise a language in which we could converse and communicate so freely that our understanding of each other and of the world around us would give rise to a harvest of satisfying explanations and solutions; become in practice one structure that would provide us with a vehicle – the latest and most comfortable model – for the rest of our journey through a bewildering and increasingly hostile wilderness of a world. If I were ever to persuade her of the truth of this analysis, to move her to a point of view from which it became self-evident and even exclamatory, I needed the time and attention it takes to construct a subtle and convincing exposition of a new theory. This would have to include the seminars of silence: the irony of our living in the same house, looking at each other and withholding essential parts of ourselves from each other, day after day.

' "Have you read this?" Amy said. ' "Why I Refuse To Pay My Income Tax." '

'It was an article in a Welsh weekly magazine I subscribed to that Amy did not often read – or claimed not to. She was waiting for Dr Thomas to arrive to ferry her to a County Council education sub-committee meeting to do with health and sanitation in rural schools. It was worthy public service. She was wearing one of her committee hats that made her

309

look both chic and formidable. I could not restrain the thought that if there were a distinction to be made between community service and sluicing one's ego in people, my wife would never be the one to make it. Of course, she could have retorted, as sharply as she liked, that any form of human warmth was preferable to the chill of her marriage.

' "Do you know this man?" she said. "He sounds very much like one of your lot."

'A schoolteacher called Davies had resigned his job to prevent the government, in the shape of the local authority, deducting income tax from his salary and using it to send national servicemen to Korea. Is it from such simplistic gestures that prophets are born? "One of your lot" means almost anyone holding what she has now come to regard as extremist views, about war, about the language, about the land and the community, about self-government or about anything that might inconvenience a Labour Party and government in which she had invested her unflagging hopes of advancement. She nibbled at her lower lip as she devoured the article and I saw her party allegiance shadow the paper like the hat on her head.

' "Well," she said. "It appears that Mr Davies has vowed to go to prison before he will allow any pennies he earns to be used to arm young conscripts and send them to Korea."

'She was smiling as she said it. She found Davies's stand outlandish and eccentric in the extreme. She didn't find it in any way related to her own behaviour when she was young and glowing with ideals. She had been beautiful in her defiance. I tried to remember what Davies looked like. I had met him at an Eisteddfod. A small, tubby man in tweeds full of jokes as I recalled; too many for my taste. He and his cronies eddied around the eisteddfod field held together by what I took to be a mucilage of mutual admiration, feeding off their own wit and hoping to collide at any moment with groups of kindred spirits.

' "He has great faith in the peoples of the earth getting to know each other," Amy said. "The brotherhood of man and so on. How does a North Korean get to know a South Korean except with a bullet?"

'She was roused by the article in spite of herself. It was an

310

opportunity, it seemed to me; an opening. We could initiate the kind of dialogue in which I longed to engage. It wouldn't be easy. I was inhibited, tongue-tied. Our modes of communication were stiffened, if not completely seized up, through lack of exercise. Amy inclined to voice her opinion now on any subject with the bland objectivity of the member of a wireless brains trust; although, where I am concerned, her comment is more penetrating. I marvel, even as I wince, at her capacity to fabricate brief phrases to pierce my incomplete defences.

' "At least he sticks up for what he believes in," she said.

'Dr Thomas arrived in his Lanchester, beaming with the prospect of escorting my wife to her committee. Her words reverberated in the room and in my head after they had left. The doctor was engaged in his own little crusade for the installation of hand washbasins in school cloakrooms. He would not rest, he vowed at regular intervals, until every school in the country was equipped with them. Our green and pleasant land would at least be equal with England and Jersusalem. All power to his elbow. She was implying that I did not stick up for what I believed in, because I no longer had anything left to believe in. Was it only contempt I heard in her tone of voice or was there a challenge there as well? Was I being subtly invited to show her what in the last resort I was made of? It was the ambiguity of her remarks as well as the way she made them that sent them circulating in the mind like a feverish infection in the blood.

'I had to involve myself in Davies's cause. He would need any support he could get, I reasoned. A refusal to pay income tax would slowly deprive him of everything he owned. His house would be sequestrated. His furniture sold. Eventually he would be sent to prison for a substantial period. He would emerge, take up some form of employment, and then the slow grinding process would begin all over again. The more I pondered his predicament the more involved I became. What guilt was this little man attempting to expiate? Was I expected to suffer similar forms of mild persecution to make my own tenancy of a brutish world tolerable? Each war seemed dedicated to being more destructive than the last. In my youth I had seen

311

the end of a war to end all wars that was in fact the first phase of a cycle of conflict in which each raw encounter is dedicated to evolving a technology more deadly and all-consuming than the last. There was even a pattern established for survivors to observe. During a war the active intelligence consoles itself with designs for a better social order and improved standards of living once it is all over; post-war it recovers an ability to live as though the misfortune had never happened and would never occur again – until it does occur and populations summon up the strength to cover themselves with the shreds and tatters of human dignity as they submit once more to the hammer blows of mechanized Fate. It seems so simple and yet it abides beyond analysis and beyond rational control, like love. Perhaps Davies, being abnormally innocent, had touched on a possible solution. Each individual needs to embrace his share of responsibility for the present like a reconditioned sense of guilt until whole populations shuffle barefoot through the streets wearing sackcloth and ashes.

'Notions bubbled in my brain as I motored south to the small town where Davies had been employed as a teacher. I was excited. A venture of this sort was more important than writing poetry. It did more for me than revive the spirit of the old days. I was able to sing as I found myself travelling along country roads I had not used since the day of Val's funeral during the war. This was a corner of our country that still retained its medieval magic. I couldn't wait to hear those accents again and the poetry of the dialect that Val used to say "tasted of the rich earth". This was the kind of action that would help me to shed the shame and guilt that accumulates in years of inactivity. To atone for the obscenities of Belsen and Hiroshima and the present destruction in Korea, there had to be set in motion massive acts of innocence. That was the gist of Davies's article in the magazine. The West had to learn the lesson of leaders like Gandhi, or be doomed to some unspeakable form of self-destruction, and the little man was right. His vision gave him a right to lead and laid on me the obligations to follow.

'Davies's friends were already assembled in his favourite Temperance Café when I arrived. The hero himself was in hospital having his appendix taken out. This was the subject of some hilarity. Competitions were being initiated for the best *englyn* and the wittiest limerick to celebrate the event. So much teasing, familiarity, laughter; the atmosphere, the hot tea, cigarette smoke, and good fellowship, both attracted and excluded me. I was made aware of how little I knew about Davies and his circle and how they knew even less about me. Someone mentioned I had been a "national winner" in the twenties and I was awarded with brief glances of curiosity as an odd survival from another age. Yet none of them could have been more than ten years my junior. My poetic fame had been briefer than the track of a shooting star.

'I didn't know that Davies was an accomplished Sunday painter. I had never seen one of his pictures. I had never heard of his adventures on a bike in the West of Ireland or of how he had got lost in Paris or how he made up for turning up late at his best friend's wedding, or how quickly he had gone bald in the last three years. I didn't know he was a notable swimmer, a tenor soloist or a Sunday School teacher. I knew so little about him it seemed for a while that I was an intruder unqualified to be present at such a gathering, until they noticed my unease and made a good-natured effort to include me in what was going on. Davies wasn't present but I could sense the affection he had for people in the esteem in which he was held by his friends. The warmth of their companionship made me feel at ease. It put me in mind of descriptions of religious experiences where sin and guilt fall away and the individual finds rebirth and the new strength of a fountain of youth.

'The meeting was brought to order. A Baptist minister with a gruff voice and bushy eyebrows was appointed a temporary chairman. There did not appear to be an agenda other than a general feeling of goodwill towards Davies and support for the stand he was taking. I was not at all clear whether the support was occasioned by the person of Davies himself or the principle on which he was taking a stand, but it didn't seem to matter at this stage. The chairman tried to envisage with accompanying gestures the sequence of misfortunes that would overtake Davies as a result of his determined protest. Someone suggested they made out a rota of families prepared to take him in, provide him with bed and board and so on, for as long as his ordeals would last. The chairman said that frankly he could see no end to them in the foreseeable future. The way he said it and the gesture he made caused a certain amount of comment and laughter which was immediately followed by an intense and troubled quiet. There seemed very little further to be said except that everyone present would offer Davies a home for as long as he should ever need one, however often the bailiff's van rolled up.

'It was right at the end of the meeting, with an urgency that may have obscured the basic simplicity of my proposal, that I stood up to speak. My suggestion was that we should open a fund to which all supporters of Davies's stand could contribute on the basis of a tithe of their annual income. Our tax, the "Peace Workers' Tax", would have graduations that corresponded to a rate at least ten per cent above the current rates of the state's income tax. We would in effect, I added, be establishing a form of an anti-war church founded on more generous contributions than the money we were obliged by law to hand over to the state. My attempt to sound amusing fell very flat. My proposal was greeted by a puzzled and embarrassed silence.

' "Dear friend," the chairman said at last. "Your heart is obviously in the right place. But I'm not sure an informal gathering of friends like this is the appropriate place to launch such an ambitious undertaking – if I have understood exactly what it is you propose we should do . . ."

'He was about to make a light-hearted remark, a joke even, that would dispel an uncomfortable moment and absolve everyone present from any obligation to consider my proposal seriously.

' "I am prepared to pledge half my annual income to this Fund, if this meeting will undertake to give my tithe proposal serious consideration."

'I made the offer on impulse; but having made it, I was prepared to laugh and joke with the best of them like a man who has suddenly divested himself of an intolerable burden. There was laughter. There were also murmurs of dissent. A voice piped up.

314

' "Have you asked your wife then?"

'It sounded like a joke, especially the squeaky way it came out. The chairman seized on the point.

"No, fair play to Jacob," he said. "It is important, isn't it. We've got families. You can't go giving away a tenth of your income, let alone a half, without the old lady's permission, can you?'

'They chose to regard my proposal as an outburst of emotional goodwill with which they were in general sympathy without being under any obligation to study it as a feasible plan. It was time to leave and I sensed they were relieved to be able to distance themselves from the intensity of my preoccupations and propositions. I was leaving as I had arrived, an unaccompanied stranger. In spite of its attractions this wasn't my part of our country. A poet should have his square mile and all the attachments that went with it: a field full of his own folk. I seemed to have lost mine. I had been turned out of the garden, sentenced to indefinite exile for a transgression I was still unable to identify.

'The following week a garbled report of the meeting in the café appeared in the same weekly magazine. We had a young guest staying with us, Harry Duff by name, a nephew of Margot Grosmont. It was an attempt on Amy's part to rekindle her old friendship with Margot. I suspected there was some political or social advantage in the gesture. Margot's passion for relief work now encompassed projects in Africa and the Indian sub-continent. I know Amy envied her the scope of her activities and the glamour of her connections with powerful political figures in the countries where relief work was in progress. Young Harry Duff found us more puzzlingly foreign than any of his aunt's Indian or African associates. He and Peredur stared at each other in silence as though they belonged to two different species. I tried to make jokes and humorous remarks to improve the atmosphere but met with little success. It was hard going for all of us.

' "What on earth . . .?" Amy had picked up the magazine. The boys were drifting about the back garden wondering what to do next. "Have you seen this?" She held out the open magazine in my direction. "What on earth have you been saying?"

315

'The answers were ready to slip from my lips even before the question was completed.

' "Nothing you would disapprove of, I hope."

'I hadn't intended to sound sarcastic. There was always a part of me that longed for her approval.

' "You are so . . ."

'She was lost for words. I resisted a temptation to supply her with them.

' "You are like . . . a helpless fly. Do you know what I mean? Caught in a spider's web of spinning, ineffective, half-baked protest. That's no way to survive. No way to save anything. You know that, surely? You're a grown man. You've lived long enough, for God's sake."

'Her words went on feeding the fuel of her indignation. I couldn't allow her to crush me like a beetle underfoot. I had to have a residue of respect for myself as well as my objectives.

' "You may as well understand," I said. "I have every intention of carrying this out."

'That silenced her for a moment. She held on to the table to keep her balance.

' "You're mad," she said at last. "You have no right whatsoever to sacrifice your family on the altar of your ridiculous idealism. You are impossible. Don't you know that everyone looks on you as a figure of fun? The boys get teased in school about the way you look and your ridiculous behaviour. You must know that. Are you going to make things worse for them? Have you lost all sense of responsibility? How do you think I will be able to cross the street, let alone appear in public . . . You are mad. Did you know that? Out of your mind . . ."

'My lack of response made her scream. Her face went red and ugly. I was appalled by the transformation: my beautiful Amy turning into a screeching hag.

' "And wicked . . . You think you are too good for this world, so why don't you leave it? You are evil. Don't you dare grin at me."

'She picked up a bread knife on the table and hurled it at my head. It smashed through the window to land in the back garden. I saw the boys with their mouths open look up at me as if I were an apparition.'

X

'She wants me committed. I grow more certain of it. I've seen her confer with Wilson Thomas, their heads too close together, whispering. Watching them gives me a sense of Fate closing in. I am the quarry and I have to think of somewhere to hide where they will never find me. The things she used to say about him: fulsome flatterer, purveyor of placebos and soft soap. He still likes to sidle up to me with a double whisky in his paw and slobber fatuous remarks about poetry and make mock innocent enquiries about the secrets of poetic processes. Amy used to say he was unbearable and that she only put up with him for the sake of his wife. She made remarks in his hearing about doctors and lawyers being natural enemies except when they were covering up each other's mistakes. She was quite sharp with him. He seemed to like it. Now she allows him to approach her more closely and that can only mean she wants his signature; she wants to make use of him to trap me. He can help her remove this obstacle to her progress. What public could not be sorry for an able woman tied to a husband committed to an institution for the insane?

'The gulf between us is tragic because I know my mind has never been clearer. Clarity hurts. That is of no consequence so long as it helps in the process of understanding the universe. Let questions fall, I say, instead of tears from the fountain of heaven and they will bring their own light with them. I cannot agree that I am unfit to be a father. My sons will come to know me in the fullness of time. I never knew my own father in any useful sense. He enters my memory as a studio photograph and the object of my mother's unassuageable grief: the darkened room at Glanrafon, the smell of sickness, the oak floorboard that creaked as I tip-toed past her door in my stockinged feet. Hereditary evasions.

'At first it was the search for the oldest burial places that offered me release. I bought books about cromlechs and stone circles. I visited them when I could. They held more

317

significance in a landscape than atomic power-stations. They taught us that we should learn to do with less and that the entrance to the underworld was still inside ourselves. The cavern with many gateways and many voices to listen to, whispered music issuing from a hundred throats. I needed to tell her that we have this space inside us that can accommodate all the stars, all the living and all the dead. We can try any case including our own in the tribunal of our own minds. What we need most urgently is a reassessment of our relationship with death; as a society, as individuals. I had valid points to make.

'I went to her bedroom door and tapped it gently. I did not raise my voice.

' "Amy," I said. "You were right. I want to tell you. We would have been happier in a house surrounded by a garden. All of us. It's not a question of separate development or a space to count the drops of dew on the petals of the roses or composing half a dozen pastoral pieces or diversions of that kind. There is a simple relationship between roots and stars that can only be absorbed by staying in one place. So you see how right you were. Whatever grows has the space of the sky to bloom in. If a family can't share a garden what hope is there for the brotherhood of man?"

' "Will you leave me alone!"

'Her scream electrified the house. The boys' bedroom door was closed and locked. I could hear her sobbing. I was there to comfort her and my arms were empty.

' "You know I'm not well."

'I did know. Wilson Thomas had made light of it when he spoke to me.

' "It could be nothing," he said. "On the other hand it could be something. So we'll take her in. Just for a biopsy in the first instance. And a few tests. She could do with a rest. She works too hard. I don't know if you've noticed."

'He and his partners had this private clinic attached to the hospital at Glaslyn. A delightful spot, everyone said, and I could agree with them. Higher than the hospital, facing south with a view of the mountains, of course, and the broad estuary and the submerged sand bank where Owen Guest held the tiller under his arm and sang if he were the master of his fate and I rolled on the bottom of Harri Bont's boat expecting any moment to be swept overboard into a sludge of sand and salt water and all eternity.

'The French-windows of Amy's room opened into a rose garden. I stood there as speechless as a shadow. There were goldfinches in the rose bushes waiting to be fed. We had reached an extremity of silence where I longed to say everything to her. Within sight of each other we could drift on a timeless ocean, equal and opposite, reconciled to life and to death, if not to each other. Our positions were reversed. She was interned, committed, and I was the visitor free to leave. If I could find the words and the form, I could compose the poem that we could share together. Like reconciliation it lay just outside my reach.

' "It's your fault."

'He was sitting on the stairs leading to my office. Miss Price said he had been there for more than an hour and that he wouldn't come in. The powers were assembling to defeat me. I could no longer save myself by removing out of their reach.

' "You made her ill. If she dies it's your fault."

'This was my son of prophecy, and this was his message. He had spoken to me at last. I could not bear to look at the distress on his face. He shrank from me when I touched him. His tears were mixed with desperation and hatred. The boys were not supposed to know. That was the one instruction she had given me.

' "Don't tell the boys. Do you hear me?"

'I heard her. But a terrace is not a place to keep a secret. Information spreads like a draught from house to house. I saw Clem Cowley Jones's aunts standing in a second floor window as Dr Wilson Thomas drove my wife away. They looked curious and worried and I saw the word "cancer" shape on Menna's pouting lips.

' "I hate you."

'He was groping blindly along the wall of the stairwell, putting a distance between us. He couldn't see me lying above the abyss, on the cliff-edge of eternity, or hear anything I said.

' "I hate you. We all hate you."

319

'He left the curse with me and chased off into the street. My son of prophecy. That was his message. All I could do was retire to my office. I try to write. Scraps of verse. I sit with the silence against which I have to be judged.'

Nine

i

The evening light flooded through the window. I was glad
Wenna was with me. Her face in the gilding light was like an
icon, the transience of beauty fixed for all time, like my
accumulated guilt. This empty dining-room was designed to
be a chamber of revelations. The setting sun tinted the pink
wallpaper with gold and I sat on the floor among the
scattered fragments of my father's life, appalled by the
knowledge I had acquired from his papers of a self I did not
even know existed: a self capable of bringing off a deception
as monstrous as any which the most sophisticated
propaganda machine could achieve. How had it been done?
Unobserved by a vaunted critical apparatus, so refined by
rigorous and rational academic training, this other self inside
me had transferred my hatred of my father to my mother,
and laid my own responsibility for his death like a severed
head in her lap. She was no more or less guilty than I. By
some process beyond rational understanding we had
conspired to destroy him. Was it he or his message that was
too unbearable to live with? Who will bother to conduct
impartial inquiry apart from participants already tainted
with guilt? In light as bright as this the golden air is polluted
with floating secrets, a minefield of infected information. Let
the light speed up the process of disintegration already at
work in these mouldering notebooks. There was no known
apparatus that could filter and make safe the contagion you
were liable to take in.

'I told you to burn them,' Wenna said.

A reverberation in the unfurnished room made her verdict

sound detached and distant. She was gazing expectantly through the long sash-window. Her whole appearance was resonant with glowing colour. The light on her face was a manifestation of inexorable change and yet her stillness overcame it. This meant something, if only my intellect were released from its bondage to explore the phenomenon and find a definition. Her presence made manifest the mystery of the relationship between the unchanging whole and our state of flux, between reality and illusion. She was legend, she was history. All insufficient reasons for the strength of my attachment to her. The light flowed. She stayed still.

'And I'll tell you this,' Wenna said. 'If you allow the past to overwhelm you, you are finished.'

The voice of the oracle. Sibylline responses. I longed to hear her laugh. That would bring release. Laughter was an essential part of her divinity. It was music without malice, a young girl already capable of laughing at the ingrained folly of mankind. It made my miserable shortcomings less unbearable.

'Take my father,' she said. 'My ever-absent father. Poor old Giuso. I've got a father, too, you know. Poor old thing. He chose to do his research on Ennius's *Annales* and he admitted to me he had never enjoyed reading them! Do you know what he said to me once? We were standing in the Colosseum when he said it. He said what he would have most liked to do was emigrate to the Rockies. Live in Idaho somewhere and study wildlife. And instead what does he do? Teach Latin in a dusty classroom in a dusty Roman suburb. So there you are . . .'

Where was I? The laughter I loved, but her father was not really a case in point. He was still hale and even hearty. He may not like his job but his family has a holiday house on Isola del Giglio, the sort of place my old colleagues in the Department of Social Analysis at Redbatch dream about. He has his wine and he can dine out of doors of an evening. This laugh she had, his daughter had inherited from him. Gay as the light on the Mare Tirreno. His discontent and disappointments were different in kind from the legacy of defeat and betrayal and guilt and inescapable responsibility I was inheriting from my father.

'Scarborough was a very odd place for him to . . .'

I was touched by the effort she made to sympathize and understand my distress. Accidental death or driven to his death. To dull the pain, too much to drink. His old obsession with the sea. Lost at sea. Swallowed up, drowned in the watery wastes. There were steps cut into the cliff-face he should have followed . . . I heard Wenna's voice.

'If it was a cliff he was looking for, did he fall or was he pushed?'

She had a perfect right to be as detached as she liked. It was what I wanted. I did not want her to take account of my feelings and sensibilities. It wasn't a tragedy. This was a man who had failed to cope. That's all there was to it. It was a concern for my immediate well-being that brought her to this room. She was entitled to distance herself from my visceral involvement with my father's fate.

'He was pushed,' I said. 'And I was the one that pushed him.'

'Rubbish!'

Her response was calm and yet vigorous and uplifting. I loved her for it.

'You were just a kid worrying about his mother. Very naturally. Pleasing. Normal. You just blurted something out. As far as I can see you had every right to. You can't hold yourself responsible for the enlargement he chose to make out of it. If it hadn't been that he would probably have seized on something else. He had a need to. You know what I think? We make our own fate.'

The beauty of her in the evening light was certainly mine. When she spoke her voice took the facts and the suppositions and turned them into words that were so cordial and reviving.

'Shall I tell you something else, Peredur? While I am about it!' She moved away from the window carrying the liquid intensity of the light with her, my angel of annunciation with the uncomplicated grace of a Florentine fresco. 'Political frustration breeds frustrated people.'

These were great truths and there was even greater truth in the detached way she uttered them. The perspective she had picked up from the events of last summer in Paris. From the redoubtable Sven. Was he in her thoughts at this moment as she moved in this room between the glowing walls? I had to learn to be more generous. She was here and he languished in his hygienic German cell. I could leave room for the breadth of her affections. My love would be profound and not possessive. She had seen the uprising of a new generation, the days of hope, the popular will in motion. In Paris earthquakes, here earth tremors. I needed to discuss with her questions of scale. Dictators can massacre thousands, even millions: the life-giving force had to be faithful in the small things, reviving each human spirit as it breathes.

'They never broke the arrogance of the occupying power,' Wenna said. 'The grip of the ruling class. They had wounds of the spirit that would never heal. They explained everything away and solved nothing.'

She was kneeling alongside me, speaking so quietly it was as though our thoughts were mingling in the rapt attention I gave her. She pushed at the exercise books with a stiffened finger. The light was deepening, the colour of the walls changing.

'We live under occupation,' Wenna said. 'Not obviously oppressive, except on occasions like this when for some ritual reason the occupying power feels the need to rub our noses in it. They have this need to teach us to cheer and even worship the symbol of our degradation. They never understood that, your father's generation, because servility and passivity softened the marrow of their bones.'

Bars of purple clouds had begun to stretch across the light of the setting sun. Moments of enlightenment cannot last. Wenna moved back to the window. I wanted to study her face for ever. The light sculpted the exquisite precision of her lips, fed into the pupils of her eyes. I had to stand as close as I could to her because she was the future. We were still and thoughtful. We had to be sorry for our parents; their impotence, their pitiful incompetence, their fragmented hopes. Wenna had the strength of her exotic origin. She was alive with a confidence to intervene in and even direct the course of events.

'You prescribe the limits of power by your capacity to hit

back,' she said. 'Maybe you can't make a revolution any more. Nobody is going to abolish money when everybody loves it so much. But you can push out the limits. That is perfectly possible. Bend the system even if you can't break it.'

There was a figure moving down the path of my overgrown kitchen garden. There was sufficient light for me to recognize the large, shambling figure of Elwyn Garmon in his greasy overalls. As far as I knew there was nothing wrong with my Triumph Herald. Wenna had lost her stillness. She sounded angry.

'He should have waited,' she said. 'It's not dark yet.'

He was lurking sheepishly under the narrow portico when I opened the back door. He seemed to know already that Wenna would be cross with him. She made him sit down by the kitchen table and drink a cup of tea while she lectured him on discipline and the need for training.

'Military operations need constant rehearsal,' she said. 'You realize that, don't you? And even then anything can go wrong. Anything or everything. The whole point of discipline and training is to minimize the risk. Do you understand that, El? Really understand?'

I listened as intently as an eavesdropper. They belonged to some form of clandestine organization and they did not mind me knowing it. I hadn't taken any oaths, made any vows Eoka-style. What tied me in more effective bondage was my attachment to the girl. When the lumbering mechanic glanced at me from the corner of his eye all he saw was an homunculus in a state of childlike dependence on a female figure that in one light could pass as a virgin, but in another looked as fierce as a goddess with a girdle of serpents. She put up her hand and that was enough to stop me as I moved to switch on the bare bulb of the kitchen light.

'After dark,' Wenna said. 'And no one should see him coming. Those were the orders.'

She was talking about someone else who had not yet arrived. Elwyn Garmon had his excuses.

'What could I do?' he said. 'You see how I was placed. The bugger was making a fuss, so I had to get here first.'

Wenna had arranged all this. Made my manse a rendezvous without telling me but I didn't really mind.

'He's got cold feet,' Elwyn Garmon said. 'Our fine farmer friend. The fearless nationalist. He said the police had been sniffing around. He wanted them off the place. That instant. There and then.'

'Where are they now?'

Wenna was not prepared to waste time contemplating the shortcomings of the nervous farmer.

'In the boot. Bouncing about.'

He wanted Wenna to relax discipline a little so that he could make a joke about his experience.

'I've never seen such a terrible bloody road. I hit a rock with the nearside wheel. The stuff went up and down in the back. I thought my time had come.'

Wenna ignored him. She paced up and down the kitchen of the manse like an army commander in the throes of making a fateful decision. She spoke at last.

'We'll store them here,' she said. 'It's not good to have the gelignite and the detonators in the same place. In theory anyway. But we have no choice. You won't mind?'

Did I mind? The detonators were still to arrive. Brought here at her behest by the mysterious third party. Did I have any choice? Would the surge of events, their sense of urgency, allow them to pause long enough to hear me raise a point of principle? I spoke.

'There's just one thing. What precautions are we taking to ensure that no one gets killed or maimed?'

I could barely see their faces in the dusk. It didn't help me to elaborate the point I wanted to make. I heard my own voice and it sounded finicky and irrelevant. It shrank the epic dimensions of an heroic enterprise to the small print of a life insurance policy. I had to endorse my concern.

'Violence against property,' I said. 'Symbolic violence. Avoiding human injury. To make people think. Teach them to protest.'

'You won't mind?'

That was all Wenna would say. She was no longer prepared to enter into theoretical discussions. All I had to do was make my mind up. Lift my foot and step outside the

326

limit prescribed by the law. Had I refused I would have been in danger of losing Wenna when I needed her more than anything else in life. That was the risk I was not prepared to take.

'Of course not,' I said.

There was nothing else I could say. There were arguments that could be carried on some other time. In the dark, Elwyn Garmon carried sticks of gelignite in a bucket and hid them in the cupboard under the stairs. I had chosen my side and I had to learn to be comfortable with the choice. Wenna was quite motherly towards me. Elwyn Garmon went outside to speak to a third person I had not realized was waiting in the dark. He had brought a large supply of detonators. Wenna decreed they could be stored in the dining-room under some of my father's papers. She led me by the hand to my bedroom where we could watch El Garmon reverse his vehicle without switching on his lights. Her fingers in my hand were soft and submissive. She was pleased with me and prepared to show her affection. Before we moved from the window to the bed, the lights of the car were suddenly switched on. We caught a brief glimpse of a thin man in airforce uniform before the headlights were abruptly swiched off again. In the darkness I could still see the metal buttons on the man's uniform before he melted out of sight.

'The idiot.' Wenna was cross. She judged Garmon had made yet another stupid mistake. 'He's such a bloody fool. But what else can we do? We have to recruit where we can. People willing to take a risk. Are you willing?'

I felt the sweet shape of her face with the tips of my fingers. I was ready to embrace her.

'Of course I am,' I said.

ii

There were three possible entrances at the rear of the Hall and they were all locked. Wenna was intrigued with everything she saw. It was warm in the stableyard and the inner courtyard. I didn't know whether she expected me to display pride in the place or at the least proprietorial knowledge. In reality, it was still as alien and remote to me as it must have been to her. I certainly preferred the working areas at the back to the ponderous self-importance of the front. Brangor Hall. My mother owned it by right of marriage as a substitute for right of conquest. The ascendancy she had failed to gain on the hustings she had quietly acquired by conquest in the bedroom. The story of her life. I had to learn to be more forgiving towards her, to make large-scale exercises of empathy and see her captivating the late Lord Brangor as they watched the great Atlantic rollers smash against the solid sea-front of Monte Estoril.

'Peredur. What's this?'

Wenna pulled at my arm. I responded instantly to her childlike enquiry. She was squinting up at a coop, shaped like a pavilion on wooden stilts. It had window spaces covered with fine mesh to keep out the flies and let in the air. Years ago it had been painted with pitch and there were still black stains on the exposed rock under the structure.

'Some kind of prison or something?' She was fascinated just as I had been when I first saw it.

'A food store apparently,' I said. 'That's what old Connie told me. For meat and for bread. In the old days.'

The barred window in the semi-basement belonged to Connie Clayton's room. The model housekeeper loyal to the traditions that went with her status; the courtesy 'Missus' in front of her name and the keys of the castle attached to her waist. She had been really more at home here than my mother or myself or my brothers. Our souls belonged to the sand dunes, the silting harbour, the terraced boarding houses. Poor old Connie. I frightened the life out of her when I was rummaging in one of the rooms over the old kitchens. She was waiting for me at the foot of the stone staircase with a steel poker that looked too heavy for her to hold. My ridiculous researches. My obsession with a memorial to my father. Not so long ago and now also consigned to the painful past. The kitchens had been modernised. Stove-enamelled oil-fired ranges for the benefit of creative ladies who had come and gone.

'You see how it is.'

Wenna was prepared to be understanding and philosophical.

'Your mother chose one way out. She is a very practical woman. She chose to compromise in order to acquire. It must have seemed fair enough to her. She could take things your father couldn't accept. The language wouldn't let him do it because being a poet bound him – like a liegeman to a lord. It was a bond he dare not break. He couldn't break his word. On the surface it might appear that she was right. She has a certain wordly success and has become part of the ascendancy. But at what cost? The path of compromise leads to assimilation and oblivion. And all is lost.'

She made a mock-tragic gesture as we passed down the cobbled passage between the outbuildings that led to the walled garden and the greenhouses. The evening air was filled with the fragrance of flowers and fresh growth. I could see the Huskie sisters working in the middle greenhouse. They both wore straw hats and clearly fancied themselves as ladies of the manor pottering among the cuttings and flowers. May Huskie came to the open doorway to greet us.

'Oh it's you then, Peredur, is it?' The words tumbled out in her congealed accent. She was smiling at Wenna and her eyes rolled cheerfully as she put her problem to us. 'Where are you going to get daffodils at this time of the year? That's a tough one isn't it? There's a drought in Kenya, did you know that? So they'll never get here in time. They're going to try New Zealand, so I'm told. You can't have an Investiture without your national flower, can you? It would never do.'

Her eyes rolled again, overcome with the global drollness of the situation. I had to make an appropriate remark.

'You are very lucky, May,' I said. 'You're English so you don't have to worry about it.'

'Oh, I don't know,' May Huskie said with a sudden glottal intensity. 'He's our Prince, too, you know.'

It wasn't a subject worth pursuing. I looked up at the lintel of the greenhouse door, and then pointed.

'Is there a spare side-door key still hiding up there?' I said. 'I thought I'd show Miss Ferrario a bit of the house.'

May Huskie hesitated before raising her arm and feeling

along the dusty lintel. I knew she was longing to ask me whether my mother had given me permission to take a stranger into the house. Some years ago she would have done. Now what little authority that remained to her needed any scrap of family goodwill it could garner.

'Bedwyr hasn't been down,' she said. 'Your mother was expecting him. But he hasn't turned up yet. Here it is.' She turned away to blow the dust off the key before handing it to me. 'And what about the film Gwydion was going to make? We haven't heard anything much about that either. I would have thought it was a chance too good to be missed. Make Brangor Hall famous all over the world. Put it on the map.'

She could see Wenna and I smile briefly at each other, and I could see how much she longed to share any crumb of inside information. She would not have believed me if I said we had none to give her, any more than if someone had told her we were a pair of terrorists.

The back door creaked as I opened it. The corridors and kitchens were cold and silent. Wenna began to whisper in spite of herself.

'What was he like?' she said. 'The late Lord B. I suppose you could call him your step-father, couldn't you?'

That was something I had never wanted to do. An inner inflexibility would not allow me to pass myself off as something I was not, and had no desire to be; and whatever it was, it went even deeper than my loyalty to my father's memory and the culture he represented.

' "A verray parfit gentil knight", otherwise a jolly decent chap,' I said. 'Except he was a lord. A model Englishman, except that he was Welsh. He adored this house and worshipped his family tree although he was descended from rapacious jumped-up Tudor hangers-on. His reading of history was very selective. The Empire was part of God's will on earth and whatever the naughtiness or obscure illegitimacy of his origins, it was his duty at all times to behave like one of God's Englishmen.'

Wenna wasn't listening to me. She was examining the interior with a rapt concentration that suggested she was memorizing every twist and turn of the passages and corridors. This made me a little nervous. The cellar door was

330

open. She asked if we could go down.

'No gunpowder plot, I hope,' I said.

She ignored the joke. I took down the inspection light from a hook on the wall and began to unwind the length of insulated wire. We passed an ancient central heating boiler and a series of underground rooms filled mostly with furniture that needed mending.

'Look at these,' she said.

On racks thick with dust there were rows of muskets that dated back to the Napoleonic Wars. There had been a Brangor Milita under the command of one of Lord Brangor's ancestors. Was it the fifth or the sixth Baron Brangor? Should I be bothered to know?

'Of course you should,' Wenna said. 'It's history.'

We were inspecting the racks in the wine cellar when I heard my mother's voice calling out above the cellar steps, sharp and authoritative in spite of the sepulchral echo.

'Hello! Who is it down there?'

Our visit was meant to be secret. Now we were caught out, found wandering through the cellars for no apparent reason. It was embarrassing. I had no means of extinguishing the inspection light in my hand. I waved it about as though I were searching for an area of darkness that would hide our predicament. Wenna had begun to laugh. She was already prepared to enjoy the encounter.

'It's only me,' I called out. 'We were just taking a look around.'

My mother, too, seemed ready to be amused. She was not alone.

'And who are "we", may I ask?'

I held the light down so that Wenna could see the steps out of the cellar. She was smiling and at her most charming, and so was my mother. Behind her stood Lord Mared. He was nattily dressed and there was a red rose in the lapel of his navy-blue jacket. There he was, the former socialist politician posing like a senior army officer having his portrait painted, his thinning grey hair immaculately dressed. With his rather florid good looks he could have also posed as an advertisement for port wine or winter cruises. The more he smiled the more I disliked the cunning bastard. He was the

331

one that stopped me getting the job that had been virtually promised me. No question about it. The old woman choked with pearls and the old man with a face like a grandfather clock must have been putty in his hands. It was all his doing. My mother was only making excuses for him. Arrant knaves with candied tongues. At least my father lived and died with his integrity intact. And here they were now prepared to make a fuss of Wenna because she was young and charming. She wore her black mini-skirt and voluminous dark blue jumper with a fashion-house ease and elegance. When they shook hands Lord Mared bowed over her hand as if he was about to kiss it. The smooth bastard. And what was he up to with my mother? She was dressed to kill. There was a scent about the place. An atmosphere of compulsive ardour.

'I was going to ask Lord Mared to select some wines for the occasion. It's such a mess down there. I really don't know anything about wine. It was never part of my education. And since Gwydion and Bedwyr aren't here . . .'

There was a reproach there that included me. Once again her three noble sons, on whom she had showered benefits all the days of their lives, were unavailable at a time when she needed them.

'We are in the Oak Room,' my mother said. 'I'm trying to give the house an airing. Don't be alarmed if you hear music. There's a quartet practising in the old music room. Why don't you show Miss Ferrario the rest of the house, at least as much as she might want to see, and then join us for a drink – in the Oak Room. That would be nice wouldn't it? What do you think?'

Wenna seemed to like the idea, so I had to agree. Lord Mared took over the inspection light. My mother called him Gilbert. It would have been difficult to have thought of a name that suited him better. Born Gilbert Ainsley Jones in Merthyr Tydfil before the Flood, out of which morass of depression and unemployment he had swum via the Law and the Army and the House of Commons to his present position of demi-eminence, a large fish in a stagnant pool, about to display his vinic expertise among the cobwebs and the warmth of my mother's honeyed encouragement.

Wenna tried her best to raise my spirits. She made light-

332

hearted remarks about the portraits of Brangor ancestors, about the Blue Drawing-Room, the Chinese Room, the Japanese Room, the Royal Bedroom; but her high spirits put me in mind of Maxine Hackett and a whole episode of my own folly that I had tried my best to forget. Wenna herself belonged to such a higher plane of significance that she shouldn't allow her own idle chatter to reduce her to the level of an adventuress like Maxine out to exploit any man she could find for whatever she could dig out to her own advantage. Wenna was being particularly tolerant about my mother.

'It's understandable,' she was saying. She was admiring a fireplace in the Japanese Room made of white marble. 'It's not just if you can't beat 'em, join 'em. There is something deeply impressive about empire building. There's a dignity about it. A visionary nobility. An assumption of largesse. Dispensing the benefits of civilization throughout a savage and barbaric globe. It was an ideal of sorts. A dead ideal as it happens. Stone dead. Still, a place like this deserves a certain respect. As a monument at least. Or a museum. We can't possibly blow it up.'

She touched her lips with the tips of her fingers as she laughed, and I was relieved and enchanted. She looked as sweet and as innocent as a cherub. And yet she was the one with a vision. Through her an entire continent could make a fresh start and this little culture of ours in its state of continuing crisis could have its appointed part in the new pattern of existence – beyond the imperialism of capitalism and of communism to a confederation of communities. From code words to key words. The girl knew what she was talking about and she radiated unqualified delight.

In the Oak Room I was able to bask in Wenna's reflected glory. I could see that my mother and Lord Mared were much taken with her. She appeared demure and yet forthright: an attractive combination. And there was the impulsive frankness of youth, quick to appreciate a picture or a view. She pointed out the deer wandering nervously in the park on the edge of the trees on the knoll where the ruined castle stood, and an eighteenth-century painter's vision in oils of the same view as it was two centuries ago, the composition dominated by the antiquarian properties of the fashionable taste of the time.

It was June, but the evening was chilly. A lavish wood fire burned in the grate and Lord Mared perched himself on the leather club fender to nurse a generous helping of whisky and water in a cut-glass tumbler.

'Ferrario,' he said. 'That's not very Welsh, is it?'

Insolent bastard. I had to restrain myself from pointing out that he wasn't conducting an interview for some job or other within his tentacled gift.

'It's all very puzzling,' he said. 'To a simple Welshman like me. It really is. You must tell me. Just what is it you people have got against the Investiture?'

"You people". What nauseating overlap between blood-sucking leeches and wet-rot fungi did the noble lord have in mind? My Lord Mared. Faithful to the Travellers, the Athenaeum, and the House of Lords Library. Ex-man of the people. His ties with Merthyr Tydfil, he had given us to understand, with a winning gesture of informality that sent the whisky and water swirling in his glass, had weakened to dissolution since his eldest sister died five years ago. He gave it out in confidence but with an unspoken understanding that if we were approached at some future date by an accredited biographer, the information could be passed on.

'It's not something we shall allow to be imposed upon us,' Wenna said. 'It's as simple as that.'

She was cool and polite. I was seething inside with a dyspeptic mixture of indignation and admiration. What a girl. I was ready to cheer or even fall on my knees in front of her. Lord Mared was concealing his unease and disapproval with a theatrical attempt at light-hearted urbanity.

'Tell me, how do you propose to stop it? Taking on the Household Cavalry in hand to hand combat?'

He was looking towards my mother for signs of appreciation of his wit. She was trying to laugh. It surprised me to notice that she appeared more anxious about my reaction than anything else.

'My grandfather's father ran away from Lucca to join Garibaldi,' Wenna said. 'And then my remote ancestor on the Penybryn side was out with Glyndwr. So, you see, I have my credentials.'

334

Everything she said delighted me. Her youth was an asset, not an obstacle. She had the strength of personality and that unexpected intelligence capable of wrong-footing the older generation just as they were at their most patronizing. She was a credit to Garibaldi and Glyndwr.

'You have plans,' Lord Mared said.

'Oh, lots of plans,' Wenna said. She laughed in that self-deprecating way that I found increasingly delightful. She pointed her glass at me. 'Not that Peredur would approve of them. He doesn't want to kill anyone. I think he must be some kind of a pacifist. I can think of lots of people I'd like to kill.'

Mared and my mother treated this as an imaginative sally. Not to be outdone, Mared poked his thumb into his own chest.

'Me, for instance?'

'How did you guess?'

Their laughter had become a form of intimacy. We were all friends drinking together and pleasantly relaxed.

'You'll stay for supper, won't you?' my mother said.

Wenna looked at me. 'If Barkis is willin',' she said.

While Mared chuckled and preened himself in front of the fire my mother took me by the arm and drew me into the next room. She put a finger to her mouth as if she were about to let me into a secret. She was accompanied by the strings of a quartet rehearsing a difficult sequence in the Music Room down the corridor.

'I like your girl, Peredur,' she said. 'I really do. So lively and intelligent. I think when all this circus is over you'll find we are really on the same side.'

She must have noticed how sceptical I looked.

'We mustn't let it become an unbridgeable gulf,' she said. 'Whatever happens. It's really a case of some of us being moderate so that others can be extreme. And as far as any plans you have for this place are concerned, cultural ecology and so on, there's nothing I would like more than to help.'

Her anxiety to please put me on my guard. I had to watch her and not be carried away by the music. These were the beguiling tones I remembered from my childhood when she took my head in her lap and ran her fingers through my hair.

'There is something else you ought to know.'

335

She pointed nervously at the half-open door into the Oak Room. There was more laughter in there. Wenna and my Lord Mared were enjoying each other's company.

'You mustn't be too surprised,' my mother said. 'You probably think of me as an ancient relic. Gilbert, Lord Mared, has asked me to marry him.'

'Christ . . .!'

The shock was so great I had to look around for a chair to sit on. I was muttering unintelligibly as though I had been temporarily deprived of the power of speech. My perception of the world was in traumatic confusion. How could I see or understand anything when my own feelings were so fevered and out of control?

'I haven't given him a firm answer yet,' my mother said. 'Only an agreement in principle.'

She was talking as if she had been offered a job and still hadn't made up her mind whether or not to take it. She needed to consult the appointment board, no doubt, and particularly the old woman choked with pearls and the old sod with a brass face polished like a grandfather clock. My emotional upheaval was subsiding.

'What's he after?' I looked my mother straight in the eye.

'What do you mean?' she said. She was at her stiffest and most authoritative.

'A man like that has to be after something. It's his way of life.'

My mother breathed deeply. She glanced at her wristwatch. 'If that's your attitude,' she said. 'If you're determined to be offensive . . .'

My anger made me venomous.

'That man is the incarnation of everything I hate and despise. It's funny. I thought you would have known that. Or at least guessed. I suppose that only goes to show how little we really know about each other.'

Discordant notes from the Music Room underlined the silence between us. She would not unbend and neither would I. We carried our unnatural quiet back with us into the Oak Room. It was not long in quenching the merriment. Lord Mared's resonant baritone brought a colourful anecdote to a close. I had no idea what it was about. As soon

336

as I could I claimed to remember that Wenna and I had to leave for a previous appointment and we hurried away.

iii

I had to come to grips with it. I was being haunted by shadows and symbols. They had taken possession of the world and ordinary people's lives moved at such a distance from mine that when I looked out of the window of my bedroom in the manse, the village had become as inaccessible as a settlement in Outer Mongolia. In this state of inactivity and expectation nightmares and premonitions could only increase until they tyrannized my existence. I was no longer fit to be left to myself in this empty house. I found a key to the dining-room and locked it. This gave me so much temporary relief that I heard myself laugh aloud. Guard duty was bad for the nerves. I had to pretend to be busy but there was nothing I wanted to read or write. My father's papers were locked in with the detonators and it wasn't a door I wanted to open. Wenna should not leave me alone. A new recruit is too easily demoralized. Sometimes I trembled as I talked to myself, both reactions unnecessary and ridiculous. What was the use of teaching myself the importance of being committed and in the next breath conjuring up yet another argument in favour of doing nothing?

Gareth Hopkin called. I didn't ask him in. I could only resent the fact that the man knew where I lived. That, too, was my mother's fault. Talk about anthropology and the basic historical process. I contrived to lead him through the sagging iron gate that led into the chapel graveyard. The grass had not been cut and the tops of the headstones, mostly slate, peeped out of the green haze in their own hesitant forms of resurrection. Hopkin clasped his hands behind his back and spoke in a tone of sonorous melancholy.

'The appetite for invitations,' he said. 'You wouldn't believe it. The parades and the parties. Among so-called socialists. My own sister. Trembling with excitement because she's been asked to sing at an evening party being

337

given in honour of the Snowdons. I haven't the heart to stop her. In any case she wouldn't listen. Like everyone else she's been intoxicated by the media. I told you didn't I? That day at the Rally. What can you do with such people? They are nothing more than the raw material of the agencies of manipulation. What has become of the proletariat? The masses we are supposed to cherish? What can we do? What sources of power are available for the process of rationality? Do you follow me? Do you see what I mean?'

I gazed at information chiselled on a slate I hadn't noticed before: one son killed in 1917, the other in 1944, and the widowed mother dying in 1962 at the age of 82 after a lifetime of mourning. Hopkin was an historian. The sons were killed in action. One in France. One in Italy. Had they brought the bits back here or was the inscription a memorial to the mother's prolonged grief and pride? The world was a strange place and getting stranger. And here he was visiting his fevered cogitations on my defenceless head.

'It's a manufactured myth, of course. A political ploy. Obviously. Will it become part of an imbedded culture embraced by the bulk of mankind? In which case, what price the Revolution? "There is no point in separating historical prognosis from the acts by which they are fulfilled". Okay. Just what prognosis is this sticky circus meant to fulfil? Do you follow me? Do you see what I mean?'

He was no comfort at all. I wished he would go away. I would prefer to be alone to wait for Wenna. All he wanted was a witness to the purity of his marxist faith and mental strife and determination not to bend neck or knee to prevailing idolatry. I should just slap his back and send him on his way.

'Nothing we say, however loudly we say it, can make the slightest difference,' Hopkin said. 'The media and the apparatus of state are in collusion and a modern juggernaut is in motion. You can't stop a tank division with a shopping bag and a guitar. We never had a hope.'

He raised his arm in a rhetorical gesture and I saw him become part of the statuary of the graveyard. Behind him a marble angel glanced down in modest sorrow at the human condition.

338

'I don't know whether this appeals to you,' Hopkin said. 'I have this idea. Get away from it all. A strategic withdrawal, you could call it . . . What I have in mind is a trip to Dublin. I mentioned it to Hefin Mather and he was quite keen. Very keen in fact. There would be a couple of dozen at least. Perhaps more. Mather has a list. Kindred spirits, shall we say. A symbolic assembly on the banks of the Liffey. Call it a weekend school or extra-mural trip. Arrange one or two talks on Jim Larkin, say, and James Connolly. It wouldn't cost much. Mather has worked it out. Sail from Holyhead, close enough to the royal yacht to spit on it, and spend three days in the free air of Dublin's fair city . . .'

His jaw was stretched as he waited for my response to what he clearly regarded as a signal honour. I could be one of a select company, an intellectual elite. An awkward invitation . . . an ignoble retreat. How could I reject it without giving anything away? In what way would playing truant on the mythological day of reckoning reinforce our claim to nationhood, should I ask? The only appropriate place to be on such a day was in prison. We could each of us squat in his separate cell, bringing the philosophy of praxis to bear on the preservation of the dregs of sovereignty among a demoralized and defeated minority. The graveyard or the prison.

'Somebody wanting to see you?' Hopkin said.

The bulky figure of Elwyn Garmon in his dark blue overall was weighing on the sagging gate and grinnning at us. When he saw me look at him, he raised a grimy thumb.

'Ah', I said. 'He's come to . . . he's come to see to my car. He put a gasket in upside down . . . Wasn't thinking what he was doing. Would you excuse me . . .'

I had to put a distance between Hopkin and Elwyn Garmon. From the gate I led the mechanic to the back of the house. He seemed amused by my state of agitation. I noticed he had taken to chewing gum lately. He wanted me to see he was enjoying his role as amateur bomber.

'We need some of the stuff,' he said. 'Exercise tonight. Commander's orders.'

'You must be mad,' I said. 'Coming here in broad daylight.'

339

'I can take it,' he said. 'Or you can bring it. Please yourself. I'm supposed to be taking a look at your car. No harm in that.'

While El Garmon's head was under the bonnet of my car, Gareth Hopkin appeared under the overgrown lilac tree. He was curious but also concerned to show he was capable of rising above vulgar curiosity. He had the dignity of a man who could, at a more auspicious time, have been adopted as a parliamentary candidate with sufficient weight and presence to win even a marginal seat.

'Shall we put your name down then?' It was a straightforward question that could be overheard by anyone who cared to listen. He had the confidence of a man exercising a democratic right. 'We can settle the sub later, but we need to have an idea of the number. Shall we put your name down?'

All open and above board. No law against. El Garmon was listening as he pretended to be absorbed in my Triumph Herald cylinder head. I was his associate, not Gareth Hopkin's. Never comfortable to be pig in the middle, balancing between two stools, mixing his metaphors into an impalatable mash. Where was Wenna? I needed her to make a decision for me. Already my head was nodding as it were of its own volition. My excuse would be if she called me to account that a trip of this sort might prove to be an escape route and at the very least could serve as some kind of cover. At a time like this one had to think of everything and as I once told my students at Redbatch, thinking of everything invariably ended up as thinking of nothing.

'Thank you,' I said. 'Very nice of you to invite me. Yes. Put my name down, please.'

iv

Wenna was in a state of permanent elation. To touch her skin was like an electric shock. She had powers that I never knew existed. She had shifted my world into a zone of danger that created an alternative landscape through which I had to follow her as closely as I could. This patch between life and death obliterated the difference between day and night, between truth and falsehood, between illusion and reality. When our night-time reconnaissance began I was liable to delay our departure with an attack of diarrhoea. Wenna was patient with me. My nervousness gave her strength. I could see that. She even admitted it. She said she would transfer her own fears into my custody for the duration.

The first lesson of active service is the necessity of lying. Not an easy lesson for a dedicated seeker after Truth with a capital 'T' to learn, Wenna said. Morfydd Ferrario had to be lied to and misled on a regular basis for her own good. Similarly motherly Mrs Lloyd Tai Hirion, who had doted on Wenna all her life, and anyone else whose ignorance or unwitting collaboration was essential to our campaign. My job, my appointment, was to be Wenna's driver and trusted but untrained number two. I had to make up for my lack of technical qualifications with more intense devotion. In various cars, including Mrs Lloyd's reliable A35, which El Garmon maintained for the dear lady with such care, we distributed the gelignite and detonators from the manse to strategic hiding places that would contribute to the campaign: a coal hole near a quay, a quarry shed, a derelict shepherd's cottage, an allotment near a railway siding, an old lime kiln next to an electricity pylon.

My life in this unchartered career depended on blind obedience to a girl who said she could only tell me what was healthy for me to know.

'Don't worry,' she said. 'You've been vetted.'

Her slightest remark could set off a debate in my head that could rage all day and all night and never come in sight of a comfortable conclusion. Vetted by whom, and how, and why? A council of war? An appointments board? I agreed not to question anything; but that did not stifle the questions echoing inside my skull.

'We are handicapped of course,' she said.

We sat in her mother's car, pretending to be lovers courting in the lane. In my loose embrace, her eyes were wide open studying the target.

'It complicates things, not being allowed to kill anyone.' She was thinking aloud as I held her in my arms; musing on

341

the nature of violence. 'The word is, this is a propaganda battle. Do you understand that, Professor?'

I couldn't decide whether or not she was teasing me. She liked to make disparaging comments on the ineffectual complacency of academics. More than once she picked up my hands and said how soft they were. I wasn't inclined to think. My tongue licked the lobe of her ear and I longed to feel like her; to be as aware, as alert, and as unworried.

'It's not a war,' she said. 'We are just punctuating a people's mental processes. We have to take into account this very sensitive Welsh nonconformist reverence for human life. Okay. I don't mind. Blood has substance and meaning or I wouldn't be playing the organ in chapel when called upon, would I?'

Was she talking to me or to her German, Sven? Echoes of old café debates. He was writing to her. She told me that as we scuttled around our secret landscape. She did not show me his letters. We were part of a worldwide movement, she assured me. There were blows that had to be struck from one end of the continent to the other and we were privileged to have been chosen to strike them. This did nothing to assuage my sense of troubled isolation.

'Who chose me?' I said.

'You chose yourself.' Her answer was sharp and abrupt. Then she laughed again. 'But of course you've been vetted.'

By whom? Whatever it was, the process had reduced my psyche to a primitive level, where every step I took was watched by gods and demons equally divided for and against my continuing existence. They followed me day and night, demanding continuous propitiation. I could see their faces peering at me enquiringly through the windscreen of the car as we drove through the night.

'Think of wildlife,' Wenna said. 'The life that comes out at night, under the cover of darkness. Try to be part of it.'

He knew us all, whoever was in charge; but none of us, however few or many we were, knew him. And Wenna said that was how it should be. It couldn't work in any other way. This invisible creature was the physical embodiment of the sovereignty of our national identity and therefore we needed to obey him. He could appear without warning, like an

342

apparition, and activate a cell. We were certainly active now. We passed a police car on the road outside the inn where El Garmon had already parked the car with the gelignite in the boot. Wenna snuggled up to me and laid her head on my shoulder with the care of a young girl on a night out trying not to disturb her coiffure.

'The whole country is swarming with police,' she said.

She said it to comfort me, to point out that this was the normal state of affairs. Cars couldn't be anonymous as long as they had numbers. Nothing was too nondescript to be noticed. Gods and demons and policemen studying every step. The countryside is never empty. However deserted it may appear, there are always eyes that are watching. The world is a dream kingdom. I am not master of the situation or the subject. There are hours and hours to wait. We could be weighed into the ground with waiting. 'Always two detonators, girl.' he said. 'You'd be surprised how many of the buggers are duds,' El Garmon, the great expert. 'Have you brought the bulb then?' he said to me. 'What bulb?' I said. 'The bulb to test the circuit, you bloody idiot,' he said. It was no use me resenting that. In this business I was the 'bloody idiot' and he was the man of action, the hero, deserving honour and respect.

I wanted to burn my father's papers in the back garden of the manse. Wenna stopped me. I was to do nothing to attract unwanted attention. I was to leave them where they lay on the empty dining-room floor. Morfydd Ferrario would have been very ready to tell anyone that enquired that her lovely daughter and Mr More the extra-mural lecturer were on their way to attend summer school in Quimper . . . Another example, she would hint, of intellectuals shaking the temporarily polluted dust of their native land off their feet. That sort of thing. She would say how much she wished she was going with us. The summer school was advertised under the intriguing title of 'Arthur Lives!' with an exclamation mark and, Mrs Ferrario would say, she could not imagine a subject more 'up her street'. El Garmon would return to the boozing party at the Football Club's annual dance where his friends by two o'clock in the morning would be too pissed to have noticed his absence; while Wenna and

I, our bags already neatly packed, would drive south in my faithful Triumph Herald to catch the ferry from Plymouth to Roscoff. It was all planned.

By daylight the target looked soft and easy. El Garmon winked and rubbed his hands together and I had to admire his hands: hardened, thickened, ingrained with grease, elected to wield the modern equivalent of the sword of freedom. Our enterprise as I understood it would be a secondary diversion. Another active service cell had been allocated the destruction of the pier that Wenna had photographed. She professed disappointment. I was openly relieved. This one was meant to be easy. The lover's lane was hidden by trees and undergrowth and yet it offered a perfect escape route. Five hundred yards into what appeared to be a dead-end in a disused quarry, a sharp turn to the left and you were on a track that became a minor road that swung north and then south and fed you neatly, breathing lightly, on to the main road and the long journey to Plymouth.

The steep bank below the railway siding was covered with rose-bay willow herb. The gap we would use was covered with lanky campion and dog daisies, nettles and long grass. Above this colourful assembly of weeds and wild flowers stood our target. Wenna and El Garmon had come to speak of it with a certain affection. A drab-looking camouflaged railway carriage to be used as a stand-by communication centre by an American television company. And alongside it a stand-by generator. Our intelligence informed us it was unlikely to be used except in an emergency. This amused Wenna. She said we would create the emergency by knocking it out. It was guarded by a local security firm that tended to take on too much business and too little staff. Long live the profit motive, Wenna said, so long as it conflicts with the power of the centralized state. Our reconnaissance on successive nights confirmed that the carriage was visited by two elderly security men every two hours. The company did not use Alsation dogs, we were informed, because they cost too much in food and upkeep. El Garmon said it was a piece of cake.

It didn't feel like that as Wenna and I waited in the dark.

344

Darkness changes everything. We had pencil torches for emergency and no other light. It was essential that we lay still and silent like bodies in a tomb. If the police did chance upon us we were lying on the back-seat like a pair of exhausted lovers. We couldn't even share our thoughts. In the darkness every sound was magnified. There were bullocks in the field behind the trees on our left. Bullocks are curious creatures. Born informers. If they heard us they would give away our presence. And so would pheasants. Those colourful timid creatures. On a previous recce I had disturbed a cock and a hen and their young, and the noise they made frightened me even more than I frightened them.

At least Wenna was in my arms. I couldn't tell whether or not she was sleeping. I recited to myself long litanies of justification for what we were doing. The thoughts were mine but the voice was hers. 'We are not finished. It's up to us to shake off the shackles of an official version of history sponsored by the power of the state that says we are scheduled for polite extinction. This absurd fancy-dress festival of mesmerizing majesty is a perfect example of the state stage-managing history to its own advantage. No self-respecting people could allow themselves to be so blatantly hoodwinked for one moment. No self-respecting people could allow themselves to be deprived by an alien power of their separate identity, be deprived of their one remaining foothold in their original corner of the world . . . Only the interpenetration of our language and our landscape could preserve and nurture our native social patterns. All we were intent on doing this night was asserting that minimum degree of sovereignty without which a distinct people cannot continue to exist . . .' We had logic on our side. It was comforting to follow out our thoughts to the point of composing manifestos, while owls hooted and clouds sailed across the moon. A fine rain began to fall creating a damp mist. Was the girl as nervous as I was? I had taken kaolin and morphine and my bowels should hold out. Who exactly was it that said logic was the very devil?

El Garmon was late. This roused Wenna. She kept looking at her wrist-watch with her pencil torch and muttering under her breath. When I managed to decipher the sounds she was making they were nothing more than a repetitive sequence of childish swear words. Wenna believed in meticulous planning. It was more than her philosophy; it was her creed, her faith.

He lumbered out of the darkness, laughing, and slapped the bonnet of the car with the palm of his hand. He had the dynamite strapped to his back. Easier to transport he said, with pride, since he wanted both hands free. I could smell beer on his breath and I knew he was over-confident. Wenna was angry. El Garmon was making too much noise. She pointed out to him in furious whispers that the pre-arranged timing device could not now be used because the guards would be back before it went off and they would be maimed or killed. El Garmon took the huff. Drink made him less submissive to Wenna than usual. He said he would do the job himself and we could bugger off to Brittany as soon as we liked. All we had to do was give him the detonators and the battery and the trenching tool and we could clear off. I felt quite ready to oblige him but I said nothing. I could just see Wenna lift her hand and touch his cheek and his teeth glimmer as he smiled. She took the explosive off his back.

We would stick to the plan. She insisted on carrying the bag with the sticks of gelignite and the detonators and the battery so that he could be free to dig the holes in the soft ground between the generator and the carriage. It would be as rehearsed except the timing would be reduced to a minimum.

El Garmon would make his way back to the car-park and the party at the Football Club and she would take the path that led down the slope nearer the disused quarry where I would be waiting with the car. All I had to do was push the car quietly to that point two hundred yards away and then wait.

Waiting. A form of agony I had not felt before. I should have gone with them. I could see El Garmon's hands. He was the expert. His hands never trembled. I'd watched them on more than one exercise in the hills and learned nothing except a condition of dependence that was like free-fall. I saw his fingers fiddle with wires like a gorilla trying to thread a needle. So domestic. Kneeling over the timer he said he

346

had taken it out of a lamp-post and thanked the Electricity Board. He was proud of his improvisations: cigar cases as bomb containers, alarm clocks, plaster, wires and winding levers. I should have paid more attention. Acquired the skills. Become an executive instead of a lackey. I couldn't sit in the car. There was more comfort in the wet grass. I could walk and count the paces, so many yards in a second. Walk back and forwards and rehearse in my mind driving without the lights, on a mental printed-circuit, in the dark.

I was turned into ice by the explosion. The earth shook and I fell to my knees. A flash of light peeled off my eyelids for a fraction of a second. I saw everything and nothing and there was a soft thud as something fell into the ferns at the side of the lane. I was gasping with a wave of terror from which death would have been a release.

But there was no release. I could not escape into nothing. I had my pencil torch. I had my pathetic thin beam of light in the dark and it was with this that I saw lumps of flesh. Torn tissue, bone, clothing bloody mutilations. Part of her face. Her eye and her mouth wide open. They were both dead. How could I leave the spot? I was no less bound to her body because it was in bloody bits. It was my duty to gather what was left of her and treat it with reverence. Arrange for proper disposal. Their bodies were mixed up in an unrecognizable wreckage. One flesh. Nothing I could sort out. A warm vapour exuded from a mass of flesh and clothing. I switched off the pencil torch and leaned away to vomit in the grass.

I was paralyzed. I could do nothing. Until I heard the sirens of police cars in the distance. They were coming. All I could do was escape.

v

Voices swarming outside the bedroom door. Out of the confusion I hear my own voice insisting that it was her head. No one else's. I was prepared to swear to it no matter what the sentence. It belonged to her. I should have brought it away with me, or failing that, I should have buried it.

Wrapped it tenderly in fern and buried it in the soft earth under the rose-bay willow herb. A place that the enemy could not desecrate. Carry it away or bury it, honour demanded. I did neither. I fled the field with empty hands leaving the dead unburied. The voices outside the door were all reproach, echoing my disgrace. To bring her travelling case so neatly packed and not to bring her. Death and oblivion were too good for me. I was condemned to be alive.

I was bolt upright in the narrow bed. This was the attic bedroom of my brother Bedwyr's house. I had no right to be here. No right to be anywhere. My mouth and my eyes were wide open. Strange sounds welling up in my throat. I was choking and no breath could escape from my lungs. I was trapped inside myself and only this animal noise over which I had no control could escape from me. Sian opened the bedroom door. She was in her dressing gown, pale as a ghost, and yet all tenderness and sympathy. She sat on the edge of the bed and placed her hand on my shoulder. It helped. Bedwyr stood in the doorway. He was in his pyjamas, his thinning hair standing up. He had been woken from his much needed sleep. Such a worker he was. I wanted to say I was sorry and every hour that God sends he needed his sleep and that . . .

'For God's sake, get him to shut up Sian.' I heard his voice from a great distance. 'He'll wake the children. He'll frighten the life out of them.'

Sian's voice was much closer. As close as the orbs of concern in her wide eyes.

'Should we get a doctor? He's got a temperature. I'm sure of it. Bring a glass of water. That won't do any harm, will it? Peredur, drink this.'

And I drank it. I looked at her as grateful as a dumb animal, unable to speak. I sank down into the bed as they both watched me. I was resolved not to frighten the children. Night was around us, holding out a dark hope of oblivion. My centre had emptied and a dullness crept over my body and dribbled spittle from the corner of my mouth into the white pillow-case. To oblige them I closed my eyes.

I hid in that attic bedroom for three days and nights. I ate nothing. Not that I had the will to starve myself to death.

348

The children did not come near me. My brother Bedwyr, my refuge but not my strength, went about his honest business, restoring and reclaiming derelict sites, preserving and defending bits and pieces of our meagre architectural heritage, designing what was rumoured to be the very last university extension in our country. Life went on. Anything I had to say had to be said to Sian first, if there was anything left to say. The thought that she might have come to love Wenna almost as much as I did reduced me to tears and speechlessness that lasted a day. Daylight was too much for me. Newspapers were filth. I threw them on the floor. From them headlines like fanfares stared up to mock and accuse me. What did she die for? The drums and ceremonies roll on like the caterpillar tracks of tanks and crush our cause and ferns and flowers and flesh with impartial ease. How could we have ever stopped it, that procession of English heraldic modes in league with the calendar itself? The English press had occupied the cave on Mount Helicon and all the sacred springs. It had suborned the weavers and the muses but it was my days and not the press's that were numbered. There would be no mention of her heroic death or Elwyn Garmon's except as obscure incidents or accidents in a paragraph of one or two lines. All I could do now was absent myself from history and remain silent.

Sian brought the minister along. Cadvan Watkins. C.W. of the booming voice and pullover that needed darning. She understood I was suffering from some nameless grief and needed consolation. He stood with his head bowed outside the bedroom door. I wouldn't agree to see him. I might have done to please Sian. These were good people. So safe and respectable and domesticated. There was an abyss between us. They didn't know the streets were dangerous. You could help a blind beggar across the road to his pitch and as you left him he could shoot you in the back. That was the world's custom. Any form of tenderness was fraught with danger. Departments of state existed to exterminate and be exterminated. Revolutions were baptized in blood. The midwife who unwinds the twisted cord around its wrinkled neck could save the hangman and the apparatus of state so much expense and trouble. I had questions he could never answer. So let the crisis pass, let the victims be buried and gather history from postmarks on faded letter-cards. *I am well. I am in hospital. I have been wounded. I am dead.* Cross out the messages that do not apply. Write nothing on the left hand side except your signature . . . Keep the card with lavender and tenderness in the top right-hand corner of the chest of drawers. I could see C.W.'s broad back as he bent his head going down the stairs. He was taking something of my sorrow with him in spite of my refusal to share it with him.

My brother Gwydion turned up on the fourth day. I heard him move about downstairs, abnormally breezy and cheerful. On the stairs he made loud, reassuring remarks so that I could overhear them. He wanted me to know he knew more than Sian or Bedwyr. Sian's voice was subdued and cautious. I felt her silences heavy with restraint and suspicion. I knew she distrusted Gwydion. Her reasons for unease may have been different from mine. I had heard her say she despised everything he stood for; and then laugh and say that in fact she had no idea what he did stand for, except his own personal advantage and continued well-being, and perhaps after all, that was the normal human condition. He was the rule, we were the exceptions. I lay in bed and remembered how much I liked Sian's laughter. I wondered how Gwydion could tramp around the premises, in and out of the farmhouse, the outbuildings, the gardens, driving cars about and controlling a sequence of obscure activities with the authority of a master. Whatever the procedures, it was plain that Bedwyr had given his consent.

When he eventually came to my attic bedroom, he closed the door behind him and conducted the interview in a strident, incredulous whisper.

'My God,' he said. 'What the hell have you been up to?'

I would tell him nothing. That way I would discover how much he knew.

'It's always the same,' Gwydion said. 'It's the quiet little buggers that get up to the worst mischief. They drift around balancing the butter in their mouths and then suddenly . . .'

He raised his hands hoping I would enlighten him by finishing the sentence. I did not oblige him. He bent his head to avoid the low beam as he moved around my bed. He was closing in on me.

'There have been little bangs about the place,' he said. 'Bombs. Bombs and bangs. Lots more than the media let on, naturally. They wouldn't want to distract attention from their one day wonder. The apotheosis of a renaissance prince. Didn't want to spoil it. A couple have blown themselves up. A man and a woman. Our old lady mother seems to think you knew about it. Had something to do with it even. She says I must whip you out of the country, *piu presto possibile*! Have you understood that?'

I admitted the minimum of understanding.

'That's all right then.'

Gwydion breathed deeply. He considered sitting on the edge of my bed and decided not to. He was seeing me as something different. A man with a plague that had to be disposed of.

'Don't ask me how old Amy knows. She makes it her business to know. Spider in the political web and all that. She's just a frustrated politician. That's what she is. Ordering people about. That's her forte. I've had my orders. Plus funds. Right? So I want you up and running, little brother. No more moping up here. If all goes well, tomorrow evening we should be on our way.'

My mother remembered Wenna. She liked her. Any recollection that came to me in this room intensified the pain of irreparable loss. I wanted to confess to Sian. But what would be the confession? And I couldn't do it while Gwydion was strutting around suppressing his curiosity with the effort of being a decisive man of action. My car had gone. He put his hand on my shoulder and led me into the orchard.

'The knacker's yard,' he said. 'Sorry about that. I got twenty-five quid for it. No use having it around any more. Nothing the police enjoy more than going over a suspicious vehicle. Toothcombs aren't in it. Now what about the lady's travelling case?'

He didn't ask which lady. I turned away so that he would not see the tears welling up in my eyes. I was powerless to stop them; even to lift my hand to wipe them away.

351

'Unless you instruct otherwise, I'm putting it into the incinerator.'

The children were watching us. They knew something was wrong. The solemn expression on David's face was so like his father's. Sian said David was driven by a desire to please his father in everything he did. And the two little girls were intent on pleasing David. On the edge of the orchard they looked pretty and innocent enough to be admitted into the Garden of Eden. Not everyone who cries out father, father . . . how long has it been going on?

'You've got your passport?' Gwydion was demanding my attention. 'I'm taking you along as consultant,' he said. 'Have you got that? Marsala. Ever been there? Taormina, was it? I could swear you told me you'd been to Taormina. You sent me a postcard. I'm sure of it. Bit hot this time of the year. Still as far as you are concerned, little brother, not half as hot as here.'

'Consultant?' I said. 'For what?'

'Sicily. Tourist film. Greek and Roman remains. I'll give you a book to brush up on it all.'

'What happened to the film you were going to make about the eisteddfod?'

He slapped my back as if I had been trying to tease him. 'Water under the bridge, boy,' he said. 'I'm sorry to have to say this to the son of a national winner. But the fact is the world in general doesn't give a fourpenny fart about the eisteddfod. Or the place it comes from, for that matter. Sad, isn't it? The world in general much prefers Coca Cola.' He reached up at a branch of apple tree and pulled it down to inspect it closely. 'And I'll tell you something else. The royal circus was the same. Like a Coca Cola advert. Just a colourful flicker on the t.v. screen. Sound and flummery, signifying nothing. Here today, gone tomorrow and the place thereof shall know it no more. Hardly worth dying for, was it?'

Ten

It was a surprise to find my mother in a public ward. Six beds
on either side and the sister's desk vacant in the middle.
Twelve beds and six patients spaced out and spruced up like
vases in a display cabinet, for visiting time. I could see at
once my mother ruled the roost. She was surrounded by cut
flowers, tributes from admirers and loyal retainers. She sat
smiling among the foliage and all the other women watched
her out of their dwindling reserves of wonder and envy.
Public ward or no, she was Lady Brangor still, pale, ethereal
and smiling among her hothouse flowers. She stretched out
her arms towards me and I saw how slack and thin they
were. She was glad to see me, resolutely joyful.

'My boy,' she said. 'My Peredur. How well you look.'

I had to surrender to her embrace. Under the surface of
perfumes and powders that should have stirred ancient
animosities and affections, there was the more disturbing
sour smell of her sickness.

'Here I am,' she said. 'Amy Parry reverting to type. I like
people . . . much more than I like myself anyway! That's
why I'm a socialist, for heaven's sake. I believe in the
National Health Service. So why shouldn't I enjoy it? No
nonsense about private wards this time round. Whether it's
the same complaint or not. Do you like my flowers?'

I felt a tinge of guilt. 'I haven't brought you anything,' I
said.

It was more of a confession than an apology. Bedwyr had
said the least I could do was get here as soon as possible.
'Where the hell have you been?' That was his first greeting
when he opened the door. He hadn't the slightest interest in
my Italian pilgrimages. He was worried about Amy. It was

serious. A form of cancer. The real thing this time. It got on his nerves to think of me drifting around Italy while my mother was lying ill and without any news of my whereabouts. 'Four months,' Bedwyr said. 'Or is it five? And not a bloody word.' He was irritable and impatient. Sian was as sympathetic as ever. She gave me to understand that there was nothing at all to connect me with the bombing campaign. I was free to come and go as I liked. 'Put your skids on, will you,' Bedwyr said. 'Or come down to earth or whatever it is you have to do. She wants to see you. If you don't hurry you could be too late.'

'You've brought yourself,' Amy said. 'That's more than enough for me. And looking so well.'

She wanted the other women in the ward to admire me. The youngest of her three sons who were all devoted to her. The sunburn was convenient to conceal any signs of embarrassment.

'I was telling Mrs Roberts,' my mother said. 'I saw this place being opened. Over forty years ago. Or forty-five was it, Mrs Roberts? Dear Enid and I stood on the sandhills and she was worrying about the platform being too small and giving me a history lesson at the same time. "That's not the real Prince of Wales," she said. And I wouldn't believe her. She was right, of course. Dear Enid. Always right about the things that mattered most . . . Things don't change much, do they? And now here I am. An old woman and a patient in the very same place. It makes you think, doesn't it? But what about I have no idea!'

She laughed and the woman called Mrs Roberts laughed obligingly too. Visitors were straggling in. A bouncy probationer nurse brought in a gift of fruit, grapes on a plate, for Mrs Roberts in her corner bed, and addressed her in English. My mother raised a warning finger and made a reproachful noise.

'Now then, nurse! *Cymraeg*! That's what we want in here. Isn't that so ladies?' They all agreed with my mother, with varying degrees of fervour. 'Didn't I tell you?' she said to me. 'Amy Parry reverting to type.'

She pointed to a chair and made me move her locker to one side so that I could sit near enough to her for us to engage in private talk. The women without visitors were watching us closely as the most interesting piece of theatre available. My mother didn't seem to mind. I placed the chair so that I was facing the wall like an actor showing his back to the audience. That made my mother giggle, which implied that I was behaving true to form.

'These are from some friends of yours,' she said.

She meant the chrysanthemums. They were arranged like bronze altar flowers with their own profuse reverence. My mother was longing to surprise me.

'Mrs Ferrario and Mrs Lloyd, Tai Hirion. Two wonderful women. They come to see me every week. We understand each other so well without a word being spoken. Without reproach. They know that all I want now is to pay my debt to the culture that made me. Will you promise me something, Peredur?'

A dangerously familiar formula. How many times had I heard it before? A royal command from the queen of the dark subterranean depths of emotion. Calculated to disturb. Ancient patterns shimmering to the surface, disturbing the calm it had taken me so many months to attain.

'Mrs Ferrario,' Amy said. 'Will you go and see her? I shouldn't say this, but I think she's a little hurt that you haven't been in touch with her.'

She saw the smile spread on my face and her eyebrows raised to show she would like to know why. She couldn't see me trudging through the streets beyond the Aventino, shadowing Giuseppe Ferrario on his way to school. The trouble I took to find the man. Looking through those massive grubby Roman telephone directories. Walking around Lucca in concentric circles. Standing outside the factory and the family villa. A self-imposed task in my uprooted, aimless existence. In Rome my consciousness rattled around a complex of streets like a tram-car stuffed with weary people on their way home from work. He had a black moustache and white hair. In public transport he was a man wrapped securely in himself and his eyes looked at me and saw nothing. Outside in conversation with a passing acquaintance he looked handsome, cultivated and infinitely patient. I followed him for days, longing to speak to him. He

355

never noticed me. Who on earth could I say I was? A chance acquaintance of his daughter? Was I the messenger appointed to tell him that she was dead? How could I begin? I stood in the street and watched him disappear into the shadows of his school.

My mother had caught a nurse speaking English to one of the patients again.

'*Cymraeg!*'

Out came the order. This enthusiasm of hers embarrassed. She understood as much, and it amused her. I was there to witness her rediscovered zeal.

'I nag them about it all the time,' she said. 'It's the only way. "For goodness sake, girl, take some pride in your ancient heritage". That sort of thing. I think them up when I'm lying here in bed. "Stop worshipping pop stars and princes". That worked quite well. "Stop parading scraps of second-hand English to hide your cultural nakedness". That wasn't so good. Just made them scratch their heads.'

She could have been getting over-excited. There was no one around I could refer to about her condition. She snatched at my hand and leaned closer to whisper.

'You were quite right, you know,' she said.

'About what?'

It was an effort to withhold my affection. Perhaps an effort I no longer needed to make.

'About everything. About the great Lord Mared, for example. Whatever it was he was after, it wasn't me once he discovered I'd got cancer. It was quite funny really. He wanted to make a graceful withdrawal and he popped off like a man who'd trodden on a snake.'

We were holding hands and smiling at each other. As though at long last we had discovered how we should have been all along.

'Do you mind me being on your side?' She sounded so young as she said it. 'I've been reading a lot since I've been in here,' she said. 'All of a sudden there are so many things I want to know. Isn't that silly? Your poor father. The things he had to put up with. He should have married an intellectual like himself. I can tell you one thing. One conclusion I've come to. I was wrong and your Wenna was right. She died to prove it. I've got to admire that.'

My response was too slow for her, too measured.

'I don't care if it was an accident or not,' my mother said. 'She was willing to risk her life. And she gave it. No one can ask for more than that.'

I tried to look wise and experienced and conceal the panic rising inside me. My mother was trying to please me. All she was doing was activating the unbearable debate in my head that my pilgrimage in Italy had tried to stifle with the anaesthetic of diversion, distance, detachment. Can anyone stage a revolution without violence? Does it have to be a revolution? Or should you condemn your class and your country and yourself to a condition of permanent grovelling servility and sycophancy? How was one to bear it?

'You must promise me this, Peredur. You must live from now on to see that she didn't die for nothing. Do you understand me?' Her voice was low and urgent. 'She gave her life and now you must give yours. And I must give you Brangor Hall. You must do all the things with it you said you wanted to do and more. Cultural ecology. A centre of excellence and culture renaissance. Call it what you like, but do it. Build, build, build! In every way you can think of. I've told Bedwyr and Gwydion that this is what I want to happen. If they want to play a part, all well and good. But the burden and the privilege is on you. Your father's son. That's as it should be, Peredur. You must say if you are willing. Are you?'

Her hand was in mine. It was thin. It had begun to shake. She had taken off her rings. They slipped off too easily. I lifted her hand to my lips and kissed it. What else could I do?